The Endless Wars:
The Descent
By, Blaine Atkinson

ISBN: 978-0-615-38057-5

This novel is dedicated to the two guys without whom this novel wouldn't exist, Adam and John. I can't think of two guys I'd rather have watching my back if I were ever to embark on any kind of quest.

I: Curtain
November, 2001

Dark, ominous clouds. Lightning. A flood of rain pouring down. Decaying, long dead buildings. Streets that look like they haven't been repaved since the rule of Louis XVI. A cop substation in the distance. More rain.

That was the landscape that was sucked into Taran's eyes. His view shifted around, as if he was desperately trying to find something not dying, not gray, at which to stare. He could feel the lifelessness infecting him.

Taran Walker was twenty three years young, and possessed the body of a man. His height and build were just about average (roughly 5'8, with a fair amount of muscle.) His dark brown hair and brown eyes added to his almost average appearance. His face was adorned with a beard that circled his mouth, and his eyes contained a coldness that looked very heavy.

His room was covered in dirty laundry, various magazines and books, boxes of CDs and other belongings, empty beer bottles and cigarette packs everywhere. A bare mattress was in the corner, with an ashtray and a digital alarm clock next to it. The walls had probably once been white, but those days were long since gone.

Of course he loved her. Of course he did. Not "in love," mind you. But he did love her. How could he not? An inch shorter than him, red hair, green eyes, tiny waist, perfect curvy body, and that weird Jedi Mind control over guys. She was one of those girls that was great at convincing you that you needed her above all else, and by the time you realized that you didn't, you had already wrecked your life so badly that your best strategy was to cower in her shadow until you thought of some really clever escape plan.

Rosaline was really something.

But, Taran had learned. About four months prior, she had cheated on him and dumped him for a military school cadet three years his junior. After four years of something that almost reminded him of perfection.

So, there she stood. Fighting and pleading to be taken back.

"I'm done with you." Taran said, surprisingly calmly, though he let out several ragged breaths after-wards

"I can't fucking believe you. It's really interesting, really, really interesting, Taran, how this 'honor' that you always talk about comes and goes whenever it's convenient for you! Isn't 'forgiveness' included in your little 'code of conduct?'" she paused, inhaled a sniffle, "Taran, listen to me. Please. I'm standing here telling you that I love you."

Taran's mind raced, trying to decipher her tactic. He had known her for a long time, and knew that every single word that left her beautiful, pale lips was part of a larger strategy. She never did or said anything unless she was going to gain something from it. He had been brilliantly manipulated by her over the last year, and was done with it. Just done with it.

First, it had been the gaps in her schedule. Hours of time that were missing in her life that she would claim had been used for napping, which she never did, or extra homework, which was also unusual. She always plowed through her homework in a very short time, a testament to her intelligence. Sometimes, she would even manufacture reasons to explode at him, so as to avoid him for the hours it took to be with her lover.

Then, Taran had caught them.

Rosaline arched her back and touched her breasts in a way she NEVER did with Taran...she bounced up and down on him [GRINGO] in a way she never had with Taran...her gasps and [FAKED] orgasms sounded much more violent, more felt, more appreciated than they ever had with Taran...Taran moved away from the doorway...wished he had been noticed by them...

She had claimed that not only was Taran losing "it," but so was their relationship. She had said that things hadn't been the same since...

She saw Taran lying bloody on his couch, shards of glass embedded in his face...white powder caked under his nose...she knew he was supposed to be dead...

He figured that she, being only 19, had gotten bored and curious. He had been warned that she had been too young when they started dating, and here he stood, the biggest goddam fool in the world.

He continued to stare out the window and absorb the rather depressing landscape. He took another drag off his cigarette, exhaled, and turned to face her. He hated this moment. The moment after you've been facing away from a lover or an ex you've been fighting with and then, suddenly you turn, look at them, and remember why you were facing away. They're the most beautiful individual in the world.

He very calmly approached her. He caressed her cheek with his hand and smiled at her.

"I will always love you, I'm sure. I just don't ever want to see you again," he whispered, his smile trembling, "and please, just let me go. Please. I can't-"

"Taran, I left you for Johnny Gringo. Another guy. You are not the first person this has happened to. You're acting like this is some horrible new problem in the world. It happens all the fucking time."

He pulled away from her, his unstable smile dissolving into a sigh. His eyes rolled as he threw his hands up in the air.

"Ya know, Roz, there was a time when I thought you might actually be capable of feeling guilty for something, or actually really, truly loving someone. I suspected you were incapable of having a shred of humanity a year ago, and now, I'm sure of it."

Rosaline looked away from him, her green eyes flicking all over the place. She bit her lip and nodded her head.

6

"Taran," she began, her voice quieter and sweeter, "Can we just… start over, or something. Please? I-"

"NO! NO! NO! NO! NO!" Taran exploded, slapping a beer bottle off of his window sill and into a wall. Rosaline jumped away from the glass shards that sprayed out.

"Calm down!" she yelled, pointing a long, perfectly sculpted finger at him. The red nail shined from the light of the street lamp outside.

"Then stop! It's like you can't decide if you want me back so that you can torture me some more or because you actually do love me. Just leave! Go!"

"Taran, stop it. Look, let's calm down and just talk, okay? No more yelling, okay? Let's just relax and talk this out." Rosaline offered, almost speaking in a whisper.

"No." Taran grunted through gritted teeth. He turned and stared at the dying night through his window again.

Rosaline's voice cracked as she spoke.

"Don't you understand? I made a mistake. If I wounded you, I-"

Taran whirled to face her, smashing his cigarette into the ashtray as he turned.

"Some wounds heal and some wounds scar. Do you know what it means to be wounded? Do you know what it's like when that wound comes from someone you love? When that wound is accidentally inflicted, that is easily forgivable. When that wound is intentional, it is not. When it is intentional and repeatedly fucking inflicted, it goes into a realm beyond hatred and sadness. I believe the term 'inhuman' was fashioned for just this kind of act. You have never loved me and are incapable of doing so. Leave now."

He turned back to the window. Tears dripped off of his rough cheeks and into the ashtray, extinguishing the burning remains of the cigarette.

Rosaline stared at him for a few moments, then finally spoke in a choked voice.

"What happened to you? You used to be…"

Still staring out the window, never turning to look at her, Taran responded.

"Never mind what I used to be. It's no concern of yours any longer. You will never have to worry about it again. I've relieved you of that. Good bye."

All Rosaline could do was stare. Or, at least attempt to. The tears were flowing so heavily she had to repeatedly blink. He was gone for good this time. Forever. And, yet, there he was. Standing maybe a foot away. He was right in front of her! She could reach out to touch him. One last time. Her last memory of him could be the feeling of their skin touching.

However, she was convinced this would not be their last shared memory.

She bent down, picked up her purse, walked out of the room, and began to head down the stairs.

For whatever reason, he didn't feel that great sense of victory he had expected.

Taran stared out of his window, his hands clasped behind his back, and watched her exit the building and run to her car. Rosaline was gone.

The dying city lay before him, waiting.

II: The Knight and the Thug

Listening to his friend and roommate Milk Bone's pointless and sometimes idiotic babbling usually cheered Taran up. This is why the two of them ended up at a bar a couple of hours after Rosaline made her exit. They looked very odd sitting together. Taran, in all his plainness, with his short spiked hair, plain white t-shirt and blue jeans, stood out in contrast to Milk Bone, a short, wiry white guy wearing a backwards blue road Cardinals hat, white wife-beater shirt, sagging blue track pants, with broken teeth. He was convinced he was a "gangsta," as he put it.

They were sitting at one of the sidewalk tables outside of their favorite bar, M.P. O'Reilly's. It was busy that night, and the two men were surrounded by couples, either with their own table, or with other couples. Taran tried his best not to notice this.

For November, it was pretty nice that night. A little chilly, but tolerable. Taran was fine in his Shell coat (from working there a few years prior,) and Milk Bone slid on a Cardinals jersey, in addition to all the fake jewelry in which he covered himself.

And, sure enough, Milk Bone was on a roll tonight.

"So, I was like, 'ight, bitch, you wanna do it like that, that's coo. I mean, shit, man, I ain't gonna have no bitch talk to me like that. Know what I'm sayin'?"

As amusing as Milk Bone, or just "Bone" sometimes, could be, when Taran was in as foul a mood as he was now, he dreaded actual conversation.

"Sure, Bone, so what'd you do?"

"I was like, 'Bitch! I am Milk Bone T! Ain't no woman gonna play Milk Bone! Fuck na!' So, I grabbed her by her nappy ass hair, flipped her around, started fuckin' the hell outta her, and she's all like," Bone switched to his girly voice here, "'Oh, Milk Bone! Milk Bone! Fuck me, you big horny nigga!' The bitch was lovin' it! But, that ain't the fucked up part! Ya ready for this shit?"

"Oh yeah, Bone. Hit me." Taran snorted.

"So, I'm fuckin' the hell outta her, right. And, she starts panting like a dog. I'm like, 'ight, that's kinda whacked out, but people do weird shit when they're fuckin' sometimes, so I was like 'okay.' Then, get this! The bitch starts fuckin' barkin', dude! The bitch started fuckin' barkin'!"

"No pun intended, right? 'Bitch barking.' Get it?" Taran said, cracking a tiny smile, then realizing that Milk Bone's comprehension of this was nil.

Bone stared blankly before resuming his narrative.

"I was like, 'HELL NA!' I saw that Snoop video where he turns into a fuckin' dog and shit! So, I'm like 'what if this bitch fuckin' turns into a...bitch?!' Fuck na, man! Fuck na! So, I fuckin' kick her skank ass outta my bed and I'm like 'Bitch! Go back to your damn dog house. See ya!' Damn, nigga..."

"Ah, the epic tales of Milk Bone T. Did you ever see her again?"

Taran asked.

"No, man, but I did find some dog shit on the front porch the next week, so-"

Taran held up a hand.

"I get it, I get it. Real quick, was wondering if Rosaline had called the house phone recently? I heard it ring a few times...just thought..." Taran trailed off.

"Huh?"

"You heard me."

Milk Bone sat there, hesitating.

"Nah." he nearly whispered.

Taran couldn't decide if he was surprised.

"What?" he asked anyway.

"Um, no." Bone answered again, just as hoarsely

"Okay." Taran didn't know what else to say. He didn't even know why he bothered caring.

Milk Bone's eyes suddenly widened as he leaned forward and attempted to shift the conversation.

"Why? You still want her? Look, man, come with me to Cherokee Street and we'll get you a nice cheap ho. I know this one chick that me and my brother used to get. Her name was 'Queeffie Lou' or some shit, and anyway, she fuck pretty good. She's real cheap, man. I remember this one time-"

"That's alright, Bone. Don't worry about it. I just wanted to know if Rosaline had called."

"Okay." Bone stopped and thought. "So...what the fuck is you gonna do about her?"

Now, it was Taran's turn to stop and think.

"I don't know, man. I do know I don't wanna be with her. I just want to hurt her. And hurt her. And hurt her. Etcetera and so on."

Milk Bone stared at the base of his beer glass and admired the way the wrought-iron table as he tried to be invisible and just let Taran do his thing.

Taran continued, "I know you don't understand. That's fine. I don't care. Revenge. That's all it's about. As soon as I'm done, I can move on."

"So, when do you think you'll be done?" Bone asked.

Taran paused and thought again. "I don't know. Whenever I'm fuckin' done, man."

"I'm just sayin', dude. Don't pass up a fine little honey just 'cause you're trying to fuck up your ex."

"We'll see, man." Taran said.

"So, what have you done so far?"

"What do you mean?"

"You want revenge on the bitch, right? So what have you done to get revenge so far?" Bone asked.

"I don't know, man. Nothing yet."

"Why?" Bone asked.

"I just haven't had any good opportunities yet. As soon as I do, though..."

"Taran, all you gotta do is get a ride out to West County and-"

"Drop it, man. It's my problem. Don't worry about it."

"Whatever you say, dawg." Milk Bone said, leaning back and grabbing his Old English 800.

Taran sighed, grabbed his pack of American Spirits, pulled one out, lit it, and looked around. Almost as soon as he turned his head, he locked eyes with a young woman in a black cloak. She smiled at him. He just stared back at her.

She had small, delicate features, and was almost painfully petite. Little locks of short brown hair spilled out from under her hood.

"Ya know her, dawg?" Milk Bone asked, leaning over and looking at her.

"No. I don't know. She looks very familiar, but...I don't think so."

She looked away. Taran and Milk Bone followed her gaze. A man, close to Taran's age, sat down with her, but he was dressed in a rather outdated fashion. He wore a white, loose fitting blouse that was covered with a leather vest. His hair was pulled back into a ponytail and a thick, light brown beard covered his face. It was as if he had just walked off a Gettysburg reenactment.

"That blanket she's wearing is kinda hot. It's all like 'Dark Crystal' and shit," Milk Bone chuckled.

"It's called a 'cloak.'"

"Whatever. It'd look better balled up on my floor while I fucked her."

Taran shook his head. He looked back at the woman. She was engaged in conversation with the old-fashioned man next to her.

"I wonder who that guy is and why he's dressed like that. Must be an actor." Taran pondered, turning to Milk Bone.

"What guy?" Bone asked, looking around the young woman.

"The guy sittin' next to her, man." Taran said, surprised, and subtly pointed with his thumb.

Bone continued to stare at the girl, then shook his head.

Taran rolled his eyes and drank his Bud Light.

Milk Bone shrugged.

"He is sitting right fucking next to her." Taran pointed.

Milk Bone looked at Taran, then cracked a confused smile.

"Are you, like, messin' with me, dude? Do you really seriously see some dude over there, 'cause there's nobody with her. That little girl is a-lone, dawg." Milk Bone said, looking directly at Taran.

Taran looked at the old-fashioned man. Something was definitely odd about him. Not just his style of dress, but something else. His skin was too white, but there was more.

11

The man looked up at Taran and nodded, halfway smiling.

"Hey, Bone, let's go over and introduce ourselves." Taran suggested, standing up.

Bone grabbed his beer, tucked a cigarette behind his ear, and jumped up.

The two men approached the young woman's table. She and her male companion looked up.

"Good evening," she said to Taran, smiling at him, "I'm Sasha." she offered her hand at this, which Taran graciously took.

"I'm Taran Walker. This is Milk Bone." Taran turned to the old-fashioned man, "What's your name?"

The man smiled, leaned forward, and spoke.

"Can your friend see me?"

Taran looked at Milk Bone.

"Can you see this guy?" he asked, pointing at the man.

Milk Bone shook his head, stared at the ground, and mumbled to Taran.

"You's gonna freak her out, dude. Don't fuck up my game, dawg. Knock off this invisible friend shit."

Taran turned back to the man and shook his head. The man began to speak again.

"I didn't think so. He doesn't strike me as one of…the type, though it is hard to tell. I'm just relieved that you've returned."

Taran screwed his face up and looked at Sasha, then back at the man.

"'Returned?'" he asked.

"Yes. Look, this is going to take some time to explain. You've been drinking, and I'd rather wait until you were sober. Can you meet Sasha and myself at Coffee Cartel tomorrow at around six?" the man asked.

"Hang on. What's your name and why can't Milk Bone see you?" Taran demanded.

"I think the more pressing question is-"

Sasha cut him off.

"Ghost, enough with this stoic crap. His name is Richard Barrywood and your friend can't see him because he's a ghost. The reason that you and I can is…well…we're different from Milk Bone. Look, Ghost here will explain everything tomorrow."

Milk Bone sat there, staring at the empty chair, his eyes wide.

Taran turned to Ghost, annoyed.

"Guess what? I'm having sort of a bad day. I had a bad breakup earlier, and have ZERO fucking patience for more lies. And YOU," Taran pointed at Milk Bone, "I should kick the shit out of you for agreeing with these people to play some kind of stupid joke on me. I'm going home, and the next person who tries to fuck with my head better be ready to defend themselves. I'm out."

Milk Bone stammered.

"Dude, I…I…I dunno shit about no ghosts, dude. I'm goin' witchoo."

Sasha stood up.

"Taran, she wasn't lying to you earlier. She really loves you. She wasn't sure of it, but now that she's lost you, she knows. She-"

"Sasha, stop it." Ghost cut in.

Taran exploded at her, pointing a finger at her as if it was a dagger.

"Don't talk to me about Rosaline like you know her! I swear to God, I don't hit women, but I will knock your fucking head off if you don't-"

Milk Bone grabbed Taran and started dragging him away. Taran struggled, trying to wrench himself free. People at other tables watched the scene, whispering between themselves.

Suddenly, Sasha stood up and interlocked her fingers, then flicked each one, one by one, from thumb to pinky on each hand. She turned them palm up, her fingers still locked together, then muttered, "Peace," and raised her hands up to her mouth. A little ball of light formed. She pressed her lips together and blew. The ball leaped out of her hands and slipped into Taran's chest.

Bodies flew away from the scene as people confusedly began to panic. A roar began to pass through the bar.

A feeling of severe intoxication hit him. Not quite intoxication, he decided, but rather, peaceful exhaustion.

"What…the…ugh…" Taran mumbled. Milk Bone looked confusedly at Sasha, who was preparing a discreet exit with Ghost, then hoisted Taran up by his arm, walking him home.

III: A Summons

"It would seem that a hundred years hasn't soothed Taran's temper. In fact, it seems worse. You shouldn't have spoken so plainly to him. You shouldn't have lost faith in me." Ghost said to Sasha as they walked down Euclid Avenue.

"I didn't lose faith in you. I got impatient, I'm sorry, but we don't know how much time we have."

Layne struggled to reel his mind back in from hers. Lucia lay on her bed, struggling for breath as blood poured out of her ears, eyes, nose, and mouth. Layne had only been curious, he hadn't meant to unlock the wrong parts of her mind. He ran around in her head, trying to untangle himself from her.

Almost.

Finally.

Out.

As he reassembled in his own mind, he noticed that the acid was really starting to kick in. He blinked his eyes open, he noted the increased sharpness in his vision, and the enhanced colors of everything around him, and giggled.

He sat up, having collapsed his body on the floor when he entered her. He checked his limbs and clothing. The clothes were as tattered as they had been before his entry. His body was still in its wraith-like state. He glanced in the mirror, and checked his gaunt face for damage. None. He had shut his pain receptors off a long time ago, as he had found the constant physical agony intolerable. His own sharp nose, visible jawbone and eye sockets always freaked him out a bit. His skin was so thinly stretched over his facial bones, he sometimes worried that he might come out of one of his mental probings to find his skull partially exposed, as some of the skin had snapped from tension. His hair, which had been reduced to white patches on his 22-year old head, made him look far older than he actually was. Most of his bald pate was exposed, but there were portions that had modest croppings of long, white hair.

His reflection was so much more interesting when he was tripping.

He began to smile, then remembered Lucia.

She wasn't breathing anymore.

"NO!" he screamed and launched himself up onto the bed.

Lucia was his girl...

Alexandra brushed her long, curly blond hair out of her face with her fingers. She looked in her compact mirror.

It was the same face she had been looking at for well over a century. That of a maiden in her early 20's. Her pale skin, dishwater blond hair, and bright green eyes had been a fairly exotic look during the Reconstruction period, but thankfully, she blended in much more now.

She snapped her mirror shut, dropped it into her backpack, then tossed her backpack onto the seat next to her.

Now that the darkness had crept out, she had been able to emerge from underneath the bed in her cabin on the train, and prepare to disembark in St. Louis. She hadn't been back there in over thirty years, having traveled abroad much of the time. St. Louis contained too many straining memories for her.

But, something had compelled her to return. It was just a feeling in her, a strong compulsion, something bordering on a need.

Alexandra supposed she felt she belonged in St. Louis. She had lived there from the time she had been a small girl to right after the "Fall of the Nine," as some in her old coven had referred to it.

She grimaced when she thought about the Fall.

Alexandra shrugged the memories off, and prepared to exit her cabin. She stood up, grabbed her eight-foot rainbow scarf, and tossed it around her neck. She glanced at her reflection in the window, checked her new black turtleneck and black stretch pants, blew a kiss to herself, then opened her mouth and ran her tongue along her fanged canine teeth. She smiled, waved goodbye to herself, then spun around. She grabbed her black backpack and exited the cabin.

As she deboarded onto the train platform, she pulled her cellular phone out and called her condominium. A woman's voice answered.

"Matilda, how are my quarters? Are they livable?" Alexandra asked sweetly.

"Yes, Mademoiselle Boliviere, they are. It took quite a bit of dusting, and there was some unpleasantness in the powder room, but everything has been taken care of. I also rearranged the furniture, as you asked."

No memories.

"Thank you, Matilda. Go ahead and go home, and come by tomorrow for a check, if you like. I'll be out –

asleep in the ceiling

- if you'd like to let yourself in and pick it up. I'll leave it on the kitchen counter."

"Thank you, Mademoiselle, I'll do that. I am so happy you're back, though I was hoping you'd be *Madam* by now. No nice men in Europe for you?"

Alexandra walked out onto Market Street to hail a cab.

"No, there were plenty of nice men overseas, just none for me. Maybe someday, I'll meet someone –

Taran

- who will do it for me, but I refuse to lower my standards until then."

Alexandra ached at the thought of her old lover. He had given his life too willingly. Nothing had ever been enough for him, not even sheer existence.

"I understand, Mademoiselle. I'll see you tomorrow, hopefully."

"Hopefully." Alexandra agreed, then snapped her phone shut.

Nigel set the acoustic down on his dorm bed as the girl softly clapped and approached him. Nigel smiled at her, his light brown goatee and long hair mussed up a bit, just enough to convey the rock star thing.

"So, what was that song called again?" she asked, setting herself gently onto his lap. She gazed deeply into his blue eyes.

"In My Head, from my old band." he paused, swelling with just the right amount of pride in one place and blood in the other, "I wrote it."

"Yeah? I liked it. A lot." she whispered, then threw herself on him.

They began kissing and tearing at clothes. She nibbled at his amazing assortment of earrings in each ear. He wrapped his arms around and pulled her tank top up and off. She slid her hand to his jeans and began to slowly work his belt. He unsnapped her bra and she slowly shimmied it off, revealing her generous breasts.

As his pants began to slide down, she realized he was still wearing his coat and shirt.

"You look a little top-heavy. Come here."

"Um-"

She gasped as she opened his coat and saw his guns in shoulder holsters.

"Why do you have guns?" she asked, backing away and covering herself.

He smiled at her, thinking.

"Um...well...my mother was brutally murdered...but I don't wanna talk about it...I don't use them...they're not even loaded...just makes me feel like I can protect the girls that I care about...like you..." he smiled sadly.

"Oh..." her face curled back into a smile, "I'm sorry...but that's really sweet." and she slid back into his arms as he removed the jacket and shoulder holsters.

That reminds me. Gotta call my mother tomorrow. Nigel thought.

Taran, feeling a bit recovered, and Milk Bone walked into the Halfway. The sanctuary.

Their friend, Sebastian, was more or less left in charge of the place by the plastics company next door. Basically, Sebastian used to install alarms and he did a job for the plastics company in this building. It was a three-story abandoned halfway house in barely livable condition. Sebastian had fallen in love. He decided to just flat out ask the owner if he could live there. The owner said yes, as long as Sebastian acted as caretaker and fixed the place up.

Sebastian moved in. Phone was on and paid for. Same thing with the electric and gas. He got himself a great discount on the cable. Overall, it was a pretty kick-ass living situation.

Sebastian, however, was nowhere to be seen at the moment. He was probably out at work. He drove a cab for a living now.

"Remind me to avoid the bitches in cloaks next time." Milk Bone laughed.

Taran, still feeling a little wobbly, just shook his head.

"I'm going to bed. I hope I die in my sleep."

IV: Taran Wanderer

Taran awoke with a start. He jerked his head off the pillow and looked around as the last few hours of the previous night came rushing into his head.

It felt like a dream, though he knew it wasn't.

Rosaline.

The thought of her sent a rocket of pain through his body. He sat up, leaned his head forward, and buried his face in his hands. He fought the weakness as hard as he could, but when he broke, he let himself break completely, and the sobs came out like muted screams.

When the release finally tapered off, he rolled off of his mattress, and onto the floor, lying in the pile of garbage. He didn't know why, but he needed to just lie there for a while.

"I am losing my goddam mind." he chuckled.

The sight of a cockroach was enough to get him off the floor about 30 minutes later. He grabbed a towel, headed for the bathroom, and got his day started.

He called Nigel because he had promised to, and that was about the only reason why. He wasn't very interested in renewing their friendship, as he knew that Nigel had made some rather obvious romantic overtures to Rosaline after she and Taran had split. It was as if Nigel was friends with Taran, all the while waiting for his moment to slither his way into Rosaline's heart/pussy. He wasn't even sure that Nigel had waited until they were broken up, either.

Taran dialed the number, then waited, hoping he would get Nigel's voice-mail at SEMO, where he went to school. SEMO (Southeast Missouri State) was located in Cape Girardeau, about an hour and a half south of St. Louis.

"Hello?" Nigel sighed into the phone, sounding like he had been asleep.

"Hey." Taran croaked, realizing he was speaking to someone for the first time that day.

"The fuck are you doing up already? You get knocked out early last night or something?"

"Something like that. What time is it?"

"Hang on. Shit, man, it's 9 fucking 30. Call me later."

"No. Are you still coming today?" Taran asked, not sure what answer he preferred.

"Yeah. I'll be there some time this afternoon or evening."

"Cool. See ya then."

"Wait." Nigel said, sounding more awake, "Why are you up already? Bad shit?"

"Just had a fucked up day yesterday. We'll talk about it later."

"Roz?" Nigel asked.

Taran paused, unsure how much he wanted to disclose right now. Anything he told Nigel was something that Nigel could potentially use to win over Rosaline. His thoughts also drifted toward Sasha and the man claiming to be a ghost. He didn't want to broach that right now.

"Something like that. We'll talk about it later when you're here."

"Alright, man. See ya later."

"Yeah." Taran replied, then hung up. He began to filter what he was going to tell Nigel, to make sure his "friend" stayed away from her.

Taran walked up to Milk Bone's door and knocked.

"Who is it?" Bone bellowed.

"Taran!"

"Come in, it's unlocked!" Bone yelled.

Taran rammed the door a few times with his shoulder until it opened and stumbled in, clutching that shoulder. The door frame wasn't quite the right shape anymore, so it took a little effort to open and close it. Milk Bone was blaring "Boyz n' the Hood" by N.W.A (he didn't care for the newer hip-hop). His room was in its usual perfect, neat condition, a major contrast to Taran's. Milk Bone had everything in its place. For a guy that put so little emphasis on personal cleanliness, his affinity for neatness was almost shocking. He also had the strangest stereo setup Taran had ever seen. Milk Bone had a Neolithic age T.V. blasting through a sub-woofer and about 6 other speakers. His favorite show was the Simpsons, too, which meant hearing Homer yell "Doh!" throughout the entire three-story building.

A cloud of pungent pot smoke wafted past Taran into the hallway.

"Three things." said Taran.

"What?" Bone responded, his eyes containing more glass than any of the windows in the Halfway. He tapped his glass pipe into an ashtray.

"One, how many different people could possibly be knocking on your door? Two, There's no lock on your door. Three, You don't even really need a lock." Taran said, rubbing his shoulder. "Four, what's the plan for tonight?"

"Huh?" Bone responded, perplexed.

"What are we doing tonight?" Taran asked.

"I don't know, man, get some chronic, get some movies, get some pussy, ya know, whatever." Milk Bone responded, obviously having thought this all out thoroughly.

"Tonight's more of a beer night for me, man. Kinda like every night. Remember? I don't do anything anymore."

"Like at all, dude?" Bone asked, genuinely surprised.

"Like drugs." Taran explained, extending his hands toward Milk Bone like he was delivering a precious object.

"Ooohhh! Hahaha! I thought you meant like anything, man. Like shitting and breathing and shit! Hehehe…you're really funny, Taran."

Bone laughed hysterically.

"Jesus, Bone. Anyway, we'll see what happens. I'm running over to Rally's. You want anything?"

"No, dude, I'm chill. If they're still dealing through the drive-thru, though, pick me up a quarter."

"Right. I'll do my best." Taran laughed as he reached for the door knob

"Taran!" Milk Bone called out as Taran was about to close the door.

"Yeah?" Taran answered, poking his head back into the room.

"I didn't play a joke on you last night, dude, I swear. I know you were pissed, but I really wasn't fuckin' with you or nothin.' I'm serious, dawg. But...I mean...the only person there with us was that hot girl. I dunno, dude, I mean, did you really see...ya know...did you really see that guy you were talkin' about? That ghost guy? Maybe she spiked your beer or somethin' to make you see shit. I know sometimes when I smoke too much of this shit, I'll see shit outta the corner of my eye, but never like a fuckin' guy that wasn't there."

Taran smiled at the earnest look on his stoned friend's face. This was why they were friends. Milk Bone was many things, many of them negative, but Taran (when he was calm and rational) knew that the kid valued their friendship above almost all else.

"I don't know what I saw, man, but I believe you. I know you wouldn't fuck with me like that when I was having a bad day. I just hope it's the last hallucination I ever have."

"At least that you didn't want to have." Milk Bone chuckled.

"We'll see. I'll be back."

"Word." Milk Bone called out as Taran shut the door.

As Taran headed downstairs, he heard the T.V. going in the living room. This meant Sebastian was home. Sebastian was kind of the master of the building. He more or less ran the show at the Halfway, and it was running pretty tight. No major emergencies. No wild parties. A close eye on any drugs that came and went. A near-endless supply of free beer for Taran. A fully-functional recording studio/jam space in the basement. His security setup competed with the NSA's. And hot girls seemed to flow in and out every day. It was pretty cool.

As he descended the stairs, he looked around the foyer and his heart sank again. This place was starting to depress him. Maybe it wasn't so cool. Off-white cracked walls, filthy linoleum floors, and uneven doorways more or less summed up his life at the moment. The front door reminded him of a prison. It was a huge, two-inch thick mass of solid metal, with only a tiny, face-sized portal at the top.

Taran reminded himself that prisoners had been the previous occupants, as it had been a halfway house.

The first floor was made up of three offices, a bathroom, an industrial kitchen, and a huge mess hall. The second and third floors were identical to each other, each one containing eight bedrooms and two public bathrooms. Each bathroom held four shower stalls and four toilet stalls. The basement had originally been for storage and laundry, but Sebastian had converted much of it into the aforementioned band practice and recording space.

Sebastian had originally met Taran through the local rock scene, when Taran and Milk Bone had been homeless, and after hanging out and jamming all night, Sebastian had decided they should help him keep the Halfway up and running.

It was a pretty cool place to live, but for some reason, it just depressed him at the moment. He was incredibly grateful to Sebastian, but knew he needed to start getting his life together.

Taran walked into the living room. Sure enough, Sebastian was munching away on a salad and watching some Buddhist spirituality video.

Sebastian was a short man, maybe five and a half feet tall, had a decent semi-muscular build with buzzed red hair and blue eyes and lots of freckles.

"Hey." Taran said, walking into the living room, stopping at the end of the couch.

Sebastian looked up, smiled, and nodded.

"What'th up?" he asked with a mouthful of salad, purposely spraying some out.

"Not much. Just heading over to Rally's to get some food. Need anything?"

Sebastian swallowed his mouthful and smiled.

"Nope. I got my salad. Hey, what are your plans for tonight?" Sebastian asked.

"I'm probably gonna chill here with Milk Bone and Nigel and do some drinking and whatever. What about you?"

"Some friends and I are going to Fuel, then we'll probably head back here. You pretty much summed it up with 'whatever.'" Sebastian said, grinning.

"Yeah, I suppose."

Taran looked at the clock on the VCR and his eyes bugged out.

"Jesus, it's only 11! I can't believe I've already been up for a while." Taran muttered, genuinely surprised. Usually, Taran stayed up all night working on a book or a song, but last night, he had been too stunned from whatever the freaky girl had done to him, so he had gone straight to bed.

"Yeah, I was wondering about that, too. You're usually not up for another hour or so. I thought you fuckers were nocturnal." Sebastian laughed.

"I think I've been up for at least a couple of hours, too. Oh, yeah, I'm going to Cape tomorrow, just so you know." Taran informed him.

"Cool."

"Well, I'm out. You going back to work or are you done for the day?" Taran asked.

"Just taking a break. I'm going back."

"Well, if I don't see you when I get back, live long and prosper."

"Yup."

"See ya."

"Bye."

Taran left the living room and proceeded towards the back door. He hadn't had Rally's in a while, and was very much looking forward to it. He hadn't had the money to afford Rally's in ages, and he actually had money for it now. He was very glad he had decided to rummage through all the pockets of his coats and pants.

Taran went out the back door and walked through the back yard. His broken motorcycle was right where it had been for the last two months, next to the basketball hoop and Sebastian's truck. Sebastian's cab was next to the truck, on the basketball court. There was also a plastic table with chairs off to the side.

A huge skeleton of a tree seemed to loom over the entire view, waiting to snatch Taran up in its evil branches and end his dead-end life. The back yard would've been plenty depressing without the tree, too. There was a concrete slab the size of a small Middle Eastern country which served as the basketball court, weeds popping out through the cracks, and ivy covering all the fences, walls, and anything else slow-moving enough for it to constrict.

He looked at the scenery, trying to find something to cheer him up. Storm clouds loomed ominously, so that was no help. The Plastics warehouse next door offered no consolation, nor did the SLU frat-house to his right. He looked down the alley at his old apartment building, from which he had been evicted back in August. He had been thrilled that moving consisted of he and Milk Bone breaking into his old apartment and running everything down the alley as quickly as they could. That had been much easier and cheaper than using a U-Haul.

Nothing cheery in his view. Hopefully, Rally's would boost him up a bit.

Taran opened the back gate, went through, closed it, and wrapped the chain around the bars to give the illusion of being locked.

Taran turned around and found himself in his old apartment.

He gasped and whirled around and around, trying to understand what he was seeing.

All of his furniture was gone and it was very dark, but somehow, there was an unknown faint light source right above him. All the damage to the walls and carpet was still there. There was none of the usual bass humming from other apartments or endless cars outside. It was dead quiet. Taran ran to the window and looked out. Nothing. McDonald's was there, but there were no people. He ran to the door and tried to open it, but it wouldn't give. He tried unlocking it, but the deadbolt was jammed. He looked around, hoping that maybe someone else was trapped here. As he was doing so, he noticed another odd thing. It was daylight outside and he had ripped the blinds out years ago, but no daylight was coming in. He could see the day outside, but it didn't shed any light on the inside. And that unknown light source followed him everywhere he went. He walked to the window again and looked outside. Still, there was no one. He looked at the Halfway, hoping to gain some kind of clue. He gasped.

He saw himself collapsed on the ground in the alley.

He couldn't understand. It didn't make any sense. Where were all the people? Why were there two of him? What was with the weird lighting? Why couldn't he-

Rosaline was standing in front of the door of his apartment.

Taran just stared.

She approached him slowly, seeming to almost float toward him with an inhuman grace. Against his will, Taran opened his arms for her. She slid right into them, fitting perfectly as ever. Her warm body pressed against his. Her head rested on his shoulder. He could feel her heart beat. He could feel the rising and falling of her breathing against his chest. She ran her hands through his hair, lifted her head, smiled at him, then put her head back on his shoulder. He could feel tears welling up in the two of them. She embraced him with all of her strength. Like love crushing him. Then she was gone. Vanished.

Taran's knees began to buckle as his heart emptied. He clutched his chest and looked up again.

Nigel appeared in the kitchen, holding a beer and a pack of smokes. He smiled broadly. His long hair and grunge-era clothes emanated comfort and familiarity. Taran smiled back, knowing that he had misjudged Nigel. They had always been friends, and always would be. Nigel was not capable of betrayal. It had all been Taran's paranoia.

His old friend walked up to him, extending the beer forward, just as he had done almost every weekend throughout high school, and most weekends after. Their six-year friendship had kept Taran going at times when he thought he might break, and it was invaluable. How could he not have seen that? How could he have been so blind?

He took the beer from Nigel, who fished a smoke out of his pocket for Taran. Nigel lit it for him. Taran opened the beer and took a swig. He then noticed that Nigel had another beer, which he opened for himself. They raised their beers in a toast, then each took a generous swallow.

Taran opened his mouth to apologize to Nigel and nothing came out. He couldn't speak. He wanted to apologize but he had no voice.

Nigel cocked his head, looking confused, or perhaps even disapproving.

Taran shook his head, then tried again.

Nothing.

Nigel shrugged his shoulders and turned his back on Taran.

He reached out for Nigel, but his friend disappeared.

All Taran could do was keep smoking and drinking his beer. He walked to the window and stared at the dead city. Maybe there was some great analogy in this. Taran really didn't feel like having deep thoughts right now. He stared at his seemingly dead body in the alley. He just wanted to get the hell out of this shitty little apartment and go wake himself up so that this would stop. He wasn't a huge fan of reliving the past. This was bad. He was losing his goddam mind.

He sensed someone behind him and whirled around.

Mom and Dad.

He hadn't seen them in over two years. There stood his father in his usual attire, expensive business suit, custom made undershirts and things like that. 6'6, skinny, fairly muscular, the beginnings of gray. And his mother, short stature, long brown hair, skinny. She was wearing jeans and a red turtleneck. They were standing maybe five or six feet away and smiling. Taran didn't know how or why, but he somehow sensed that he had their approval. They were proud of him. They began to approach. He really wanted out now, but he was locked in place. His mother hugged him very tightly. He didn't know how to process these feelings anymore. His entire mind had broken down. His father came over and put his hand on Taran's shoulder and smiled the fatherly smile that Taran was so unfamiliar with.

They really approved. They actually cared again. He hadn't known what it was like to have his parents be happy with who he turned out to be. It was always "he had so much potential" or "he should've gone back on Ritalin." Now, they loved him for who he was. Finally.

Maybe he could come over for dinner again and see the dogs.

They vanished. Like the others.

Maybe not.

Taran collapsed on the floor and stared at the blank wall. He would not show weakness. That was not an option. He was a warrior. He believed in honor and integrity.

Taran had always known he was different from others. He had always seen the world differently from them. He had always felt alone.

But, never like this. Never, ever like this.

Raphael appeared.

Taran jumped up, set his beer and burning cigarette down on the window sill and stared down his old adversary.

Raphael stood there in his kimono, hand on his sword's hilt, which hung at his waist. His old enemy and dojo master.

His mind suddenly flooded with memories of the lessons he had learned from Raphael, of the great sparring sessions, of the intimate conversations they had. Raphael was always interested in Taran's life, and had become a good friend, as well as a great teacher of fighting.

Raphael had rarely discussed himself.

Then, THE memory took hold. Taran clenched his teeth and

assumed a fighting stance.

Raphael took a step toward him. As soon as his foot hit the floor, his dojo outfit began to dissolve.

Underneath the disintegrating threads, he wore plated black leggings and red plated body armor that resembled scales. A green scaly cape hung off his shoulders. His long black hair fell freely, the band that held it dissolving. His pale, clean-shaven face stared at Taran, hatred burning in his eyes.

This was not a memory. Taran had never seen this armor before.

Raphael took another step forward. As his foot slammed down on the ruined carpet, a ring of fire shot out and instantly ignited the floor. The ring spread at an incredible speed, and smoke quickly filled the room.

Taran jumped back, trying to avoid being consumed by the flames. They raced toward him.

Taran tried to break the window behind him, his only possible escape route. Around him, the walls were already starting to burn. The carpet in front of him was almost completely gone.

Raphael just stood there, staring stone-faced at Taran.

Smoke began to suffocate him. Each of his coughs were silent.

The window wouldn't give. He slammed his elbow into it over and over, and the window held, not even rattling in its frame.

Suddenly, he felt heat underneath him. He looked down, and his pants were on fire. He renewed his effort with the window, slamming elbows and fists into it in a panic.

The fire raced up his clothes, consuming him. First, he felt heat, then pain, then numbness. His skin was bubbling and popping. The fire covered his face and his vision went black. He tried to scream, but there was no sound.

He fell to his knees, screaming silently. Consciousness began to fade...

Then, he found himself lying in the alley again, screaming at the top of his lungs. It echoed and reverberated throughout the city.

He stopped screaming and sat up. He breathed in deeply, and his lungs burned. He coughed several times, shook his head, and tried to comprehend what had just happened.

Between the ghost and the vision, he had no doubt that he was going mad.

Maybe it had been an acid flashback.

But, why did his lungs burn? Could it be a psychosomatic response?

He looked at his skin and clothing, both of which were unmarked, but he doubted anyone had ever hallucinated being immolated and actually had their skin burn.

I hurt.

Taran whirled around, trying to find the voice.

"Now what?" Taran asked the alley, exasperated, "Please…just let me…" he knew more words were supposed to come after that, but he didn't know them anymore. He shook his head clear, then looked around.

There was a homeless man at the east end of the alley, digging through trash, but the voice had been within a few feet of him, and the man was too far away.

There was a dog sitting at the edge of the McDonald's parking lot, however.

Taran shook his head. He didn't feel like dealing with talking dogs today.

Hurt.

Taran looked at the dog again. It was a mix, but looked to be mainly chow and black lab.

I hurt I hurt I…

Taran walked up to the dog, which immediately stood and began to back away from him.

"Are you…no…" Taran began, then stopped himself. He tried to assert rationality, but nothing was making sense.

Not dog. Idiot.

Taran looked around again.

"Well, screw you, too, then." he spat. He stormed down the alley. If he ignored the voice, it might stop. Maybe one was less crazy if they heard voices, but didn't acknowledge them.

Milk Bone walked into the living room and found Sebastian on the couch, eating a salad. It amazed Bone how content Sebastian looked eating that stuff.

"Hey." Bone mumbled.

"What are you up to?" Sebastian inquired, munching away.

"About to take a shower and shit." Bone said, plopping down on the couch.

"You and Taran got up earlier than usual today." Sebastian commented.

"Yeah, well, it's hard as fuck to sleep once his ass is up." Bone explained.

"Why?"

"'Cause, he wakes me the fuck up every five minutes, man!" Milk Bone exclaimed.

"Why?"

"Hell if I know, man. He just comes in there with his big-ass boots stompin' around like, 'Bone! Milk Bone! Wake the fuck up!', throwin' shit at me."

"Why does he do that?"

"Different reasons every day, man. One day, he wanted to know if I drank all his Schnucks soda, another time he wanted to know if Eazy-E really was an original member of Bone Thugs-n-Harmony, then one time, he wanted to see if it was me or Standellini that shot a load all over one of his Playboys, and then, one time, he wanted me to get a job."

"Sorry to hear that, man." Sebastian chuckled.

"Well, not much I can do about it."

"Maybe you could, like, shove furniture in front of your door or something." Sebastian suggested.

"I should probably try that."

Layne Wood shuffled down the alley, clinging to a dumpster to keep himself from sinking into the concrete. He gasped raggedly as the burning spread from his stomach upwards and outwards.

The world wobbled as he proceeded forward. The Halfway wasn't much farther. He had seen the leader leave, and had tried to show him what he needed to see.

He knew Taran understood "the burning," but didn't think he was going to let himself feel it completely yet.

Snow started to come down. Layne sighed and began to heat his body to compensate. He was already burning too hot from the heroin, but that wasn't real heat.

If he made it into the Halfway, he would be okay. He would be able to share the images with Taran and Sasha, and they might be able to help him decipher them.

He just wished Lord Dell would leave him alone.

He suddenly felt a hand on his shoulder. He spun around too quickly, and his gaunt, too-thin body fell onto the cold, wet concrete. The new snow began to soak into his rotting t-shirt, and his holey jeans offered almost no protection.

A smelly man stood over him, smiling an almost toothless grin.

It was Ricky, one of the other junkies.

"You holdin', Wood, I know you are. You always are. How you got no money, but you always holdin'?"

Layne stared at the man, a darkness building in him. He knew the man meant to take his powder.

"So, you holdin' or what?" Ricky asked, reaching for something in one of his back pockets.

Layne closed his eyes and ignited the burning in himself.

"Fuck it. Dumb ass mothafucka." Rickey muttered, looking down both ends of the alley, then producing a huge blade from the back of his pants.

He bent down, grabbed Layne by his shirt and started to drag him behind one of the dumpsters. The frail man offered no resistance as he kept his eyes closed, as if he was in a coma.

The burning was hot now. Layne reached forward with his mind, found his assailant's mind, then unleashed the burning.

Ricky dropped the knife, and reeled back, clutching his skull. He screamed, fell against the opposite side of the alley, then began to make a choking sound.

Layne wandered about in Ricky's mind, finding the tender spots. The bad memories. As he located each one, he made a note of it, then hit it with the burning, his own pain.

He looked up and down the corridors of Ricky's mind. Each door was an experience. All one had to do was listen through the door to find the bad things. Sometimes, the doors were marked, which made things much easier. The obvious ones, the repressed ones, were boarded up, or in this case, painted over, to hide it. Those that had the defense mechanisms built in were also the easiest to destroy. In most cases, simply ripping open those sealed doors was enough to crush the person.

Ricky's mind was dirty. The walls and doors of his mind were crumbling, coming apart. Layne knew he was supposed to feel sympathy because of this.

There were dead things littering the hallways. They might have been animals, possibly even disfigured people, but he wasn't sure. They were pink masses of flesh, with protrusions that looked a bit like limbs, or tentacles, or something. Layne stared at them impassively.

As he walked past another door, something pounded on it, then screamed. Layne cocked his head curiously, then slowly walked to the door. He reached for the handle, turned it, and found it wouldn't open.

He lowered his eyes to the handle, studying it. As he did, he caught a sight of his own shoes and smiled.

His appearance during the mental links always shifted a bit. His mental image of himself was what would have been. He was tall, tanned, with a thick head of black hair. He always wore a suit, too, but the suit seemed to alter a bit every time. The shoes were the key difference here. They were now boots instead of dress shoes. Layne marked this as very odd.

The scream again.

Layne looked back up, and focused himself on the task at hand.

He leaned his eye into the keyhole, looked around in it, then looked down at one of his hands. A key slowly materialized.

He grabbed the key with his other hand, inserted it into the lock, then hesitated. He had no intention of killing Ricky, or even scarring him. He just wanted to scare the man into leaving him alone. If he opened this door, he might kill or mentally destroy Ricky.

The scream rang out again. A woman's scream. No...no...it was a child's scream.

Something slapped the other side of the door. A hand. A small hand.

"Anyone there?! He's hurting her! He's hurting my momma! PLEASE!" the child cried out.

"Ricky..." Layne whispered, and slowly backed away from the door. He would do too much damage here. Ricky had to open this door himself.

Layne yanked the key out of the lock and tossed it onto the floor. He would leave it for Ricky to find when he was ready.

Layne retreated from Ricky's mind, and reassembled in his own.

As he blinked his eyes open, he looked around. Ricky was crumpled on the ground, next to the building on the opposite side of the alley, sobbing. A black dog looked at them inquisitively from the McDonald's parking lot, east of them, the direction that Taran had walked.

As he always did, he looked at himself to see if the suit had gone.

It had. His emaciated body had returned, as had the rotting, ripped clothing.

The exhaustion from the burning began to overtake him. His mind began to whither again. He crawled behind the dumpster, out of view, and fainted.

Taran walked into the Halfway feeling more than a little agitated. At least he had his Rally's. That made him happy. He was going to sit down on the couch, watch "Natural Born Killers" and eat his BBQ Bacon Burger and fries. He was going to enjoy this and just start this day over.

Apparently, Sebastian had left. This suited Taran, because he really wanted to enjoy his time alone with his burger. It was nothing personal against Sebastian, he just wanted the burger more than a friend right now. He set the bag down on the table and went over to his movies to find the DVD. After rummaging for a minute or two, he found it. He popped it in his PS2 and sat down on the couch. He withdrew the coveted burger and set it on the table. He began the unwrapping process. Slowly, it began to reveal itself. The sweet scent permeated the air in the living room.

Then, another scent filled Taran's nostrils. He lifted the top bun.

"FUCK!"

They had put pickles on his burger. It had been contaminated. He couldn't eat it now.

"WHY?! WHY WHY WHY WHY?! All I wanted was a burger..." Taran hung his head and fought the stupid tears, "I just wanted a burger, man. Not much."

Maybe Milk Bone would want it.

At least he still had his fries. Rally's had great fries.

As Taran shoved the last of the fries into his mouth, Milk Bone walked into the office that had been converted into a living room.

"Wassup, foo?" Bone greeted him, then plopped down on the other couch, "Good movie." he commented when he saw the movie on the TV.

"Yeah." Taran nodded, "Want a burger?"

"Hells yeah! Wait. Where's yours? You eat that shit already?"

Taran looked at his friend for a moment, wanting to convey his own madness, then just nodded.

"Yeah. Dig in, man."

Milk Bone grinned broadly, then snatched the burger, consuming it as if he hadn't had a real meal in weeks.

He probably hadn't.

They both sat in silence for a while, watching Mickey and Mallory Knox go on their killing spree.

The phone buzzer went off, sending a piecing shriek through the entire building. It was one of the last bits of evidence of what the building had once been.

"God, I hate that thing." Taran muttered.

Bone ran over to the cordless phone next to the TV and picked it up.

"Hello?"

A piercing, nasal voice penetrated the line.

"Okay, I need three large pepperonis, a medium sausage and onion, two 2-liters of Coke, and an order of bread-sticks" the guy on the phone said.

"Uuuhhh..." Bone frowned and looked over at Taran, who looked back at him with a questioning look.

"Oh, and I'd like that delivered please."

Milk Bone shrugged his shoulders at Taran, then froze, suddenly breaking into a grin and holding a finger up.

"Can you hold on one second, sir?" Milk Bone asked.

"Sure." the voice on the other side said.

Bone covered the phone receiver and looked at Taran, "Still got your Pizza Slut shirt?"

"Yeah." Taran didn't like this. Bone was scamming. He had to be. Taran knew that look, "Why?"

"Wanna make some money?" Bone asked, still wearing that evil grin.

"Maybe."

"Cool. I have an idea."

"Who the hell is that?" Taran asked, standing up and walking toward Bone.

"Hold on."

"Bone!"

Too late. He was back on the phone.

"Sir?" Bone said, as politely as possible.

"Yes?" the guy responded.

"Sir, um, all of our drivers, are, uh, really, really busy, so do you mind coming and picking it up?"

The man sighed.

"Fine. We can do that. How long?"

"Well, we're swamped today, sir, so 45 minutes. Is that okay?"

Taran's hand snatched the phone out of Milk Bone's, and hung it up.

"No." Taran hissed, "No more idiotic adventures. No more drama. We're done with that."

"WHAT?!" Milk Bone cried out, "Dawg, that woulda been hilarious! And we woulda make some cash! I need smokes, man, I need smokes! And it woulda been hilarious!"

"I need to take a walk, and I'll grab ya some smokes. Reds?"

"Hells yeah, dawg. How you got so much money?"

"Persistence."

With that, Taran grabbed his Shell jacket, and made for the door.

"Hurry, man." Bone said, falling over on the floor.

"Yeah, yeah." Taran said, exiting and beginning his journey.

Right after Taran left, Sebastian arrived home, and found Bone slouched in the corner of the front hallway, part of a burger hanging out his mouth, cradling his pipe.

"Need some help?" Sebastian asked, grinning.

"Uh...yeah." Bone said, blinking, confused, and somewhat embarrassed.

Sebastian extended his hand, and lifted Bone up. He steadied the little guy as they walked into the living room and helped him onto the couch.

"Thanks, man." Bone said.

"No problem." he answered.

Bone sat on the couch and stared at the blank TV screen, trying to will BET to come on. He was hoping that Jedi mind trick that Taran always talked about would work, but apparently, Milk Bone just wasn't down with the Force. He would have to remember to ask Taran exactly how that worked.

"BET?" Sebastian asked.

"Yeah, dude...you read my fuckin' mind, man." Bone said. Apparently, Sebastian knew how to use that Jedi stuff. Everyone but him could do it.

"I try."

Sebastian picked up the remote and switched it to BET.

"Aaahhh...much better. Thanks, man." Bone sighed, melting into the couch.

"Hey, no problem."

Milk Bone took out his bag and started to pack another bowl in his pipe.

"Jesus fuck, man, aren't you stoned enough?" Sebastian laughed.

"Hahaha...I forgot I was stoned, man. That's really funny. Hahaha..."

"Wanna share?"

"Abso-fuckin'-lutely!" Bone exclaimed, excited to actually be getting stoned with someone else again, since Taran wouldn't even touch the stuff anymore.

"Better get packin', 'cause we're goin' on a journey!" Sebastian yelled.

Milk Bone sat there and began packing the bowl. This was one of his favorite parts of the ritual. Packing a bowl was a skill. If you didn't do it properly, you didn't get very high. If you packed a good bowl, you got HIGH. Milk Bone was quite skilled at this.

"We're gonna get so high we're gonna see God, dude. Yeah." Milk Bone laughed as he packed the pipe.

V: The Descent

Taran proceeded down Vandeventer Ave. at a comfortable pace. Vandeventer was the immediate cross-street for West Pine if one walked east, and also acted as a border for SLU. He was now walking south on Vandeventer toward the gas station, trying to decide how he felt about the snow.

Darkness would come soon. He glanced at his watch. 16:00. He hated this time of year. The sun rose late, and always set far too soon.

He heaved a sigh, and continued walking.

His thoughts were a jumble as he tried to process everything that had been happening over the last 24 hours. He had ended things with the former love of his life, seen a supposedly invisible man, been hit by a magic spell from a small woman in a black cloak, had a vision, then heard a voice.

Taran suddenly stopped walking, looked around, then sat down on the curb. A mix of ancient sedans (the locals) and brand new coupes (SLU students) raced by him as he stared into nothing.

He played back recent events again in his head. None of it made sense. It had all started right after the confrontation with Rosaline. Was all of this connected somehow?

He thought it might be.

He looked up at the darkening sky above him, just above the dingy rooftops to the west. He could feel the darkness slowly settling in around him, insulating him from the potential human connections.

The slap of running shoes to his left snapped him out of his thoughts and he whipped his head around.

A cute female jogger, wearing running shorts, a SLU sports bra, and a pair of headphones was running down the sidewalk, in his direction. She glanced at him, smiled, which he returned with a nod, then she quickly shifted her gaze away and continued running by him. Taran looked back up at the setting sun, and thought about Rosaline while wondering why a woman would jog in shorts and a sports bra in new snow.

On August 8th, 1997, Taran was standing in the locker room at the dojo, changing out of his sparring gear when Raphael came around the corner, wearing a long red robe.

"Taran. I would speak with you." the master said.

Taran's spine straightened itself as he turned to Raphael and nodded. Raphael continued.

"You fought with great desperation today. Your confidence was down. Why?"

Taran looked away, brushed his long hair behind his ears, then turned to face Raphael again.

Raphael and Taran both had long hair at this time, though Raphael's hung to about his waist, while Taran's went just a bit past his shoulders. Raphael's black hair was also unnaturally silky, almost shiny, whereas Taran's was usually unkempt and greasy. There were many other physical differences between the two men, but the most obvious was body shape. Raphael was very tall and well-sculpted, while Taran was about average height and muscular, almost stout-looking.

A lock of hair slipped out from behind one of Taran's ears. He sighed, reached into his book-bag in his locker, and fished out a hair-tie. He stared at the pink elastic circle and froze. A moment later, his eyes looked up at Raphael through the lock of hair.

"This belonged to a dead woman. She died a year ago." Taran rumbled.

Raphael nodded.

"Jill." he offered.

Taran nodded back, then placed the tie between his teeth as he pulled his hair back, then used it to wrap around his pony tail.

"I miss her, Raphael."

"That much is evident. However, I would advise that you don't carry the past on your shoulders. Let it slide off of you and into the abyss, before it drags you down. You are a man of passion, Taran, and thus, you are often tangled in your own emotions. You must learn to untangle yourself and channel these feelings properly. Rather, you should channel them into something other than trying to take my head off."

Both men chuckled a bit at this.

"Yeah, sorry about that. It's just that I thought I was a bit more past this, but anniversaries are always strange things. I just sorta thought I had let this go. Guess not."

"No apology is necessary, as you did not remove my head. May I ask you a few questions?"

Taran sat down on the bench in front the row of lockers. Raphael continued standing as he placed his hands behind his back, clasping them together.

"Uh, sure."

"How did she die?"

"She was asthmatic. She was walking her dog over by Euclid and Westminster, and apparently, she had an attack. Something must've startled her badly, or who knows what, but someone found her gasping for breath on the sidewalk, and she didn't have her inhaler for some reason. I dunno, there were a lot of odd details, like what caused the attack, and why she didn't have her inhaler, and shit like that, but…whatever."

Taran went back to stripping his *dougi* (sparring outfit) off.

Raphael remained frozen, like a statue.

"How long had you two been dating when this happened?"

Taran pulled a t-shirt on, then looked up at the dojo master.

"Only six months, but I had known her since high school, like '94 or so. I don't know why it took us so long to get around to dating, but it did. I loved her. The cops said that her dog, Cerberus, was guarding the body when they showed up. She had stopped gasping for breath about ten minutes before the medics arrived. Cerberus is a huge fucking dog, too. If someone did...startle her...the fucker's lucky she had him on a leash. The dog was going nuts when the cops got there. They ended up...they had to put him down. It took several bullets, too." Taran paused, rolled his tongue back and forth across his teeth for a moment, then spoke again, "Anyway, yeah, we dated for about six months."

Raphael finally moved. He approached Taran, placed a hand on his shoulder.

"You are a good student. The last two years have been a pleasure. You are...fun to teach. You learn quickly. However, I fear that your passion, particularly when it comes to women and drink, will be your ultimate destruction."

Taran's face shot up at Raphael's.

"What?"

"You must guard yourself carefully. I can only teach you what you are willing to learn. Your potential is probably the highest of any student I've ever had, but your anger over the past will only bring you more anger in the future. Guard yourself carefully."

Raphael nodded sharply at him after this, and exited the locker room. Taran just stared after him.

Later that night, Taran sat in the back of the Hi-Pointe at his own table, watching the band on stage. They were called *Siren*, and were quite good. They were a five-piece with a black dread-locked guy on drums, a rather pudgy, tattooed guy on bass, a tall, lanky bald guy on lead guitar, a tiny girl with short pink hair on rhythm guitar, and a goddess on lead vocals. Each person was dressed in ripped-up denim, leather, and chains, except the vocalist. She was pale, with dark red hair, black eyeliner, bright green eyes, pouty lips, and a voice like the sweetest violin. Her full breasts were obscured by a tight v-neck black belly shirt, and her pale white legs appeared beneath a black leather miniskirt, and they led down to a pair of black Doc Marten's.

She moved back and forth across the stage, her eyes and throat tightening with each beautiful resounding note, the guitars laying the perfect rough backdrop for her vocal smoothing of the songs. Taran nodded in time to the music, sipping his Michelob (which he had acquired with a decent fake ID.) He pulled out an American Spirit and lit it.

His favorite part about going to unknown bands' shows was reliving the excitement of his old band's early shows. When Basement had first started playing out, back in '95, they had been nothing more than obnoxious high school kids with a shared passion. In early 1997, they were considerably more refined (after a few lineup changes), and had a decent following in the St. Louis area. They had started out playing a lot of shows at Bernard's (down at Laclede's Landing), then graduated to Kennedy's (also at the Landing), right before it closed, then shifted a lot of their shows to places like the Hi-Pointe (near the Loop) the Red Sea (actually in the

Loop), and the Side Door (downtown.)

As Siren continued playing, Taran tossed more beers back. The few moments that he looked away from the singer, he took in the interior of the Hi-Pointe. The bar sat to his left, filled with a few older folks just wanting a beer, while the majority of the rest of the club was filled with close to 80 or so of the trendiest people of legal drinking age or at least with decent fakes, like Taran. It was a sea of baggy shirts with ironic logos (guys with Girl Scout shirts, girls with Charlie's Angels iron-ons), baggy pants with chain wallets, and Converse One-Star shoes.

Taran sat in the back, his eyes returning to the singer of Siren.

The music was loud, pulsating through him. The crunch of the guitars and bass, the smashing of the drums, and the singer's soprano voice grabbed him, held him at his table. The more he drank, the stronger this paralysis became.

The ghost-like singer leaped forward during a breakdown in one of the songs, and as her eyes passed over the crowd, she and Taran finally locked gazes.

He stared into her green eyes and pleaded with her to notice him. She held his eyes, continued singing, and a smile came across her face.

Taran sat on the curb on Vandeventer, reminiscing, when someone sat down next to him. He snapped out of his daydream, and looked over. It was the same cloaked woman from the night before. She was still wearing the black cloak, but he noticed another layer of black beneath, a black blouse and black skirt. He still wasn't able to make out much of her face, aside from burgundy lipstick against her pale complexion.

"Sasha?" he asked.

"Hi, Taran. Am I interrupting a zen moment or anything?" she asked, smiling at him.

Taran hesitated. She actually was interrupting a thoughtful moment, but it was far from achieving "zen." He looked at her as he considered this.

She spoke before he could answer.

"Do you believe in God, Taran?"

Taran looked up at the now dark sky. There were no stars visible, due to the city's pollution and clouds.

"No. At least not one that sends redeemable people to Hell. I don't think I ever did. Why?"

"Did you grow up thinking that there was something greater than all of this, but not a true 'god?'"

Taran rolled his tongue around in his closed mouth, and glanced at her again. He considered her idea, then shook his head.

"No. I used to think about this a lot in my teens, and I think it all came down to exponents. The universe beginning. Ya know, like there was one action, which spawned two actions, which spawned four, which spawned sixteen, etc. and so on. That seemed to make the most sense. It was the most logical explanation I could come up with. Forgiveness is divine and Hell isn't. Why?"

The burgundy lips pursed together for a second, then she began to speak, a bit hesitantly.

"What brought about that first action? I mean, you must've considered that when you were-"

"Yeah yeah yeah. I know. Actually, no, I don't know. I just can't...I just can't accept a god. It doesn't make any logical sense. At least not from where I'm looking at things. I can appreciate a different opinion, no problem, but it doesn't 'fit' with everything else. Everything I've ever seen in life has some scientific explanation. Well, at least until...anyway, it just seems like the notion of a god upsets that simplicity, like it removes the need to better ourselves. If we're all fighting to improve life as a whole, then there's no need for a god. If there is a god, there's no need to worry about anything. All we gotta do is follow the laid out instructions in whatever text we're supposed to believe in, remove all the passion from our existence, then die someday, and we're cool. I'm sorry, but that's a bullshit existence."

Sasha nodded vigorously.

"I was right. You're ready."

And there sat Milk Bone and Sebastian. Baked. Very, very baked. Milk Bone had finally regained his composure and Sebastian was trying to remember what he was supposed to be doing.

And there they sat, chillin'.

"Wanna get some food, yo?" Bone asked, his eyelids droopy.

"Yeah, man. That's cool." Sebastian responded, staring at the ceiling.

"What do you wanna get? I hear Pizza Hut's got some specials goin' right now."

"I don't feel like pizza right now, man. How about some Chinese?"

"Chinese what?" Bone asked, grinning wildly.

"Chinese food, man. Duh...haha..."

"I don't like Chinese food. I like Chinese people, though. They're really nice."

"You wanna eat Chinese people? Hehehe. You're kinda weird. I'll tell you what. I'm gonna go find some Chinese people. I'll be back later."

"Coo."

Sebastian pulled his cab keys out of his pocket and stumbled for the door.

After Taran had picked up the cigarettes for Bone and himself, he and Sasha headed back to the Halfway.

"So, this is it." Taran said, gesturing towards the building.

"I know." she said, smiling.

"What?" he asked, surprised.

"I know a lot about you, Taran. I've been tracking you for the past couple of years."

"Excuse me?!"

"Look, I'll explain it all to you in a sec. Off topic, who's that prick of a roommate you have?"

"Sebastian or Milk Bone?"

Just then, Sebastian walked out the front door.

"Hey, man, what's up?" Taran nodded.

"Hey hey hey. Not much. Just gotta find some Chinese people for Bone. He's got the munchies. See ya."

"Uuuhhh...right." Taran said, more than a little confused.

Sebastian fell into his cab and took off.

"Nice." Sasha commented.

"I...he's...I don't know...he's not normally like that. I think he's stoned."

"Right on. Which one was that?"

"That's Sebastian."

"In that case, I guess I'm referring to Milk Bone. He seems like a total misogynist."

"Oh he's not that bad, but he can be a pain in the ass sometimes." Taran said, lighting a smoke.

"I could tell."

"Before we go in, what am I ready for? I just kinda let that thought hang, assuming you'd tell me."

"Soon. I know, I know...but really, it's a long conversation. Just trust me."

Taran rolled his eyes, then nodded.

"Wanna go in?" he said, pointing to the front door.

"Yeah."

Taran and Sasha strolled down the cement walkway to the front door. Taran got out his keys, unlocked it, and let her in.

As they walked in, the first thing she noticed was the thumping bass of the stereo in the living room. It was playing some rap song or another that she didn't know.

The next thing she noticed was the green smoke billowing out of the living room.

"That's Milk Bone." Taran explained.

"Great." she mumbled.

They proceeded into the living room. Milk Bone was sprawled out on the couch, smoking out of a pipe made from an oxygen mask. He was nodding his head in time to the music and flipping through the channels on the TV.

"Hey." Taran said to him as they walked in, tossing the homeboy his smokes. Milk Bone was staring intently at the TV.

Milk Bone looked up at Taran, then noticed Sasha.

"Hey, you're the bitch with the 'cloak,' right?" he asked.

"Excuse me?"

"Um...uh..."

"Fuck you."

"Okay. I just don't like the games you were playin' with my boy." Milk Bone shrugged his shoulders.

"Don't even pretend to understand what's going on here, child."

"Look, bitch, my boy's got enough problems without some fuckin' mental patient wannabe slut thing stalkin' his fuckin' ass. I don't give a fuck what you say, I'm gonna protect Taran."

"Look, 'Milk Bone,' why don't you go 'chill' with the rest of '2 Live Crew' and pick up some 'bitches.' And, when you're done, you can go 'fire up a doobie' and 'flow.' I hate to break it to you, but you are not black and you are not of urban origins!"

"What?" Milk Bone said, feigning surprise.

"What?" Sasha spat, actually surprised.

"You was usin' some big words, like 'black' and 'urban.' I mean, I be totally reeetarded, ya know?" Bone responded, smiling.

"What an asshole. Taran, wanna get some food?"

"Yeah, sure." he said.

He and Sasha walked out into the foyer.

"I was thinking that we could head over to-" she began.

"Wait. I wanna see your face."

She giggled.

"Oh. Okay. I'm sorry, but I just have this thing with people seeing me...I don't know, it sounds crazy, but it's just this weird neurosis, I suppose...anyway, fine, I guess we're going to be together a while, so I'll just..."

Sasha reached up to her hood, started to pull it back as she faced straight down, then, as her black hair was being revealed, she hesitated. She sighed, yanked the hood off and onto her back, then looked up at Taran.

It was almost surprising to see her face, and to be able to associate it with her identity. She was actually quite stunning. She had jet-black chin-length hair (which perfectly matched her outfit; he didn't think that was an accident), turquoise blue eyes, heavy black eyeliner, pale white skin, and very small features. Of course, she could've only been a bit over five feet tall, but still, her nose was tiny, her ears were small, and she struck Taran as perhaps the most "petite" woman he'd ever seen.

"I don't understand why you would want to hide such a pretty face, Sasha." Taran offered, smiling at her.

Sasha started to grab for her hood nervously, when Taran grabbed her wrists and stopped her.

"Wait. What's wrong?" he asked, gently lowering her arms to her side.

"You don't need to mock me or flatter me, Taran. I'm-"

"Wait wait wait. That's not what I was doing. I swear to whoever, Sasha, that I was genuinely flirting with you. Come on! Relax!"

Sasha blushed, and looked away from him, smiling.

"Okay. Um...sorry." she almost squeaked.

"No need to apologize." Taran gestured toward the door, "Shall we go to dinner?"

Sasha nodded, then quickly moved for the door.

Taran and Sasha were walking west down Lindell. The mix of the rotting buildings and new commercial structures, like Wendy's and Blockbuster, always jarred Taran a bit. It reminded him of the blending of the rich SLU students and the homeless.

His thoughts then turned to the crazy events of the past 24 hours. Who was this girl he was walking with? What was that weird power she had last night? Why was he seeing and hearing things that weren't really there? His head began to spin from the chaos.

Anxiety began to creep in him, as he suddenly felt a lot of pressure on himself to do something about all of it.

"What are you thinking about?" Sasha asked after a while.

Taran looked at her, then forced a grin. He adjusted the waist on his Shell coat a bit, then looked over at the New Cathedral as they crossed Newstead Avenue.

"Well?" she asked again, nudging his arm.

"I don't know." he answered quietly.

"How can you not know?" she asked, laughing.

"I just don't. I don't know. I...don't get asked that a lot. Anymore."

"I see. Well, I'm asking you. Now, answer my question."

"I...when I understand all the madness flying around in my skull, you'll be the first one I tell."

"Agreed." she said, smiling again.

"So, what are you thinking about?" Taran asked, countering.

"You."

"What about me?"

"Just that...I'm finally meeting you."

"Big fuckin' deal."

"You'll understand later."

"I guess." he muttered, dread being added into the mix with anxiety, "So who are you? Really? What was that...thing you did to me last night to knock me out?"

Sasha's grin faded as she picked a random spot to stare at now.

"Yeah..." she started, almost dreamily, "Okay, the truth. Well, I'm Sasha Rosetta Stone, for starters."

"What, are your parents like archaeologists or something?" Taran chuckled.

"Yeah, they are. They're in Afghanistan now, trying to work with the so-called government to try to protect some artifacts from falling into looters' hands. I guess some stuff also got messed up during some of the combat between the Taliban and the U.S. forces. Anyway, so yeah, that's my name, and yes, the middle name comes from the famous tablet. I've more or less lived on my own since I was in junior high. My parents have taken care of all my expenses for the last few years. I'm 18 right now, I graduated from Clayton High School this past spring, and yes, I have a good fake ID, so if you ever want to go drinking, we can…" she blushed again here, took a deep breath, then continued, "As for the Peace spell, I'm what's called a White Mystic. I handle healing and defensive spells. A Black Mystic handles the more…attack-based spells. After we eat, to help convince you further of my powers, I can demonstrate some of them."

"That'd be sorta cool to watch after a few beers. Anyway, what about this 'Ghost' guy? Who's he?"

"It's all in the name, really. He'll explain everything in a bit."

"Cool. Let's go to Spoon's on Euclid, what do you say?"

"Sounds good."

I HURT GODDAMIT YOU YOU YOU HELP!

Taran and Sasha both stumbled briefly, grabbing onto each other for support.

"What the hell was that?" Sasha asked, pain coming through in her voice.

"I heard it earlier, right after a really fucked up…well, a really strange hallucination." Taran explained, rubbing his forehead with his thumb and index finger.

Sasha let go of him, and nodded.

"Hallucination? So he penetrated your mind and you survived? How…never mind. I thought I sensed something like this earlier, but I had my hood up so…anyway, yeah, that's…oh no." Sasha almost whispered the last two words, and her head slowly turned to Taran, "I think that might be a really strong Psycho Mystic. If he's targeting us, we're in deep trouble. Let's get moving. I'm not kidding. If he gets into close enough range, he can kill us with a thought. Let's get into a crowded place. He won't be able to focus as easily." Sasha explained, throwing her hood back up, then grabbing his hand and almost dragging him forward.

"What the hell is a Psycho Mystic? Black and White I get, I mean, I've played like every Final Fantasy ever, they got black and white mages, and actually FFX is coming out soon, which I can't wait for, oh man, that game's gonna rock, but anyway, what the hell is a Psycho Mystic?"

"Put him out of your head for now, or that might strengthen his reception, and I'll explain as soon as we get to the restaurant." Sasha said, breathing hard as she ran down the sidewalk, still holding his hand.

"Right on. If he starts messing with us, though, I got a piece in my coat. Walther P99."

"Unless you're the fastest draw ever, I don't think that'll make much difference."

"Huh. Okay." Taran said.

VI: Truth

They had barely spoken over dinner. A few casual flirtations and lingering touches of their feet, but little more.

They had since migrated.

Taran and Sasha sat in the Coffee Cartel smoking section and stared at each other. Sasha threw her hood back again. There was a weird energy in the air. Taran didn't know if it was from the excitement of finding out the truth about what was happening to him or from his hormones responding to her.

He stared into her eyes. He was surprised. What he saw was utter concentration and seriousness. She seemed to swing from this very girly/giggly/cutesy girl to the most focused person he had ever met.

Sasha returned the stare. She had trained her whole life for this mission. She didn't understand why, at the key moment, she would choke. She simply looked into his dark brown eyes and had nothing to say. She knew exactly what she was supposed to tell him. She just couldn't. What was wrong with her? *Just tell him. Easy. Just tell him.* Somewhere in that black hole of a head of hers, the entire speech was in there. She needed time to remember it.

"I'm getting the quad mocha. Do you want anything?" she asked, trying to stall.

"20 oz. Cherry Coke, if you don't mind." Taran said, handing her a dollar bill.

"20 oz. Cherry Coke?" she said, taking the dollar bill from his hand.

"Did I st-st-stutter?" Taran smiled.

"Right." Sasha said, walking away.

Taran watched her get in line, noting her tight little butt, and stand there looking troubled and moody just like the rest of his generation. Sasha was cool, but he could tell she had some "issues."

He looked around. The cool thing about Coffee Cartel was that they always had a new artists' work on the walls, like they did now. At the moment, it was some guy named Layne Wood. Taran wasn't too knowledgeable about painting and such things, but this was some great stuff. One picture was of two men standing in a field with snow coming down. The taller, thinner man on the left was wearing a long green cloak made out of dragon scales with red body armor covering the rest of his body. The armor was shaped so that every curve and contortion in his real body was shown in the armor, so that the armor, in essence, looked almost like someone had taken red latex and just stretched it over his body. This man had long black hair pulled back in a pony tail and one of the most beautiful swords Taran had ever seen. The sword was long, slightly curved, and incredibly skinny. The handle was black with what appeared to be rubies, sapphires, amethysts, and countless other shiny rocks embedded in it. The artist had done a wonderful job of capturing this person so perfectly. The warrior on the left had just leaped to attack the man on the right. The guy on the right was very different from the guy on the left.

The man on the right was wearing a white T-shirt, blue jeans, and black boots. He had black hair and was in semi-decent shape. This guy was almost a joke. His T-shirt was filthy, blue jeans were muddy, and a cigarette was hanging out of a mouth surrounded by a mustache and goatee. However, the beauty of his sword rivaled that of the other man's. T-shirt man had a more plain-looking blade. The beauty in this sword was in its simplicity. Curved, silver blade with a black leather handle. No fancy ornamentation. Nothing. He stood in a defensive position.

Taran noticed something else. The T-shirt the guy was wearing was identical to one he had. In fact, the guy on the right was starting to look a lot like him. The only problem was that the faces of both men were distorted, like someone had taken their thumb and rubbed it over their faces.

And the other guy…Taran thought back to his vision…

The title was "Slaying of the Slayer."

Taran looked at the next painting. This one was even more interesting. It was a blond woman with blood dripping from her mouth cradling a dead redhead woman. The blond was obviously a vampire, judging from the fangs and the hissing look on her face. She was also the most beautiful woman he had ever seen.

Taran stood up and approached the painting, wanting to reach into it and just touch her face. He couldn't even breathe.

So this is what it's like to have your breath taken away.

She had barely blond hair past her shoulders and green eyes. Perfect skin. Very nice hands, too. He noticed an engagement ring on her left hand.

Alexandra.

Taran almost collapsed, he was feeling so dizzy. He had to sit down.

He walked back over to the table and turned to look at the painting again. As he did, something caught his eye outside.

He looked out the window at the tables outside.

Blond hair.

Green eyes.

Perfect skin.

Nice hands with the engagement ring.

Alexandra.

His stomach exploded in butterflies and he began to see red. There she sat. She was wearing a tight, long sleeved, black V-neck velvet top and black pleather pants, topped off with a very long rainbow scarf. He tried to get up to talk to her, but his legs had become so weakened that he couldn't move. He would watch her until he could walk, then go talk to her.

He tried to look at her teeth, but she would never smile. She looked so sad.

Alexandra.

How did he know that? He knew her. He knew her. Where? How?

Taran knew Alexandra. This was really starting to piss him off.

Look at me, he cried out to her in his head.

She kept staring at nothing, as if in a daze.

Look at me, he pleaded.

Suddenly, she snapped awake, looked up at the stars briefly, then fell back into a waking coma.

Look at me, he practically screamed inside his head.

Her eyes shifted momentarily, but no results.

I love you, he thought.

Suddenly, she started whipping her head around, as if trying to find someone. She began to turn in Taran's direction.

"Here's your soda." Sasha said, appearing right in his line of sight.

"Sasha! Move your fuckin' ass!" Taran screamed, finally finding the strength to get to his feet. He shoved her to the side and looked at Alexandra.

She was gone.

"Fuck!" he yelled, running for the door.

"Wait!" Sasha chased after him.

Taran got outside and looked west, then east. She was gone. He couldn't believe it. Sasha stopped right next to him.

"What's your deal?" she asked, shoving him, "You nearly threw me through the wall!"

"She's gone. Shit. I don't suppose you saw her, did you?"

"Who?"

"Alexandra." he said, realizing he had just spoken her name for the first time. Her name felt good on his lips, "Alexandra."

"Alexandra?"

"I...I don't know. She and I...I don't...I don't fuckin' remember! I just...I just know her! She's..." he trailed off, staring down Maryland Avenue.

"She's what?" Sasha asked, annoyance beginning to reveal itself.

"I'll show you. Follow me." he said, leading her back inside.

Taran and Sasha reentered the coffee shop, smiling at everyone they had just scared the hell out of. He walked up to the painting portraying Alexandra cradling the dead redhead. Taran pointed at the blonde.

"That's her. That's the girl. That's Alexandra."

"Wow. Nice girl." she leaned in and squinted at the signature, "Layne Wood, huh? He's good. Maybe it's his girlfriend or something. Or maybe she's just a friend. Or maybe she's his sister, who knows? Look,

Taran, you're rebounding big time." Sasha sighed, "And, quite frankly, we have bigger fish to fry. Can we talk now?"

"I hate that expression, and yes, let's talk. Sorry if I threw you into a wall."

"It's okay."

Taran and Sasha walked back to their table. He thought about telling her about the other painting, but didn't want to come off as a complete psycho, so he kept it to himself.

They sat down on opposite sides of the table and faced each other again. Taran opened his Cherry Coke and took a big slug. Sasha took a sip of her quad mocha. They both lit up, inhaled deeply, and exhaled with even more force.

"Okay," Sasha began, taking another drag and exhaling quickly, "here goes. Who do you think you are? I mean, deep, deep down inside, who do you believe yourself to be? Be completely honest."

"I...I am just a man."

"How very humble of you, Taran. Don't give me this Atticus Finch crap, just answer the question from your heart. Who are you?"

"I'm Taran."

"Jesus, you're dense. What do you want to do with your life? Come on!"

"I...want to change the world."

"There you go! You're getting close. Okay. How?"

"Through my music and writing."

"Now you're sounding like every moron on MTV or VH1, whichever one shows music stuff now, if either. How about something more direct?" Sasha said, cocking an eyebrow.

"Like what?" Taran asked, cocking an eyebrow back.

"What is the main thing that keeps people from freeing their minds and their lifestyles?"

"Easy. Religion."

"Very good. Now, I'm going to tell you something and you're going to think I'm a lunatic."

"What if I already think you're a lunatic?" he said, smiling.

"That should make it easier for you to take, but in the meantime, just shut up and listen."

"Look-" he began

"Please! Just listen!" she yelled, almost pleadingly. Taran could see the near-desperation in her eyes.

He took his fingers and made a zipping motion across his mouth.

"Thank you. Anyway, here it all is.

"There is a god. He created this universe and everything in it. Everything but you, me and seven other people. But, we'll get to that in a second.

"Anyway, he created all this stuff billions of our years ago. Time passes differently for him, since he's from...I don't know who he is or where he's from. I know nothing about him. What I do know about him is that he's not a very kind or patient god. He created all these people in his image. That's why most people are the way they are. They have a disposition towards violence and power."

"So do I." Taran countered.

"Yes, but you, me, the seven others, and all these people in this world have limiting factors. You have things stopping you. Your need to be loved. The fact that you need food, oxygen, and sunlight to live. Your need to mate. Your susceptibility to things like allergies, fatigue, drunkenness, physical wounds, harsh words, and..." Sasha looked him in the eye, "and a broken heart."

Taran rolled his eyes again.

"He doesn't have these. As far as I know, there's nothing stopping or controlling him. He's, by our definition, evil. Now, from what I've heard, he's had it with this planet. He wants to start over. He wants to let this planet destroy itself, and if it doesn't, soon, he'll do it. We're supposed to stop him."

Taran looked at her again.

"Ha." was Taran's only response.

"What?" Sasha asked him, confused.

"Why hasn't he already done it?" he asked.

"I don't know."

"What?"

"I don't know, Taran. It still doesn't make sense to me, and I've known of this mission for years."

"Sounds like a lot of crap, to be honest, but it's amusing, so I'll listen."

"Taran...please..." she begged, looking pathetic. He liked her. He really did. He wanted to give her the benefit of the doubt.

"So, if he didn't create us, who did?"

Sasha looked out the window and pulled her hair behind her ears.

"Taran, I honestly don't know. All I've been told is that we're supposed to stop God from destroying this planet."

He looked at the painting of the guy who looked exactly like him and the other swordsman.

Raphael.

Something clicked. He turned to Sasha.

"Three questions. One, who else is on the team? Two, what's my role? Three, what's the opposition?"

Sasha stared at her cigarette and sighed. She turned and looked around the coffee house.

The strangely dressed man from the previous night approached their table. He had simply come from around a corner, as if he had been waiting there the entire time.

"Hi." Taran said, eager to hear the rest. Whether it was excitement stemmed from amusement or serious fascination, he wasn't sure yet.

He almost wanted Sasha's story to be true.

Ghost sat down to his left.

"I heard your questions, Taran, and here are your answers. One, so far, it's you and Sasha. The other seven you will know when you meet them. Two, you are the leader. Three, the opposition is the power of God. Any more questions?" Ghost spoke.

"Yeah, a ton more. Why am I the leader?"

"Because you were created by another force to be so. You were all created for the same purpose, but with different strengths. As of this moment, Sasha and seven others are under your command. Sasha is what you would call a White Mystic. In training, I should add. She was born with a predisposition towards healing and defensive magic, as you witnessed last night. She is part of the Mystic's Guild, an underground group of White and Black Mystics. White and Black meaning what type of Mystic, not the color of their skin, obviously."

"Obviously." Taran snorted, "So who the hell are you?" he asked, pointing to Ghost.

"I am Sasha's mentor."

"Great. So, who the hell are you?"

"I am Ghost. I defied God's judgment in the afterlife, and I was cast down to earth, to spend an eternity unable to interact with any of his creations. To spend an eternity in solitude, wishing I had taken his judgment. Since you all were created by someone else, I can interact with you all."

"How did you defy his judgment?"

"I'm not 100% sure, but I think that I did something to shake some of his hold on me. Over time, you will come to know everything I know."

"Why not just tell me now?" Taran asked, rolling his eyes and throwing his hands up in annoyance.

"I would rather that the group was together first."

"Whatever. What's next?"

Sasha jumped in.

"Well, as far as we know, he doesn't even know we exist yet. We know his creations can hurt us, but he might not be able to. The reason for this is that he can't manifest himself in his actual form here. He hasn't figured out how yet. Also, we are virtually identical to the humans here. The only difference we've noticed is slight improvements in different faculties. I am much stronger in white magic than other White Mystics. Granted, I'm still learning, but I've accomplished in eighteen years what most Mystics take thirty or forty to accomplish. In fact, I'm the youngest member of the Guild. But, to answer your question, our vulnerabilities are the same as anyone else's."

"Alright. Where do we start?"

"I would suggest rounding up the team would be a good starting point." Ghost offered.

"They could be anywhere."

"I'm guessing they're all very close to here. Whoever wants us to do this is probably going to make it as easy as possible for us. They're probably all within the area. In fact, you may already know some of them. Look into your heart and you'll know." Ghost told him.

"Nigel." Taran said, looking almost dumbfounded.

"I suspected him, too." Sasha stated, taking another drink of her mocha.

"How?" he asked, surprised.

"I told you. I've been trailing you for a while now. I know about Nigel and Raphael and Rosaline and the band and your…breakdown last year and…the addictions." she almost whispered.

"That's enough." Taran raised his hand to stop her.

"Sorry. I'm just kinda nervous, since it's all starting to happen now…" Sasha stammered, picking her cigarettes up, then setting them back down.

"What else do you know?" he asked, deadpan.

"A lot. Don't worry about it. Look, we're going to be spending a lot of time together over the next few months or years, so I probably would've found out a lot of this anyway."

"Whatever. This is so unfair." he hissed at Sasha and Ghost.

"Taran…why are you so…upset by this?" Sasha asked, touching his hand.

"I don't know…my head is just freaking. My heart's pounding. I'm sweating. I don't know why. I just feel all this pressure now. Like everything that's happened yesterday and today is some attempt to force me into being someone I'm not. Do you know why I live in a fucking abandoned building? Why I'm unemployed? What happened to my car? Why Rosaline…"

He trailed off and looked out the window.

"Taran," Ghost began, "Sasha is not trying to hurt you. She cares about you. As do I. You overcame-"

"Fuck what I overcame! I didn't overcome anything! I still have anxiety attacks! After I quit using, everything fell apart. It turns out I don't even need drugs to ruin my life. Hah!" Taran laughed, throwing his hands up, then slamming them down on the table.

Ghost continued.

"If feeling sorry for yourself is what you need to do, then so be it. That's how I felt when I was first cast back down to earth by God as a ghost. Taran, you've been receiving one blow after another for a few years. Some of it, you've brought on yourself, and some of it, you haven't. We need you. There is much honor to be gained from this, and you might even find redemption."

Taran looked at Ghost now, his resistance lessening a bit in his face.

"Interesting."

"Taran, can I show you something?" Sasha asked quietly.

51

Taran turned to her and felt his heart melt a bit. As soon as they locked eyes, he felt guilty for having spoken so harshly to her. This girl would do anything for him.

"What did you have in mind?" he asked, gently.

"Give me your left hand." she said, more confident now.

Taran shrugged, extended his hand palm-up to her. She clasped his hand with her left, then ran the tips of her right fingers from the inside of his elbow to the scar tissue on the inside of his wrist. Once her fingers found the scars, they stopped. She covered the scar with her right palm.

"Dermal regenerate." she said quietly.

The hand on his wrist grew hot, and he glanced at her nervously. Red light began to seep out from underneath her palm. He felt a bit of pain, tried to pull his hand away.

"Trust her, Taran." Ghost whispered.

Taran nodded and relaxed.

Sasha gripped his wrist tighter and tighter. She stared down at her hand intensely, her face frozen.

"Heal." she whispered, then squeezed one more time, then let go.

She fell back in her chair and exhaled.

Taran leaned forward and stared at his wrist.

The scars were gone.

"Oh my god, what did you do?" he asked, looking at the healed wrist, then her, irritated.

"I healed the scar tissue." she explained, closing her eyes and relaxing.

"That was a part of me. I'm not saying I necessarily wanted it there, but you took a part of me. I can't believe this." he pointed at the healed wrist, then looked at her, his eyes misty.

Sasha leaned forward, looked at him, then hung her head.

"I give up. I can't appease you. No one can. It's never good enough for you. Forget it, Taran, let's just let the world be destroyed while you refuse to move forward and refuse to let yourself heal." she sighed, shaking her head as she stared into her lap.

Taran scowled at her, then looked over at Ghost. Ghost just stared back, shaking his head disapprovingly. Taran looked away and stared out the window at the seat that Alexandra had been sitting in. He and Jill probably sat at that table once. He and Rosaline probably sat there once, too.

She's gone. I have nothing to lose.

"I'm sorry, Sasha. You've kinda caught me at a weird time. I haven't been myself in a while. Maybe even ever. As for the scar, thank you. I was pretty attached to it, but it was getting kinda heavy."

He smiled at her and she smiled back.

Ghost bowed to them.

Taran and Sasha both waved to him and bid their respective farewells.

Once he was gone, Taran suddenly felt like his parents had just left him alone in his bedroom with a pretty girl.

"So…" he started, looking deeply at his almost empty Cherry Coke bottle as he swished it around.

"Yeah." Sasha giggled.

Alexandra's apparently engaged, Jill's dead, and Rosaline is evil.

"So…boyfriend?" Taran asked, leaning back, looking at her, and doing his best to look like he couldn't care less what she said next.

Sasha shook her head vigorously.

"No."

Taran made a motion for her to continue.

She picked up on the gesture after a few seconds.

"Oh. Well, I've never, um, never had a boyfriend." she shrugged as she said this.

"Why?" Taran asked, disbelieving.

"Long story. I don't want to talk about it right now." she paused, bit her lip, "I'm sorry, it's just…I don't feel like being embarrassed tonight, and we have more pressing issues, so…"

Taran nodded understanding.

"So, let's get to it, right." he finished for her.

Sasha immediately shifted the conversation.

"Look, how do you feel about everything Ghost and I told you?"

Taran looked at the painting, "Slaying of the Slayer." He stared deeply into it and could almost see the two warriors come to life. He could feel the sting of the snow and heavy wind. He could hear the "whoosh" of his attacker's blade. He could feel his muscles tense up, preparing to fend off the assault. He felt the imminent victory.

"I…it's a lot. It's a lot to take in. I'm excited, but…Jesus Christ, Sasha, I mean, what do you say to that? I don't know. Let's do it."

She grinned hugely, dropped her cigarette into the ashtray, jumped up, ran around the table, hugged him, then pecked him on the cheek. She ran back to her chair, sat back down, picked up her cigarette, then started ashing it like crazy.

"Wow! You're taking this a lot better than I thought you would!"

"Seems you don't know everything about me."

"Perhaps not."

She smiled at him, blew smoke out of her mouth, and he smiled back at her. Once eye contact had been held for too long, they both shifted their eyes.

Taran and Sasha looked around the coffee house, trying to think of a way to pass the uncomfortable moment.

What Sasha didn't realize was that he didn't fully believe her. If it was true, it would be great. A life of meaning. If it wasn't, it was okay. He hadn't really lost anything.

Taran noticed all the people passing in and out of the place, talking about everything from their favorite Misfits album to "my place or yours?"

53

It seemed that no one had noticed the issues he and Sasha had discussed.

He also realized that he had never really been one of them, even before this. As what he had been told sank in, it felt right. If it was true, and he wasn't sure, all of his identity as a human had potentially been ripped away in the past few minutes. He watched the dumb SLU guys hit on the art school girls and the really "deep thinkers" discuss pseudo-intellectual subjects such as whether or not a fork really does have consciousness.

However, he found himself already missing a normal life. He realized he would never again be able to go out and relax and just chill with his friends. His entire life would be dedicated to...this "mission."

That wasn't so bad. It would ensure an honorable death. Given his beliefs, this was very good. His beliefs came down to two words: honor and victory. He had a code of honor, but didn't see the need to have a god scare him into following it. Unlike standard religions, he chose a moral, honorable existence of his own free will, because it was good for the species, instead of doing it out of fear of retribution from a deity.

But, a part of him was really going to miss the "normal" life. Growing up to be a husband and father with the nine to five job. That was very tempting.

"Sasha?" he asked suddenly.

"Yeah?" she asked, snapping out of a daydream.

"What happens to this universe and us when we're done?"

She looked down again, shifted, then looked back up.

"Uh, well, Ghost and I have discussed this, and, uh, we don't know."

"Huh. Okay. Well, as long as it doesn't affect the Cards' chance at the pennant, it's cool." he said, smiling again.

"Right."

Taran suddenly stood up and grabbed his Cherry Coke.

"Going somewhere?" Sasha asked, looking up at him.

"I'm going for a walk to soak this in. You gonna be okay here by yourself?"

"Yeah. I'll be fine. If you even suspect the Psycho Mystic might be messing with you, hurry back here."

"Yeah. Be back in a bit."

"See ya."

Sasha smiled at him as he turned and walked away. She realized that he really was the ideal leader for this group. Very tough mentally and physically, but also highly intelligent. He wasn't the most book smart person, but he was very, very intelligent. Intelligence and knowledge were, by definition, very different. Taran had much intelligence. She had much knowledge. They complemented each other very well.

Taran strolled down Euclid (this was the street that intersected with Maryland, which Coffee Cartel is on the corner of) and looked at the stars. Where was this all-controlling creature? Was he up there? Was his existence intangible to them? How were they gonna pull this off? Was his team going to be any good? If they were, would he be a good leader?

But how does one even fight a god? Maybe that was in a later "briefing."

So far he knew he had Sasha and Nigel. Sasha he was sure would work out. Nigel he wasn't sure about at all. He knew that Nigel would never betray him outright, but there were still a lot of question marks surrounding his friend. Nigel's betrayal would be something subtle. Or, maybe, it would never come at all.

He never knew when it came to Nigel.

Taran was starting to come up on "the alley." The alley was exactly what it sounded like, but the only reason that it was referred to as such was because Taran and his friends used to frequent it. Back in the day. When the "old crew," as Taran called it, was still around. Before the breakdown. Taran's little losing-his-mind thing. All that was left now was Nigel.

Did he have all the bases covered?

He turned and walked down the alley, towards Kingshighway. It was just like he remembered. The back of Spoon's on the left, brick walls hiding houses on the right. Various pieces of trash on the ground. Parking lots coming up on the left, while the brick walls continued on the right all the way down. Very dimly lit and uninviting. Dead trees and cats.

He and Sasha would go to Cape Girardeau tomorrow with Nigel and explain the whole deal to him. Ghost should probably come to, since he was good at batting cleanup for Sasha.

The next issue was weapons, or if they would even need any. Needed or not, they would still be a good idea. And fun.

Weapons brought up finances. Or lack thereof. Who knows, maybe Sasha had been saving for a rainy day.

Part of me knows that everything I've just been told is true. I'm already planning.

He was being followed again. He felt a presence. This person was very good. Completely silent and keeping a safe distance. Blending in with the shadows. He didn't even need to see her to know. He could feel her.

Then, something else took hold of him.

He stopped and spoke.

"Dismal days and starry nights are the only moments that draw my attention. Dismal days, because they cause your tears. Starry nights, because the stars reflect off your tears so beautifully. It's time to wipe away the stars and look into an empty sky full of possibilities. Our future begins now." he spoke, then touched his mouth.

His follower gasped and halted, causing her boots to scrape on the ground.

"Taran…" a weeping female voice whispered behind him.

He turned and looked over his shoulder at the girl. She was staring at him with almost catlike eyes. She spoke again.

"You're...still alive." she said.

"And here I deserve to be. Is that the question?" he asked.

"How...step into the light. Let me see if it's really you." she mumbled with a hint of command, stepping toward him.

Taran stepped into the light from one of the backdoor lamps of Spoon's. He stopped, put his arms out, and slowly turned. She approached him.

"You're hair's shorter. You still have your mustache and goatee. You've put on some weight. And your style of dress is different. But it's definitely you." she said from behind him.

He turned to get a look at her. She was still in the dark.

"Did I know you in high school or something?" he asked, thoroughly confused. She had described the way he looked in high school fairly accurately. He had long, black hair and his mustache and goatee back then. He had been thinner and dressed much more flamboyantly.

"You don't remember?" she asked, about to go into tears again.

"I don't remember a LOT from high school. I'm sorry. Did we date or mess around or something?" he asked, half laughing.

"Taran...you died that day. I saw you. I died right next to you. We both survived, apparently, but I still remember. Why don't you remember?"

"Look, baby, I never died in high school. At least not all the way. I'd remember THAT."

"What year were you born?" she asked, beginning to come into the light.

"1978."

Just as she was coming into the light, she whirled around and grabbed her head, cursing under her breath. She walked in circles for a moment, then stopped and looked at him, still hidden in shadows.

"I'm sorry. You look just like him and have the same name. But, if you were him, you'd remember me and be 121 years old. He was born in 1880. So was I. I'm sorry. Goodbye."

She turned and began to stroll off.

"Alexandra?" he whispered, narrowing his eyes to penetrate the darkness that enveloped her.

She stopped and whirled around.

"You...it is you!" she whispered back, sniffling as she did so.

She ran to him and threw her arms around him, covering him in kisses.

"You do remember! God, you feel exactly the same in my arms! I knew if I waited, you'd eventually come back to me! I remember you told me that nothing could ever keep us apart, not even death! You were right! Taran! Oh, it feels so good to say your name again! Taran!"

"Alexandra." he said, grabbing her shoulders and trying to get her attention.

"Taran, why aren't you holding me? It's been over a century! Haven't you missed me?" she asked, finally prying her face off his shoulder.

It was her. It was Alexandra from the painting.

"Alexandra, look. The first time I saw you was about an hour or so ago in a painting. Then, I saw you outside. During this whole thing, I felt something. I do know you. I don't remember from where, but I know you. You seem to know me rather well and seemed to have missed me. I'm very glad we've found each other, I just don't know why. It seems like I'm asking a lot of people this question lately, but who are you?"

She pulled away from him, looking very hurt.

"Painting? Where? What? Taran...you really don't remember anything?"

"Apparently, I died quite a while ago, which I don't remember, nor anything that I guess preceded that death. All I remember is growing up here, in St. Louis, during the 80's and 90's. I'm sorry. What I do remember is hearing strange voices today, meeting a dead guy, a witch, and my apparent destiny. I'm guessing you fit into all this madness somehow, huh?" he flapped his arms in the air, then let them slap against his side.

"Maybe you were reincarnated? It's all starting again, isn't it?" Alexandra asked, her eyes lighting up.

"What? You mean the 'killing God' thing?"

"You know! That must be why I found you. Where's Michael uuuhhh and uuuhhh Evangela and Wil and uuuhhh Layne and-"

"I don't know those people. Wait, Layne painted that picture I was talking about. I know Sasha, Nigel, and Ghost. Ghost isn't part of the team, he's...he's more of a consultant."

"Ghost? Oh, you mean Richard. But...maybe he's fixing some of the mistakes from before. Maybe that's why there's new members. Wow." she said, smiling for the first time, revealing those teeth. Taran stared in disbelief. She caught him gazing at her teeth, "Oh those. Yeah, I've undergone a few changes since we last saw each other. We'll discuss that later. Right now, I just want to enjoy you."

She grabbed him with amazing strength and pulled him to her. Their lips locked and Taran received the most powerful kiss he had ever known. Their tongues were in perfect harmony, like they had become one being. She also had incredible strength with her tongue. It was without a doubt the best kiss he had ever received. It was beautiful.

Suddenly, something pricked his tongue and his mouth began to fill with blood.

He jerked back, covering his mouth.

"Ow! What the hell?" he yelled, giving her an icy stare.

"Sorry! I'm sorry! I've not kissed anyone since I've been a...this way."

"Are you a vampire?" he asked, smiling.

"What do you think?" she asked, smiling back.

"She is!" a deep, hateful voice echoed from farther down the alley.

Taran turned, shoving Alexandra behind him. He knew that voice. He prayed it belonged to who he thought it did.

"Oh shit. This guy's been chasing me for years now. Taran, I'll take care of this. There's no reason for you to get involved." Alexandra said, trying to pull Taran behind her.

"Alex, I might have all the reason in the world." Taran said menacingly, his eyes glazing over with anger.

The figure began to come into view. Long, black hair. Long, shiny, scaly green cloak. Black and red body armor. He had been in Taran's hallucination like this. Two swords crisscrossed on his back. The man in the painting.

The man in the painting.

"RAPHAEL!!!" Taran screamed, throwing Alexandra back a few feet and rushing at the man.

"Hahaha…good to see you, too, Taran. Patience!" Raphael laughed at the man coming towards him.

Taran was now about twenty feet from his nemesis. Raphael suddenly rushed at him, spun around and tripped him. Taran skidded across the concrete, then clutched his scraped-up arm. He immediately jumped back up and turned to face the warrior.

They locked eyes.

Alexandra stood back, a look of confusion on her face as she glanced back and forth between the two men. She was ready to jump in at any moment.

Taran suddenly felt the hatred flow through his veins, giving him what felt like infinite strength. A madness had overtaken him. He hated Raphael a thousand times as deeply as he had ever loved Rosaline. He felt as though he could simply approach Raphael and rip his head off with little or no difficulty.

Raphael was wearing a thin smile. The kind that the bullying sixth grader wore when he booked you in school. However, Taran could see Raphael was struggling to maintain his composure. He, too, felt that hatred that had years and years to build up.

He wanted to kill Raphael.

He would kill Raphael.

"Taran." the enemy spoke.

"What?"

"I have something that I want to give back to you."

"Feel free, asshole."

Raphael pulled a sword and its sheath off of his back. Taran got into a defensive stance. It was a long, curved blade with a black leather hilt. The sword he had held in the painting. His old sword from the dojo.

Raphael threw the blade and sheath at Taran's feet.

"I cannot kill you unless you are holding this. I ask you to pick it up so that I may kill you." Raphael said, very respectfully.

"Fair enough." Taran said, shrugging.

He bent down and reached for the blade. As he picked it up, he never took his eyes off of his enemy. To think that a man who observed honor so steadfastly could brutalize a woman as he had…

It was incomprehensible to Taran.

He lifted the sword carefully, unsheathed it, tossed the sheath to Alexandra, then he saluted Raphael with the blade, who returned the gesture.

He spun the sword around in his hand, coming to a stop in an offensive stance. He charged toward Raphael, screaming.

Raphael laughed, unsheathed his sword, parried, and purposely nicked Taran's left cheek.

Taran didn't even check his wound as he spun to a stop and faced Raphael again. The blood began to trickle down his cheek. It was Taran's turn to force a laugh now as he taunted his enemy.

"Stop fighting like a child, Raphael! Fight me like a man! Of course, if I had spent my whole life a cowardly traitor, such as yourself, I wouldn't know how, either."

"You will die for that." Raphael snarled.

The two stood about six feet apart, circling each other.

"So, how have you been, Taran? Are you still dating that child?"

"No, she left me for a younger guy. You?"

"I've been well, actually. I've now slain over seven hundred vampires and I'm looking to add another head to my collection. What happened to that little whore, I wonder?" Raphael wondered aloud, looking in Alexandra's direction.

Taran took advantage of this to attack.

He charged and slashed across Raphael's body armor. A huge spark shot out, but he didn't pierce the armor. Only a deep groove shown where he had hit.

Raphael stumbled back and laughed again.

"Nice." he commented, silently applauding Taran.

Taran had about much as he could stand of this opponent. He angled his blade so that the flat part would strike and smacked Raphael across the face with it.

Raphael's face trickled blood, and he fell back clutching his bloodied nose and mouth.

"Ah!!! Well done!" Raphael yelled, falling on his back.

Taran stood there, almost marveling at his utter brutality. He looked at the blood on the blade of his sword and smiled. He looked at Raphael, lying on the ground, wrapped in his cloak, blood oozing through the hands covering that condescending face of his. He wanted more. If enough force was applied, this blade would penetrate his skull. Taran began his approach.

At that moment, Raphael somersaulted backward and jumped up, blood still dripping down his face. He grinned at Taran, his teeth stained red.

"Thought you'd catch me unawares, did you? Not tonight, kid." he smiled that smile again.

"Wouldn't dream of it."

"Liar. Come. Just try to kill me."

"Okay." Taran said

Sword clashed against sword. They whirled back and forth. Taran kept jumping, dodging, whirling, swinging, and fighting. The only problem was, he was in terrible shape and starting to tire already. Months of inactivity were starting to catch up with him. Raphael was fighting with the same vigor as he had at the beginning of the contest. He was just hacking away, slowly wearing Taran down. The hero kept swinging and blocking and swinging and blocking and Raphael just kept coming.

Jesus fuck, how did I end up here? Taran thought.

It was January 29th, 1998. Taran and some of his friends and band-mates were hanging out at Nigel's new apartment in south St. Louis, down by Arsenal and Grand.

Lots of the other local musicians had come to Nigel's housewarming party, some of them to hang out with them, and some of them to hang out with the free keg beer that Taran had sponsored. Guys who had once had long hair milled around, slapping each other on the back and spilling beer everywhere, though no one but Nigel seemed to mind.

"Well, Taran, aside from never getting my deposit back, this was a great idea." Nigel muttered, leaning against a wall with his girlfriend, Puck, and Taran.

Taran laughed, set his beer down on a speaker, then began to pull his hair back into a ponytail.

"I'll help ya clean it up tomorrow, fucker, don't cry." Taran reassured him as he held his hair tie in his teeth.

Nigel rolled his eyes, then turned to Puck.

The two of them were as rock n' roll of a couple as one could have. He looked a bit like Taran, except with much lighter-colored hair, both in his recently trimmed hair and goatee. He had pierced ears, a pierced nose, a black tattoo that stretched around his arm, and an ironic t-shirt. She had short, clipped brown hair with blonde streaks, bright, flashy makeup, a million piercings in her ears, a pierced eyebrow, and a pierced navel, exposed so invitingly.

"Yes, dear?" she chirped sweetly, pecking him on the nose.

"I need you to throw everyone out of here. Now." he commanded, sweeping an arm across the living room, where most of the crowd was located.

Puck giggled and cocked an eyebrow at him.

"What, you want me to get out those dirty pictures we took the other night and show them to everyone?"

"Yes." Taran's voice boomed as he grinned and looked at Nigel questioningly.

Nigel rolled his eyes again.

"I guess I'll get over this, won't I?" he asked Taran and Puck.

Both nodded.

"About those pictures…" Taran began, then trailed off as a woman entered the room. It was the singer from Siren that he had seen a few months before, "Nigel, that's her. That's the girl I was telling you about." he pointed at the girl. She was wearing jeans and a Hello Kitty tank top.

"Rosaline? Her?" Puck questioned, looking at Taran like he was crazy.

"What? What's wrong with her?" he asked, never breaking his stare at Rosaline.

Nigel broke into the conversation.

"We'd have to move about a million more records before she'd even consider you, buddy. She has two sisters, and all three of them are exclusive to successful artists. Some weird thing about the Paris sisters. Like it's some family code or something. I think that one, Rosaline, is the only one who actually does something in the music scene here other than bang members of the Urge and Nerve and fucking Gravity Kills and whoever else has made it beyond I-270. I heard she's actually dating one of the guitarists from Missile Silo Suite."

Taran snapped his head around and glared at Nigel.

"You mean the one who wears that stupid fucking hat all the time?!"

Nigel, again, rolled his eyes.

"It's called a fedora. I don't think it's that dumb-looking. I'm not sure if it's him or not, though."

Puck grinned evilly.

"I think he's actually kinda hot. That cute little hat and that baby face. Yummy."

Taran and Nigel both rolled their eyes now.

"Taran, you should go talk to her." Puck suggested as she lit a Marlboro Menthol light.

Taran grabbed his beer off the speaker.

"That settles it. I must save her from fedora hell. Wish me luck." he saluted Nigel and Puck.

Puck turned to Nigel as Taran walked away.

"Don't you like how I'm not like her? See? Aren't I, like, the best girlfriend ever? Give me compliments, Nigel." she mock-whined to him as she kissed his neck repeatedly.

"Um…you're the only woman I know who is still hot even when she talks and…uh…I appreciate the fact that you're willing to date unsuccessful musicians as you so tactfully pointed out." he snickered.

Puck playfully hit him on the arm.

"You're lucky I'm the best girlfriend ever. A lesser woman would dump you for a musician from the east side of the river."

"Oooh...now that's slumming it. Hey, look, Taran's talking to her. Well, it looks like he's at least got his foot in the door now."

Puck turned and followed Nigel's gaze.

Taran was telling Rosaline some ridiculous story. He was gesticulating with his arms all over the place, nearly knocking beers out of hands, and making Rosaline double over with laughter. Nigel knew he had to be a nervous wreck, but there wasn't a bit of evidence. He had to give Taran credit for one thing.

He never showed fear.

"Nigel," Puck whispered to her boyfriend, "Rosaline will not make him happy. Do what you can to stop this from developing."

Nigel looked at Puck, then over to Taran and Rosaline.

"Little tired, Taran?" he snarled, getting that grin again.

"Fuck...you..." Taran wheezed.

Then, out of nowhere, Raphael stopped and just looked at Taran with a very curious look. He didn't know what to make of this. He stayed in a defensive stance and stared Raphael in the eye. Then, the enemy spoke.

"Your whole world is crumbling, Taran. You are losing everything you love, everything you're familiar with."

"I don't love anything anymore."

"Liar!" and Raphael slashed at Taran, cutting his left arm from the elbow to the hand. Taran groaned and dropped his sword. He suddenly felt the point of Raphael's sword piercing into his throat.

He turned and looked at Raphael. His rival was grinning.

Taran cocked an eyebrow.

Raphael returned the gesture.

Suddenly, Taran spit in his face. Raphael pulled his head back to dodge it, failed, and made a sound of disgust.

Taran ducked, rolled onto the ground, kicked Raphael over, and loosed the sword out of his enemy's hand. Raphael jumped on top of Taran and began to choke him. He knocked the attacker's hands off of his throat, pulled his legs up and wrapped them around Raphael's throat, choking him right back. Raphael clawed at the heavy boots and began to gasp for air. Suddenly, he felt Taran's boot knife, unsheathed it, and drove it into the meat of Taran's thigh. Taran let out a scream and Raphael got loose and rolled away. Taran pulled the knife out and felt the hot, wet blood gush out all over his leg.

Raphael got to his feet and froze, watching what Taran would do next. Taran attempted to get to his feet and collapsed again.

Raphael let out a cackle as he picked up his sword.

He began to approach Taran's exhausted body.

Taran was starting to black out from the oxygen deprivation and blood loss and pain.

"Wait..." Taran coughed, looking up at Raphael.

Raphael kept slowly walking toward his adversary.

"I...I need to show you something." Taran wheezed, as he reached behind him, then produced his Walther P99 and began firing.

Raphael's eyes lit up, then he crouched down and spun his sword in front of himself, deflecting the entire clip.

"Damn...dammit." Taran coughed again, trying to stand again as he reached behind himself for another clip.

Just then, he heard feet land right in front of him. He shook his head and tried to see straight. He saw a pair of womens' Doc Marten's. Alexandra.

NO!, he thought.

Alexandra picked up Taran's sword.

"Alright, asshole, you two have had your fun. I will not let you kill him. You want to hunt a vampire, then hunt a vampire."

"You know, Alexandra, this blade is made of a silver composite. The second it pierces your heart, you're dust."

"Fine. At least I died well."

"Very respectable."

Raphael leaped at her and within a split second, she vanished. Suddenly, he was thrown forward, over Taran, into a parked BMW. His sword clanked to the ground. He sat there, dazed, for a second, then shook it off, rolled off the car, and picked up his sword. Taran and Alexandra were gone.

"COWARD!!!! FIGHT LIKE YOUR VAMPIRE NATURE TELLS YOU!" he roared.

Once again, he was suddenly hurled across the alley into a brick wall, which, impressively, knocked a few bricks loose.

"Dammit! Enough of this sneaking around! Fight me like a warrior!"

"If you don't like the way I fight, then crawl away and beg for your life." she said, her voice coming from everywhere.

Raphael kept his back to the brick wall. He looked around, waiting for the undead creature to pop out at him. He was also keeping a lookout for Taran, making sure not to repeat his mistake of forgetting that there were two of them, both formidable in their own rights.

The night was dead. Occasionally, he would hear the scratch, scratch, scratch of some rat, or the roar of laughter in the distance from M.P. O'Reilly's. He inched closer in the direction of Kingshighway, deciding that would present him with more options, since the alley got wider down there.

Suddenly, he got an idea.

"Alexandra! How good is your swordsmanship?! Answer this question!" he bellowed to the open air.

A long, quiet time passed. He pondered whether this was good or bad. If she fought him in the open with swords, he would no doubt win. If they fought hand to hand, it could go either way. If they continued the way they had, she might kill him. He waited and waited with his back to the wall for what seemed like ages. She might have also taken off to protect Taran. The only way that she could do that was if Taran had been completely unconscious. Taran would never leave a fight unless his opponent was unconscious or dead. And, Raphael was neither.

Suddenly, Alexandra appeared right in front of him, completely unarmed.

"Okay, Hunter. We'll compromise here. You'll fight your way. I'll fight my way. Is that fair? Or do I need to give myself a handicap in order for you to kill me?"

Raphael stared into her eyes, trying to detect any kind of self-doubt or fear. He found none. She was pretty convinced she could win. But, he was, too.

"No. Let's do this."

She vanished again.

"Shit." Raphael muttered to himself, bringing his sword up and backing up against the wall again. He had been tracking vampires for a long time and she was one of the fastest he had ever seen. Maybe even THE fastest. She was the only one who had the ability to move so fast that it really did look like she vanished into thin air. It was probably the combination of the vampirism and the fact that she was one of the Nine. He had heard of them before. They were an irritation then and looking like they would be an irritation now. He had suspected that they were enhanced before, but Alexandra was proof.

He heard a noise to his right.

He looked down the alley and saw nothing. He squinted and studied every shadow he saw. Nothing. She wasn't down there.

Suddenly, he was soaring through the air in that direction. Right before he smashed into a dumpster, he heard her giggle.

He went face and right shoulder first into it. He landed with a thud, aching all over. His head swam and his shoulder throbbed. He couldn't believe this vampire was getting the best of him.

Raphael jumped up and spun around. Alexandra stood there, smiling at him, fangs glinting in the pale streetlight. He began to walk towards her, very slowly. He focused his eyes on her, hoping that if she moved again, he would be able to follow her movements. She began to walk towards him, too, also slowly.

"Alexandra…" he nearly whispered, feeling his moment of triumph approaching.

"Raphael…" she whispered back, mocking him.

They were about ten feet apart now. She stopped and got into a defensive stance. He kept walking toward her, never taking his eyes off of her. She began to back away a little bit when he got too close.

64

"Afraid?" he asked her, smiling.

"No, I-" she looked over Raphael's right shoulder and her eyes widened, "Taran, no!" she screamed.

Raphael felt something hard hit his shoulder. He got an idea. He began to turn his head to look at Taran, faking Alexandra out, then whipped back around and plunged his sword forward. Right through her chest. He felt another hit on his shoulder. Still didn't hurt. He heard the girl screaming, accompanied by a hissing sound. This was the silver of his sword burning her insides. He twisted the blade around, so the wound wouldn't close up.

Suddenly, he felt himself being picked up. The vampire slid off of his sword.

"What the-" he began to exclaim, before he was dropped straight down on Taran's knee, which was kicking up.

Raphael yelled in pain as he came down on the upward limb. He then fell to the ground, trying to catch his breath, as the wind had been knocked out of him. He looked up and saw Taran.

Taran stared down at him, one of the fiercest looks he had ever seen. All he saw was hatred and the need to destroy. He didn't utter a word. Taran stood there, a cold statue. A monument to hate and killing.

A breeze kicked up and the two continued to stare at each other. The wind blew Taran's hair around a little. He didn't even blink.

"Taran...what...what happened to you?" Raphael asked, puzzled. He might have betrayed his remnant of affection for the young man. He also realized that the vampire had fallen silent. Maybe she was finally dead.

Then, in the blink of an eye, Taran moved. His right hand shot up his left sleeve, pulling out a dagger. Raphael rolled. The dagger stuck into the concrete with a "ping" right where his face had been. He swore it clipped a couple of hairs on the back of his head.

Raphael jumped back up and turned to face his old nemesis. Taran had retrieved his sword. They locked eyes again. They both raised their blades. They both began to rush each other. They both let out a roar, charging into battle.

Suddenly, something exploded on the ground, sending them both flying back. Raphael hit the wall again (he was getting really tired of this) and Taran hit the BMW that Raphael had hit earlier.

"HUNTER!" a female voice bellowed. It was Sasha.

Raphael stood and looked at the woman who had summoned him by his title.

"Hunter, I understand what you're doing here. But, perhaps it would be better if you didn't try to kill a member of my team. If you did, I would be very angry." Sasha said, her eyes narrowing as she continued to walk towards him.

"Excuse me, little girl, but this is none of your business. Who are you, anyway?" Raphael asked, offended that someone as unimportant as this baby would dare address him by his formal title.

Sasha walked up to him and turned her back. She pulled the back of her top down and revealed a symbol on her left shoulder blade. The mark of the Mystics. It resembled a planet with two lines through it with four points at each corner.

His eyes widened.

"Mystic? You're kidding." he said, studying the tattoo.

"No, I'm not. But, if you think you're taking…" she pointed to Alexandra's motionless body, "…that, you're kidding yourself." Sasha said, fixing her shirt and turning to face him.

Taran walked over to Alexandra's body to examine her. She was breathing. He didn't realize that vampires even needed to breathe, but he also knew nothing of how their bodies worked. This did mean, however, that she was alive, at least relative to her vampirism, he supposed.

She was lying on her left side with her back to him. He rolled her on her back.

"I have pursued this vampire for quite some time, Mystic. It has been my life for the past five years. Will you really deny me this moment of glory now? She means nothing to you! Let me kill her!" Raphael said, trying his hardest to be respectful.

Taran looked at Alexandra's face. The whitening skin. The almost blond hair. The light pink lips. The blood dripping from her mouth. If she died, so must Raphael.

"You're right, she means nothing to me. But, apparently, she means something to him. Look at how he cares for her even in his poor condition. She is ours." Sasha said, pointing to Taran crouched over Alexandra's body.

Taran opened the hole in her shirt and looked at her wound. Blood was still gushing out of it. She would probably die soon.

"So, there's no way we can resolve this with diplomacy then?" Raphael asked, shifting his eyes from Sasha to Taran.

"That is up to you." she answered.

"Sasha! Tend to her!" Taran said, standing and turning to face Raphael, sword in hand, "Wanna finish killing each other?"

"More than you can imagine." Raphael answered, smiling again.

"Taran-" Sasha started.

"Fix her, NOW! That's a fucking order!" Taran screamed, on the verge of madness.

"As you wish." she responded, softly. She knew, in her heart, he was making the wrong decision, but she was unable to undermine him. She knelt over Alexandra and began looking at the wound.

"Oh, man." she said, seeing the girl's situation as nearly hopeless. This was a death wound for a vampire, "GHOST! HELP ME! PLEASE!" she screamed into the air.

"Who's Ghost?" Raphael asked Taran.

"I don't know. Some dead guy she hangs out with." he replied.

"Fair enough. Killing each other, remember?"

"Right, right. Sorry."

They leapt into action. Taran had become a monster. He knew no pain. He knew no defeat. He knew nothing other than victory. And vengeance. He would not be denied it. Again. Raphael would be defeated tonight. One way or another. His body, despite his injuries, moved fluidly and without fault. He matched every single one of Raphael's attacks and initiated many of his own.

Raphael was actually quite amazed by how well his former student was fighting.

Their sword play increased in speed and intensity. Sparks began flying every time their blades met. They became a blur of sparks and metal.

Taran faked Raphael out with a swing to the left, spun around, connecting with Raphael's right bicep and finally piercing his enemy's armor.

Raphael let out a cry, but didn't slow down. He flipped over Taran, kicked him in the back and raised his blade to deliver the death blow. Taran rolled, somersalted back up, and met Raphael's blade with his own.

Ghost finally appeared at Sasha's side. He looked down at Alexandra, his eyes widened, but quickly hid his recognition.

"Vampire Hunter?" he asked, looking at the fledgling Mystic.

"Yes. And as you can probably tell, he had a silver blade. Ghost, if she dies, we might lose Taran, too. Maybe not in body, but in spirit. His life has been filled with too many tragedies already. I don't know what his deal is with this girl, but I sense love in him towards her. I don't understand it. I don't even know who she is. I need your instruction. Tell me how to save her." Sasha pleaded.

"I know who she is. I also know why Taran feels as he does. I'll explain all that later. For now, let's fix the vampire. First, vampires heal just like humans, only faster."

"Right. I knew that. But, look at the wound. He twisted his sword so that it would be oddly shaped and wouldn't close."

"I see that, but, understand that these…creatures can tolerate many more injuries than humans. There's an exit wound, right?"

"Yes."

"Take your hands and place them on her stomach over the wound."

"Okay." she did exactly as he told her.

"Now, do your Fire Stream spell."

"What?!"

"It'll cauterize her wound! Just do it!"

Sasha channeled her spirit through her arms and into her hands. She then envisioned the result she wanted and forced it out.

"Protective Fire." she whispered.

Fire shot from her hands and through Alexandra's body. Alexandra let out a cry and became conscious again. She thrashed about and threw Sasha off of her.

Ghost looked down the street and his eyes widened. He took off running in the direction of whatever he saw.

"What did you do to me?!" Alexandra hissed, sitting up, her eyes burning into Sasha.

"I saved the life of a vampire, if you can believe it." Sasha replied, glaring at Alexandra.

Alexandra stopped, took this in, clutched her wound, and winced. As she was doing this, the battle between Taran and Raphael was reaching an impossible point. Neither had inflicted a new wound. Neither had begun to win or lose. They were matched. Perfectly. Each man's hatred had consumed him and become him. Their hatred was equal. So was their ability to kill each other.

Alexandra and Sasha had both noticed this.

"Witch, what is happening?" the vampire asked.

"They won't stop until one of them is dead. And my name is Sasha."

"Oh, sorry. I'm Alexandra. Um, I don't want to sound pessimistic, but I don't think Taran's in the best shape to take on the most legendary vampire hunter of all time."

"I agree, but I don't want to distract him. Raphael might use the opportunity to kill him."

"True, but if I interfere, Taran could get away."

"You really think Taran would run away from Raphael?" Sasha asked in a "duh" tone of voice.

"Why do they hate each other so much?"

"That part of Taran's past is hidden from me. I don't know."

"What do you mean, 'hidden from you?'"

"I'm a Mystic." Sasha explained, "I am part of their White Coven, meaning my powers lean towards healing and defense. One of my abilities is to sense thoughts and feelings. If someone's unconscious, I can usually penetrate into their memories and learn their entire history. I did this to Taran when I was tracking him to find out if he was really our leader."

"It is happening again!" Alexandra exclaimed, "Am I to be part of a new team? Of the Nine?"

"'New team?' Why do you think you're included? There's no way in hell a blood drinker is part of our team."

She began to open her mouth to let this child of a Mystic have it. Unfortunately, she wasn't in great shape, either.

She moaned and collapsed again. She began wheezing and writhing around. Her eyes were rolling into the back of her head. She was dying again.

"NO! Now what?" Sasha yelled, running over to Alexandra to

reexamine her. Suddenly, she realized what was happening to her. She had lost so much blood, what her entire existence depended on, that her body was shutting down. Alexandra needed to feed. NOW.

This meant interrupting the battle. This was going to be very bad. How was she going to pull this off? She thought about using her Baby Bolt spell again, the one she had used to split them up initially, but decided she needed something that would render Raphael immobile for at least a couple of minutes.

Unfortunately, all of spells were of the White Coven, which was all defense and healing.

Taran's knees buckled, but he quickly stood back up. His face was beginning to go slack, and his breathing was a series of moans.

Raphael redoubled his efforts, swinging like a man chopping down a tree in triple speed, and Taran collapsed.

Raphael raised his blade to finish Taran. After this, he would take care of Alexandra, then render the Mystic unconscious. He couldn't kill her, as the Vampire Hunters often needed cooperation from the Mystics on some joint missions.

Taran looked back up at his old master.

"You killed me a long time ago, Raphael, and I still walked away from it. You may kill me now, again, but you won't end me. Apparently, I died over a century ago, too. Good luck, you piece of shit." Taran mumbled.

Raphael hesitated.

CRUSH YOUR HEAD CRUSH YOUR HEAD CRUSH YOUR HEAD!!!

Raphael screamed, dropped his sword, and fell on his side. He curled into the fetal position and vomited.

Sasha gently set Alexandra's head onto her jacket and ran over to Taran. She grabbed his arm and started lifting him.

"Get up! Now! Come on, Taran!" she yelled, jerking on his arm.

He began to sit up and placed an arm around Sasha's tiny frame.

"Look, I can't lift you, but I'll try, okay?" she said, pecking him on the cheek. He looked at her, smiled, then shook his head.

"I…walk. It's cool." he heaved a sharp breath and slowly stood up, teetering to the right, then the left. He eventually centered his gravity, then began looking around.

"What? Let's go." Sasha barked, walking back to Alexandra's body.

Taran continued looking around the alley for something.

"Taran, she is going to DIE. Let's go. I don't know what happened to Raphael, but I don't want to see if he gets back up. Either way, Alexandra is going to die soon, unless I can do something. Taran?"

At the mention of Alexandra's possible death, Taran gave all of his attention to Sasha. After she was done speaking, he looked at Alexandra, then at Raphael. He did this again.

Suddenly, a wraith-like creature floated out of one of the parking lots by the alley. It was carrying Taran's sword and shambling toward them.

HI TARAN HI SASHA HI ALEXANDRA

Taran and Sasha both cried out in pain briefly, then looked at the gaunt figure that was approaching them.

Raphael stopped moving or making noises and now appeared to sleep.

"Taran..." Sasha started, but trailed off as the figure revealed itself.

It was a human male, Caucasian, but horribly withered. His white t-shirt and jeans were torn to pieces and hung off his body like rags. Lesions and rashes were all over his skin, as were endless trackmarks from repeated hypodermic needle use. He had three or four thin clumps of white hair on his head, and his age was indeterminable.

"Sorry...don't talk...people...much..." the man mumbled hoarsely.

"Right. We're leaving. Give me the sword." Taran said, looking back at Sasha briefly and nodding.

His sword floated out of the man's hands, then flew at him. Taran ducked and threw up his hands in a futile effort to protect himself.

It stopped an inch in front of his face and floated there, suspended in thin air.

Taran slowly uncovered his face and looked at the levitating sword. Its point almost touched his nose. As he backed away a bit, the sword began to float down a bit, and it began to turn so that the handle faced him.

Taran quickly seized the sword, then gathered up his sheath.

"Okay, Sasha, I'll carry her. You carry my sword and we're getting out of here now."

"Wait, what about...him?" she asked, pointing at the emaciated man.

"I don't have time for fucking junkies, especially not now." he snapped, lifting Alexandra, whose breathing was extremely shallow now, "I can't fucking stand them. We're leaving."

Sasha looked at him strangely, almost in disbelief.

"Okay, but we need to talk about this later." she said, taking his sword from him.

I AM ONE OF NINE

Both of them winced again, and Alexandra jolted a bit in Taran's arms. She blinked her eyes open.

"Bullshit. Goodbye." Taran yelled, not even looking at him.

"Layne..." Alexandra whispered, trying to point at the thin man, "...one of us."

Taran fumed, breathing through his nostrils quite loudly, then turned to Sasha as he lifted Alexandra completely off the ground.

"Fine, he comes, but no hard drugs allowed in the Halfway."

"Okay." Sasha squeaked, then waved for the man to follow them, "Layne, huh? Nice to meet you. We're going to the Halfway, so follow us."

He started floating toward her.

VII: Dialogue

Taran and Sasha burst through the front door, carrying Alexandra. As the huge steel door started to slam shut behind them, it suddenly froze, then swung back open and smacked against the wall. A few seconds later, Layne shambled in.

Taran and Sasha hung a left, then scrambled toward the living room.

"Taran, set her down on the couch in there! MILK BONE! MILK BONE!" Sasha yelled and let Taran take the vampire.

Taran ran into the living room and flung her down on the couch. He looked at her face again. Her skin was no longer pale pink and soft. It was now pale white, drawn, and basically outlining her skull. It was almost see-through now, too. He touched her skin, hoping his touch would single-handedly revive her and make her all better.

Then he noticed it.

She wasn't breathing anymore. He felt for a pulse on her neck and felt none. Maybe vampires didn't have pulses.

"Sasha." he almost coughed.

She didn't answer.

"Sasha!"

Still no answer.

"SASHA!!!" he screamed, whirling around to see what she was doing.

She came running into the room, Milk Bone behind her.

"Holy shit, she's hot!" Bone exclaimed, pointing at Alexandra, then paused, "Holy shit, she's dead!"

"How is she?" Sasha asked, coming over to the couch where Alex was laid out.

"She's dead."

Raphael couldn't believe this. He had lost a total of four battles in his entire existence. In this world and his home world.

Tonight, he had been beaten by an out-of shape reincarnate, a vampire, a Psycho Mystic, and a White Mystic.

No, he had not lost. He had not been defeated. Just delayed.

He lifted himself off the ground, felt dizziness start to overtake him, then slumped back onto the cold concrete.

He knew Taran had been part of the original team. The 'old' Taran, he should say. So had Alexandra. He knew that the Psycho Mystic had been, too, since he had been the second most notorious out of the group. Maybe this child Mystic was part of a new team.

The man assisting "Sasha," as Taran had called her, must've been the legendary Ghost. He had heard stories about him, too. He had defied this universe's god and been punished.

The legend of the Nine was very popular discussion among the Vampire Hunters. They were regarded as heroes by many of the younger

Hunters. He knew they were little more than pawns.

Raphael sat up, focused, got his head back in order, then stood.

He wobbled for a moment, put his hand up against the brick wall behind him and took a few deep breaths.

Of course, if word got out that a "new" Nine were working with a vampire, the Hunters would be enraged and he could lead an attack that could wipe out the rest of his enemies.

Raphael finally stood on his own, stretched his limbs, then bent down to grab his sword.

He sheathed it and began running back to the local Vampire Hunter's Guild.

Sasha and Taran stopped for a moment and stared at each other.

"What?" Sasha asked, slowly approaching the body on the couch.

"She's dead." Taran mumbled, then leaned back on his knees, stunned.

She knelt down and looked at the girl's wound. It was cauterized alright. Like a big, black hole in her body. She wasn't breathing, either. No heartbeat. Her mind raced. One last option.

"Taran, give me your hand."

"Why?" he asked, giving her a cautious look.

"Asshole! Give me your hand!"

Taran put his hand out. Sasha seized it, pulled a dagger from his boot and slashed his hand.

He screamed and tried to grab it with his free hand, but Sasha yanked it away.

She put his hand over Alexandra's mouth and squeezed it, dripping blood into the vampire's mouth. The drops were collecting on her lips and a few were dropping in between her teeth.

"Come on, vampire." Sasha muttered. She took her other hand and began to force the girl's mouth open more.

Suddenly, Alexandra's eyes flew open. She seized Sasha's hand and bit into the Mystic's wrist. Sasha let out a scream and tried to pry herself from the vampire.

"Alex, no!" Taran yelled, tackling Alexandra and shoving Sasha onto the other side of the room. Milk Bone pulled his shirt off and wrapped Sasha's wrist in it.

Alexandra lay under Taran as he straddled her on the couch, trying to wrestle her way free. He held her wrists, felt her weakened strength in her contracting arm muscles. Eventually, she sighed and gave up, going limp underneath him.

"Taran...I'm sorry. I need blood...now. Tar-"

He shoved his bleeding hand onto her mouth.

She immediately pushed it away.

"No, I can't. I...need an evil...person...I..."

"Shut up. Drink." he shoved his hand into her face again. She turned her head away.

"Goddammit, Alex! Drink my fucking blood!" he yelled, putting his face right up against hers.

Suddenly, she grabbed him and sank her teeth into his neck. A horrible sucking sound began. Taran jerked around under her iron grip. It lasted for a only a minute or so, but it felt like an hour. He could feel the blood passing out of the wound and into her cold, moist mouth. He felt the precious and necessary red life force drain out of him. He was dying. He was convinced of it. His heart was pounding and sounded like canons going off. His life was passing out of his body and into her mouth. He was dying. At the worst time. He was on the verge of something huge and-

He was thrown off of her and landed with a thud on the floor. He lay there, trying to make sense of what just happened. Sasha lay on the other couch, glaring at Alexandra. The vampiress lay on the main couch, getting her composure back.

Ghost appeared in the doorway, with Layne behind him. Everyone saw him, but Milk Bone.

Ghost was a tall, slender man. Dark brown hair, bearded, narrow face, and very strange eyes. Taran couldn't believe that this was the first time he was noticing this. Ghost had no pupils. His eyes were solid white. Very odd.

Alexandra's eyes widened and her elbows buckled. She sprawled out on the couch on her stomach, looking like a beautiful beached mermaid.

"Richard, you're back, too? How...what's happened? We're really doing it again, aren't we? I always knew I'd have my second shot. How have you been? Where have you been? I've been trying to find you for years. I went back to the bar and all the places we used to train and spend time and everything. Where did you go?" she paused and looked down, "I'm sorry, it's just that...I was afraid I would wander forever and never... never get a chance to...well, make things right, you understand?"

"It's good to see you, too, Alexandra, though your...'condition' troubles me. Last I saw you, you were dead over by the riverfront. Taran and Layne had been shot, too. It's very relieving...and frightening to see you two again." Ghost explained, looking as though he was struggling to keep control of himself.

"Shot?!" Taran spat and whirled to look at Alexandra, then Sasha, then Ghost.

"Who the FUCK is you all talkin' to?!" Milk Bone yelled.

"Bone, would you excuse us, please?" Taran asked.

"But, who-"

"Now." Taran said, staring daggers at him.

NOW a voice thundered in his head and Layne crept past him, into the living room.

"Whatever, dude..." Bone mumbled, looking at Layne, terrified,

then walked toward the basement steps in the hallway.

"Ghost, what're you two talking about?" Sasha asked, securing a wrap around her wrist as she stood again and approached the specter.

Layne sat down on the floor in the corner of the room and stared at Ghost.

"Hang on. Sasha, why don't you just heal that?" Taran interrupted, pointing at the reddening towel around her wrist.

"White Mystics can't heal themselves. Anyway, Ghost, what's going on?" she asked.

"Sasha, I wanted to wait until everyone was together again. It's not like I lied to you, it's just-"

Sasha finally exploded.

"Again?! What the hell is going on, Ghost? I mean, 'Richard.' How have you met them before? Why have you kept all this from me? You've been my mentor and friend for as long as I can remember. You had a responsibility to tell me everything. We can't do this unless you are completely and totally honest with us! You know everything about us. Everything. And now, it turns out you've been lying to me for eighteen years! Why? Why?!" Sasha screamed at him, clutching her wrist. She shook her head, sighed, then walked over to Taran and seized his bloody hand. She wrapped her hands around it and whispered something almost inaudible as she closed her eyes. A quick flash of light sparked under her hands and he winced. When she removed her hands, his previously slashed palm was scarred, but healed.

"Thanks." he offered, then grinned weakly at her. She turned from him before he could say anything else.

With her back to everyone else, Sasha spoke again.

"So? Ghost?"

Ghost looked at all of them, trying to figure out where to start. He began to realize that his plan of explaining "everything else" when the team was finally assembled wasn't going to work. He had really believed that all the originals were dead. He couldn't figure out how Alexandra had been susceptible to vampirism. She wasn't of this universe. It couldn't have worked. However, it had.

"Richard, tell her." Alexandra said, finally sitting up, then nervously glancing at Taran. His neck had healed already. She double-checked this with another glance, then turned her attention back to the dead man.

Ghost closed his eyes and thought about the consequences of this. If he told them what happened before, it might convince them to give up this near-impossible quest. That would be everyone and everything's destruction. On the other hand, Alexandra had lived through all of it and seemed more eager to fight than before. He also realized Sasha wouldn't relent until he had told her everything. And, telling them might help them avoid the mistakes the originals had made.

He decided to talk.

"Okay, I'll explain everything. However, my story stops almost exactly a hundred years ago. After that, Alexandra will take over and tell all of us what happened after the executions. Are we agreed, Alexandra?" he asked.

"Yes, we're agreed."

"Okay, here's the story of the Nine."

VII: The Legend of the Nine

"I'll tell you what I can remember. No one remembers every detail, especially not one who has walked the earth for 161 years. The story of the Nine took place a while ago, and not all of this will be verbatim.

"In 1865, I died. My human name was Richard Barrywood. I had been a lifelong resident of Fairfax, Virginia. I had always been a sickly person, so, much of my time was spent buried in books and researching things of interest, usually in bed. In my readings, I discovered many great authors with all sorts of interesting thoughts. Many of these thoughts dealt with things like the existence of deities, where we came from, how the universe was made up, and other assorted timeless questions. I read these books with great fervor and interest. In the long run, it became my obsession in my mortal life. I was a person who craved answers, but perhaps new questions even moreso.

"In all my readings and ponderings, I never found anything that convinced me one way or another. Then one day, as I was nearing my death, a priest came to see me, to do my last rites. When he was finished, I asked to speak to him in confidence.

He agreed and I asked the question that had been burning in my mind throughout my life. I needed to know before I died.

"'Father, is there a God?' I asked.

"He almost recoiled from me, shocked that a man about to appear before God for judgment would be crazy enough to verbalize such a question to a priest.

"'Of course there is! Why would you even question such a thing?'

"'Because I do. Why do we yawn? We can't help it. Because we do. If the question is in my heart, it's in my heart, and this God will know this. Besides...well...it's also about...it's just...there's so much perfection in this world.'

"'That's exactly why there must be a God. Do you honestly believe such perfection could come out of chaos?'

"'But, what else would come out of chaos? Isn't it possible that the only two results from chaos would be perfection or utter destruction? Perhaps we are still in chaos now and the only reason that I see perfection all around is because my world has been books. At least in books, good and evil are perfectly balanced. That's perfection. The God you speak of wants no evil. If you have no evil, how can you define good? You have nothing to contrast it with. If you have no good, then God's defeated himself. It's all contradictions. It's not a very well thought-out religion.

"'A person, I believe, Father, is like a small universe. There's a constant battle between good and evil inside them. Your God wants purity. Purity is achieved only in the womb and after death. The time in between is called life. I believe that each individual leans toward good, but they have differing interpretations of good and differing objectives in life. They also have quite a bit of evil in them, it's just less than the amount of good."

"I disagree, Ghost, I-" Taran interrupted.

"That's very nice, Taran, now please continue to stay quiet and listen."

"Prick." Taran whispered to himself, joining Alexandra on the couch. She slipped into his arms and rested her head on his chest. He looked down at her questioningly, then returned to his attention to Ghost.

Sasha looked over at the couple and scowled.

Ghost began again.

"Like I was saying, each individual is inherently good, just with different interpretations and different objectives. Allow me to explain.

"It is possible to have two men, both righteous and good, who have different goals. If these goals conflict, these two men become enemies. Some people will perceive one as the 'hero,' and the other as the 'villain.' Another side will see the reverse. These two men are both good in their hearts, but are mortal enemies because of a conflicting agenda.

"Or point of view." Taran interjected, "What if we have the same set of values and whatever, just different perspectives on 'what happened?'"

"Taran..." Sasha began, then shut her mouth and shook her head.

"No, Sasha, he's got a good point. I wish I had thought of that 136 years ago. Anyway...

"So, I explained my views to the priest and he seemed very interested. It took much longer than it has with you all, so after about an hour, he put a question to me.

"'You tell me, Mr. Barrywood, is there a God?'

"I weighed this question heavily. I already had my mind made up, but I wasn't sure what consequences my answer would have.

"'No.' I answered.

"The priest hung his head and shook it. He muttered a curse in Latin and looked at me.

"'Why?'

"'Because, Father, a living being could never create perfection. Everyone creates based on opinion and feeling. To create perfection, one would have to be completely unfeeling and unbiased. This is impossible. I believe in no god. I'm sorry to disappoint you, Father. I truly am. I've always respected you and loved you and what you do for people. I'm sorry. A thousand times.'

"'Richard, do not worry about me. Worry about your soul.'

"And I died at that exact moment.

"That sucks." Taran cut in again.

"TARAN, YOU...I'm sorry, I'm sorry. I really need to hear this, so please keep your comments to yourself. Please." Sasha asked with pleading eyes.

Taran opened his mouth to respond, then sighed and smiled at Sasha. He nodded in acquiescence.

"Taran, you haven't changed one bit." Alexandra sighed, "Richard, continue. If he spits out another of his one-liners or arguments again, just continue as though he said nothing, okay?"

"Fair enough, Alexandra. So, I died.

"I can't decide if I was unconscious or if it's possible to be unconscious when you're deceased, but-"

"It is." Alexandra added, then quickly looked down, "Sorry."

"Regardless, I 'awoke' in what looked like a jail cell. I sat there for a bit, alone in the prison, until a lawman came and got me and informed that He was waiting for me. I was a bit surprised at this, as you can probably imagine.

"Anyway, I ended up in this place that looked like one of those interrogation rooms on that television program, 'Law and Order.' Except no two-way mirror. Just white walls, white ceiling, white floor. Not even a pure white, either. A dirty white, like it was very old and had been used many times. There was a black metal table in the middle of the room, and a man was seated behind it. This is the very puzzling part.

"First of all, his appearance was exactly as Jesus Christ is commonly pictured. Long brown hair, brown beard, Caucasian, everything. If you pictured what you know as Jesus Christ in your head, that is exactly what I saw. But, one very strange difference.

"He was approximately eight to nine feet tall. I stood and stared at him. I couldn't believe it. I was very confused. Not about his existence, I mean, he was sitting right in front of me. I was confused about what this meant. Was he an all-powerful godlike being or just a more evolved being? As far as I know, no one had ever asked that question. Most people either believe in God or didn't. They never questioned the nature of his existence. Then, he spoke.

"'Hi, Richard, how are you?' he asked, sounding sincere.

"'Probably the same way most people are at this point. Very confused. By the way, how shall I address the Almighty?' I asked, playing it safe.

"He laughed and gestured for me to sit in the chair opposite him. I sat and faced him, waiting for an answer.

"'You may address me as…God. How's that?'

"'Are you really?'

"'Of course I am. Would you be more comfortable if the afterlife were run by your beloved President, Mr. Lincoln?'

"'Actually, 'God,' I would. I mean no offense, by this.'

"'Of course you don't. Unfortunately, I saw Mr. Lincoln right before I saw you, Mr. Barrywood.'

"'What do you mean?'

"'He died just before you, Richard. Didn't you hear? Very unfortunate. He was shot.'

"I was shaken by this. I had been a huge Lincoln supporter in a time when he was hated by many. The Civil War had ended just days before my death, and I died knowing that one of my heroes had achieved a great victory. Now, it seemed that the price of victory was a high one. Of course, I had died with no great accomplishments or victories in my life, which left me, understandably, with somewhat of a feeling of regret. But, this is not the focus of my tale.

"I paused for a moment, deciding to use this opportunity to gather some of the answers I had craved throughout my life.

"'Um, God, why did you create me? I mean, why create a worthless being? Did you intend to create me or am I a product of a system that you've either let get out of control or that you can no longer control?'

"He stood up, sending his chair thundering into the wall behind him and pointed a huge finger down at me.

"Suddenly, the anger melted from his face and a smile a appeared. His enormous finger was still almost touching my face.

"'Boo.' he whispered, then started cackling, 'I'm not telling you, Dicky boy. You needn't know these things. That's my domain.'

"I didn't accept this.

"'But we are all affected by this. Surely, you can see how it's not just your concern. We all have a right to-'

"'YOU AMERICANS AND YOUR FUCKING RIGHTS!' he screamed, withdrawing his finger, then slapping the table with that hand. He stared down at me for a moment, then melted his face back into a grin, 'Richard, look, I'm God and well…that's kinda it for you, my loyal subject. You can keep asking me questions, but if you bug me too much, I'll send you to Hell for eternity, and then you'll have a newfound familiarity with regret. You've been warned. Don't be stupid.' he muttered as he pulled his chair back up and sat down again.

"'I don't see you as God. You failed and won't admit it.' I told him.

"What followed was actually somewhat amusing.

"His jaw dropped and he stared at me in disbelief.

"'YOU…I created you. With love. I infused you with life. I can take it away…well, I guess I already did, but you get the point. Anyway, you owe me your-'

"'I understand, I just don't think that you have a complete understanding of how your own universe works. That's…almost funny.'

"'Quite frankly, it doesn't matter what you think, Richard. The fact is, I run the universe and you don't. I created you, not vice versa. I'm your god. Say it.'

"'You created me, but you do not control me. I can hurt you.' I said, standing up and staring down at him as he sat there.

"He then stood and I took in his full size. He was huge. He stared down at me with the cruelest, most hateful stare I had ever seen at that point.

"'What went wrong with you? Every other one has been either

very submissive or became so after I explained to them what kind of eternity I could give them if they upset me. You're different. Why are you different?'

"'I do not know. I do not care.' I said and lunged at him. When my body collided with his, he was so surprised he fell back. I punched him in the face three times before he launched me into the opposite wall. I sat up and looked at him. He was holding his face in pain! He held his face in pain! If God could be hurt, he could most likely be killed! I rejoiced in the agony I had delivered to him! I had been right (at least about the conclusions I had reached after I had died)!

"God stood up and looked at me. He was bleeding.

"'You know now that I am ageless but mortal. You shall never be able to share your secret with any other soul. I condemn you to an eternity on Earth in the form of a ghost. You are no longer the mortal Richard Barrywood. You are now nothing more than a ghost. You can never interact with any of your once fellow mortals nor can you ever sleep. Your soul shall slowly go mad. I condemn you, Ghost. I condemn you to a fate worse than Hell. An eternity of watching life go by and never including you. Forever. I sentence you to silence. No one shall ever know what you've discovered. Have fun.'

"And, in a very cliché manner, he snapped his fingers and I appeared right where I had been before, except my room had been cleaned and emptied.

"I verified what that wretched god-thing had told me about never being heard or seen and never sleeping. As I suspected, he wasn't joking.

"So, after a number of rather painful incidents in Fairfax, I headed west to St. Louis, where I found that I could walk on water, so I laid down and...well...

"Before I continue, however, let me talk about what I became exactly.

"First, I couldn't pick anything up or shove anything or apply any force to objects. I could, however, touch them. Please, call your friend 'Milk Bone' back in here."

Taran jumped up and ran to the doorway.

"MILK BONE!!! GET UP HERE!!!" he screamed, cupping his mouth with a hand and aiming it down the hall.

Silence. Silence. Silence. Suddenly, he heard that familiar thud of Bone flying up the steps.

"What? You done talkin' to the air?" Bone said, emerging from the basement.

"Where do you want him to stand?" Taran asked Ghost.

"YOU STILL DOIN' THAT?! What the FUCK, man?!" Bone yelled.

"Just bring him in the room." Ghost said.

"Milk Bone, I swear I'll explain everything to you in like five minutes. I just need you to stand in the middle of the living room for a sec, okay?" Taran asked.

"Whatever, dude." he answered and walked into the living room, standing in the approximate center.

"Okay, everybody watch closely. I'm going to punch him as hard as I can in the face."

Ghost reared back.

"What's everybody fuckin' starin' at man?" Bone asked nervously, noticing the wide-eyed stares around him.

Ghost's fist flew into Bone's face and stopped as soon as it made contact. Milk Bone didn't flinch. He hadn't felt it. He was completely oblivious to the whole thing. It was like Milk Bone was brick to Ghost.

"What the fuck, man?" the homey asked again, starting to get agitated.

"Taran, tell him 'one more minute.'" Ghost said.

"Bone, just one more minute of staring, okay?"

"This is fuckin' stupid, man. Whatever."

Ghost spoke again.

"Okay, now watch this."

Ghost climbed up on top of the TV and VCR. Since they were like stone to him, they didn't budge, no matter how much he was to one side or the other.

"Watch closely. This is one of my favorites." he said, getting in a jumping position.

He launched himself into the air and landed on Milk Bone's head. He pulled himself up and stood on top of Bone's head, bowing, waiting for applause. Taran, Alexandra, and Sasha watched in awe, not moving a muscle. It was quite a sight. Milk Bone stood there, looking around uncomfortably, while a dark-haired, pale white-skinned man stood there, on top of his head, wearing Reconstruction era clothing. They all began laughing and clapping, except Layne, who continued to stare at Ghost, unblinking.

"Ya know, 'ight, fuck this. See ya!" Milk Bone spat, moving to storm out.

"Oh!" Ghost cried out, falling and hitting the ground.

Bone slipped out, humiliated, though he couldn't quite understand why.

Ghost stood back up and bowed again. They all (except Layne) resumed laughing and clapping. As soon as he righted himself, he pointed to Sasha and motioned for her to approach him.

She stood up and walked over to him.

"Here's the strangest part."

He scooped Sasha up and twirled her around. She giggled, slinging her arm around his neck and smiling broadly as her black hair fluttered as they went around in circles. Finally, he set her on her tiny feet as she pecked him on the cheek, then sat back down.

"As you'll notice, I can interact with you all just fine. That was more for your benefit, Taran, since Alexandra and Sasha already knew that." Ghost explained.

"Well, I have a plan. We'll simply walk around downtown and have Ghost try to pick up every person. The ones he can lift are on the team." Taran said, laughing.

"Perhaps." Sasha chuckled, "Anyway, Ghost, where does the 'original team' come into play?" she asked, smoothing her clothes and curling up on the couch again.

"Well, this one's a little more elaborate, so I'll try to summarize more here, then Alexandra will take over. Also, Mademoiselle Boliviere, feel free to add anything as I'm telling the story."

"Alright." Alexandra nodded.

Ghost sat down on the other couch next to Sasha, who lit another cigarette. Taran and Alexandra untangled for a second and Taran lit a smoke, too.

"May I have a cigarette?" Alexandra asked Taran.

He stopped in mid-drag and looked over at her.

"You smoke?" he asked, a little surprised.

"It doesn't affect me at all. I smoked a little when I was alive and after I was first turned, I lost my addiction. Now, it's more for mental comfort than anything."

"Mental comfort?" Taran asked, curious.

"He's about to tell a very sad story, and I'm one of the main characters."

"Oh." Taran said, putting the cigarette in her mouth and lighting it for her.

"Thanks." she said, touching his face, "Go ahead, Richard."

"Alright. Well, without further ado, here's the story of the Nine.

"1888, I had just…come out of a, uh…a, uh…well, despite what 'God' had said, I had more or less been in a deep slumber on a lake, when I was awakened by a pair of vampires."

"Vampires?!" Alexandra gasped, "You never told me that. What were their names?"

"Gawain and Aunica. Do you know them?"

Alexandra sat up and pulled herself away from Taran. She ashed her cigarette, then looked at Ghost again.

"Yes. I…what did Aunica say to you?"

"Nothing. They couldn't see me. I was awakened by their whispers, and followed them into town.

Alexandra's look of shock hadn't faded.

"Until today, I felt that Aunica had preserved the final chance for one of the Nine to get revenge. I don't know. Look, I'll explain when you're done, Richard. I'm sorry, go ahead."

"No, problem." he nodded and grinned, then began again.

"I was admiring the vigor and energy of a new city, walking along the riverfront and watching the men unloading the steamboats and the

85

ever-expanding industry of the beautiful little port city. Everyone was scrambling around frantically to do their part in the ant farm of society in this area. It was a refreshing change from the east coast.

"One particular day, I was taking a stroll through the downtown around sunrise, when a woman and her young boy were walking by. As they were passing me, the boy stopped and looked at me.

"I froze, not sure what to make of this. Understand that no one had looked at me in years. He looked up at me and spoke.

"'Why are you so white, sir? Are you an albino?'

"I just stared at the child. I looked at his mother to see if she could see me. She was staring at the boy, too. Probably trying to comprehend who he was talking to.

"'Taran,' she said, 'who are you talking to?' she asked.

"'The man right there, mom. The really white man.'

"I couldn't speak. I was too shocked. This child was defying his creator by seeing me and speaking to me, or so I thought. I also hadn't spoken in many years, so I was more than a little out of practice.

"'You didn't answer my question, sir, why are you so white?'

"'Taran, let's go. There's no man there. You're starting to upset mommy. Come on.' the mother said, beginning to haul the child, Taran, after her. He held his ground and stared at me.

"'Taran, your mother can't see me. Tell her you're kidding, and I'll meet you after school, okay?' I suggested, looking at him pleadingly.

"He considered me for a moment, then turned to his mother.

"'I'm just kidding, momma. I'm sorry.'

"She rolled her eyes and jerked on his arm, pulling him after her.

"Once he was out of school, I met him a few yards away, by a large tree, where we both sat and spoke. I explained a little bit of what had happened to me, minus the God stuff. Luckily, psychiatry wasn't nearly the huge industry it is now, or Taran would've been hauled away rather quickly. One of the reasons I didn't approach you as a child in the 1980's, Taran, was because of this. Sasha, on the other hand, has been more or less independent since she was a girl, since her parents have been one archaeological project or another for the last seven years."

"So, do they just send you money every month?" Alexandra asked, looking concernedly at Sasha.

"Not really. I have a bank account I can use whenever I want." Sasha answered, not looking at Alexandra.

SASHA WHY DO YOU HATE HER? Layne asked.

All of them but Ghost winced a bit again, but not as badly as before.

"Huh?" Alexandra chirped, looking at Layne, then at Sasha.

"Who is he, anyway?" Sasha asked, looking at Alexandra and Ghost, and pointing at Layne, who was still sitting in the corner of the room.

"It would appear that, like Taran, he is another reincarnate, though he is quite different from his predecessor, at least physically and verbally. He is Layne Wood, I'm assuming." Ghost offered.

YES

"So, wait a minute, if Sasha is our White Mystic, then that means that..." Alexandra began, then trailed off, shaking her head, "It doesn't make any sense. No sense at all. Anyway, Sasha, do you hate me?"

Sasha lolled her head back and blew smoke out of her mouth.

"No, vampiress, I don't hate you. I just don't like vampires all that much."

"Most mortals don't. It's okay." Alexandra said, offering a slight giggle. Sasha didn't return it, "Anyway, Richard, please continue."

"We spent much time together over the following years. I educated him and offered counsel whenever he needed it. My only regret, looking back is that I think he would've done better had he had more contact with the living. He didn't have a lot of friends. I'm pretty sure this was due to my existence in his life. I took up much of his time since he was the only person I could talk to.

"By the time he reached his teen years, we had pretty much covered all the basics of my existence, including me being cast out in the Judgment, my present state, my story back in Fairfax, etcetera and etcetera. I had given it to him in bits over the years, so as not to overwhelm him.

"I'll jump forward a few years here to where things start to tie in a bit more.

"Taran had been working on a novel for about a year and had just finished it. He took it to a printing press to have copies of it made, paid for by inherited money. I followed him there, since it was a big part of his life and he was my best (and only) friend. He and I walked in, and there was a woman and her daughter there. The daughter was about Taran's age and should have been married by this point. This caught Taran's interest right away. He walked up to the woman and explained that he had a book, he wanted several copies printed, money wasn't a problem, and asked when he could pick it up. The woman flipped through the book, told him when it could be ready, and they set a date. Taran, this whole time, kept glancing at the daughter. He was quite fascinated. Every time he looked at her, he was terrified, but he also couldn't bear to look away. She was beautiful. Long, dirty blonde hair and green eyes. The body of a goddess. Very athletic build. Slim, smooth neck, breasts no larger than a handful and very perky."

"Good Lord, Richard." Alexandra muttered under her breath.

"You couldn't really see her legs, due to the long skirt she wore, but if they were anything like the rest of her body, they were probably perfect. He also loved her presence. She seemed to command respect that bordered on worship. Every move she made was done without any hesitation, as if confidence was as natural to her as breathing. She was almost intimidating him. He was losing his nerve quickly. As soon as they were done, Taran made a quick, nervous exit. When we got outside, I began teasing him.

"'Afraid of her, are you?' I asked, laughing.

"'No...no! I don't...I don't know how to talk to her. I've known her, well, vaguely, anyway, for a few years, but...Richard, help me! How do I talk to her?'

"'Do you wish to marry her?'

"Taran stopped and pondered. It was his nineteenth year, and he was a man now. It was a bit young to do so, but if he chose to, he could approach her father.

"'You only live once, right?' he laughed.

"'Right.' I answered, not knowing what I know now.

Everyone listening chuckled morbidly at this.

"Taran looked up at the sky, and I wanted to warn him not to pray for guidance, when he looked at me again. His long hair was pulled back and flipped around every time he looked at me, looked at the ground, looked at the sky, and looked back at the building, hoping for a glimpse of her. His gaze fixed on me, but he kept biting his lip and nodding his head.

"I folded my arms and stared back at him, smiling.

"Finally, he returned the smile.

"'Richard, I wish to marry her.'

"'Okay, follow me.' I said, walking hurriedly down the street.

"I led him to a flower patch just outside of downtown.

"'Okay, Taran, lesson number one. Never underestimate the effects of flowers on a woman. It's almost a cliché, but it should get you results. Now pick the five prettiest flowers.' I instructed.

"'Which ones are 'pretty?'' he asked, screwing up his face and staring at them as if he had never seen nature before.

"'Think with your heart, not your head, boy. Which ones will make her remember you?'

"'I don't know.'

"'Look, almost every woman in the thousands of books I've read has had a deep appreciation for flowers and the aesthetic aspects of simple natural objects. I myself have never courted a lady, but I've read virtually every text on the subject, and they all stress the basic importance of flowers. Now, pick five.'

"Taran rolled his eyes and crossed his arms.

"'Look, I'm not some goddam naturalist. I don't know which... can't I just take her to a baseball game or something? That's where I first talked to her when we were kids and...well, these things are just gonna wither and die after I give them to her and...this is silly...'

"I nearly smacked him all over that flower patch. I couldn't believe he was so dense. He had amazing strength, not only physically, but also mentally and morally. He was virtually a tower of honor and dignity. He was a living tribute to ancient, more civilized times. But, he couldn't 'woo' to save his life. I had never seen a man so incompetent with winning women. He was drowning. And fast. He needed my help.

Badly.

"'Okay, Taran, pick that one, that one, that one, that one, and…that one!' I said, pointing, 'Now, you're going to give these to the young lady as soon as she steps out of her family's shop and she's out of viewing distance from her mother. When you hand these to her, I'll be standing behind you to tell you what to say. Got it?'

"'Yeah. So, what do you we do in the meantime?'

"'We go stand nearby and wait.'

"'Okay. Let's go.'

"Taran and I walked to a general store across the street, Broadway, and sat. We decided it was safer to not engage in any conversation, so as not to draw any unusual looks. We sat and sat and sat. Taran was quickly losing his patience. And his spirit. As more time passed, the more and more convinced he became that she would hate him, that she would be insulted by the fact that he thought a man like himself could ever be with a woman like her. I assured him that if he acted like himself, stayed relaxed, and made her laugh a bit, he was in the clear.

"About an hour later, she appeared. She was covering herself in a shawl and heading down the street, presumably to go home.

"Taran burst off the chair he had been sitting on and began running down the street like a madman. I gave chase and caught up with him, right before he caught up with her.

"'Okay, Taran, here we go! Listen carefully and repeat!' I yelled.

"Taran stopped right in front of her and extended the flowers, looking her in the eye for the first time.

"'Sweet young lady,' I began.

"'Sweet young lady,' he repeated.

"'Please take these flowers into your hands so that I may have the honor of saying that I have been fortunate enough to touch the same thing that you have.' I spoke into his ear.

"'Please take theses flowers so that I may be fort…no, wait. Your hands are…shit! Oh, please, I beg your pardon! I-'

"She spoke.

"'Taran, why are you repeating everything that man behind you says?' she asked, looking annoyed.

"Taran and I froze and looked at each other. We both shrugged and stared back at her, wide-eyed.

"'He was with you in my father's store earlier. I remember seeing both of you.'

"'You can see me?!' I asked, shocked that not one, but two people knew I existed.

"'Is this a joke of some kind? If it is…did Wil put you up to this?' she seemed to be getting increasingly annoyed.

"'Miss, please do me a favor. Try to introduce my friend to any three people you choose, and see what they do.' Taran requested, smiling.

"'Why?' she asked, putting her hands on her hips and eying Taran suspiciously.

"'Do this, and you'll understand why my comrade and I were so surprised by the fact that you could see him. Just do it.'

"'Very well. What's your name, sir?' she asked, smiling viciously.

"'Richard Barrywood. And yours, miss?'

She tossed her hair back and commanded her most haughty look.

"'I am Mademoiselle Alexandra Boliviere. Follow, please.'

"Alexandra and I approached a couple of gentleman loading a cart with boxes.

"'Excuse me, gentlemen, I'd like to introduce you to my dear, dear friend, Mr. Barrywood.' she spoke, smiling, and gesturing to me.

"The two loaders stared at her, then looked at each other and shrugged, going back to work.

"'Excuse me, aren't you going to say hello to my friend?' she repeated, crossing her arms.

"The loaders stopped and looked at her again. They seemed confused. Finally, the one on the left spoke.

"'Forgive me, Miss Boliviere, but we don't have time to play games today. We are very busy and have little interest in talking to your imaginary friend. Tell your mother and father I said hello. Good day.' and he went back to his work.

"Alexandra was very perturbed by this. She was, however, determined. In her mind, it was possible that we had rigged this. She stopped and thought for a second. She needed to think of someone that we hadn't gotten to. Suddenly, she lit up.

"'Wil!' she exclaimed. 'Follow me, please.' she said and began walking down the street again. We followed.

"We came to a bar at the end of the street. It was probably one of the oldest buildings in this still fairly young city. It seemed as though Pierre Laclede had arrived here, built several bars, then the rest of the city. This particular bar, judged by its condition then, would've had to have been the first ever constructed.

"We went inside and were less impressed with the interior than the exterior. Though it couldn't have been that old, really, it appeared to be on the verge of collapsing in on itself. Ivy and other assorted plants were growing through the walls, the floor was covered in vomit and animal droppings (the owner, I found out later, had six dogs that were never let outside), the patrons were either passed out drunk or hopefully would be soon, and there were a few rather sizable holes in the ceiling. There were eight customers there that particular day. Six were all seated around a table, apparently playing poker. The other two were seated up at the bar. One was passed out and the other seemed to be working very hard at acting sober.

"'What the hell are we doing here?' Taran asked, shooting Alexandra a strange look.

"'I'm trying to find my...friend, Wil. He'll settle this for us.' she answered.

"We walked over to the bar. Alexandra stopped the bartender and whispered in his ear. He shook his head, shrugged, and pointed to a door leading to the back.

"'Follow me.' she ordered and began to walk towards the door. Taran and I shrugged and followed her.

"We got to the door and Alexandra knocked.

"'Who's there?' we heard, then also heard a shotgun click.

"'It's Alex!' she yelled.

"The latch on the door turned, then the door came open. There stood a very handsome, but very wild-looking man, about the same age as Taran and Alexandra. He stood at about six feet, was skinny, but slightly muscular, had brown hair about down to his shoulders, in a semblance of a pony tail, had a thin mustache, and very small, beady, blue eyes.

"'Come in, Alex. Who are your friends?' he asked.

"'You can see me?' I asked, shocked again.

"'Uh...yes, I can. Do you believe yourself to be a ghost or a haunt of some kind?' he responded, smiling and setting his shotgun on the desk at which he had apparently been sitting.

"'No, of course not.' I answered, 'It's just...will all of you follow me?'

"'Look, no more silly games!' Alexandra yelled, and turned to the man, 'These two were trying to convince me that this man was invisible to everyone but myself and this boy here.' she said, indicating Taran.

"'Boy?!'" Taran exclaimed.

"'Please, just follow me out into the bar. I don't know why you two can see me, but I assure you no one else can.' I pleaded.

"'Alright, I'll play along.' the man said, shrugging.

"'Oh God, fine!' Alexandra pouted.

"So, the four of us walked out into the bar. The same people as before sat around, drinking themselves into a stupor.

"'Okay, watch. I'll prove to you all beyond a shadow of a doubt that I am a ghost to this world. Just watch closely.' I explained.

"I jumped up on the bar, ran back and forth, imitating a chicken, clucking and everything. On occasion, I would jump up and down on the bartender's head, and leap from table to table.

"'Look at me! Look at me!' I was screaming at the men in the bar. Not a single one took notice of my antics. After a sufficient amount of time, when Alexandra and her friend looked convinced, I jumped down from the bar.

"'Well?' I asked.

"'Could I see you in my office?' the man asked.

"'Sure.' I answered.

"So, the four of us went back into his office and he closed the door.

"'I'm Wil. What in the name of God are you?' he asked, almost shaking.

"'It's funny you should put it quite that way…' I began.

"So, I sat there and told him and Alexandra my story. I answered their questions and explained further about what I could and couldn't do. Then, we tried to figure out why they could see me and everyone else couldn't. We couldn't come up with a thing.

"About six or seven months passed before anything new developed. In that time, we all became pretty good friends. The three of them were very close, though. They were able to enjoy the world. As stated before, all I could do was look at it and admire its beauty. They, however, would go swimming, or shooting, or drinking, or whatever. They were having the time of their lives. It was nice. Taran had never really had any close friends that were alive. He was finally emerging into the world.

"There was one problem that was apparent then, but hadn't really surfaced yet. He and Wil were both in love with Alexandra.

"Anyway, one night, we were all sitting in the bar after close. We were able to do this, since Wil's father was the apparent owner of the bar, and Wil was slowly taking on more and more duties there (which included renovating the place, thankfully.) Wil and I were discussing what direction the country was taking during the Reconstruction, and Taran and Alexandra were having a drink at the bar. Wil seemed genuinely interested in the conversation, but kept looking back at Alex and Taran. After the twentieth or thirtieth time in five minutes, I finally said something about this issue.

"'Wil, are you in love with her?' I asked, staring him dead in the eye.

"He shifted in his seat, poured another shot of whiskey from the bottle that was sitting at our table, threw it back, and returned my stare.

"'Our mothers were best friends. I've been in love with her since the day that she and I were born. We were born on the same day, in the same house, twenty feet and two minutes apart. She's been my sister, my mother after mine died, my best friend, my obsession, my first kiss, my first crush, and the only woman I've ever cared about. You're damn right I love her.

"'Have you ever told her?'

"'She knows. I've never had to tell her.'

"'You're sure?'

"'Uh, yeah, she's engaged to me, so, yeah, I'm pretty sure.'

"I froze when he said this. In six months, no one had ever discussed this. I knew if Taran wasn't careful, he might get himself into serious trouble. The only thing was, though, that Alexandra constantly flirted with him.

"Anyway, that's a whole different story. There was much more discussion about the topic that night, but it's irrelevant to the story. I'll get to the interesting part.

"About an hour later, the front door was busted open my a man in rich clothes, but covered in filth. He appeared to be either very ill or very drunk, for he was stumbling all over the place, and his eyes looked dead. Wil and Taran jumped up.

"'Three of the Nine! It really is true! I'm one of you! The ghost is here, too! I can't believe it! It's true! I-' and he collapsed on the ground.

"Wil ran over to him.

"'Taran, come here and help me carry him into the bedroom in the back! Alex, get some water!'

"So, Taran and Wil carried the man into the bedroom in the back and put him in bed. Alexandra brought water and dabbed a damp towel on the man's face, cleaning him and trying to revive him. No luck. Taran tried shaking him awake, but the man just wouldn't stir. After a while, I offered an idea.

"'Look, I never sleep, so I'll stay here and watch him. You three go sleep and I'll wake you if he stirs, okay?'

"'Agreed.' Wil said. Taran shot him a look of annoyance, for the fact that Wil was speaking for all of them, but ultimately let it go.

"'Where are we going to sleep?' Alexandra asked, looking around and seeing nothing but tables and the bar.

"'Grab a table.' Wil said, smiling.

"'Fine.' Alexandra said, obviously dreading even touching the rather filthy furniture that inhabited the bar.

"So, they each curled up on a table and I retired to the room with the stranger.

"I stood over the stranger and looked at him. He was almost unhealthily skinny, with short blond hair, and very pale. I couldn't really tell what color his eyes were, since they were shut. He was dressed very richly, almost obnoxiously so. He was almost pretty. After a while, studying his features became boring.

"I sat on the floor and stared off into space, trying to figure out all the questions going through my head. Why could they see me? What made them special? Who was this raving lunatic babbling about 'three of the Nine' and 'the ghost?' I was pretty sure the ghost was me. Apparently, he could see me, too. How did all this fit together? I sat on the floor pondering all of this when I suddenly realized I had company. Alexandra was standing in the doorway.

"'Hi.' she said, semi-nervous.

"'Hi. Are you okay?'

"'Um, no.' she laughed nervously.

"'Have a seat. Let's talk.' I said, gesturing towards the one chair in the room.

"She plopped down, hung her head and began to weep.

"'Mademoiselle Boliviere, why are you crying?' I asked, standing and approaching her.

"'Wil...I'm...shit!' she looked up at me, 'Why do always address me so formally?'

"'I address a lady like a lady. I also took note of your French heritage, so I included that out of respect.' I smiled at her.

"She returned the smile and touched my face.

"'You're so sweet, Richard. Please, I would be more comfortable if you addressed me as Alexandra or Alex, okay?'

"'Alexandra. Very well. What's on your mind?'

"'You're an intelligent man, so I'm sure you noticed this before any of us, but anyway, it seems I'm at the center of a love triangle.'

"'Yes, actually, I noticed immediately. They're both in love with you. And, I found out tonight that you're engaged to Wil.'

"'I'm not engaged! I'm...promised to him. Look, I thought I knew what love was three years ago, but I only recently uncovered what it really is.'

"'What is love, then?'

"'Taran.'

"'Oh.' and yet another surprise, 'You love Taran?'

"'Yes, but more than that. I'm IN love with Taran. But, I'm promised to Wil. I do love Wil, but...like a brother. In a more 'friendly' fashion, you might say.'

"'A rather nasty state of affairs, if you don't mind me saying so.'

"'Yes, it is.'

"'What are you going to do?'

"'I don't know. I feel obligated to marry Wil, and he is a sweet, loving man, but Taran...there's something there. Something that compels me to...want to touch and feel Taran in ways I that I would feel embarrassed if I were to speak of them plainly here. I want your advice, Richard.'

"'Honesty. Break the engagement...I mean, 'promise,' to Richard, then tell Taran how you feel. Simple. It'll be painful, but in the end, you'll be glad you did.'

"'What if Taran says no?'

"'Ha. He'll say yes.'

"'You're sure?'

"'You just told me you think he's in love with you!'

"'Am I right?'

"'Ask him!'

"'But, Richard...you're right. I'm sorry. Look, I'm just going to take a few days to think this over, then I'll talk to you about it again, then I'll act. Okay?'

"'Alexandra...' a raspy voice hissed from behind me.

"Alexandra and I realized it was the stranger.

"She approached him and sat next to him.

"'How are you feeling?' she asked, very sweetly.

"'I'm quite thirsty, but now that I've finally found you all, I'm much happier. He was right. You're exactly where he said you'd be. Tomorrow, we'll set out to find the others. Where are Taran and Wil?'

"'They're in the other room. I'll go wake them and get you some water.' Alexandra said, jumping up and leaving.

"'Thank you. I take it you're Richard Barrywood, the ghost.'

"'Yes, I am. How do you know this?'

"'The creator of the Nine. A true god. Taran, Wil, Alexandra, and myself are members of this group. I don't know who or where or what or anything. All I've been told is that we must destroy the god of this universe.'

"'What?! Why?' I asked, a little skeptical.

"'Because he will destroy this planet.'

"'What do you mean?'

"'I don't know. That's what he said to me when I asked the same question. All he told me was how many people, where to find some of them, and our mission. That's it. Look, I can see in your eyes that you don't believe me, but listen! Have you been wondering why only we can see you? Because we're not made by the same maker as you! That's why we can interact with you! Richard-'

"'Okay, okay, I believe you. What's our next move?'

"'We-'

"Suddenly, Taran and Wil burst into the room.

"'Richard, how is he?' Taran asked.

"'He's fine. Move out of Alexandra's way, so that she can bring him water.' I said.

"Taran and Wil stepped into the room, moving out of the doorway. Alexandra slipped past them and handed a glass of water to the stranger.

"'What's your name, stranger?' Wil asked.

"'Layne. Layne Wood.'

Suddenly, the modern Taran interrupted and stared at the modern Layne.

"So, how come the old version of you can talk?"

HOW COME BOTH VERSIONS OF YOU SUCK ASS?

"Excuse me? You wanna repeat that, little man?" Taran shouted, standing up and gripping his sword.

Layne stared at Taran, who began to unsheathe the blade.

"Taran…" Alexandra began.

CALM YOURSELF I WAS TEASING YOU WE ARE VERY MUCH ALIKE

"I have NOTHING in common with you." Taran hissed, pulling more of the blade out.

"Please sit down, Taran." Sasha gently pleaded.

"I'm not like you!" Taran snapped at Layne, who still sat calmly in the corner.

WE SHALL SEE

"Fine, Taran, you're not like him. Relax." Sasha tried to soothe him, standing up and slowly approaching him.

A cold hand slid onto the back of Taran's neck. He gasped and turned, seeing Alexandra's china-white complexion.

"It's the past, Taran. Your past. As you're about to learn from mine, it's inescapable. However, you can just accept it and move on. As for you," she turned to Layne, "please leave it alone. For now."

Layne shifted his stare to Alexandra.

YES VAMPIRESS

Taran glared at Layne and plopped back down on his couch, where he was quickly joined by Alexandra again. Sasha took a seat next to Ghost again. Layne continued in his same spot, but shifted his eyes back to Ghost.

"We were talking about the other...Layne..." Taran prefaced, his eyes darting toward the corner.

"Okay. Thank you, Taran. Anyway, he told us his name and explained the things he had told myself and Alexandra to the other two. We sat around and exchanged what we knew and what we didn't know. Layne explained that he had been given a destination where we could encounter others like us, but he had been given no names or faces or anything. He had been told that we would somehow know when we found these people. At this point, I noticed Taran was looking troubled.

"'Something wrong, Taran?'

"'Yeah. Layne, why is it that this 'being' has tried very hard to be as vague and mysterious as possible? If he really wanted so badly for us to kill God or whatever, why didn't he just tell you exactly who, exactly where, and basically everything we need to know to accomplish our mission? It seems kind of silly that he would hinder us in our mission like that.'

"'I don't know. I'm telling you everything, I swear.'

"'So this is everything, huh?' Wil asked, a little calmer than Taran.

"'Yeah...well, there is one more thing. He said that Taran will be the only one who survives.'

THAT IS CORRECT

Everyone turned and stared at Layne.

"What?" Sasha half-laughed, disbelief leaking from her eyes.

"He was wrong then, and he's wrong now." Alexandra rolled her eyes, "There is no fate, there are no guarantees. Let's move on."

"No! Hang on!" Sasha wheeled around to face Ghost, "Well? Is that true? Am I meant to die?"

Ghost grimaced and stared sadly into her eyes.

"I really hope not. You mean...everything...to me."

Sasha shook her head and looked at everyone else in the room.

"This is crazy." She heaved a sigh and sat back down, still a little in shock, "I guess I don't have much of a choice, do I?"

NONE OF US DO WHICH MAKES IT EASIER

"Whatever." Sasha sniffed, "Please go on, Ghost."

"Based on Layne's info, we headed west and came across a very small village. There, we found Evangela and Cole. We spent the night in that village and explained everything to both of them. Evangela and Cole took it pretty well.

"I guess I should tell you a little about each person. I'll start with Cole.

"Cole Hamill was a mercenary. He claimed to have done secret 'jobs' for the government and organizations affiliated with the government. I still don't know if he was over-exaggerating or flat-out lying or what, but he was definitely qualified. He was a master swordsman and an excellent shot. He had an arsenal that, for the time, was amazing. He had a Colt Peacemaker and a long, beautiful rapier. He was 22, about 6 feet tall, very muscular, had long, brown hair in braids, and a face like stone. Personality-wise, he was a hot-head and and seemed to always be looking for an excuse to fight or kill. However, he was highly intelligent and very cunning. He had a great head for strategy and fighting tactics. He was a man who really loved what he did. Killing.

"Evangela Boliviere."

"Boliviere?" Taran cut in. He looked at Alexandra, "That's your last name, isn't it?"

"Yes, it is." Alexandra began to look like she might begin to weep, "She was my cousin. And my best friend in the world. I try to not to think about her. I almost envy you, Taran. You don't remember. I treasure these memories, but at the same time, they hurt like hell. Especially the good ones. I'm sorry, Richard, please continue." she said, a single tearing falling from her left eye.

"Are you alright, Alexandra?" he asked.

"Yes, I'll be fine. Go ahead."

"Okay, but if you need me to stop, just say so."

"Thank you. I'll be okay."

"Alright. So, Evangela. She was the equivalent of what Sasha is to us. A White Mystic. The only difference is that Evangela was what's known as an 'Accomplished Mystic,' meaning that she was one of the most powerful Mystics in her region, and hence on the Regional Council. She was probably the most cooperative of these two. Partly because she was so close to Alexandra and partly because she had a very deep understanding of the workings of the world, and much of what we explained to her seemed to make sense. She looked a lot like Alexandra. She was 19, like Alexandra. The long, dirty blond hair, similar features. The only real difference is that she had two different colored eyes. One was green, like Alexandra, and the other was blue. She, to this day, is probably the kindest woman I've ever met. Her death was a huge loss to the world."

Alexandra pulled Taran closer and buried her face in his chest. He could feel the warm wetness of her tears. He cradled her in his arms and kissed her on her forehead. Richard paused, eyed her for a second, then continued.

"The next day, Layne felt we should go south. We bought more horses early that morning, and took off. In case you're wondering, I rode with Taran by riding in front of him, with him holding me steady. Anyway, we arrived in Cape Girardeau. There we found Nicole.

"Nicole Michaels was a Black Mystic and quite a character. She wasn't an Accomplished Mystic, but she was very powerful and very respected by the Black Coven. Why wasn't she on the Regional Council? Because of her attitude. The Coven strictly forbids ever using spells to settle petty disputes. Nicole's claim to fame was that one night, she had been caught in the throes of passion with a black man, who was then beaten severely by many of the idiot men of that town. The men who beat the negro were never seen again. Nicole never would say what had happened to them, but she was capable of...monstrous acts, but even my words can't properly convey the anger in that poor girl's soul. Anyway, the council ordered her to Cape Girardeau, one of the more remote outposts. Well, needless to say, she was more than happy to join us. She was 19, fairly short, had dark red hair down to her chin, brown eyes, and very tan skin, almost Indian looking.

"The next day, neither Taran nor Layne had any clue where to go or what to do, so we returned to St. Louis to begin planning our mission.

"About three days after we got back, the inevitable Wil-Alexandra-Taran triangle exploded.

"Wil was sitting in his bar, doing the monthly paperwork. All of us but Taran were there, talking and joking around, getting to know each other.

"Suddenly, the door flew open. There stood Taran, drunk as a skunk.

"'Alex! I love you! In a very, very, very...serious and manly way...uh...I, uh, don't think you should marry Wil.' he cried out.

"Wil stood up slowly, biting his lip, and began to skulk towards Taran.

"Taran eyed Wil, teetering back and forth, while getting his fists up.

"At this time, Alexandra snapped out of her dream state.

"'Taran, no! Don't do this! Please! I beg you, Taran, don't hurt him! Please! Taran, I love you!' she yelled. Wil spun around and looked at her.

"'Alex, I...but, I love you. I thought we...' he trailed off, staring into her beautiful green eyes. He reached out, caressed her cheek, almost reduced to tears and turned to look at Taran.

"'Let's do this.' he said, almost hissing. They began to head outside.

"'NO!' she screamed, jumping up to stop Taran."

"I kicked his fuckin' ass, didn't I?" Taran asked, laughing.

"Wil held her back, looked at her, and asked, 'Will it hurt you more if we fight?'

"Alexandra looked up into his eyes, and slowly nodded.

"'I'm sorry.'

"'You love him?'

"'Yes, I do.'

"'Which means you don't love me.'

"Taran stumbled forward, the rum in his breath so dense it was nearly flammable.

"'So we gonna fight or talk, hoss?'

"Wil looked at Taran.

"'She's yours.'

"With that, Wil seized the promise ring that hung on a chain around Alexandra's neck, snapped it off, and dropped it at her feet. Her eyes began to well up with tears, and she whimpered.

"'No, not like this. Don't be hurt.' she requested quietly.

"'You're free." Wil hoarsely responded and walked back to the office. The rest of the day, he didn't say much, but by the next day, he was more or less back to his old self, though there was always a bit of iciness to him after that. Understandable, I suppose.

"And that's how things continued for another five months. He and Taran continued discussing the next plan of action, unable to come up with a single good idea. There was little or no friction between them. On occasion, it was obvious that Wil was bothered by all of this. For one, he would barely speak to Alexandra.

"A lot changed in that five months. Taran, Cole, Alexandra, and Nicole became pretty good friends. Layne was researching nonstop to find some kind of clue as to what they should do next. Taran and Alexandra seemed to fall in love more deeply everyday. I was the only person Wil would talk to a whole lot.

"He would stay up late almost every night, drinking himself into a stupor, going on and on about how much he loved her and how he was trying to move on but she was all he had ever known and ever loved and how he didn't hate Taran and how he understood and he was determined to get past this and eventually, he would fall asleep crying. Every night.

"Then one night, it all came together. Wil, Layne, Evangela, and I were sitting around discussing an idea that Layne had. All of his visions of where we'd find people had been based on landmarks, most of which he had recognized, but there were a couple he didn't. He pointed out how, so far, all the members seem to be found in a circle around St. Louis. He suggested we cross the river and head into Illinois to see what we could find there. Wil agreed that it was a good idea and he would discuss it with Taran whenever he got back.

"And, at that moment, Taran, Alexandra, Nicole, and Cole walked in, drunk again. Apparently, they had gone down to one of the bars by the river, which was pretty normal for them. Except, this time, Taran and Cole had managed to get into a brawl with a couple of men who thought Cole had once cheated them in a card game. Midway through the brawl, Nicole, who was probably the drunkest of all of them, made the mens' pants burst into flames. She had found this very funny. Of course, so did Taran, Cole, and Alexandra. The men ran outside, fanning their asses and threw themselves into the river. The four drunks took this moment to make a quick exit, before the bar accused one of them of being a witch and a burning was scheduled.

"Evangela immediately began to scold Nicole. Since Evangela outranked Nicole in the Coven, she was allowed to do this. Nicole had a smart mouth but an even smarter head. She stood, bowed her head, and listened to the tongue-lashing she got from Evangela.

"'…and last but not least, Nicole, I'm putting a week-long binding spell on you, to teach you a lesson. You will be reduced to the same powers as a normal human.'

"'Evangela, please don't. You all need my powers! What if-'
"'Silence!'
"Then, Wil cut in.

"'Evangela, do whatever you like. This is obviously a dispute within the Coven, but I think that Nicole might have a point. We might need her powers in the coming week. Tomorrow, we might be leaving for Illinois, and we'll need some firepower if we run into any trouble.'

"Then, Taran cut in.
"'Illinois?!'

"'I was going to wait to discuss it with you tomorrow, when you were more sober.'

"'Oh. Okay.'

"'I hate to say it, but you're probably right, Wil. Nicole, you have been scolded and warned. Now, go sleep it off!'

"Nicole nodded, literally biting her lip, and was about to walk away when nearly-silent footsteps were heard right outside the bar. We all looked over to the door, which was suddenly thrown aside, revealing a tiny figure. A young girl, maybe two years old stood there, holding something in the shadows.

"'Liz?' Nicole asked the young girl, 'Liz, what are you doing here?'
"Liz considered her older sister with an icy, deathlike stare.
"Nicole recoiled from the stare, then began to slowly approach her sister.

"'Liz? What's going on? If you're here, where's-'
"The little girl's head jerked up suddenly and looked at Taran.

"'Seven you are,' she began, in an androgynous voice, 'and Nine you will become, but threaten me, and I will hurt you so badly that the pain I am about to inflict on you will be but a pleasant memory.'

"Taran's entire body tensed, his hand shot down to his gun, and he waited, ready for whatever was about to come.

"Liz's head jerked painfully back to face Nicole. Her sweet, two-year old face suddenly began to come back, as if the possessing entity was moving on.

"'Nikki!' she cried out as she lifted the revolver in her tiny hands

100

and put it to her own head.

"Nicole lunged forward as the revolver fired.

"'NOOO!!!' she screamed.

"Liz's little body thudded to the floor, along with the gun.

"Nicole fell to her knees next to her baby sister's body, and began to bawl. Evangela, her mouth covered in horror, approached Nicole from behind, and slowly placed a hand on her shoulder. Nicole tried to shrug it off violently, but Evangela had a solid grip. Nicole kept trying to jerk away, and Evangela kept kneeling and pulling her closer. Eventually, she had Nicole's head pushed against her chest, and while Nicole kept kicking her feet out, like she was trying to scramble away, she sobbed freely in Evangela's arms. After a few more kicks, she stopped and both women held each other, as Nicole screamed into Evangela's blouse.

"Taran turned to Cole and quietly asked him to remove the body. Cole solemnly nodded and moved toward the little body.

"After about two and a half days, we finally found a small town. In it, we found Michael and Jessica.

"Michael Thomas was a scholar and published author and really, one of the most intelligent American philosophers I've ever known of. His ideas on society and religion were, at the time, pretty radical, which is why he lived in a tiny little town in the middle of Illinois. He figured his best chances for survival were to avoid a lot of human contact. He was 23, a bit on the lanky side, had short blond hair, blue eyes, and always wore black. He had a very mild temperament and seemed to almost always be in a dream-like state, like he was contemplating heavy issues all the time.

"Jessica Star was the funniest out of the group. She was 18, had a small frame that was betrayed by an almost-chubby baby face, had long black hair, green eyes, a mole right beneath her right eye, and was probably the most innocent looking woman I had ever seen. Her image suited her well. She was the most innocent woman I had ever met. She had never left the town she grew up in, was deeply religious, and had never even thought about drinking, having sex, or ever questioning anything around her. I think we might've presented her first real temptation, her chance to escape sameness. Either way, I was puzzled that the others felt the connection to her so strongly, but they all said it was there.

"After that, well, we had the Nine. Then, all we needed was some kind of clue as to what we were supposed to do next.

"Six months went by fairly uneventfully. The only points of interest were Taran and Alexandra announcing their engagement, Layne began painting some strange things, like symbols and scenes from a bad epic, and the group began to really solidify.

"Wil had everyone training with various weapons, Michael helped them develop their minds, and at my request, Jessica and I educated them in various religious myths.

"The biggest problem, what I think proved to be fatal, is that there was no overall plan, no direction to any of it. It was six months of heavy thinking and even heavier drinking.

"At the end of that six months, though, is when the inevitable tragic ending was set in motion.

"Nicole, Jessica, Cole, and Michael went out to one of the local bars to get drunk and laugh at everyone but themselves, when Nicole ruined us. One of the customers recognized Michael as a man who owed him quite a bit of money. Michael tried to explain to the man that he must be mistaken, when the man, drunk off whiskey, stabbed Michael in the stomach. Nicole and Cole told Jessica to get him back to Wil's bar and have Evangela see what she could do for him.

"Cole unsheathed his sword and explained to the man that he had three seconds to get out of town or Cole would relieve him of the burden of his testicles."

"Awesome." Taran grunted to himself.

"The man," Ghost continued, hardly noticing, "along with the rest of the bar, laughed at him, telling him to put his toy away and fight like a man (meaning use a gun). Cole obliged them. He put away his sword, pulled out his revolver and shot the man in the head. He dared the rest of the customers to challenge his manhood.

"They dared. All of them.

"Before Cole knew what was happening, about a dozen or so shotguns and pistols were out and began firing. Cole was hit three times in the torso and twice in the left leg. Nicole dragged him outside and hid him behind some boxes that were at the side of the building. She was infuriated at this point. I think she might've been in love with him. She walked back into the bar, where the men were laughing about the 'idiot boy.'

"'You dare puncture my friend with your bullets?! Do you?! He did nothing to any of you! He killed a man that might have killed a friend of his! Vengeance! Apparently, you all don't understand vengeance! I'll explain it to you and make it very, very easy to understand! You want blood?! Have some fucking blood!' and she raised her hands straight up in the air, screaming the shrillest, most maniacal scream those man had ever heard. She stared up towards the ceiling and began doing strange motions with her hands, almost like she was writing with her fingertips, each finger doing a different letter. Suddenly, a blackness appeared over each fingertip. She screamed even louder and flung her hands at the frightened crowd.

"Now, it was the group's turn to shriek. Blood vessels all over their bodies began to swell, growing larger and larger. Some of the frightened ones looked at their hands, unable to move, speak, or do anything. Others ran around, frantically swatting at their skin, as if some invisible insect was causing this. Others just collapsed on the ground, shaking and sobbing.

"Soon, the blood vessels began to explode. The ones who were staring at their hands like morons saw their hands explode into almost nothing but bone. The explosion went up their arm, slowly blowing off more and more flesh and exposing more bone.

"Nicole laughed and laughed.

"The ones running around, raising their blood pressure, pretty much just exploded in one loud, wet sounding 'pop.'

"The ones on the ground went almost identically to the ones who had just been staring at their hands.

"Soon, all that was left were twitching mounds of stringy muscle and bone.

"Nicole, when all of this was done, exited the bar quietly, covered in blood, trying to hide a smile. She went over to Cole and checked his pulse. He was still alive. She scooped him up and got him back to Wil's.

"By the time Nicole and Cole were back, Michael was pretty much patched up. Evangela sewed his wound up and gave the healing rate an acceleration. She told him he would feel better tomorrow.

"One thing that I should add is that the spell that Nicole performed is almost impossible. Many Mystics have died trying to do that spell, since it saps so much strength, both spiritual and physical. When Nicole got back, she was fine. Not only did she have enough strength to carry a man twice her weight several miles while running, but she seemed more powerful from the experience of casting the spell and running with Cole. This was not right.

"Evangela set to work on Cole while Nicole explained to Taran, Wil, and myself what she had just done (out of earshot of Evangela.) What was even more 'not right' was that she was beaming the whole time that she was telling us this horrible, gruesome story.

"When she was finished, Wil jumped up and started berating her. Taran calmed him and told her to go assist Evangela in any way she could. She nodded and went over to the other Mystic's side.

"Then, Taran and Wil talked, with Wil starting.

"'Taran, she's finished us! How long are we going to allow her to go around pulling this kind of shit?! She just killed thirty or forty men with practically a snap of her fingers!'

"'Wil, relax. These are the same men that tried to kill Cole in cold blood. These are the same men that all laughed when they thought that they had. If you ask me, they deserved to die. Also, this is a great demonstration of Nicole's power. Think about how useful she will be. And, another thing. It doesn't matter whether or not they deserved it. Nicole's already decided that for them.'

"'I agree with you, but you're forgetting one thing. We still need to hide our true nature. If anyone, and I mean ANYONE, knows what we're up to, we'll have to find somewhere else to hide! If someone saw her doing what she did to those men, they'll accuse her of being a witch! And, when they come for her, they'll grab us, too. Even if they don't, if we lose any member of this team, we've probably already lost.'

"'You're right. Well, if that happens, we'll harm anyone who tries to harm us, agreed?'

"'No, we need to leave. Now.'

"'No. We don't budge until we know, for a fact, where we're going. Also, Cole's in no shape to travel. No, we stay and stand our ground if anyone opposes us.'

"'Taran, you're wrong! Stop being so goddam thick-headed! Listen to me! You're going to get us all killed!'

"'Wil, shut up! I've told what we're going to do and that's that. I've listened to what you have to say and I don't agree with it. I'm in command. You're not. Once Cole is okay to travel, I'll reconsider your idea. Until then, we kill if we're attacked. Do I make myself clear?'

"'Yes.' Wil hissed.

"Taran got up and walked over to where Evangela and Nicole were working on Cole.

"'How is he?' Taran asked Evangela.

"'He's going to live, more than likely, but he won't be fighting again for another two or three weeks.'

"'Shit. Alright. Nicole, did anyone see you?'

"'Anyone who did is a pile of meat now. Worried?'

"'Yeah, they might accuse you or all of us of being witches or some other fanatical religious shit. I really hope no one followed you, Nicole. You've killed us all if they did.'

"Nicole just stared at him, unable to speak.

"'Nicole, what did you do?' Evangela asked, already looking upset and worried.

"'I...performed a Mass Execution spell.'

"'WHAT!? How?! There's no way...you're not strong enough! It would've killed you! Nicole! Why?! Why?!'

"'Evangela...it made me stronger. Isn't that strange?'

"Evangela stared at her, almost frightened. The Accomplished White Mystic had spent almost her entire young life trying to improve the quality of life of those in her charge. Now, she was always around this Black Mystic that was bent on punishing the world. Now, Nicole had slaughtered God knows how many. I think Evangela was beginning to fear her.

"Alexandra noticed the look on her cousin's face and approached her.

"'Are you alright?' Alexandra asked.

"'No. Will someone please remove Nicole from my sight?'

"'Nicole, come walk with me.' Taran requested.

"'Alright.' she shrugged.

"'Alex, would you mind assisting Evangela?' he asked, looking at his lover with that 'please help me out' lover look.

"'Yeah. No problem.' she said, putting her hand on Evangela's

104

shoulder.

"'Let's go, Nicole.' he said firmly, and he and Nicole exited the bar for the last time.

"Alexandra turned to Evangela.

"'What happened?'

"'Nicole, tonight, has done the unspeakable and the impossible. She performed a Mass Execution spell. She has slaughtered many people. Please, Alex, take my mind off of this.'

"'Okay.' Alexandra paused, thinking, 'Well, Taran and I set the date for a month from now. And, if you're okay with it, I'd like you to be the Maid of Honor.'

"Evangela's face slowly shifted from deathly stone to wedding joy.

"'Really?! Thank you! Oh, Alex, you should wear your mother's dress! I'm sure my mother would fit it for you and everything! Oh, I can't wait! What a happy day! Are you nervous at all?'

"Alexandra smiled, blushing.

"'Yeah, a little, it's just…he's the one, Evangela. I know it. He is.'

"'What about children? Have you all discussed that at all?'

"'Yes, a little. Taran insists that our firstborn must be a male, so that he has a proper heir, but I told him it's the luck of the draw. I also told him a female would make just as good of an heir.'

"Evangela laughed.

"'What did he say to that?'

"'He told me that I am a woman and don't understand what it means to be a man. I told him that if he can find a way to pass the child instead of me, I would think much more highly of men in general.'

"Evangela laughed again.

"Meanwhile, Taran and Nicole were sitting in the darkness of the nearby woods, talking.

"'So, mighty Black Mystic, any regrets?'

"'No. You?'

"'I wish I had made the need for secrecy more evident to you.'

"'Taran, I'm sorry, okay? Watching Cole collapse into a bloody heap made me a little mad.'

"'So, you really killed thirty of forty men, huh?' he asked, lighting a cigarette.

"'Yeah, I did.'

"Suddenly, five figures burst out of the bushes.

"'Nicole, get back to the bar!' Taran yelled.

"Nicole made a break to get past the attackers, but they were quicker. They had her pinned and bound in no time.

"Taran pulled his gun

"'Alright, assholes, let's dance.' he said, motioning with his fingers for them to try attacking him.

"Two of them leaped at him, attempting to pin and tie him, too.

"He quickly took both down.

"The other three stood there, confused as to what to do next.

"Suddenly, one of them, on Taran's right, attacked. He moved so fast that the dagger seemed to literally shoot out of his hand. It buried itself deep in Taran's bicep.

"He yelled and dropped his gun.

"He and Nicole were both unconscious within a minute.

"'We got 'em, sir!' one of them called out.

"'Good work, Watts! Jonas, tell the De-fencers of the Faith or whatever they call themselves that we found two of them from the bar!' the sheriff called out.

"'Yes, sir!'

"Meanwhile, Alexandra and Evangela had just finished with Cole and put him to bed. They were just getting settled to match each other shot for shot, when the door burst open. There stood several men clad in very strange, ancient looking armor. It was baby blue and yellow, and covered every part of their body, but their eyes. It appeared to be made out of a very, very thick metal. They stood at nearly seven feet tall, were about as wide as a standard doorway, and had the loudest footsteps of any creature I had ever heard. I wasn't even sure that they were human.

"They walked in, threw the unconscious and tied-up Nicole and Taran onto the floor and drew their weapons.

"'The Nine shall die together. Where are the rest of your members?' the largest and most decorated soldier asked.

"Wil looked up and spoke.

"'Two others are injured and the rest are about. And armed. I ask you to please leave my property and see the tailor down the street. Good night, gentlemen.' Wil said, smiling pleasantly.

"'Bring the other two out here. We will kill the nine of you now.'

"'I think not. Good night, gentlemen.' Wil repeated, sounding a little more frustrated now.

"'Very well. We kill all of you, then kill your injured, then find her ourselves.'

"'Who?'" Wil asked, surprised.

"The soldiers stopped and looked at each other.

"'I am surprised that you don't already know who she is. You don't know who we are, either do you?' the big one asked.

"'No, I don't know. Care to introduce yourself?' Wil asked.

"'We are the Defenders of the Faith. You are a threat to the Faith."

"'You flatter me needlessly. To imply that I am, in some way, jeopardizing an entire belief structure...wow...you just made my night. However, I do believe that you're, to put it exceeding politely, bat-shit crazy. You've found the wrong people. Please, leave us alone. These are just friends of mine hanging out at my bar.'

"'You lie like a heathen pig, William. You will be the first to die, then. Step forward.'

"'What is it with villainous cowboys and swine-based insults? How did you know my...never mind. Very well, take me.' he said, approaching the soldiers.

"'Wil! No!' Alexandra cried out, being restrained, once again, by Evangela.

"Wil approached the head soldier, stopping three feet in front of him.

"'So...you gonna kill me or what?'

"The soldier unsheathed a huge sword and raised it above his head.

"Suddenly, Wil reached behind himself, pulled out a revolver, stuck it one of the leader's eye slits, and fired. The soldier fell back, instantly dead.

"The other soldiers were not. They were very alive, and infuriated. They charged at the five conscious warriors. Wil ran for his shotgun, Alexandra, and Layne pulled out revolvers, Evangela relied on her spells, and Jessica ran to get Taran and Nicole to safety.

"At first, the battle was going fairly well. Wil ordered Jessica to get Taran and Nicole into the same room that Cole and Michael were in, then barricade it. She dragged them in with no problem. Evangela kept knocking the Defenders back with a Repulsor spell, and Wil, Alexandra, and Layne kept firing away. As time went on, though, bullets began running low, and Layne realized they weren't penetrating the armor. Evangela was becoming weary.

"Suddenly, smoke started coming out of the soldiers' armor and they started screaming. The heroes could hear their skin crackling and popping, like they were in a frier. The attack stopped as they collapsed on the ground, trying to pry their armor off.

"'Thank you, Nicole!' Layne called out, letting out a deep breath.

"'Wrong!' a female voice from outside yelled.

"Wil stumbled over the burning, armored corpses, and looked outside.

"Nobody was there.

"Suddenly, Taran burst into the room.

"'What the fuck is going on? Who are these guys?' he asked, pointing to the still smoking armor on the floor, 'Who knocked me out? Where's Alex?'

"'I'm here.' she said, standing up from behind the bar and running over to Taran, 'How's your shoulder?' she asked, lightly stroking his long hair.

"'Hurts like hell. Look, we need to move to a more hidden location. Someone's on to us. Wil, you're in charge of moving Michael and Cole. Alex, your family is very respected in town. See what you can find out about how much the town knows. Layne, go with her. Take care of her.

"Nicole had joined the group again by this point.

"'Taran, I can protect us from these...' she motioned to the cooked metal shapes, '...things with no problem."

"'I can see that.' Taran nodded, almost grave at the thought of Nicole being this powerful.

"'It wasn't her.' Wil rumbled.

"Nicole shook her head, 'I was still unconscious when this happened. My point is that, in the future, I can handle this, and we don't need to move.'

"'So, who did this?'

"Wil shrugged. Taran shook his head.

"'No, Nicole, we need to move. Both for our protection, and that of any innocents that you may accidentally immolate.

"'Listen, I will bathe this whole planet in blood if-'

"Taran wheeled around and put a finger to her lips.

"'Well, regardless of how many millions you want to slaughter, we need to get moving. Wil, Alex, Layne, you all have your assignments. Take care of them in a timely fashion, please. The rest of us are going to find a new place to stay. Wil, I'll be back here in two hours at the most to let you know if we've found a place. Alex and Layne, come back in two hour intervals to report to Wil and let him now what you've found. If you're fifteen minutes or more late, we're going to come looking for you. Please don't make us do that if we don't need to. Any questions?'

"Nobody said anything, so they got underway. I went with Taran, since I had a pretty good place in mind.

"As we rode across the city, we noticed that the Defenders of the Faith were patrolling all over the place. I could tell this was really worrying Taran.

"'Taran, maybe we should leave the city. Head north, hide out and recover for a while. Staying here is suicide. They'll find you eventually.' I told him.

"'But, Richard, they might hold the key to how we accomplish our mission. Think about it. They're HIS soldiers. There has to be a way that using them can help us. If we stay, we win.'

"'If we stay, you die.' I countered.

"We came to the spot that I had suggested. It was the cellar to a house that had recently been abandoned by a family. It was going to be auctioned off in a month. Taran shot the lock off the storm doors and we all went inside. Taran, Evangela, Nicole, Jessica, and myself.

"It was actually very spacious and in great shape.

"'It'll do.' Taran said after less than a minute, 'Evangela and Jessica, I'll need help bringing Michael and Cole back. Nicole and Richard, you stay here and guard the new place.'

"'Taran, let me go! I would feel much better insuring that Cole gets back here okay myself!' Nicole said, immediately realizing everyone was more than a little surprised by her outburst.

"'Nicole, you're a wanted woman.' he responded.

"'Taran, please.'

"He stopped and considered it for a while. He looked at Jessica, then at Nicole.

"'Very well.

"The five of us hurried back to Wil's bar. We brought Wil up to date, and started moving the injured. Taran stated that he would wait for Alexandra and Layne. Wil protested somewhat, but Taran quickly shut him up.

"So, Wil took everyone else to the storm cellar.

"I waited with Taran. We both sat down at one of the tables and he poured himself a beer.

"'So,' I began, attempting conversation, 'any thoughts?'

"Taran paused for a while, staring at the ground. After a few minutes, he looked up at me, smiling, a single tear falling.

"'Yeah. I screwed us completely.'

"A silence fell between us. We looked at each other, smiling.

"'Why? How do you mean?' I asked.

"'Because we'll never have the peace that we deserve.'

"'Ah, I see.'

"We paused again, taking in the moment.

"'I miss this, Richard. Quiet. It's been over a year since you and I really just sat and talked. It's been fun, but it's been wearing me out at the same time.'

"'Yes, I can see that. You've actually aged noticeably.'

"'What?'

"'You act quite differently and your hairline's receded a bit. You're much more mature now. And not nearly as fun-loving.'

"Taran stared into his beer, taking this in.

"Suddenly, Alexandra and Layne burst in.

"'Taran, we need to leave town NOW!' Alexandra screamed.

"Taran jumped up and faced her.

"'Why? What's happened?' he asked.

"'They're organizing an army to come find us. Taran, they know our names, they know everything about all of us! We need to leave now!'

"'Okay, Alex, okay. Let's go get the others and we'll leave.' he said, holding her.

"She jerked back.

"'They're not here! Where the hell are they?!'

"'They're at our new place. Look, just follow me. We're getting them now. Come on!'

"They all mounted their horses and raced over to the cellar. When they neared it, Taran spotted Defenders walking down the street.

"'Stop.' he whispered, 'We'll do the rest on foot. Follow me.'

"They all got off their horses and proceeded towards the storm doors. Taran pulled them open and walked down.

"The cellar was empty. Everyone was gone.

"'No! No!' he yelled, falling to his knees and hanging his head.

"'Taran, maybe they realized what was happening and left already. Maybe there's a note around here.' Layne said, looking around.

"Just then, Layne yelled and jumped back. A Defender stepped out of the shadows and grabbed him.

"'Taran Walker, surrender or I kill him.' the soldier said.

"He had no choice. He surrendered.

"The soldier led the three of them outside and met ten other soldiers who were waiting in the street. They were then taken to a paddy wagon and taken to the riverfront.

"At the riverfront, the other six members were waiting, tied to posts. Taran was placed at the first post, hands bound, feet bound, and tied by his neck, waist, and ankles to the post. Next to him was Wil, then Evangela, Alexandra, Layne, Cole, Jessica, Michael, and Nicole. They all stood there, silently attempting to think of a way to get out of this.

"What seemed like the entire city began to form a mob around the execution area.

"That night was one of the strangest nights I had ever seen. The clouds were swirling around the moon like a ring of fire. Defenders were stopping the mob from getting near the prisoners. There was one Defender who stood in the middle of the scene, looking very much like the leader. He had the standard baby blue and yellow armor, but was highly decorated and had a long, black cape draped from over his shoulders. He seemed to be shouting orders to the other Defenders.

"'I think they're going to kill us, Taran.' Wil suddenly said.

"'You always were the brains of the operation, Wil.' Taran chuckled.

"Taran looked out over the crowd, trying to find his parents. He didn't see them. That was for the best. No parent should ever have to watch their child die before them.

"He looked at his crew.

"Wil was staring straight ahead, frozen like a statue. Evangela was leaning her head back, eyes closed, her lips moving. Taran was praying that she was about to pull of the greatest stunt ever. Alexandra, his beautiful Alexandra, was hanging her head and sobbing. This nearly killed him. He was supposed to be defending her. He was supposed to give his life FOR her, not WITH her! He couldn't stand watching her cry anymore, so he moved on. Layne was looking at him, smiling. This was even more surprising. He mouthed the words, 'It was fun.' Taran smiled and looked at Cole, who was still unconscious, or maybe even dead. Jessica, who had never done anything wrong, was bawling. He felt horrible for this. She didn't even really want to join them, had been talked into it, and now she would die with them. Next to her, Michael and Nicole were engaged in idle conversation, like nothing unusual was happening.

"'Amazing, isn't it?' Wil suddenly spoke up again.

"'What?' Taran asked, coming out of his dream world.

"'How different we all are, and we're still in this together, even at the bitter end. We're all upset, but none of us have really broken. I was looking at all of them, too, and marveling at how they face death differently. They're real men and women, Taran. We could've won.' Wil said, hanging his head.

"'Wil, pass this down to Nicole and Evangela: can they cast a spell to free at least one of us?'

"'Yeah.' Wil smiled, and asked Evangela. She said no and passed the word down. He watched the heads turn back and forth. Eventually, the verdict came back: Nicole could free one person at a time with a very minor fire spell. Mystics require their hands to gesture in order to conjure magic, but Nicole could make a litte fire with just a few fingers.

"Taran absorbed all of this for a few seconds, then acted.

"'Wil, tell Nicole to free Alex. Tell Alex to jump in the river and ride the current until she gets to safety. When she's safe, she's to forget all of us, everything that happened, and to live a long and happy life. Understand?'

"Wil hesitated.

"'Yeah," Wil said, then hesitated and spoke again, "and thank you.'

"'For what?'

"'For choosing her.'

"Wil passed this down. Suddenly, Taran heard Alexandra.

"'Taran, no! Please! This isn't fair! If you're going to die, I'm dying with you! Damn you for denying me that!'

"'Alex, please! When your bonds are gone, just go! Please!'

"'Taran-' and she fell, her ashen bonds sprinkling to the ground.

"'ALEX, GO!'

"She turned to him, tears pouring out of her eyes and began to walk towards him.

"'I won't leave you!'

"'ALEXANDRA, GO! PLEASE!' now Taran was in tears, too.

"She put her arms around him.

"'I love you.'

"'I love you, too, Alex.'

"They stayed frozen in that position for at least a minute before Taran noticed the Defenders approaching them.

"'ALEX, GO!'

"Suddenly, they all heard a commotion coming from the crowd.

"'Alexandra! Alexandra! I'm here!' her father yelled.

"She spun around.

"'Daddy! Daddy! Oh God! Dad-' she was cut off by the Defenders grabbing her and dragging her back to her post.

"'DADDY! DON'T LET US DIE! DADDY! PLEEEASE!' she screamed.

"Her father began to run towards them.

"'Alexandra! Put her down! Alex!' he yelled.

"'DADDY!' she sobbed, still screaming while she was being tied to the post again.

"To this day, I don't know how she did this, but Alexandra got free again. She immediately ran back to Taran, kissed him, whispered in his ear:

"'I'll be back for you, my love. This is not our last day together.' and began to run to her father.

"'DADDY, I'M-' Alexandra's chest exploded like a volcano and she fell to the ground. A Defender about twenty feet away lowered his shotgun. Her father collapsed on his knees, lifting her up and cradling her in his arms, crying uncontrollably.

"'MY BABY!' her father screamed.

"'ALEXANDRA!' Taran cried out, unable to say more. He was overcome with suffering. He looked at her body again. Alexandra was dead. This couldn't be. Alexandra was dead. He looked at Wil, who looked as though he had finally lost his mind. His eyes were bulging out of his head and filled with tears. Drool was dripping out of his mouth and he was whimpering. Evangela was crying endlessly. He couldn't bear to look at the rest of them.

"'Baby, please don't be dead.' Taran whispered to himself and looked up again to see if maybe she was still alive somehow.

"But, all he saw was black. The last thing he heard was a bang.

"He had just been shot in the head by the Defenders of the Faith. And so were the rest of them. They started with Taran and worked their day down the line, finishing with Nicole.

"I walked away, wanting to cry, but I have no tears. And that is an overly long summary of the original Nine." Ghost finished.

IX: Come Together

They all looked at each other, unable to speak.

Alex pulled Taran close and clung to him, shaking. He rested his head on her chest and looked up at her.

"You okay?" he asked, stroking her cold, white skin.

"Yeah, I just hate remembering that day."

"So, how did you survive?" he asked.

"The gun shot didn't kill me." she said.

"Obviously. But, how?"

"Let me smoke a cigarette, talk about something else for a bit, then I'll tell everyone, okay?"

"Fine."

Ghost nodded in agreement and a moment of silence passed among the group. Taran and Alexandra closed their eyes and enjoyed the sensation of being near each other. Sasha heaved a sigh of annoyance. Ghost stood in the middle of the room, surveying the group.

For the first time ever, the silence didn't bother Taran. Just having her near was calming enough to put him into a coma. The longer he lay against her, the more he felt like he understood her. Familiarity and comfort were infecting him, the way a touch from a long-gone lover will make one ask, "How could I have forgotten all those good times?" Except, he had no memories with her. Just an impression. He was intoxicated by her.

Sasha was growing more and more annoyed with this whole Taran-Alexandra thing. She needed Taran focused. They all did. This team would know the same fate as the original one if he didn't pull his head out of her ass. Sasha couldn't argue whether or not she should be on the team after everything Ghost had just told them. She didn't like Alex. That's what it came down to. She couldn't figure out why, but there was something about her that really irritated Sasha.

Suddenly, her annoyance was momentarily alleviated. Alexandra stood up and grimaced, touching her side, where she had been wounded.

"I've really gotta feed, so I'll be back in a little while. Taran, can I borrow your key, so I can get back in?"

"Do you want me to go with you...to make sure you're safe?" he asked sheepishly.

"No. I always feed alone. When I get back, I'll tell my story, okay?"

"Sure. Yeah. Actually, I need to go on a beer run anyway. Does anybody-"

Taran suddenly heard a familiar voice.

"No need. Icehouse long-neck bottles right here." said Nigel, walking into the room, and setting 12 Icehouse bottles and 12 Killarney's Red on the coffee table in the center of the room. Taran looked up at him in shock. There stood his best friend of six years, with his long light brown hair, blue eyes, goatee, and piercings in both ears. He was decked out in his usual gear. Bright, multi-colored unbuttoned shirt with a wife-beater on underneath and blue jeans with Converse on his feet. He stood there, waiting for a reaction from Taran.

"Hey, man! Good to see ya!" Taran exclaimed, embracing his friend. Actually, both men were surprised by Taran's enthusiasm. Taran clapped him on the back, then turned to grab a beer.

"I figured we could get drunk and watch Ninja Turtles or something." Nigel said, smiling.

He turned to Alexandra, who was standing right next to him, waiting for him to move so she could leave.

"Hi. I'm Nigel." he said, extending his hand. She grabbed it and shook it.

"I'm Alexandra. Nice to meet you. I'm sorry, but I really need to get by you. Sorry." she said, trying to be polite.

"Oh, no problem. Go ahead." he said, maneuvering and plopping down next to Sasha.

"I'm Sasha." she said, cracking a cute smile.

"Since my name hasn't changed in the last thirty seconds, I'm still Nigel."

Alex spoke up, looking at Taran.

"I'll be back in like an hour, okay, babe?"

"Yeah. Please be careful, alright?"

She nodded, smiled a little, then turned and headed out.

"Babe?" Nigel asked, shooting a Taran a look.

"Yeah. New, I mean old, I...old flame that I'm getting involved with again." he explained.

"Old flame? From when? Did you fuck her when you were like eight or something? Who is she?"

"Well, she's-"

"WHAT IS THAT?" Nigel cried, backpedaling and pointing at Layne.

Layne had been studying Nigel from his corner spot, then slowly levitated his emaciated body into a standing pose.

"Nigel, there's something you should know."

Nigel nodded, not taking his eyes off of Layne, until he had floated out of the room, when he turned his gaze back to Taran.

"I know you're not queer, so that's out. Are you actually a several hundred year old being from another universe masquerading as my best friend?" Nigel forced a chuckle as he resumed his previous cool.

"No. Look, a hundred years ago...shit. Okay, back in 1860 something...no. Ghost, will you tell him?" Taran asked.

Ghost stepped out from the corner and approached Nigel.

"Whoah...discount day at the resale shop, huh?" he said, noticing Ghost for the first time.

"Nigel, nice to finally make your acquaintance." Ghost said, shaking his hand.

"Right." Nigel said, nodding uncertainly.

Taran approached his friend and slapped a hand on his shoulder.

"Ghost is going to tell you a little story. I'm going on the roof to think about some shit. Sasha, do whatever you…do. Whenever Alex gets back, have her come up to the roof. Let me know whenever Ghost is done, because Alex is going to pick up where he leaves off. I know that this all makes no sense right now, but ya gotta just trust me, okay?"

"Right. Go smoke some more crack. I'll listen to pirate-shirt here and find you when I'm done." Nigel sat and popped open a beer, "Hit me." he said to Ghost. Taran and Sasha got up and walked out into the main foyer, where Layne stood, waiting for them.

"Taran…" she began, hanging her head.

"What's up?" he asked, lighting a smoke.

YOU HAVE HOT POCKETS

Taran winced again, and nodded.

"Yeah. Did you read that from my thoughts?"

6 BOXES IN TRASH FAT BOY

"Oh. Yeah. You want some?"

INDEED

"Yeah. Go for it."

Layne floated down the hall toward the kitchen.

"I…I have some major concerns about the vampire." Sasha stated forcefully, looking up at him.

"Alex? What's your problem with her? She drinks blood. It doesn't affect you."

TURKEY BACON CLUB KICK ASS

Taran and Sasha both winced again, then resumed their conversation.

"Taran, she murders every night. Killing is perfectly natural to her. Her very existence is immoral."

YOUR LAST ONE YOU DON'T MIND

"No! It's fine!" Taran bellowed down the hall, getting annoyed.

"Sasha, I understand your issues with her. Get over it. She's part of the team. Also, I really doubt she kills indiscriminately. Give her a fair chance. Get to know her, okay?"

"Okay." she sighed, looking down again. Taran ran his fingers through her hair and made her look at him again.

"We're a team, Mademoiselle, and I'd much rather have the undead fighting for us than against us."

"I know. I'm sorry, it's just…nothing like I expected."

"Hey, at least you expected anything. This is all new for me."

She smiled.

"Alright." she said.

"I'm going on the roof now. Milk Bone's downstairs if you want a challenge in human social structures." Taran said, starting up the stairs.

"Right. Thanks."

Alexandra dashed through the alley behind the Halfway. She remembered that one of the crooked police captains in St. Louis lived right around here. His name was Vic Faye. He lived down by Vandeventer and Forest Park Parkway.

She loved this feeling. Moving at an incredible speed, she would've appeared as a blur to any passerby. She jumped nine foot fences, scaled brick walls with no problem, ripped apart chains that were locking fences as if they were putty, shot through traffic with such grace that it almost appeared to be a ballet done at twenty times speed. It was still a beautiful night. It was Alexandra's night. That was why she was now truly convinced that she and Taran were made for each other. In the near future, she knew in her heart that he would rule the day and she would rule the night. United, they would be unstoppable. She was more than excited. She was actually turned on for the first time in a century.

As she was nearing his apartment, she decided to have some fun. She saw one of Vic's thugs walking out of the building and stepping onto the sidewalk, looking for his ride to show up. He leaned against a tree and lit a cigarette.

Alex accelerated, leaped into the air, and smashed through the tree, causing it to explode in a hale of splinters. The upper part of the tree shot up, twirling around like a toy plastic tree. It landed with a crunch on top of some poor guy's '80 Malibu. The minion was laying on the ground, looking for what he believed to be the gunman that had missed him and hit the tree.

Alex was already charging up the stairs to the overlord's apartment, smiling, her mouth watering at the prospect of the fresh blood. She was in a frenzy now, in her killer mode. Nothing would keep her from the blood now.

One thing that people didn't understand about vampires is that on many occasions, when they work themselves up enough before a kill is that all their abilities (strength, vision, hearing, agility, etc.) will increase even more. Vampires are already incredibly superior to humans in all these areas, so when this heightening occurs, they become a literal death machine, virtually unstoppable. The only trade-off for this is that they will lose almost all rational thought, only aware of their need for the blood. This "death machine" state didn't occur every time they would feed, only when the vampire worked him or herself up into it.

Alexandra loved this feeling. It was like a 20 or 30 minute orgasm. She was near invincible and knew it. Vic Faye was going to become a feeding trough for an immortal.

Alex approached the door and put her ear against it.

Taran sat on the roof, looking at the city skyline to the east, marveling at how the buildings seemed to form a jagged, ugly set of teeth

116

that seemed to chew up the otherwise beautiful sky. He wondered if his predecessor ever had to deal with stupid thoughts like this.

He took another slug off of his Icehouse, waiting for that epiphany to hit, where he would figure out what the fatal error for the original team was. Did they not assemble fast enough? It really seemed like they didn't waste any time. They couldn't force the others to reveal themselves, especially since most of them weren't aware of their true nature anyway. It seemed that if you could see Ghost, you were not of this universe. That did make sense. Were some of the members not the right ones? No, they could all see Ghost. What had they done wrong? He knew that not leaving St. Louis right after Nicole's little episode had been stupid. But, there must have been something bigger than that. The Defenders of the Faith had been there so fast and overwhelmed them so easily.

Maybe after a few Icehouses, when he relaxed, he would understand. In the meantime, he should think about something else.

Alexandra.

Wow. She was an interesting catch. He really couldn't decide how he felt about her. He did feel an irresistible pull to her, unlike anything he had ever felt before. On the other hand, he really didn't know if he could handle a relationship at this moment. But, it really did seem that they were fated to be together. Once again, on the other other hand, her vampirism might cause a few problems. He could never bring her to dinner with mom and dad.

Why was he worrying about a girl right now? Stupid.

He wondered what Rosaline was doing at this exact moment.

Rosaline methodically plucked photograph after photograph from her wall, and tossed them into the box. Pictures of her and Taran at various shows, posing for the camera and throwing up metal fists, pictures of them on stage, whenever he would guest with her band, pictures of them out with friends, pictures of them at her various high school dances, pictures of them at parties.

Her whole room was a shrine to how much she'd let him totally suffocate her. Not that she hadn't usually enjoyed it. At first, she'd lapped it up, like a starry-eyed school girl, but after time...

She shook it off and kept ripping her past away from her present, dropping pictures and jewelry and trinkets into the box.

It was done.

She grabbed another photograph, dropped it in, and looked up. There must've been at least a hundred more, but they weren't all Taran. Sure, most were, but her whole life of the last five years was captured on this wall.

She grabbed another photograph. In it, Taran was lunging at the camera with no shirt on. The sides were folded back. She unfolded them, and her feet appeared on either shoulder of his. She rolled her eyes, and dropped it into the box.

Should I even bother getting the rest of these back from him? I guess he'll never post them online, given now young I was at the time.

She grabbed another photograph. She and Taran were playing beer pong with Nigel and Puck at Nigel's New Year 1999/2000 party.

Her stomach tightened, and she sat down at her desk chair.

Maybe I shouldn't be so angry with him.

"Welcome to Nigel's Millennial Bacchanalia!" Nigel called out to the crowd, "One hour left of this century, motherfuckers!"

Nigel was bathed in drunken cheers.

"Actually, it's neither the end of the century, nor the end of the millennium." Taran muttered to his friend.

"Yeah, we've been over this, Stat Boy." Nigel groaned, but still smiled.

"Wait, what?" Puck asked, tucking her hair behind her ears, and leaning toward Taran.

"He just needs to make sure no one actually enjoys themselves tonight." Rosaline yelled over the noise as she elbowed Taran.

Taran smiled, gently elbowed her back, then leaned toward Puck.

"What was the first year, anno domine?" he asked her.

"A.D? I dunno, 1?" she answered, shrugging.

"Right! Therefore, the first millennium ended in 1001!" Taran exclaimed, then turned to Nigel, "Therefore, the second millennium will end one year from now!"

"Hey, Taran." Nigel tugged on Taran's sleeve.

"Yeah?"

"I got a great idea. Let's lead a mass conspiracy where we don't tell anyone, since you're obviously the first fucking person to think of this, and just make them all look stupid by letting them all get drunk and have a good time on New Year's. No one will suspect a thing, and it'll be our secret. Sssh." Nigel cracked a grin, holding his finger up to his lips.

"Fine. But when the truth leaks out, I'm rolling over on you all." Taran chuckled back, banging his plastic beer cup into Nigel's.

"SHIT!" Nigel suddenly called out, jumping up.

"What?!" Puck asked, standing up next to him.

"We're not playing beer pong! Hurry!" he yelled, scampering away.

Puck smiled, then rolled her head and eyes as she stumbled to follow him. Taran shrugged, grabbed Rosaline, and they followed him into another room.

As the four of them stumbled through the hallways, Rosaline heaved a sigh of relief. Taran was having a good night. He had been sober (from drugs) for three months, but tended to freak from time to time when he drank.

The four friends entered into a dark room, Nigel's gaming room, when he flicked on the lights. The ping-pong table had its net removed, and it was covered in beer cups.

"BEER PONG!!!" Nigel screamed, mock-tearing at his shirt.

The girls laughed, but Taran stared, perplexed. Nigel caught his look, and stared back at him, equally perplexed.

"Beer pong, dude." he laughed, motioning at the table.

"It looks like a potentially fantastic time, but I don't understand how it's 'played.'" Taran cocked an eyebrow.

"How do you have an alcoholic parent and not know how to play beer pong, man?!" Nigel cackled, clapping his hands.

"Well, shit, dude, it's not like we'd roll out the beer pong table at family Easter every year." Taran retorted.

"Okay, fair enough, fair enough. It's real simple dude. Hit the ping pong ball into your opponent's cup to make 'em drunk. Er, drink. Er, ya know what I mean, bitch."

The four of them laughed, banged their beers together, and began playing.

Later, as Taran was preaching to a crowd of drunk disciples about how this wasn't actually the millennium, Nigel sidled up to Rosaline.

"Preacher Taran is educating the masses, I see." Nigel said, smiling, then took another sip of beer.

"God, I know. At least he's having a good time and doing what he loves."

"Oh yeah, what's that?"

"He's telling people what he thinks." she sighed, sipping off her own beer.

"Can't deny him that." Nigel agreed, nodding, then in a hushed voice, "How's he been doing?"

Rosaline stared at her beer, nodding.

"He, um, he has good days and bad days. Ya know? We're working through it."

"How about you?" Nigel asked, even quieter.

"Me? What do you mean?"

"I mean, how you been doing?" Nigel asked.

Rosaline looked up at Taran. He was having a good time, but something about him was fragile. She knew she might have to intervene at any moment.

He was a burden, and she felt guilty for feeling that way. She had been his crutch through an ordeal that she hadn't signed up for, that had been sprung on her like a bear trap.

She bit her lip as the tears came crashing down.

Nigel wrapped her in a hug, and she tried as hard as she could to disappear from Taran in his chest.

Maybe it was the alcohol, maybe it was the need to escape her burdening security, maybe it was because Nigel was just better-looking and funnier than Taran, but she suddenly found herself in the throes of his naked, wonderful embrace as his rythmic thrusting granted her a temporary reprieve from the life she hadn't asked for.

Just this one time, she thought, and gave herself fully to Nigel.

"Nooo..." a voice choked as light spilled into the dark room.

Puck stood in the doorway, trembling. She shakily set her beer cup on the dresser next to the doorway.

"At least now I know." Puck whimpered, "I can exit from this, but Taran can't. I'm going to distract him for a bit, then send him to find you, Rosaline. He never needs to know about this, since he depends on you. You two have five minutes to get your shit together, and you're not going to feel well, Roz. You bitch. You fucking whore. You and Taran will leave immediately, and then none of you will ever see me again."

Rosaline wiped at her eyes, then dropped the beer pong picture into the box.

Sasha sat down next to Milk Bone in the recording studio in the basement. He was playing with the levels for the some of the tracks he had laid down, listening to them through headphones. He was nodding his head in time to the music, really groovin' to it. After a while, he noticed the girl next to him. He stopped the song, pulled off his headphones, and looked at her.

"What?" he asked.

"Nothing. Just...didn't feel like being alone right now." she shrugged, looking at all the knobs.

"Oh. Okay."

A silence fell. The kind of silence where you realize you have nothing in common with the person who you're being silent with. Sasha's mind raced for something to say to her temporary friend. She had a hard enough time coming up with something to talk about with Taran, and he was relatively easy to converse with. Maybe Milk Bone would be good practice. Okay, Sasha, think of something. It shouldn't be this hard. Start with the basics of what you know about him.

"So...you like rap, huh?" she said, smiling.

"I guess." he mumbled, turning back to the mixer.

"You're working on a song, right?"

"I guess." he mumbled again, adjusting some knobs and checking levels.

I'm not allowed to choke him, right? Sasha thought.

Sasha was very surprised by this. Milk Bone seemed strangely subdued. In every prior encounter, he was always high energy and very outgoing. This was a very unexpected change in him.

"Milk Bone?" she said, very gently.

120

"What?" he responded, monotone.

"Are you mad at me?"

"Yup."

She was shocked. What possible reason did he have for being mad at her? She ran through the evening's events in her mind, trying to remember when she had ever made him mad. Maybe he was a little pissed about the incident in the living room, when he had no idea why they were all laughing. That might be it.

"Why are you mad?"

"Because you're sitting on Bob."

She paused.

"What?"

"You're sitting on Bob."

"I don't understand."

"Why?"

"Why what?"

"Why don't you understand?"

"Who's Bob?"

"My invisible friend."

She paused again.

"I'm very confused." she said.

"You're stupid." he retorted.

She paused again. Taran really hadn't been kidding. She could do this, though. She knew she could.

"Why do you think I'm stupid?"

"Because you're stupid."

Okay...

"Milk Bone, I'm sure we can resolve this. Just point to where 'Bob' is and I'll move away from him."

He pointed at her.

She got up, walked behind Bone, and took a seat on the other side of him.

"Nooo!!!" he wailed.

She immediately jumped up again, scared to death.

"WHAT?! WHAT?! WHAT'S WRONG?!" she yelled.

"YOU JUST KILLED FRANK!!! YOU BITCH!!! YOU FUCKING WHORE BITCH!!! AAAHHH!!!" he screamed, burying his face in his hands.

She backed away slowly.

He began to laugh wildly, clapping his hands.

"Nah, baby, I just playin'.' Siddown. Whatchu wanna talk about?"

Sasha smoothed her skirt and sat back down on one of the swivel chairs next to the recording equipment.

"So, you record your rap music down here?"

"Kinda. I mean, I do whatever down here. Sometimes I flow, sometimes I make some beats, and sometimes, I dunno, I just kinda mess around with stuff, like electronics and whatever."

"You're good with electronics?" she asked, looking at him curiously.

"Yeah, and doin' stuff with metal, too. My dads taught me a lotta shit before he went back in lock-up."

"Like, prison? Your father is in prison?"

"Yeah, I been hangin' with Taran since then. Oh, and I work on his bike and shit, too, but I'm still learnin' some of that shit. Gonna get that bitch runnin' soon, I swear." Milk Bone held up his hand as if he were giving an oath.

"Your affinity for the word, 'bitch' troubles me a bit." Sasha narrowed her eyes as she said this.

"You sayin' I say 'bitch,' like, infinity times?"

Sasha sighed.

"Yeah, I guess so."

"Well, it's better than 'cunt,' right? YO! I knew this bitch who HATED the word, 'cunt!'"

Sasha balled her hands into fists, and she could swear she felt her blood rushing throughout her body.

Milk Bone scooted away from her a bit.

"Yo, baby, chill. I just playin.' Kinda. I mean, she didn't like...that word, ya know, but I was tryin' to get atcha, ya know? I'll stop. It's cool. You fine, and you seem...kinda naïve, but-"

"Did YOU just call ME naïve?"

Milk Bone looked around for any kind of help.

"Uh. No. I don't even know that word, ya know. Like, I'm stupid, so don't hate. Don't hate. I heard Taran use that word and-"

IDIOT

Milk Bone rocked back in his chair, and then he saw Layne float down the stairs and completely fell out of it.

"WHAT THE FUCK?" he yelled.

Sasha glanced back at Layne. She tried her best to act cool, like they were old friends, but she found his presence unsettling, as well.

"Milk Bone, meet Layne Wood. Quit fucking with me."

WHO'S THE BITCH NOW

Nigel looked Ghost in the eye.

"And that's it, huh?" he asked.

"Yes, that's it." Ghost said.

Nigel sat back, lit a smoke, and popped open another brew. He thought about everything that this 'Ghost' had just told him. It was an amazing story. Action. Adventure. Romance. Drama. Beer. Not bad.

"That's pretty good, Ghost, er, Richard, whatever. Um, I don't believe you. I think Taran is fucking with me. I'm going to go throw him off that roof now. Bye." and he walked out.

Ghost rolled his eyes.

He was in his bedroom. He had to be. Alexandra backed up, preparing to launch herself through the door. She had it all worked out. She would burst through, hit him with so much speed and force that he would be unable to react. She would drain him lightning fast, avenge those poor girls, and get out before his buddies showed up. Easy.

3....2....1

She shot through the door, head first, arms pointed out, like a human bullet. She somersaulted on the floor, leaped onto her feet, and broke into a sprint for his bedroom. His door was shut, so she simply repeated the maneuver she had used on the front door. Busted right through it, head first, somersaulted again, and when she popped up, she performed a reverse flip, and landed on his bed, standing over him. Laying next to him was a whore she recognized from Cherokee Street. The girl began to scream. Alexandra backhanded the girl so hard she went unconscious. She then turned her attention to Vic.

"Hi, Vic." she hissed, flashing her teeth.

"Holy Jesus." he whimpered, "Who the fuck are you? Please don't kill me. Please don't. I'll give you whatever you want. Please!" he cried, his hands curled in a begging motion.

"Fix all the girls you've broken by abusing your power, asshole!" she roared, grabbing him by the back of his hair, and getting right in his face. She was very much deviating from the plan, but she loved scaring the shit out of these guys.

Word on the street had been that he got his jollies by raping fledgling hookers.

"Look, lady, if you're in the business of saving lives, I'm someone you want on your side!" he said, regaining his courage somewhat.

She'd have to fix that.

She sank her teeth into his jugular and began to rob him of his life, as he had so many others. This is why she believed she had held up a lot better than other vampires. She took pleasure in her work. She only fed off of bad men.

She stopped just a bit before he was supposed to die. She sat up, and looked at him. His eyelids were drooping, drool was seeping from his mouth, and his breathing had become rasps, futile attempts at preserving this worthless carcass he called a body.

"Vic?" she said sweetly.

"Wha..." he moaned, barely conscious.

"You're going to die now. Look at me. I want you to know exactly who it was that murdered you. I'm Alexandra Boliviere, a vampire, the Queen of the Night. Time to die." she hissed again, baring her bloody fangs.

She attacked his neck again, draining the rest of him in a couple of seconds. She stepped off of the bed, stretching, feeling the new blood in her veins. She was at full strength now. She looked at her wound from earlier. It was already healing a lot more. Since silver had been used, it would probably scar, but it was definitely looking a lot better. The large, gaping hole it had once been had closed up. The skin was still horribly disfigured, but it would probably be as healed as it was going to be by tomorrow night.

She needed to get out of there. Chances are, one of the neighbors heard all the commotion, saw the hole in the door, and had already called the cops.

She looked around the room, trying to figure out where he kept his safe. She tore apart the bedroom. It wasn't underneath the bed, it wasn't behind any pictures, it wasn't under any furniture, and it wasn't out in plain view. She walked out into the main room and looked around. She saw the door leading to the study. Aha.

She walked in there. And, right on the desk, was a cheap, little green safe. She smashed her fist down on it, and the door popped open. She reached inside and pulled out a fat stack of bills. She counted through them all. $50,000. Sweet.

She was making quite a killing these days, no pun intended, of course. She shoved it all into her pocket, leaped out the window, and took off for the Halfway.

IT APPEARS THAT EVEN THE UNDEAD CAN BE HYPOCRITES

Alexandra whirled around, and there was Layne, standing in that weird, shriveled way, in the alley.

"Jesus, you're a creepy one, Layne. I've heard of you before. You're a bit on the infamous side among the 'creeps' locally."

YOU JUST USED THE WORD CREEPS ARE YOU INCLUDING YOURSELF

Alexandra looked at the walking corpse, his bulging eyes reflecting in the light from a lamp post outside, and considered his statement.

"I think I fall into that term more than almost anybody. I mean, yeah, all Mystics, including Psycho Mystics, are in there, too-"

Alexandra found herself hurtling into a dumpster, then falling to the ground quite painfully. Layne's shriveled form floated toward her slowly. For the first time in almost a century, she felt terror pulsating in her brain. She shook her head, shrugged off the fear, and jumped to her feet.

DON'T YOU EVER FUCKING CALL ME A PSYCHO MYSTIC YOU ALREADY KILLED ONE OF MY SOURCES TONIGHT I USED TO BE A SOMEWHAT NORMAL PERSON IN FAR LESS PAIN AND HERE YOU COME TO

The ground began to tremor.

KILL MY ONE SOURCE YOU HAVE NO IDEA WHAT I CAN TO DO THOSE WHO WISH TO FURTHER MY PAIN

"Wait! Hang on! I'm not furthering any pain! This was a very bad man!"

YOU HAVE NO IDEA

"How did you know him?"

Layne continued his dead stare at her, apparently thinking for a moment.

Alexandra used this moment to her advantage. She burst from her position, vaulting off the wall, and knocking him down. She perched on his bony chest, baring her fangs, and holding a nail on his jugular.

I LET HIM FUCK ME FOR HEROIN

She gasped, loosening her grip a bit, at which point, she found herself sailing straight up through the air. She tumbled repeatedly as she gazed at the skyline from an impossible height.

She managed to land on her feet, albeit painfully.

Layne was standing right in front of her.

YOU WILL FIND MY NEXT SOURCE OR FACE MY PAIN

"Freeze, motherfucker."

Taran yanked his sword out and spun around. A man in the shadows was pointing a gun at him, and coming towards him slowly.

"Drop the sword, you sack of shit. A gun is a projectile weapon. A sword is not. I could put you on your back from here. Be smart."

Taran didn't move an inch. The gunman hesitated.

"Fair enough." the gunman said, "Just give me a beer and I'll put the gun down. I left mine downstairs."

Taran relaxed, sheathed his sword, and sighed.

"Jesus, Nigel! You scared the shit out of me! Where the hell did you get that fucking thing anyway?" Taran laughed, putting his sword away and handing his friend an Icehouse.

"I bought it from a guy at school...after the accident. It just kind of makes me sleep a little better at night. I brought it up here to show it to you." he handed Taran the gun, "9mm. Beretta. Pretty nice, huh?"

Taran turned it over in his hands. He brought it up and aimed it at the moon. It was nice.

"Don't know much about guns, but I assume that's a nice one." he said, handing it back.

"I think so." Nigel said, putting it away and opening his beer. He took a swig and shuddered.

"Ooohhhh, I'd forgotten how bitter this stuff is."

Taran laughed.

"I told you, it's a man's beer. This shit'll put hair on your chest." he chuckled some more and took another drink with no problems.

Nigel looked up at the stars. He realized it was one of the few city nights where you could actually see the stars. Most of the time, there was so much pollution that the stars actually seemed more like a legend.

Nigel broke the silence and spoke, finally.

"Nice try, by the way, with that whole story Ghost told me. More creepy-funny than, like, haha-funny, though."

Taran hung his head.

"Nigel, it's not a joke. It's serious."

"Remember how you told me that Matt's mom would find it endearing enough to order pizza for us if I smacked her ass, since she respected brutal men, and she ended up calling the cops on me? No, sir, am I buying into this one."

"Goddamit, Nigel! Look at my fucking arms! Look at my fucking face! You know who did this?!"

Nigel looked at Taran's face and arms. There were cuts and bruises all over him, including a very nasty gash going down his right arm.

"Jesus, Taran, I didn't even notice those. Who the fuck did this?"

"Raphael."

Nigel's blood froze. He nearly dropped his beer. He slowly looked away from Taran and looked at the stars again.

"What the hell happened, man?" Nigel asked.

"I met Alex, then he tried to kill her. I stopped him." Taran said, looking almost dazed.

"So what the hell does that have to do with the story Ghost just told me?"

Taran paused.

"I have no idea." he said.

"Oh. Swear to me that everything I've been told today is true."

"I swear. I swear on their graves."

"Their gr...oh, yeah...their graves." The two reasons Taran wanted Raphael dead.

"I also swear to the world I will kill him one day." Taran's eyes looked completely glazed now. He was almost speaking in a whisper now.

"Maybe you should just let it go. Move on with your life. I mean, just get away from...this whole cloud of...just bad memories that you've let infect you, ya know? I left, and you should, too."

"I can't. I need to settle this. You know what he did." Taran said.

"Taran, you're talking about killing a man. That's crazy." Nigel said, shaking his head.

"Nigel, I'm not crazy. The rules, the laws, they don't apply to us anymore. We're...the Nine. We're..." he trailed off.

"We're on a mission from God." Nigel commented, doing his best Dan Akroyd.

"Look, dude, I don't know how to explain it to ya. If you could've been at that fight tonight, and see what I've seen...you'd trust me on this."

Nigel sighed, grabbed another beer, uncapped it, and played with the cap for a moment.

"I do trust you, man. And look, I've not always been a great friend to you. But, I'll keep an open mind and...fine. Fine. Look, asshole, all I wanna do is sit out here and drink some beer with you, okay? Can we please do that or are you going to continue your little 'Worf' routine?"

Taran looked up at the sky and wiped away a single tear. He took a few deep breaths and nodded. After a moment of silence, he looked at

Nigel.

"Fuck you, let's drink some beer."

"Sounds good. To the beginning of a great adventure." Nigel said, holding his beer in the air for a toast.

"To the beginning of a great adventure." Taran said, knocking his beer against Nigel's.

"So, it's really true, huh? I mean, we...we're really going to do this?"

"Yep." Taran said rather casually and took a drink of his beer.

"So, what do we do next?"

Taran paused, then shrugged.

"What do you mean? You're supposed to be the fucking leader, man! I mean, are waiting on a group of fucking Hobbits to lead us toward Mordor?" Nigel laughed, exasperated.

"I don't know, Nigel. I'll talk to Layne and know by the end of the night."

"Are we still going to Cape tomorrow?"

"I have no idea. I'll let you know later."

"Well, I'm glad that you're relaxed about the end of the planet. I guess someone has to be. At least this new 'reality TV' shit will go away."

"Look, man, now it's your turn to relax. Have faith, brother. I've got everything under control. New subject. You start." Taran said.

"Okay. Who are the girls?"

"The blond with fangs is Alexandra, my...girlfriend. The brunette without fangs is Sasha. She's a 'White Mystic.' If you want an explanation, ask her for a demonstration."

"Huh? So, Alexandra has fangs? What is she, some kind of vampire? I guess she 'sucks' real good, huh?" Nigel asked, laughing. Taran looked at him and nodded with a very serious look on his face. Nigel stopped laughing and stared back in disbelief.

"Bullshit!" Nigel yelled, wanting to laugh.

"I'm dead serious, no pun intended." Taran said, "She's out hunting right now."

"Hunting like...humans?"

"No, like killer sheep, yeah, humans! Bad people, though. That's what she says." Taran explained, sighing now.

"Killer sheep would be bad, though. I mean, like, if she was killing them, I'd be down, since it'd wreak havoc on the farm industry. If that's an industry. I guess they subdivide further. Like, ya know, corn and wheat and barley and veal and shit. Anyway, though, as long as she got the asshole who cut me off in his shitty Camaro earlier, I'm cool."

They both heard a sound from the alley below. Taran and Nigel looked down and saw a form jump the fence down there.

"Alex!" Taran yelled.

She stopped and looked up, shielding her eyes from the streetlights.

"Hey! What's up?" she yelled back.

"Nigel doesn't believe you're a vampire! Prove it to him!"

She shook her head, stretched a little, and began to run at the building. They both peaked over the edge to follow her movements. She reached the side of the building and began scaling the flat wall at a blurring speed. She practically rocketed up it, leaped at Nigel and brandished her fangs when she reached the top. He fell back, gasping.

Taran burst into laughter.

"Have a seat, babe, you wanna beer?" Taran asked, still chuckling.

"No thanks." she said, seating herself next to Taran.

"Convinced now?" she asked, smiling at Nigel, the lights reflecting off her fangs.

Nigel turned to Taran.

"Okay, dude, that was sorta unnecessary right there. Like, if she had just thrown a car and smashed a killer sheep against a brick wall, I would've been okay with that."

"Killer sheep?" Alexandra asked, looking puzzled.

"I was just telling your boyfriend here that I have trouble with a woman that literally sucks the life outta people. I don't wanna get into one of those complicated discussions where I contrast you with his previous vaginal endeavors, but the fact that you rely on blood for a food source could create issues. Like, we're at Olive Garden, and I order some kinda shrimp pasta, and Taran's feeling as un-adventurous as ever, and so naturally, he gets the fettucine alfredo, and then suddenly, you're asking if you can get blood instead of marinara sauce, and it's just sorta awkward. And then, even though the waitress was super-hot, I got tip her like shit since she called the cops on my buddy's girlfriend. I'm just not seeing this 'undead girlfriend' thing panning out for Taran. I'm just seeing this whole discussion, where he's on my back porch, all cryin' and whatever, and he's all like, 'everything was fine, and then she ate the cat.' Not a discussion I wanna sort through with him. It's much simpler when the blood-drinking is a metaphor."

"Everyone you've ever loved is going to be snuffed out of existence by this universe's god, Nigel." Alexandra dead-panned.

Nigel pointed at Alexandra and looked at Taran.

"See! Creepy!"

"Alright, let me try another tactic, Nigel." Alexandra began, "We're doing this, and we need you onboard with us. I need you, and Taran needs you. And I give you my word that I would sacrifice everything to protect him. Not just because I've been devoted to him for over a hundred years, but also because I believe that every man, woman, and child on this planet deserves to have a future."

Nigel nodded cautiously as he stared into his beer and considered her words.

Alexandra continued.

"And think, if everything you've heard tonight is true, the crazy things you'll get to see. Not just getting to test your own limits, but also the exotic naked vampire women who will fawn over you. Are you seducing them or are they seducing you? And the thrill of making love to an amazing woman while never letting your gun slip too far from your grasp? Can you handle it? Perhaps you can use your own sexual prowess to completely disarm her and make her discard any thoughts of enslaving you. Then, once you're done, you roll off the bed, you check the clip in your gun, and move on to the next amazing action scene. You're one of the heroes. You get the girl, kill the bad guy, and save the universe."

Nigel nodded some more.

"She's full of shit, but I like it." Nigel laughed, then sighed.

"Well, if that's settled, I wanna talk to Taran alone for a bit before I tell my own story." Alexandra said, extending a hand to Taran to pull him up.

Nigel stood up and looked at her quizzically.

"Your story?"

"Yes, basically everything that happened from when we died to now."

"Alright. So we're crashing here tonight?" Nigel asked Taran.

"Yeah, if that's cool."

"Fine by me. I'll go see what the others are up to." Nigel said, picking up the rest of the beer, "See ya cats downstairs."

Sasha couldn't believe she actually missed Layne's company.

"I'm sorry. I don't find you even remotely attractive. Get your teeth and your hair fixed, then we can talk. I'd really like to be friends, though." she said, smiling.

"Fuck all that."

"What?"

"So what you're sayin' is that you don't wanna get with me, like, at all?" Bone said.

"That's right. Look, can we talk about something else?"

"Okay. Why you come down here?"

"I don't know. I just wanted to see what you were doing. Everyone else is busy. I was bored. I thought I'd just see what you were up to."

"Oh, I see, since you were BORED-"

"Hello! Anyone down here?" Nigel yelled from the stairs.

"Thank god," Sasha whispered to herself, "right here!"

Nigel walked down and came around the corner.

"Hi. Taran and Alex need a private moment, so I was asked to 'excuse' them. What are you guys doing?"

"Leaving with you." Sasha said, grabbing his hand and dragging him back up the stairs. She led him down the hall and entered into the first room she found, on the right. They went into a huge room that apparently used to be the mess hall. They sat on a bench at one of the tables across from each other, and just stared at each other. This went on for about a minute or so. Nigel, boldly, broke the silence.

"You have no idea how to start this conversation, either, do you?"

She breathed a sigh of relief and started laughing.

"No, I don't. I'm so glad you said that. I have to be the most socially retarded person in the world. You have no idea."

"Actually, Milk Bone might give you a run for your money on that one. I mean, I generally don't care about having any kind of social grace, but that dude...wow. Maybe that makes me a prick or...I don't know. Anyway, so, what's your excuse?" he asked, lighting a cigarette.

"Give me one of those and I'll tell you. I left mine downstairs." she said, still laughing a little.

He handed her a cigarette and lit it for her.

"Thank you." she said.

They stared at each other in silence a little longer, before Nigel broke eye contact and began to notice how interesting off-white walls can be when you really think about it.

Sasha didn't.

"So, who are you?" she asked.

He looked at her again, took another drag, and ashed. He exhaled/sighed and opened his mouth to say something before quickly shutting it again.

"What?" she asked, mildly surprised.

"Nothing. I'm nobody."

"Did you fuckers plan this or something?"

Nigel actually managed a small chuckle.

"What do you mean?"

"It's just the two of you have this shell or something that you protect yourselves with. Modesty's good and all, but tone down the 'humble' act. No. I'm sorry. I'm just a little...kinda all over the place after today."

"Hey, make no apologies to me. You seem like a very sensitive person, someone who spends all her time making sure everyone else is okay. It must be exhausting."

Sasha smiled at him, and nodded her head.

"FINALLY! A sane person!" she laughed

"Oh, I wouldn't say that, m'lady." Nigel smiled back at her, "Believe me, I have the same problem. I feel like I'm constantly shielding myself from the atrocities of everyone else's issues."

YOU ARE SO FULL OF SHIT AND YOU KNOW IT

Nigel winced, and looked at Sasha.

"What was that? Did you hear that?"

Sasha shook her head and looked around.

"I just heard this voice, like this flat, almost computerized kinda voice."

"Really?" Sasha asked, sensing a familiar phenomenon, "What did

130

it say?"

Nigel was puzzled by her easy acceptance, but then his mind raced to cover his tracks.

"Um, it said...'why are you talking about yourself when you have such a fascinating young woman sitting across from you, who is merely waiting to hear that you think she's-"

YOU ARE PATHETIC

"pathetic?" Nigel called out, looking around.

"I'm sorry, you think I'm pathetic?" Sasha asked.

"No, the voice thinks I'm pathetic!" Nigel yelled, standing up, still looking for the voice.

"Why would Layne think you're pathetic?" she asked.

"Layne? The floating dead guy? This is gonna sound crazy, but I actually forgot about him. So you heard him yelling?"

"No, he does this telepathic thing. It takes a while to get used to, but we were talking about Hot Pockets earlier, and-"

"Hot Pockets? What?"

"I know it sounds stupid, but he was really excited about this Turkey something or other thing, and-"

TURKEY BACON CLUB

Nigel and Sasha both winced that time.

"So you heard that?" she asked.

"Yeah." he nodded, shaking his head, "That hurts."

IT WAS DELICIOUS

"Okay," she exclaimed, holding her arms out to Nigel, "he had this delicious Turkey Bacon Club Hot Pocket earlier, and Taran and I heard all about it, and we got somewhat used to his form of communication. That's all I'm trying to say!"

Nigel nodded, his eyes still shifting around the room.

"Layne!" he called out, "Why don't you join us?!"

A shadow formed at the other end of the mess hall, where it connected with the kitchen, and Layne's body floated to the doorway.

"Come on! Don't be a stranger. Join us! Sit and talk with us!"

Layne's head continued to hang lifelessly for a moment, before it looked up, directly at Nigel.

"So, the three of you, Sasha, Alexandra, and Layne, each have some kinda cool power. What's mine and what's Taran's?"

TARAN DOESN'T HAVE ONE HE DEPENDS ON US

"Weird. Okay, so what about me?"

YOU ARE THE WISECRACKING SIDEKICK

"Oh! That's funny! You don't really know shit, do you? Your power is what? Floating around all dead and freaky? Nice. Guess what? You're that X-Man that everyone knows sucks! Like fuckin' Jubilee! You don't know anything! Just admit it."

I CAN PAINT THE MOMENT OF YOUR DEATH FOR YOU

Nigel gasped, and looked at Sasha, who was nodding gravely.

"My power is I'm supposed to die?"

"So, what's up?" Taran asked, starting to straighten his room for the first time, a little embarrassed.

"Well, I wanted to talk to you one-on one." Alexandra said, sitting nervously on his mattress.

"Okay. Well, um, anything in particular? I, uh, am I the same as...the other me you used to know?"

"How so?"

"I don't know. Yeah. Anyway, it's strange, because, well, we both died and here we are again."

"Technically, I never died."

"Well, whatever, you're no longer living."

"Is that what you think? That I'm this undead monster? Taran, you being here is my greatest dream fulfilled, but I was also dreading it."

"What do you mean?"

"I didn't want to have to overcome what I've been turned into in order to be with you again. I've been terrified that you'll hate me. That you'll hate what I am now."

Taran stopped cleaning for a moment, and turned to face her.

"I don't. I mean, I can't. It's like...I was looking at that painting that Layne did of you and it completed some circuit in me I hadn't been aware of."

"Painting? What painting?" Alexandra asked, leaning forward.

"There's this painting of you drinking from some woman in the Coffee Cartel, and he signed it. I'm assuming it's his."

Alexandra nodded.

"Huh. So, he's still seeing images. I wonder if that one was past or future."

"I dunno, but I saw that painting, then I saw you outside, and I...maybe we're programmed to be together, but I...ya know what? That's all bullshit."

Alexandra recoiled.

"What?! Taran, no!"

"Look, I love without all that pressure. I don't even know you, but I know you and I don't need all this crazy reincarnation shit and predestined pressure to fuckin'...ya know...come together. I'm sorry. I wanna be with you without all this craziness telling me I have to be. I know I need you, on same base level, and I just wanna pour myself into you, but..."

"Taran, I know you're not the same man I knew, but you're the same man I need to be with. Our souls are the same. I know that you've been betrayed, I know you've had your soul trampled on, I can feel all that from you. If you need time..."

"No, I don't need time. I don't. I just need to release all this pressure, ya know? Like, I've had all this expectation forced on me, which

132

I know, sounds all whiny and shit, but, it's true. I've been working a long time at being my own man, and then, all of a sudden, this scripted part is handed to me, and I know it's what I'm supposed to do, I'm not gonna turn away from it, but damn..." he sat down next to her and put his arm around her waist.

She ran a hand through his hair and kissed him on the cheek.

"I'll be fine." he said, "I just need to blow off steam." he turned to her suddenly, "And take ya out for a drink and get to know you. It's so strange, because I know your heart, but I don't know YOU. Or even the basics of...the vampire thing. Like, I'm guessing sunlight is bad."

She smiled, giggled, and nodded.

"Sunlight is bad, you're right."

"I know you drink blood, so that's outta the way. I know you're crazy strong and fast. Anything else I need to know...like, to be a good boyfriend to a vampiress?"

She shrugged and looked away.

Taran looked at her, unsure if he had upset her. He ran his fingers through her hair now, amazed at how soft and silky it was. He ran a finger along her ear and down her neck, then down her jawline and to her lips.

She kissed that finger, then slowly took his hand, and lowered it to her leg, where she rubbed it back and forth on her thigh.

He looked at her again.

Her head was angled back a bit, her fangs fully exposed. Her ears slowly became pointed, and she became totally white, even her lips.

Suddenly, she spoke.

"I don't know. I don't think it's ever been done before."

"Huh?"

"I know exactly what you're thinking about and I'm telling you. I don't think it's ever been done before."

"How-"

"It may have been a hundred years or so, but I am still a woman, Taran."

"So no vampire has ever...made love?"

"As far as I know. It's just that vampires don't reproduce sexually, so..."

"Are you okay with this?" he asked, kissing her neck.

She pounced, pinning him to the bed and covering him with kisses.

"It's just...I've burned for you for the past century, since the day you died. Then, one day, out of the blue, you're back. I just need to know you're here. I need to feel us...together."

She kissed him deeply. She was careful not to prick him with her teeth, but caution was in war with passion. Their tongues flickered against each other, moving in a perfect rhythm. She completely lost herself in the moment. The soft touch of his beard, the warmth of his mouth against her coldness, the warmth of his skin against her frigid hands.

He broke from her as he grabbed a handful of her hair and bit into her neck gently, then dragged his tongue up to her ear.

They began to kiss again. They kissed with such ferocity and vigor that she pricked his tongue. He didn't care. They shared a passionate, bloody kiss. The intake of blood only heightened the experience for her. She felt pleasure and passion wash over her body. They flipped, putting her on top. She pulled away and began to lick the blood around his mouth, almost drunk off the pleasure. She kissed him all over, eventually pulling his shirt off. She kissed his chest and his stomach, feeling his soft hair against her lips. He suddenly grabbed her and pulled her back up, pulling her shirt off. Her pale white skin looked like porcelain, almost shiny. He unhooked her bra and revealed her perfect breasts. They were no larger than a handful and felt perfect against his tongue as he caressed her nipple. She let out a gasp and dug her nails into his back.

He finished with her breasts and began to kiss her again. She pulled him even closer, running her hands up and down his sides, breathing heavily. He dragged his nails up and down her back, occasionally running his fingers through her hair. They continued kissing as he fondled her breasts again. Suddenly, she began grinding her crotch against his, breathing more heavily.

They flipped again, and he began to pull her pants off when he realized something. She was wearing combat boots.

He dropped down to her feet and began unlacing them.

"Let me do it." she whispered. She sat up, unlaced them, and kicked them off in a blur.

"Wow." he remarked.

She smiled and laid back down. He stood up, grabbed her pants by the ends and yanked them off. She lay there, dirty blond hair, the palest skin he had ever seen, beautiful breasts with pale pink nipples no larger than a quarter, and black silk panties.

"My god." he said, just before she sat up and pulled him down on top of her. They began kissing again while he ran his hands all over her. He slid his body a little to the side of her and slid his hand down the front of her underwear, finding her spot. He slipped his fingers inside of her and began gently rubbing her. She let out a gasp and arched her back.

"Oh, Taran, I need you in me!" she yelled and flipped him on his back, unlacing his boots with the same speed and yanked his pants off. She slid her underwear off, revealing herself completely. She had a very thin cropping of light brown pubic hair.

God, she was beautiful.

She slowly pulled his boxers off and immediately began performing the most amazing oral sex he had ever had in his whole entire life. Now, it was his turn to gasp and arch his back. He closed his eyes and concentrated to keep himself from cumming. This continued for another minute or so, then suddenly stopped. He was about to open his eyes when he felt a completely different sensation. He knew he was in her. He opened his eyes. She began to rock herself back and forth and back and forth, resting her hands on his shoulders, her breasts bouncing right above his face. After a few minutes, her face tensed up and she closed her eyes, and she began riding him even faster, gasping his name repeatedly. As soon as she slowed, he grabbed her, and they flipped, never even interrupting the rhythm. She rested one hand on the back of his head and the other on his back, clawing it up.

They continued the lovemaking for what seemed like an eternity.

Raphael approached the local Guild building. It was rather impressive-looking, rectangular design, a black and deep red color scheme, beautiful yet moody looking trees decorating the front of the yard, and very well hidden security measures. These included hidden cameras with infrared lasers mounted on them for night vision, land mines that would activate in case of an attack, hidden mounted guns controlled from inside, and the Hunters themselves.

The best part about the building was the way the true nature of it was disguised. A bank. The Vampire Hunters used a bank as their legal front, which was how they funded their entire operation. Union Farmers Bank. The third largest bank in the world. Each UFB had the logo "Union Farmers Bank," but right underneath it were what looked like random symbols. These symbols were, however, the language of the Vampire Hunter Ancients. The particular bank that Raphael was entering into was Vampire Hunter Guild 937867.

The Vampire Hunter Ancients were the very first Vampire Hunters. Raphael and his three brothers. The language they introduced to the land was a beautiful, flowing dialect that had been raped and twisted into various other languages. At first, this infuriated Raphael, but he got over it, realizing that it was only a matter of time before this world fell into proper control.

Raphael approached the front door, stopping about two feet away from it.

"Dekuni matata Raphael!" he declared.

Snap. The door unlatched and slowly came open, making a slight creaking sound as it did.

Raphael stepped forward, slowly guiding the door out of his way. The inside of the building was pitch black, since the bank was closed.

"Ancient, we are pleased and humbled that you would even consider visiting and inspecting our Guild. I beg you, tell me any way that I may improve your current mood or health. It would be an honor to assist the great Raphael." a voice from the dark declared.

"Take me to the Honor Hall." Raphael near whispered, disregarding the placation by the Guild Master. For some reason, the fact that Raphael was older than all the other Hunters was a source of great respect. In his world, being old indicated that you had not fought hard enough in battle. Of course, even in his own land, Raphael was different from the average warrior.

"Yes, Ancient."

Raphael followed the Guild Master to the bank vault and watched as he disabled all the security measures on the door, eventually opening it.

The two of them walked into the vault and the Guild Master slammed the vault door shut behind them, making the inside pitch black. He heard two popping sounds and a bit of light began to show from the floor, becoming wider and wider. A flood of voices began to reach Raphael's ears. Yells and laughs emanated from below. The Guild Master pulled the trapdoor all the way open and the two of them began to descend into the Guild.

The Guild Master dropped down first, offering his assistance to Raphael. Raphael waved him away and jumped down, landing in a crouched position. The Guild Master watched as Raphael stood up, taking in his full form. He also noticed that Raphael had been wounded on his arm.

"Ancient, you've been wounded! I will summon the doctor immediately!"

"Do not, Guild Master. I will fix it myself later. There is a matter of great urgency with which I need your Guild's help. I must address you and your warriors. What is your name, Guild Master?"

"Joseph."

"Joseph, just lead me to the Honor Hall."

"Yes, Ancient."

Raphael and Joseph proceeded through the Guild. It seemed to be a pretty typical one, Raphael noticed. It had the barracks for the warriors, a kitchen, bathrooms, training halls, the communications center (which held about 20 or 30 computers for online use), a weight room, and other assorted less interesting things.

One thing Raphael always appreciated was that few or no Hunters ever recognized him. No photograph had ever been taken of him, so no one knew what he looked like. Any time he was visiting a Guild, any Hunter who passed him knew he was somebody important, but always figured he was one of the Continental Commanders. They usually figured it out after a while, in which case he was mobbed, but he always had at least an hour or two of peace. This Guild Master here had met Raphael at a regional summit once.

The two men walked into the Honor Hall.

This was perhaps one of the most impressive Honor Halls he had ever seen.

Blood. Everywhere.

The purpose of the Honor Hall in each Guild was almost like a church. It was a spiritual and sacred place.

If a boy decides he is ready to become a "Votali," or Vampire Hunter apprentice, he must enter the Honor Hall and survive at least five minutes of combat with the Guild Master.

If a Votali decides he is ready to become a Vampire Hunter, he must capture a live vampire, bring it into the Honor Hall and kill it unarmed.

If a Vampire Hunter is to be wed, it is done in the Honor Hall.

If a Vampire Hunter is to be promoted in the ranks, it is done in the Honor Hall.

If a dispute between two Hunters is to be settled (meaning a duel, usually to the death), it is done in the Honor Hall.

If the Guild Master is challenged for leadership, it is settled in the Honor Hall.

"Joseph." Raphael spoke, still looking around the Hall.

"Yes, Ancient?"

"Gather your warriors. I must address them."

"Yes, Ancient."

"I got it now." Nigel snickered, setting his beer down on the coffee table as he and Sasha entered the living room where Ghost had exposited previously.

Sasha smiled expectantly and plopped down next to him. If she was intrigued by everything she had heard about Taran, she genuinely liked Nigel for who he seemed to be.

Is it possible that he's just a simple, fun, nice guy?

"Oh yeah, what's that?" she asked, stretching her feet out on the coffee table and leaning back.

I think he likes me, too. I mean, he's been talking to me nonstop for the last hour or more, and I keep catching his eyes wandering over my body. I don't know about that beard, though.

"You're a virgin, aren't you?" he snickered further, "Oh shit, I just asked if you were a virgin, which must mean that I'm a little tipsy and betraying the fact that I think you're...ya know...HAWT! And, there...there...therefore, you're actually talking to me, and therefore, wait, I just said that. Hmm. You're talking to me right now, and all I'm saying is you're talking to me right now, and, ya know, so you must not know better. Is all. IS ALL. Ya know?"

Nigel's head bobbled a little, and he smiled sheepishly. She shook her head, and hadn't lost her smile. He was definitely cute, but she was concerned that he might also be kind of an idiot.

I CAN KILL HIM WITH A THOUGHT IF YOU'D LIKE

Nigel must've noticed her wince.

"Wait! Did Corpsy the Clown just say somethin' to ya?" Nigel turned his head and back forth and glanced down the hall, "I've never been cock-blocked by a flying carcass before! Thanks, buddy! Hey, and you never answered my question earlier about each person's powers! And what the hell are you anyway?"

Taran and Alexandra entered the room and plopped down on the same couch they had been on before, with Sasha where she had been before with Nigel next to her.

Layne trailed right behind them, and with his head lolled sideways, his face slack, he smiled gently at Nigel, never taking his eyes off of him as he floated over to the corner.

Nigel raised his chin at Layne.

"Do somethin,' bitch." Nigel mumbled.

"Where's Ghost?" Taran asked, looking at Sasha.

"Shit, I forgot." she said, sitting up, "Ghost!"

Ghost immediately walked into the room.

"Yes, Sasha?" he asked, very courteously.

"Time for Alex's story." she said, motioning for him to have a seat.

"Hold on." Taran spoke up, "How the hell does he do that?"

"Do what?" Sasha asked.

"That 'instantly appearing' shit. It's like he's always just around the corner, but enough so that he's out of sight. I haven't seen him since we finished the original team's story, and apparently he's always close enough that you can summon him and he just sort of appears. That's fucked up, ya know?"

Sasha and Ghost looked at each other and shrugged.

"Okay, whatever. Please begin, Alex." Taran said, leaning back and relaxing.

"Alright. I'll warn you. This is, quite simply, my life for the past century. Please excuse me if I get a little emotional in some parts, okay?"

"We gotcha. We're here and we're listening. Finish painting the picture for us." Taran smiled, spreading out on the couch a bit, getting comfortable.

Alexandra inhaled a deep breath, blew it out, and looked at Taran.

"Just please don't hate me after what you hear tonight, okay?"

Taran waved at her like, "*please*," and Ghost nodded.

"Of course not, my dear. Please tell us your story.

X: Alexandra

"So, the entire team has just been murdered. Everyone but myself is hanging dead from a post. I'm laying, dying, mind you, on the ground. I'm not dead, though I'm not sure even I realized that. My mid-torso was basically a rather large, gaping hole.

"Then Defenders had strange men and women in hooded cloaks begin cutting the dead team members from their post and tossing their corpses in a fire. At some point, one of them scooped me up and tossed me right past the fire, into a cart next to it. This individual immediately stooped next to me and spoke.

"'If you wish to live, don't move and pretend to be firewood.'" a female voice ordered, throwing a cover over me.

"About five minutes later, I felt the cart begin to move. I was fading in and out of death.

"The next thing I knew, I was being carried into a cave of some kind. I was laid out on a table and stripped naked. The hooded female threw her hood back and revealed a pale-skinned woman of incredible beauty, with long, curly blond hair and almost silver eyes.

"'Do you wish to continue what you all started?' she asked, obviously in a hurry to move things along.

"'Taran...not without...' I murmured, completely delirious from the blood loss and the pain, both physical and emotional.

"'I'm leaving you with no choice. I know what you all have been doing, and I won't let it die with you all. You are the last chance. I will make sure that it happens someday.' she said, very serious. She then proceeded to rip her wrist open and drip blood into my mouth.

"'Swallow.' she ordered, and I, not knowing what the hell was happening, gladly cooperated.

"So, I swallowed it, and became a vampire.

"My experience is best described as...cold. I felt an extreme cold. First, I could actually tell that many of my organs were shutting down. All but the ones I still needed. Really, the main organs you need as a vampire are the heart, brain, and stomach. I also felt the rather disgusting sensation of the waste materials leaving my body. I also noticed that the unfertilized egg and uteran lining that I no longer needed were exiting, too.

All of these things were very strange sensations, but the strangest was watching the hole in my torso heal in a matter of seconds. It was kind of disgusting, but I got over it rather quickly when I realized that there were larger issues at hand.

"Such as my fiance's death.

"I sat up and looked at the woman. I couldn't believe that she had been cruel enough to not let me die. She claimed to have known what we were doing. And, surely, if she had known what we were doing, she would have known about Taran's and my involvement, right?

"I decided to ask her this.

"'What nerve you have, you undead wretch, to allow me to

continue without the rest of me. Who are you to decide that half of a being should be allowed to live without its counterpart?' I spoke, sliding off of the table and approaching her. I could already feel the added strength flowing through my veins.

"'You are the only survivor from a team of warriors on a quest to liberate this universe from an oppressor more evil than the word itself. You have my sympathies for your pain, but I assure you that your mortal life will mean little when you realize how powerful you've become.'

"'I CANNOT CONTINUE WITHOUT TARAN!!!' I screamed at the horrible woman.

"'Child, please, listen. What you all were doing is more important than a love lost. I know it hurts, but please, find a way. It is still possible. I truly believe that you can do it by yourself. I know you can. That's why I've granted you the powers of immortality. To ensure that you, one day, will finish this task.'

"Taran was gone. I knew no more joy, no more playful flirting, no more lovemaking, no more promises exchanged in the moonlight, no more envisioning the future as I lay in bed, no more communicating hours of dialogue through simple eye contact, and no more love. He was dead. I longed to join him in that bonfire of death. My place was at his side, whether it be in life or in death. And that had been violated. My fate had been destroyed. Simply because some vampire didn't want to die. I didn't care whether or not the entire universe perished anymore. I didn't care about my place in it.

"She spoke again.

"'You can avenge your love's death, too, if you choose to. The man responsible is named Gorath. He was in charge of this operation. You still have an eternity left to strike him down if you choose. You can either sit here and feel sorry for yourself or you can kill him. Which will it be, Alexandra?'

"I didn't need time to think.

"'Where is he?' I asked, fighting emotional numbness with every bit of strength.

"Aunica, as her named turned out to be, explained to me that the Defenders of the Faith were still here until the Elite's bodies were all accounted for and destroyed. Since my body was missing, they would still be around for a while, searching for it. I explained to her that all I needed to know was where they were and how many.

"She chuckled slightly and took my hand.

"'Alright, young lady, the first thing you need is to understand your powers. I'll get you some clothes, then follow me outside.' she said, smiling.

"So, I put on a man's shirt and pants (from a past victim, I assumed) and we walked outside the cave and entered into a field that seemed to go on forever.

"The stars were more clearly defined, the clouds seemed to appear as almost a gateway to the infinite expanse known as space, and I really seemed to understand that all of the vegetation truly was alive. I know, that sounds stupid, but really, how often do you remember that the grass you're trampling is as alive as you are? For the first time ever, I was able to look at the trees and know that a life force was rocketing through it! This was exciting!

"My excitement seemed to impossibly anesthetize the gaping would in my soul.

"'You're seeing it, aren't you child?' Aunica asked, stroking my hair.

"'Yes, I am.' I whimpered, almost feeling idiotic for not having realized all of this before.

"'It's alright. There was no way for you to understand. You used to be human. Humans are stupid, mindless creatures that destroy anything they don't understand. You are now evolved. You are better than they are. Come, follow me. If you can.' she said, smiling, then took off at an impossible speed.

"I stood there, speechless. I marveled at the blur she had become. I would have given chase had I not been so shocked by the fact that she had more or less disappeared before my eyes. I looked in the direction that she had run and saw her stopped, about a quarter of a mile away.

"'Run to me!' she yelled. I realized I should not have been able to hear her over the wind, but it seemed that my hearing had improved since I had been turned. I stood there, unable to move for a few more seconds, then began a light jog towards her.

"'No, run!!!' she yelled again.

"So, I quickened my pace.

"'As fast as you can!'

"So, I accelerated. And accelerated. There's usually a speed that humans simply can't break, but I somehow passed it. And kept passing it. As I was doing this, I glanced to my left and noticed that my surroundings were a blur. This made me realize how fast I was going, and my legs faltered. My feet didn't know how to operate at this speed, and I slipped, skidding across about twenty feet of grass and rocks. I don't think that a human can really understand how fast I was really going and the pain of sliding that far on your stomach across rough terrain. Imagine running down a very steep hill at top speed. I don't know if any of you have ever done this, but usually, you hit a point where you realize you're going pretty fast. As soon as this realization hits you, you slip. You fall and regret quite a bit that you had this realization.

"Aunica walked up to me, offered her hand, and helped me up. She explained to me that I was still stuck in a human way of thinking of things and that I needed to break it and etcetera and so on. We practiced the running for a bit, then jumping (which was pretty amazing), then climbing, and then fighting. That was the best part. Taran and Sasha, you've seen the very basics of what vampires are capable of. Try to imagine two of us fighting each other. It was basically two blurred images dancing back and forth across a field.

"The most interesting part of the fighting training was when Aunica realized that I was more powerful than she. Apparently, this was very unusual. Fledglings are supposed to be very weak compared to their masters. Aunica was about three hundred years old and I was a little over twice her ability. This was impossible, according to her. She seemed to become almost frightened of me. We continued the fighting training with her constantly keeping a watchful eye on me. After a couple of hours, she announced that it was time for my first kill.

"'I want Gorath!' I announced.

"'In time, in time. Let's start out simple. We'll find a common thief, an easy first kill, okay?'

"'Look, with this power that I have, I know that I can defeat him. Aunica, please!'

"'Alexandra, he will beat you. Easily. You have no idea how powerful the Defenders are, do you?'

"'Uh, well, let's see. They just killed all my friends. Hmm. No, Aunica, I have no idea. What the
hell do you think? Yes, I know how powerful they are! And, I know I can kill Gorath! Dammit, Aunica, let's go!'

"Aunica stopped and looked at me, seeming to stare right through my eyes. She approached me and caressed my cheek.

"'Child of the night, I know you're hurting, but understand that going on a suicide mission will not bring them back. I also know that a rather big part of you wants to join him in the grave, but you have things you need to finish before you can truly rest with him. I'll help you as much as I can, but you need to listen to me. Let's develop your powers before you unleash them on Gorath and his army. If we do that, you will be able to defeat not only him, but his commander, too. Are we agreed?'

"I hated her for being so correct about how I was feeling. I knew she was right.

"'Fine. Let's go.' I murmured.

"She and I ran to the outskirts of town, which was about five miles away. As we approached, we both noticed that a crowd of people were standing around a man who was ranting and raving about something. Aunica and I dropped into the shadows and snuck towards the crowd. As we neared, we could finally hear him.

"'...and those horrible, wretched demons that were destroyed today were here to do nothing but bring a reign of terror and agony to you all! We are lucky to have a god that forbids things like what you saw today from existing! When you all get home tonight, pray and thank god that these horrible creatures were destroyed. Then, by morning, forget that you even saw them! The memories will do nothing but allow evil to live on in memory! Forget them! They do not deserve to be remembered! Remember only that you love Christ and the burden he took on because of

YOU! THESE CREATURES ARE EVIL! GIVE YOU LIFE TO GOD! THEY WERE DEMONS! BEG FOR GOD'S FORGIVENESS FOR EVEN HAVING SEEN SUCH EVIL! THE FIRE THEY BURNT IN TODAY IS NOTHING COMPARED TO WHAT AWAITS THEM IN HELL!'

"The crowd roared in agreement. I wanted to cry again, but decided that enough tears had been shed already and it was time for action.

"'Aunica,' I whispered, tugging on her sleeve, 'I found my first victim.'

"'Alexandra, he's a priest.' she warned.

"'All the more fitting.'

"The priest stepped down off of the box and began smiling, shaking hands with people, making small talk, and basically kissing ass so that none dared question his infinite wisdom. After a short time, he made his final proclamation of the night, laughing.

"'Everybody! Go to bed! I hadn't realized what time it is, but it's almost one in the morning! I'm tired and I'm sure everyone else is, too. Good night.' he said, ambling inside his house, right next to the church.

"I leaped into action.

"I grabbed Aunica's hand and began a mad dash for his house. Fortunately, she stopped me right before we got there.

"'Stealth, young one, stealth. That's the only way we can survive. We can take on small numbers of humans, but large numbers can easily overwhelm any vampire. Through stealth, we avoid attracting the attention of others. That way, we only have to fight one or maybe a few. By the way, I'll let you do the kill yourself in there. But, if you hesitate or he's about to make any kind of noise, I'll take him out and we'll practice again tomorrow. Understand?'

"I nodded. We began to sneak around the house, peaking in windows and keeping a watch. We spied him crawling into bed, then downing a few shots of whiskey.

"'Alright, Alexandra, what do you think?'

"I stopped. I didn't want to rush this. I wanted to make a good impression on my new mentor. I wanted her to stop fearing me and start trusting me and think good thoughts about me, you know? After all, she was my only friend in the world.

"'I say check all the windows, sneak in through one of those, since a door might make too much noise, then tip-toe over to his room, burst in, and hit him so fast that he doesn't have time to make a sound. Is that good enough?'

"'We'll find out.' she said smiling, kissing me on the forehead and caressing my cheek again.

"'So, we began checking the windows and found that all of them were unlocked.

"'I think we should pick one furthest away from his room, so he doesn't hear it open, agreed?' I asked.

"'It's your kill.' she said.

"I shrugged and we walked over to the other end of the house. We found a window to the kitchen that was perfect. I pressed my hands against the bottom of it, pushed in and up. The window made a slight hissing sound as it slid up. I lifted my self up and slid in. Aunica soon followed. We proceeded through the rather modest house without making a sound. I marveled at my newfound abilities. I could walk like a normal human and make no sound whatsoever. It was amazing.

"We were nearing his room. He had his door already open, which was perfect. I realized then that there was no need for him to close it, since he lived alone.

"Aunica and I were hiding around the corner. I held up my hand and showed three fingers. Then two. Then one.

"We dashed through his door and I pounced on his bed, landing on top of him. His eyes flew open and he was about to scream when I covered his mouth.

"'You dare slander the dead? I'm one of the nine that was executed today. You described us as demons and, well, I've decided that is exactly what I should become. And, how dare you try to tell people that they should feel guilty for having witnesses something, or for having been born. The concept of 'original sin' is wielded by those seeking power, like you, who helped martyr me. Being a martyr is no fun. Taking revenge is. Good night. I hope it was worth it.'

"I lowered my lips to his neck. My fangs began pressing against his skin. Suddenly, I stopped. I sat back up and looked at him again.

"'By the way, see you in hell.'

"Then, I bit into his neck with every bit of rage in me. I ravaged his tender neck and drank every bit of blood in his body. By the time I was finished, his skin was almost gray and a little shriveled.

"I sat back up and enjoyed the rush going through my body. I felt even stronger than I had before. I looked over at Aunica, who was smiling.

"'Well done. Let's go.' she said, walking out of the room. I jumped up and fell in line behind her. We walked out the front door, so as not to draw any attention.

"'She leaned over and began talking in a very hushed tone.

"'You did well. However, I advise against giving speeches before the kill. That's more time for something to go wrong. We thrive on secrecy. Someone could overhear you. Your victim could find a means of stopping you. Someone could stumble upon you about to kill someone. You might hesitate. A million things might happen. You need to get in, kill, and get out. No ifs, ands, or buts. That's the way it is. Understand?'

"'Yes. I'm still glad I did it, though.'

"'I bet you are. If it brought you a little peace, then good. I'm glad you did it, too. Don't do it again, though. Especially against Gorath. Okay?'

"'Yes, ma'am.' I said, mocking a salute.

"'Anyway, Alexandra, I'm going to have my meal, then we'll retire to the cave.'

"'Alright.'

"'I'm going to show you a useful tactic for bringing a victim to you if you're female. Go hide behind those crates in the alley over there and watch closely.'

"I knelt behind the crates as she asked and peeked around them, watching her. She walked into a bar that we had passed across the street. I didn't know it at the time, but it was the same bar that Nicole had terrorized the day before.

"After about three or four minutes, I began to worry. I started to consider going in there after her to make sure whatever plan she had was working, when she emerged, on some guy's arm. She was laughing, so was he, and they appeared to be having a good time. They were walking towards the alley I was in. I noticed that he appeared to be rather drunk, since he was falling all over her and unable to walk in a straight line.

"'But, like I was saying, Miss...what was your name again?' he asked, laughing drunkenly.

"'Miss Seward.' she answered politely, despite his rudeness.

"'Well, Miss Shewarrrd, I have a proposition for you.' he said, emphasizing the 'you.'

"'And what would this proposition be?' she asked, snuggling closer to him, tickling his chin with her finger.

"'I'd like you to be one of my...main attractions.'

"'You mean a whore.'

"'Well...yeah.' he said, laughing sheepishly.

"They were almost to the crate that I was behind when she stopped, turned to face him, and drew him closer.

"'How do you know I'd be a good 'main attraction' without trying out the goods first?'

"He chuckled in excitement and leaned in to kiss her.

"Suddenly, she seized him, spun him around, covered his mouth, and bit into his neck, draining him in a matter of seconds.

"When she was finished, she dragged him over to me, motioned for me to move and threw him behind the crate, where I had been hiding. She went through his pockets and took all of his money.

"'Time for bed, young darling.'

"We walked down the main avenue, heading towards the cave again. As soon as we were safely out of view, we broke into a run and, a few minutes later, entered into the cave.

"When we walked in, Aunica and I walked deep inside. For maybe sixty or seventy feet, there was no indication that anyone lived here. Then, the cave seemed to end. I didn't remember this at all.

"'Wha-.' I began, cut off by Aunica.

"'Watch.' she said, pointing to a solid wall.

"She dug her nails into an almost invisible crack and pulled part of the wall away, revealing a passageway. She motioned for me to enter. I walked in, and she pulled the rock-door shut behind us.

"Now, a normal human would have been completely blind in the blackness. However, vampires have no real use for daytime vision, so our night vision is excellent. We need no light to see, though it does help. So, Aunica lit a couple of candles and showed me around. I recognized much of the stuff from before, but was still surprised that I didn't remember the rock-door.

"'Why don't I remember the doorway from before?' I asked.

"'You were probably still delirious from the transformation. Many of your first memories as a vampire are probably patchy at best. They will come back to you in a few days, however. In the meantime, let's sleep. I have a bed prepared for you in one of the rooms.'

"'Rooms? How do you have rooms in such a place?'

"'My master chose her cave well. I inherited it from her. The main part of this cavern is perfect for a vampire home. Do NOT go exploring without me. I assure you, you will get lost. Understand?'

"'Yes.'

"'Alright. Go to bed. I will see you tomorrow evening. Do you need anything before bed?'

"'Will I actually sleep? I know this sounds dumb, but is a vampire sleep different from a human's?'

"'Only in the way that your dreams are much more vivid and you remember them perfectly. I'm glad you asked, otherwise I would've forgotten to warn you.'

"'That makes me almost afraid. I'm glad I know.'

"'Don't misunderstand, Alexandra, there's no need to fear them. It's just like your mortal life. Most are strange or good, and only a few are bad, okay?'

"'Alright. Will you show me to my room?'

"'Follow me.' she said.

"She showed me into a cave that was rather small, but well furnished. There was a bed, nightstand, candle, dresser, bookcase full of books, coat rack, wash basin, and trunk.

"'I hope this is acceptable.'

"'Yes, it is. Thank you.' I turned to her and paused, hesitating to say what I needed to say, 'Aunica, I'm sorry about all the things I said to you when I first...became...you know. I'm sorry. You've been very kind to me tonight. I thank you.'

"She smiled at me, took my hand, and pulled me close, embracing me.

"'It's alright, child. I did the exact same thing. That's why I was prepared for it. I expected it. I took none of it personally. You're my apprentice and friend now. And, your mentor is telling you to get some sleep. Good morning and see you in the evening, Alexandra.' she said, pulling away and walking to her room, which was maybe twenty feet to the right of mine.

"There was one last thing I needed to say.

"'Aunica!' I said. She turned to face me, 'Um, my friends all call me Alex.'

"'Alright. Good morning and see you in the evening...Alex.'

"She smiled broadly and continued to walk to her room. I could tell she was touched. I walked over to my dresser and opened it, praying for proper night clothes. I had grown up a spoiled girl and wasn't about to change now.

"I was out of luck. The dresser was empty. I would have to remember to track down my clothes tomorrow. In the meantime, I would have to be less than modest. There was no way I could sleep in these clothes. They were too uncomfortable. Aunica was a woman as well, so that made it easier for me. I stripped off my clothes and slid into the bed. I stretched out and took in the extreme comfort of the bed. The sheets actually felt quite nice against my bare skin. I was a little cold, but slight cold always makes me sleep better. I blew out the candle, turned on my side, and closed my eyes.

"Then, it hit me.

"Taran wasn't sleeping with me. He was dead.

"I tried to fight the onslaught of tears, but lost. I burned for the feel of his strong arms holding me and protecting me from any hurtful force that might try to harm me in my sleep. I began sobbing uncontrollably, silently begging for him to pop out of the shadows and tell me that he was just testing me or playing a really mean joke or something. But, he never came. I began to realize that he never would, ever again. I was alone, forever.

"I didn't want to die, but didn't want to live, either.

"So, I began crying so hard that my entire body convulsed with each sob. I realized that I was being rather loud about it, and hoped Aunica wasn't hearing this. I wanted her to think me strong and unwavering, a worthy student.

"I buried my face in the pillow, shaking horribly and bawling. Every single memory he and I had ever shared came flooding into my head, nearly driving me to madness. I began almost screaming into my pillow, pleading for the memories to stop. I couldn't take it anymore.

"'TARAN!!!' I screamed into the air. I broke down, curled into a ball, and began slipping into a complete and total breakdown. Nothing mattered anymore. I had no strength anymore. The Defenders of the Faith had won. They had killed the proud woman, Alexandra Boliviere. The undead thing lying in a bed in a cave in Missouri was the ghost of that woman, reduced to haunting the streets she used to play on as a little girl.

"'Alex?'

"I barely heard her. I was dead inside, the memories rotting away what was left.

"'Alex, I'm here.' she said, laying next to me, uncurling my body

147

and pulling me close to her. She began soothing me, wiping away the tears, and kissing my face.

"'Alexandra, forget for now. Just forget for now. If you don't, you'll end up as pathetic as you think you already are. I'm here. I love you. You are my family now. My daughter, my friend, my protégé, my sister, everything. I love you. I'll sleep with you today, okay? Forget your mortal life for now. When you're strong enough, I'll help you straighten everything out. Sleep, child of the night, sleep. Sleep. You've had a hard night. Sleep.'

"And, I slept. I dreamed of murdering Gorath. Of tearing him limb from limb. Of pulling off his armor and revealing a smug, stupid human. Killing him over and over. I slept very soundly.

"That evening, I awoke to a smiling Aunica. A very pleasant sight. Her hair was hanging in her face, getting in her mouth. She spit it out, giggled, and spoke softly.

"'Darling, are you going to sleep the whole night away? Wake up! Let's go shopping! You're a new woman! You need a new wardrobe! Get up, borrow one of my dresses, brush your hair, and let's go shopping! Come on!'

"I sat up and slipped off the bed. As soon as I did, I realized I was still naked, and pulled the sheet over myself.

"'Alex, I slept next to your naked body all night, it's alright. No need to be embarrassed or modest. You have a beautiful body. I should know. I have one, too.' she said, laughing. I laughed a little, too. I tossed the sheet aside.

"'Are you sure I'll fit into your clothes? You're a little taller and bustier than me.' I asked.

"'Well, let's find out. Come look at my dresses.'

"I followed her into her room. She opened a finely polished closet of an unknown wood trimmed with gold. In it were many beautiful dresses. I picked a rather plain one, following her directive to not attract attention. I tried it on and found that it was a little loose, but it would work.

"She then led me into the main room and I found that she had been nice enough to clean up the rather unpleasant mess I had left on the table the night before. She sat me down in a chair and began brushing my hair. I have always found this very relaxing. She talked to me and explained that I needed to keep a very low profile in town, since many believed me to be dead. If they were to think otherwise, people would start talking and Gorath would come looking for me.

"I understood and asked how we were going to get around this.

"'Well, it's quite simple, actually. Just make sure no one recognizes you.'

"'And how are we going to accomplish this?' I asked her.

"'We'll give you a completely different look from the one you had before. Style your hair differently, dress you differently, do your makeup differently, everything.'

"So, she did me up and I came out looking like a princess. I don't like to brag, but damn, I looked good. She left the whiteness to my skin, added some heavy black eyeliner, red lipstick, my hair was up, and she loaned me some of her most expensive jewelry. After this process was done, she extended her hand, helped me up, and looked at me.

"'Alexandra, you look beautiful. I promise no one will recognize the little girl that played in the mud with the boys. Now, let's get going. We'll shop, then we'll feed.'

"Aunica and I headed out for town, talking the entire way. I explained a lot about my mortal life. I told her basically everything from my mother dying when I was young to being a tomboy when I was a kid to helping my father in the printing press to meeting Taran to dying. She asked a few questions, listened when I gave overly long explanations and answers, and touched my shoulder reassuringly whenever I began to choke up. As we were conversing, I realized I knew nothing about her. So, I asked.

"'So, who are you, Aunica?'

"She stopped walking, looked at the sky, and took a deep breath.

"'Alexandra, I think even I've forgotten. A few hundred years ago, I might have been the younger sister of an English noble. I never think about it, so I seemed to have forgotten quite a bit. It's all rather uninteresting anyway.'

"'How did you become a vampire?'

"'Sylvia made me. She was the resident of the cave before myself. She was my mentor.'

"'What happened to her?'

"'She was slain by a vampire hunter.'

"'Vampire hunter?'

"'Yes. There is a group of people who are dedicated slayers of the blood drinkers.'

"'How many are there?'

"'I honestly don't know. They, for the most part, blend in with the rest of society. Much the same way we do. I'm not too worried about them, though.'

"'Why? They killed your master.'

"'Yes, one killed Sylvia, but I killed him and about twenty others over the the past few centuries. Most of them seem to underestimate us. They're undertrained and overconfident. Be aware that they're out there, but don't fear them. It's quite simple. If you see one, kill him. Otherwise, they'll kill you. Understand?'

"'Yes.'

"We continued our idle conversation all the way into town. When we arrived, we sought out the best womens' clothing shops and had me fitted for several dresses. It was much fun. I was finally, for the first time ever, really feeling like a girl. Growing up, I had never really done much like this. Hell, I had never had much interest in it. Now, I was finally understanding. I was finally a woman. I just ached for Taran to be able to see me.

"When we were finally done, the tailor told us that he'd have the dresses done the next day and to please come back if we should ever need anything else.

"So, we left and Aunica asked me where I'd like to dine tonight. Not thinking, I informed her there was a wonderful restaurant just west of where we were. She laughed and hugged me and reminded me of our situation.

"'Darling,' she spoke, smiling and showing off her fangs, 'I'll show you the best dining spot in all the area. It's a little dangerous, but I'm feeling adventurous tonight. How about you?'

"'I suppose. I don't know yet. It's all still...' I trailed off, unable to access the proper word.

"'Grotesque, but it feels too good to be wrong?'

"'Exactly.' I said, turning to her, shocked. She had known exactly what I was trying to articulate.

"'Okay, Alex, prepare yourself. You're going to receive a great lesson in the kill tonight. Follow me.'

"She led me through the city, heading towards the more upscale part. We did appear to be among the high class, so I didn't really object. The area here was much nicer than what I was used to. I hadn't grown up in a bad area or anything, but this was much more design and fashion-conscious than my area. Every building and structure seemed to scream luxury and money. Every human I saw walking down the street was wearing more in dollar value than my father earned in six months. Even the dogs some of the people were walking were groomed and decorated with much care and currency.

"Aunica and I walked past many of these people, completely aware that they were unaware. I almost wanted to laugh. To think that I could reach over, rip their heads off with little or no challenge was exhilarating. They were so weak and unimportant compared to me! Vampires rule this earth, not humans! They had no idea that every night, we decide who lives and who dies!

"'You're starting to realize the state of affairs, aren't you, darling?' my master asked, smiling and turning to me.

"'Yes, I am. We rule the world.'

"'Yes, we do. I figured you'd realize that quickly. Someone who was had everything ripped away from her by this world should. You're better than them, Alex. In a few minutes, you'll have a chance to express that to many of them. Now, steel yourself. It might get a little unpleasant.'

"We continued strolling down the street, taking in the beautiful night. I glanced up at the sky. Not a cloud in view. The trees seemed to be doing a waltz for us, begging for attention. Even all the worthless humans seemed to be in sync with each other. I looked over at Aunica, trying to read her face.

"She was so beautiful. In all my existence, I, like other women, have striven to be the most attractive, the most adored, the most beautiful. She won. I'm sure the fact that I knew her enhanced her beauty, but even before I knew her, when I was screaming at her, I had noted her attractive characteristics. A part of me was really starting to idolize her. She was so many things that I wanted to be. Strong. Intelligent. Bordering on all-knowing. Beautiful. An excellent killer.

"Suddenly, she stopped and pointed across the street. I looked over and saw a huge, two-story mansion. People were filing in, all dressed very well and looking very happy.

"'See that?' she asked.

"'Yes.'

"'That's almost the entire aristocratic society of the area. We're going to kill some of them.'

"I didn't say a word. I just looked at her, not sure how to tell her that I didn't really like this.

"'Alexandra Boliviere, you can do this! They're your food! That's all. Did you ever hunt with your father?'

"'Yes, but that's different.' I said, a pathetic counter.

"'How so? When you were human, there were certain self-imposed and society-imposed expectations. Now, you're a vampire. A different set of expectations. It's okay to kill these people! They are no longer peers, they are now a resource!'

"'Aunica, I can't...I just can't...please don't be mad at me...please...'

"'Alex, I'm not mad at you. Don't worry. I just need you to trust my judgment. I'm trying to train you on how to handle many people at once. There's also a certain amount of justice in this. These were, and maybe still are, Ku Klux Klan members after the war. Many of these humans were slave owners prior to and during the war. They value human life even less than we do! Now, Alex, I need you to listen very closely. Focus on the kill. Think about the kill. The blood. The sensation of the blood trickling into your mouth and gushing down your throat. Casting their body aside when you're done. The kill. You need the blood, you need the kill. Let's go kill them, Alexandra. Kill them.'

"Aunica burst into a run. We ran to the side of the house and began scaling it to the roof. When we were on the roof, we began surveying the situation. Most of the people were on the first floor chatting and laughing. A few were out back, and a few were on the second floor. We counted about three hundred people.

"'Alright, young lady, here's how I think we should do this. Hang off the roof and crash through one of the windows we just passed. Wipe out the second floor. If we're fast enough, we can get them all in under thirty seconds. Then, jump down to the first story and begin the massacre.'

"As she was explaining all of this, my head began to swim. All I

151

wanted was the blood. I didn't want to plan, I didn't want to think. I wanted the kill. My fading humanity screamed at me to think, to feel something human, but all I wanted was excuses to make my need for blood go away.

"'Forget about the ones outside. If we can, we'll get them, but I doubt that we'll be that fast. No vampire is that fast. Ready?'

"I didn't even answer her. I slid along the roof, dropped down, and kicked through the window, sending glass everywhere. I flew in through the window, shrieking at the top of my lungs, and landed right in front a group of five men and women, who were so surprised by my sudden appearance, they didn't even have a chance to make a sound. Aunica came in right behind me and took off for the hallway out in the main part of the house.

"One of the women opened her mouth to make a sound. I reared my hand back and swiped at all of them, hitting each of their necks with such force that it decapitated them immediately. Heads were sent this way and that. All of their bodies but the first woman's fell right away. Her body stumbled back and forth, waving the hands around wildly before finally collapsing in a blood-gushing heap.

A human voice inside me wailed in sorrow at what I had just become. Its vampire twin cried out in orgasmic ecstasy. I marveled at my power and mourned my soul. The blood soaked into my skin, sending lightning bolts of pleasure and power rocketing through my body. I had never felt so good.

Still, that human voice inside me sobbed and sobbed.

I began running to join Aunica.

"I found her in the hallway holding a man by his neck in the air. She was staring him in the eye, listening to him plead for his life in a choked voice. She began to laugh suddenly. Just then, her hand punched through his chest and ripped his beating heart out. She laughed and began to suck it dry right in front of him. He began wailing and screaming. She cast him aside and began to move from one bedroom to another. I did the same. The first two bedrooms I found were empty. The third one, however, contained a little treat for me.

"Missy Williams.

"Missy Williams had been one of the girls that teased me constantly when I was young. She was rich, snotty, and for some reason, singled out the tomboy to pick on. She and her wealthy friends took great pleasure in throwing rocks at me when I was walking home from the printing press. One time, the stoning left me with a scar running from the nape of my neck to my left shoulder.

"I stepped into the room, my dress already sprinkled with a bit of blood.

"'Hello, Missy.' I said, blowing a kiss at her.

"'Oh, Alexandra, you must be one of the girls they hired for entertainment tonight. The servants aren't allowed in my room. I ask you kindly to leave. Goodbye.'

"'Missy?'

"She began to get very frustrated, approaching me and getting right in my face.

"'Leave now, Alexandra!'

"'No, Missy.' I mumbled.

"She was about to say something very loud, when I grabbed her by her arms, threw her down on her bed, and jumped on top of her. I ripped her dress away, revealing her naked, perfect body. I sat up, raised my hands in the air and smiled at her.

"'HELP! HELP!!!' she screamed, thrashing around.

"'Good night, Missy Williams.' I said, digging my fangs into her left breast and finishing the job.

"When I was finished, I realized that Aunica and I were well over our thirty-second projection for the second floor. I jumped up and ran out of the room.

"'Aunica!' I yelled.

"'Over here.' she said calmly, coming from another bedroom to my right. I walked into the room and gasped at what I saw.

"She was holding a small boy and girl in the air, one in each hand.

"'Alexandra, you do know that their skulls aren't fully formed until about the age of seven, right?'

"'Aunica, they're just children, please-

"She suddenly reared each one back and angled their heads so that they would collide top-to-top.

"'Aunica!'

"The two children began screaming and sobbing.

"'Aunica!!!'

"Their heads collided with such strength that a split-second after that horrible crunching sound, nothing remained of their heads. It was splattered on Aunica, the wall, me, their shoulders and what was left of their necks. She dropped the bodies on the floor with a thud and came to me.

"'Let's join the party, what do you say?'

"I looked at her, my vampire lust fading at such a sight.

"'No one's innocent, Alex. You'll begin to understand that in time. However, right now, I'd like to dance. Let's go dance.' she giggled, grabbing my hand, running out of the bedroom, and launching the two of us over the balcony.

"We crashed into the floor of the main room and immediately went to work.

"Aunica grabbed a middle-aged woman with brown hair, dug into her neck with her fangs and drained her in a matter of seconds. She threw the dead woman into the crowd and began slaughtering. Slaughtering is really the only correct word I can think of to describe how merciless and vicious she was.

"She ran through the crowd of screaming, hysterical people, killing right and left. She would punch through a man's stomach, grab his intestines and began running around the room, decorating with it. She would grab another man's arm and beat him to death with it. She would use her hands like claws and start mowing through the crowd, tens and twenties of people falling over dead.

"At first, all I could do was stare at the suffering. I was not like Aunica, nor did I aspire to be anymore. She had been educating me, but now I decided the education should be mutual. I was standing in the middle of the room, contemplating my deep thoughts, when I realized I was being attacked. My left arm was stinging quite badly and making a frying sound. I looked at it and realized I had been cut by silver.

"'The game is up, young Alexandra.' a voice behind me spoke.

"I turned and saw three men, swords unsheathed. The speaker was standing in the middle, with the two others flanking him on either side. The speaker had a shaved head, thin mustache, was about six feet even and very muscular.

"'Vampire Hunters. How amusing.' I spoke, not moving an inch.

"'Someone's been looking for you.' he said, smiling.

"'Friends of yours?' I asked, curious about the possibility of an alliance between the Defenders of the Faith and the Vampire Hunters.

"'Not at all. We just both want you dead now. I was actually quite amazed at you and your little rebellion, but now that you are a vampire, you must die.'

"The three were about to rush me when the windows on the first floor exploded. Vampires began flooding in. Interestingly, though, they didn't kill anyone. Suddenly, Aunica grabbed me.

"'Child, we must leave! We're in Francisco's territory! He's very powerful and gets very angry when another vampire kills in his domain! We must go now!' her eyes were wide open, pleading.

"I looked over at the other vampires, who seemed busy with the Hunters. One of the Hunters was already dead, another one very wounded, but the leader seemed okay. Six of the vampires were dead, which left about another twenty or so.

"'Alex! We need to go!'

"I looked at the carnage and death surrounding me. What the hell had I gotten myself into? It was like living in a nightmare that you were slightly enjoying in some sick, twisted sadistic way and waking up and feeling very self-conscious and angry with yourself. I couldn't believe what I had just participated in.

"'ALEX!!! PLEASE!!!'

"Vampire or not, this was not me. I realized that though I had changed forms, my soul had remained the same. It was not in my nature to massacre and kill indiscriminately.

"'ALEXANDRA!!!' Aunica screamed, shaking me. I finally came to and looked at her.

"'Aunica, we've made a mistake.' I said, deadpan.

"'We'll discuss it later. They're going to kill us if we don't leave! We must go!'

"I looked at the battle ensuing with the vampires and the one remaining Hunter. The wounded one had fallen. The one last Hunter was incredible. There were maybe ten vampires left, which meant he and his comrades must have slain close to sixteen. He was whirling around with his sword, slicing and chopping in the air, moving at an incredible speed. He decapitated two more. Eight left.

"Suddenly, the entire wall exploded and in strode the largest bipedal animal I've ever seen.

"That must be Francisco, I thought.

"He stood at about nine feet and was built like a fortress. He had shoulder length black hair, huge black eyes, an even bigger beard, and wore padded leather from head to toe. When he walked in, all fighting and panic ceased. Everyone froze in fear and dread of this beast. Aunica looked mortified.

"'We're going to die now, Alex.' she whispered.

"Francisco's eyes swept across the room, ice cold, showing no emotion at all. He looked at the dead party guests. He looked at the dead Hunters. He looked at the destruction of the home. He looked at the still-living party guests who had frozen in mid-escape. He looked at his slain vampires. He looked at the lone Vampire Hunter. Then, he looked at me. And didn't look away.

"'Who the hell are you?!' he roared.

"I was tempted to sound pitiful and show how truly scared I was, but decided I was tired of being intimidated that night.

"'I'm Alexandra Boliviere! Who the hell are you?!'

"He took a moment to think about my response, then answered.

"'I'm Francisco Carlo, the Overseer of this area. You are vampiric, are you not?'

"'Yes, I am.'

"'And you've not heard of Francisco Carlo?'

"'No, I have not. I've only been...this way for about two nights now, so I think it is slightly understandable. However, I'd like to discuss our current situation. Have we offended you?'

"Aunica grabbed my hand and squeezed it, giving me a nervous look.

"'Yes, you have. Quite badly. I keep my area nice and neat. A healthy balance, if you will. I don't allow heavy killing of the humans in my area and keep my vampire population low. I prefer to live in secret. Things are much better this way. I've known for quite some time that Aunica runs her area quite differently. She doesn't see things the way that I do. That's fine, though. We are Overseers of different areas. Now, Aunica, might I ask, what the hell were you thinking? The balance among the Overseers is delicate enough already! Why did you do this?'

"'It...it was a training exercise for the fledgling here.' she said indicating me.

"'Why didn't you do it in your area?' he asked, eyes blazing now.

"'I thought...I'm overseer of the river coast and didn't want to...I thought I could get away with it.'

"He began laughing. His vampires began to laugh nervously, too. Aunica and I exchanged worried glances.

"'Both of you, leave now.' he said, still laughing.

"Aunica grabbed my hand and began dragging me away. Many of the human guests followed suit at this moment. As we were exiting through the front door, he began to speak again.

"'And now, you, Vampire Hunter, it's your turn. We're not even going to play question and answer like I did with the idiot and her protégé. I'm just going to kill you.'

"The night's events flashed through my head again. The blood. The murdering. The utter wrongness of it. Not a single right, moral thing.

"Aunica and I were out the front door now.

"'What's your name, fool?' Francisco bellowed.

"'Frederik.' the Hunter spoke proudly.

"'Kill Frederik.' Francisco said to his underlings.

"I heard the screams of rage as the vampires leaped at him. I heard the yells and grunts of Frederik as he began fighting them off.

"Suddenly, another proud warrior that had been executed popped into my head. I saw them all. Taran. Wil. Evangela. I saw a chance to do something right for the first time since my love and my friends had been murdered.

"I tore free of Aunica's grip and plunged back into the mansion.

"Frederik stood there, now facing only three vampires. He had killed the rest. The three of them spread out, encircling him and taunting him. He turned rapidly, doing his best to keep all of them in view. He knew this was a bad position. He seemed to also be looking for a way out.

"Then, like lightning, the three vampires charged him. He decapitated one, but the other two were on him. He was disarmed. He was being killed.

"I jumped into the fray.

"I grabbed one and ripped his throat out.

"Francisco roared and started to come at me. I grabbed Frederik and tried to drag him away, but the last underling was attacking me, trying to get at my throat. Francisco was still coming at us. The underling went for my throat again. I grabbed him by his shirt and pulled him close. I bit into his neck and drained him in a matter of seconds. His blood felt incredible. I felt my strength increase. I continued dragging Frederik. We were almost to the front door. Then, Francisco was upon us. He grabbed Frederik and threw him into the wall.

"'NO VAMPIRE DARES DEFY ME IN MY LAND!!! NOT A SINGLE GODDAM ONE!!!'

"'He brought his hammer of a fist down on me, sending me into the wall, right next to Frederik. I laid there for a second, stunned. However, I managed to come to my senses quickly and jumped back up, turning to face him. My mind raced for a good tactical idea against a nine-foot vampire.

"I got one.

"I began an attack. The last thing he expected was an attack. He had probably not been challenged by another vampire in ages. I shot out of his field of vision in no time. I knew I had the edge speed-wise. I came back around and hit him from behind, knocking him down. He landed on his stomach with a crash. I leaped onto his back and reached around his head with my right hand, gouging out one of his eyes. I was about to go for the other one when I felt a hand on my back. It was his. He tore me off, stood back up and hurled me into the ground right in front of him. That time it really hurt. I lay there on my back, howling in pain. Suddenly, I was in the air again. I realized that he had kicked me across the room. I smacked into another wall, and slid down. I felt another hand on me and knew this might be it. The final blow.

"'Thank you, blood drinker. I will now return the favor.' Frederik said. He took off, limp-running over to his sword. Francisco bore down on him. Frederik somersalted, picked up his sword and faced his adversary. Francisco continued charging. Frederik held his stance, sword in front, grimacing, ready to explode into a slashing death machine. Francisco was right in front of him.

"Frederik side-stepped and spun around, cutting the mega-vampire across the stomach.

"Francisco's wound hissed, but he didn't even flinch. He stopped, twirled around, and tried to backhand the Hunter. Frederik leaped out of the way and cut off the hand.

"Francisco roared in agony, clutching the stump.

"Frederik took this opportunity to attack again.

"In vain.

"'He tried to impale the mighty vampire through the heart, but Francisco swatted him away with the stump. The Hunter smacked head first into the stair railing, rendering him unconscious.

"At this moment, I realized that I had stupidly not even moved.

"Francisco went lumbering after Frederik to finish the battle.

"I wobbled back up, and began to give chase.

"Francisco scooped him up, lifted him above his head, and stuck his knee out, intending to snap him in half, life a twig. I jumped, soaring through the air, and landed on Francisco's back again, clawing at his throat, to no avail. He dropped Frederik and hurled himself backward, squashing me against the wall. All my strength left me and I let go, dropping to the floor like a doll.

"Francisco returned to Frederik. He picked him up and set him down next to me.

"'Now, you two can die together. A vampire and a Vampire Hunter. How interesting. This has got to be a first. By the way, you two do know that by tomorrow night, I'll probably be fully regenerated, right? So, basically, you'll be dead and I'll be in perfect health. Stupid little things.'

"Frederik grabbed my hand and we both closed our eyes.

"A ripping sound and a scream filled the air. I figured it was us dying. A few seconds later, they both stopped. I was still living. Or maybe I really had finally died and I wasn't supposed to notice the transition from living to dead.

"Thud. Right in front of me. I opened my eyes.

"Francisco lay on the ground on his stomach, his face turned so that the side with the eye still intact was revealed. He was frozen with an expression of utter horror on his face. It was horrible to look at. I wanted to look away, but couldn't. My life had been filled with so much blood and killing in the past week, that I couldn't take it anymore. I was on the verge of madness. I was still functioning on the outside, but all love and life had died within me. I was grief-stricken for what had happened to Taran and the others and ashamed and hating myself for what I had more than willingly participated in that evening.

"'Frederik, get me the hell out of here.' I murmured, squeezing my eyes shut.

"'My god...' he gasped.

"I opened my eyes and followed his gaze. Next to Francisco's body stood Aunica, his spinal cord in her hand, dripping blood onto the floor. In my fixation on his face, I had never even noticed the rip down his back.

"'Now, can we go, Miss Boliviere?' she asked, seething and heaving.

"I quickly nodded in agreement.

"She dropped his spinal cord on his body and walked over over to us, helping us to our feet. Frederik needed a little more help, but was able to stand on his own once he was up. Aunica, still holding his hand, looked at him.

"'If you have the strength, cut his heart out to ensure he doesn't regenerate.' she said coldly, obviously still disapproving of his presence.

"'Of course.' he said, limping over to retrieve his sword from the other side of the room. Aunica took this semi-private moment to address her student.

"'Alex, I-'

"'Aunica, shut the hell up. We'll talk later. For the moment, know that whether or not I'm a vampire has nothing to do with how good or evil my soul is. What we did tonight is evil. I will never do anything like we just did. You can neither force me nor punish me. If you try, I will kill you. Do you understand?'

"Aunica opened her mouth to retaliate, then quickly shut it and nodded agreement.

"Frederik walked back over, dragging his sword behind him. He approached the (hopefully) slain monstrosity on the floor, raised his sword above his head and brought it down on Francisco's neck, screaming something in a bizarre language:

"'Lexon matauno noctil!'

"He then plunged his sword into the body, twisting his sword and turning it until he eventually cut out the heart. He bent down, picked up the heart, raised it towards the sky and yelled another sentence in that language:

"'Desregil loompa ont!'

"He set the heart on the floor and walked over to a lantern resting on a table that hadn't gotten smashed to pieces and cast the lantern onto the heart. It erupted into flames.

"'FORMALON!!!' he yelled at the burning heart.

"Aunica and I looked at each other, both wondering if one day a Hunter would perform this ridiculous ritual on one of us.

"'Ready?' she said to me.

"'Uh, yeah. Coming, Frederik?'

"At that moment, he and Aunica both shot me that look that instantly means they're questioning your sanity.

"I scrambled to explain myself.

"'I...I mean, he did help us...maybe...I... Fine! Forget it!'

"Aunica grabbed my arm and burned into my eyes with a horrible stare.

"'If you associate with him, IT WILL BE OUR DEATH!!! Even if he doesn't do it, others like him will follow. He may be a very nice gentleman, but we will not survive it!'

"Frederik stepped forward.

"'I'm sure it's for the best, Miss Boliviere. I owe you two my life, and for that, I will not take yours. However, I cannot protect you all from the other Hunters. Nor will I help you kill them. I am not much with parting words, so good night, ladies.' he said, grabbing Francisco's severed head and departing.

"'Why'd he take the head?' I asked her.

"'Trophy.' she grumbled.

"'Oh. Let's go home.'

"Our trip home was, at first, filled with silence and constant quick glances at each other. The last mile, though, conversation struck up. Aunica began it.

"'My entire family was executed by King Henry VIII for suspected treason. They weren't guilty, however. The night before the execution, Sylvia kidnapped me and turned me. I had lived a very cushy, comfortable life until that night. My family was a family of aristocrats. After I was turned, I learned how the other side lived. In the worst way. The details of that are not important. It's filled with murder, rape, disrespect, tears, and many nobles being drained of their blood. As soon as Sylvia and I heard about the new world, we stowed away on a ship and came over here, to start anew. Getting away from it helped at first, then the same thing happened over here. That's why I've never left that cave. I've tried to forgive them, I really have, I really have. Please, believe me. I would ask for help from you, but I think that you're the wrong one to ask about forgiveness right now. To get to the point, Alex, I'm sorry for making you do that tonight. If you want to leave the cave now, I understand.'

"'I don't know. I have no idea what I'm going to do.

"We went back to the cave, sat around and discussed various other topics before retiring to bed.

"Over the next few years, I never left, though I never indicated I was going to stay. Every time Aunica asked me, I simply responded with one or another non-committal statement. Those years were pretty uneventful. I still burned for Gorath's head, but found myself talking about doing something about it instead of, ya know, actually getting off my Victorian rear to do something about it. That night with Frederik and Francisco had really shocked something into my brain. Aunica and I would talk about rising up to take on the Defenders, but...it never happened. I don't know. Anyway, during all this, Aunica and I became like sisters. Those years were the time when I adopted my 'killing discriminately' posture and Aunica did the same. Basically this means only killing evildoers. I don't remember if I mentioned it before, but vampires can usually sense the nature of someone's soul, whether it be good or bad. Anyway,-"

"Hold on." Sasha cut in, sounding annoyed.

Everyone in the room turned to look at her.

"Yes?" Alex responded.

"I don't want to sound rude, but what the hell does any of this have to do with the Nine or any of the problems we're facing?"

"Very nearly nothing, at this particular moment in the tale."

"Then, why are we sitting here listening to this?"

"I don't know. I thought everyone wanted to hear how I got from there to here." Alex mumbled, looking embarrassed.

"Sasha, just let her continue." Taran snapped at her.

"All I'm saying is that we need to stay focused right now. All this vampire stuff is very interesting and all, but it has nothing to do with what we need to be doing."

"Sasha, shut up and be patient, please. Alex, try to stick to things that pertain to us."

"Alright, but you're not going to understand why some of this pertains to us until the end, so bear with me, alright?"

Everyone nodded. Alexandra looked Sasha in the eye.

"You will understand, okay?"

"Fair enough." Sasha said, looking away and biting her lip.

"So, what's next?" Alex paused, looking in the air and using her tongue to play with her fangs, "Okay, here we go. In my fifth year as a vampire, my training under Aunica was completed. We were sitting in the cave one night, discussing the possibility of visiting Italy. I had never been there and very much wanted to see it. Aunica felt the same way.

"'There's one problem, though.' Aunica said, looking very serious all of a sudden.

"'What?'

"'It's generally not a good idea to take a vampire still in training out of their familiar surroundings.'

"'Why?'

"'They tend to react badly. You'll understand when you have a student of your own. For now, just take my word for it.'

"'I really wanted to see Italy, Aunica.'

"'In that case, we better end your training.'

"I slowly looked up at her, unsure whether or not I understood her.

"'What did you just say?' I asked, trembling slightly.

"'It's time for you to meet the Coven. Tonight, you become a full member. When the trial is over, we leave for Europe to celebrate for a few years.'

"'I...wow. You really think I'm ready?'

"'Yes, Alex, I do.' she said, standing up, coming behind me, and resting her hands on my shoulders.

"I put my hand on hers and squeezed.

"'So, tonight is the night?' I commented.

"'Yes, it is.' she paused, sat down again and looked at me with a very serious expression, 'Alex, we need to have a conversation. About you. Something you should know before your trial.'

"I became a little worried.

"'What?'

"Aunica paused again, looked at the ground, took a deep breath and looked at me again.

"'I think you might be the most powerful vampire I've ever seen, and for that matter, the most powerful the coven has seen, at least in a long time.'

"I didn't agree with her assessment.

"'Aunica, what about Francisco? Or the Texas vampires that we barely fought off? I nearly died, and would've without you!'

"'You didn't fully understand your powers then. You didn't have much confidence in yourself. If you and Francisco fought now, I'm certain you would beat him. You are much more powerful than I am. I'm surprised you haven't noticed. When you finally have contact with other vampires tonight, you'll see it. Anyway, I just want you to be aware that you're going to get a very strange reaction from the Coven.'

"'Good or bad?'

"'I don't know. In all likelihood, they'll demand that you sit on the council. If they don't, they'll demand that you be executed. That's my guess.'

"'Wonderful.' I sighed.

"'Ready?' she asked, standing up, apparently wanting to go at that moment.

"'I...uh...sure.' I said, standing up and following her.

"The way to the meeting hall was actually rather scenic. We pressed further into the forest past our cave, over crystal clear rivers and through extremely dense foliage. The night seemed to be the blackest one I remember. The only reason I could make out any of the beautiful scenery was because of my enhanced vision. The moonlight was nonexistent. I looked up at the sky to figure out if it was blocked out by clouds or the trees, but it just didn't seem to be there.

"On the way, she explained the proper way to address the council members, which was rather simple. All it consisted of was covering one's mouth and bowing. The covering of the mouth symbolized no aggression towards them, since vampires commonly bare their fangs when trying to intimidate someone. After that, you address each council member by name, adding in 'sir' or 'madam' before, and introduce yourself and your Master. You then declare that your master has deemed you ready to join the Coven and that you are petitioning them to do so. If they accept your petition, you then proceed to endure the trial, about which Aunica informed me she was not allowed to inform me. If I passed the trial, my performance was judged. Depending on the judgment, I was either accepted or killed.

"I was beginning to grow nervous.

"We arrived at a huge dome constructed from brick and incredibly sturdy wood. The dome seemed to be at least the size of a modern sports stadium, with a moat around it. Guards were stationed about every twenty feet. Aunica and I approached the edge, at which point she whispered to me.

"'Make yourself known.'

"I looked at one of the guards, who was already studying me. I didn't know what to say to him. I had no idea what these beings would respond to. If I said the wrong word, they might decide it would be a good idea to dismember me and leave me out for the sun to finish off. Of course, Aunica had informed me that I was the most powerful vampire she had ever seen.

"'I am here to join the Coven! Step aside or be...horribly demolished!' I bellowed to the guards.

"'Horribly demolished? What the hell is that?' Aunica whispered again, stifling a laugh.

"The guards found it even more amusing. They broke out in a terrible laughter, looking at each other and pointing at me. The one that I had been looking at yelled back to me, still chuckling.

162

"'Approach me, horrible demolisher!'

"'Aunica and I leaped over the moat and began to walk towards him. At this point, I realized why the moat was effective. It was too wide for a man or horse to jump across, but close enough that a vampire could make it with some effort.

"As we approached him, I noticed a broad smile on his face.

"'So, you are the newest child to petition the Coven for membership, are you?' he asked, almost hissing each syllable.

"'Yes, I am. Do you find this funny?' I retorted, trying to sound insulted by his condescending attitude. As this exchange was transpiring, the other guards began to come closer.

"'And what if I do? If you fail, I get to do whatever I want to your corpse. I'm going to cut your heart out while I fuck you. Maybe I'll cut your head off and fuck your neck. That is funny. Now that you're on this side of the moat, your ass and any other part of your body that I want, all of it belongs to me.' he boasted.

"I realized at this moment this was probably part of my initiation.

"I shot around behind him, knocked him down, put one foot on his shoulders, grabbed him underneath his chin and ripped his head off, the body falling with a thud. The other guards took one look at this and backed off.

"'Alex, you weren't supposed to kill him.' Aunica whispered in my ear. She grabbed my arm and began to lead me inside. I was still clutching the severed head in my hand.

"As we were approaching what seemed to be a main door, I shook myself free of her grip and sped up the pace.

"I walked up to the door, kicked it open, threw the head into the main chamber and walked in after it, glaring at everyone I saw. The chamber was littered with vampires. The room was circular with blood drinkers crowded around a main room. They were talking and conversing before the head rolled in, at which point they stared at the head, then its second owner. There was an upper balcony populated with more nicely dressed vampires who appeared to be an upper class of sorts. Seated opposite the main doors were five vampires, dressed very finely. They were up on thrones, with servants scrambling away from me. I walked over to the base of their chairs and bowed, covering my mouth. From left to right, there were two men, one woman, another man, and another woman. The first was a somewhat aged man with a long gray beard. He was wearing a beautiful red cloak. Next, was a very young looking man with a thin mustache and black hair. He wearing a simple tunic and pants. The middle woman was blond and wearing an onyx-colored dress. The next man was also blond and had the look of a man in his early twenties. He had long hair hanging down in his face and a goatee. His dress was identical to the first man. The last woman had incredibly long black hair that seemed to hang to her knees. She was wearing a long, flowing golden dress. Aunica had drilled me on their names, so I was set to go.

"'Sir Francis, Sir Robert, Madam Anna, Sir Gawain, and Madam Julia, I am Alexandra and this is my Master Aunica.' as she came screeching to a halt behind me, 'She has informed me that I am through training. On account of this fact, I am petitioning to join your Coven.'

"Sir Gawain leaned forward and eyed me. He didn't seem to pleased by what he saw.

"'What was your full mortal name?'

"I swallowed hard. They would remember me from the Nine. I was afraid this would mean trouble.

"'Why do you wish to know?' I asked.

"'I wish to know. I need not explain my motivation to you. Answer the question or die.'

"'I looked at the ground. I had tried hard to forget the happy-in-love girl that I had been. I had tried even harder to forget HIM. My mortal name was no longer mine. I was simply 'Alexandra.' However, this vampire was demanding my mortal name for some reason. My mind raced. Maybe I could lie. How the hell would they know the difference? Maybe I could simply withdraw my petition and kill all of them. Maybe-

"'Answer the question!' Madam Anna barked.'

"'ALEXANDRA COLLETTE BOLIVIERE!!!' I yelled, furious.

"The council members gasped.

"'Alexandra Boliviere of the Nine?' Gawain asked.

"I stared at him and nodded. I opened my mouth to ask how he knew of the Nine when Francis held up a hand.

"'Your face betrays you. We will reveal our source, all in good time. First, I accept your petition. Now, face your trial.' Sir Francis said, right before the blackness.

"At first, I thought I had been knocked unconscious. Then, I realized it was just that I was completely enveloped by darkness. It was so dark that my enhanced vision couldn't even penetrate it. I spun around, looking for anything. Maybe even a tiny, insignificant ray of light. But, there was nothing. Only blackness. My humanity wanted to panic, but I buried myself deep inside and faced this test with courage. This was simply a test. Nothing more. Of course, Aunica had mentioned that the only way you don't pass it is if you die, which meant I could be killed during this 'trial.'

"'Alex...' a male voice to my left echoed.

"I whirled in the direction of the sound.

"'Alex?' he said again.

"I began walking towards him, my lips beginning to tremble.

"'Alex, answer me!'

"'I'm here. Who is that?'

"'It's me! Come on, where are you?'

"'I'm coming. Who is that?' I was nearly weeping by this point.

"'It's me!'

"I kept walking towards the voice. I seemed to be walking forever.

164

"'Alex!' the voice was right behind me now. I turned and looked over my shoulder. Eight figures stood lined up with a bit of light covering them coming from an unknown source.

"Taran. Wil. Nicole. Evangela. Layne. Cole. Michael. Jessica.

"My first reaction was teary eyes. However, I quickly realized the impossibility of this. They were all dead. Had been for years. This was simply part of the test. Powerful, yes. Effective, no. They all just stared at me, unblinking, dead. Dead.

"That was when I realized the horrible truth.

"They were still dead. Their bodies were right in front of me. Somehow, they had been preserved and placed right in front of me.

"'Oh, god...' I said, wanting to retch my guts out. This was beyond difficult. This was cruel. I looked them all up and down. Each had a small hole in their foreheads. Except Nicole. Knowing her, she had put up a hell of a fight and nearly got free, like myself, and had been subsequently shot somewhere other than the head, like myself. The rest of their bodies were completely intact. Same clothes, everything.

"I had to look away.

"But for some stupid reason, I couldn't

"Then, something else clicked.

"Who had been speaking?

"'Taran...' I said, choking on tears.

"'Yes, Alex?' he said, matter-of-factly.

"I tried to speak, but couldn't. I fell to my knees and lost it.

"'Taran, you upset her again.'

"'Sorry, Wil.'

"'STOP IT!!! YOU'RE ALL DEAD!!! YOU CAN'T TALK!!! LEAVE ME ALONE!!!' I screamed.

"'Alex, what's wrong?' Evangela said with an expressionless face.

"I turned and began running away from them.

"'ALEX! Come on, it's been a while! We just wanna talk!' Layne yelled.

"I ran and ran, sobbing.

"'Aunica! Help me! Please! Please!' I pleaded to the air.

"After a few minutes of running and no word from the corpses that used to be my lover and friends, I stopped and looked behind me.

"There they stood, the exact same distance that they had been before from me.

"'GO AWAY!!!' I yelled again.

"'But, Alex-'

"Nicole's fingers were twitching.

"'-why are you acting like this? After all we've been through together? Life, death, everything else?' Taran said, face as dead as before.

"I stared at Nicole. I was no longer afraid or upset. Things were not at all what they seemed.

"'Nicole, what the hell are you doing?' I asked.

"'What do you mean, Alexandra?' she asked, smiling.

"She smiled. She had smiled.

"No bullet wound. Fingers wiggling. A smile.

"She was doing this to me.

"I hurled my body at her.

Ghost stepped forward.

"Alex, are you saying that Nicole hadn't been killed? I know she was shot in the head along with the others. She had to have been killed. There is no way a mortal can survive that kind of blast. No way." he insisted.

"Richard, she isn't human."

"What?" he blurted, shocked.

"Just let me finish. You'll understand."

"By all means, finish." he said.

"Okay, so I'm flying through the air at Nicole. During this moment, which seemed to last an eternity, I'm contemplating several things. One, Nicole's probably a vampire, like myself. Two, that's impossible, because a gunshot wound to the head is instantly fatal, and one must be alive in order to be turned. Three, she's something else.

"I collided with her body and knocked her to the ground. We began wrestling. I was trying to pin her arms and legs, but her strength was incredible.

"'Alex, wait! Wait! They made me do it! I had no choice. I-' and she broke off into sobs.

"At this point, I lost all my motivation. I stood up, dropped her, and began looking around for the Coven members.

"'IS THIS YOUR TEST!? SHOW YOURSELVES!!! NOW, GODDAMIT!!!'

"Flash.

"I was back in the main chamber, sprawled out on the ground. Nicole was next to me.

"'You both passed your respective trials. Before you two are admitted into the Coven, there's a question I have for both of you.' Francis declared.

"'What's that?' Nicole asked, dusting herself off and standing up. When she spoke, I saw the fangs. She was a vampire. But, that was impossible...

"'Why are the both of you so powerful?' he asked, leaning forward and grinning a sadistic grin.

"'I dunno.' Nicole said, shrugging.

"'I have no idea.' I said, rising to my feet.

"'Is that so?' Francis said, leaning back and stroking his beard. His thin nose and beady eyes seemed to enhance his already incredibly evil look. He looked over at his peers and seemed to silently communicate with them. They all nodded to him. Then, Francis and the others looked at us again.

"'In that case, we need a sample of blood from each of you.'

"This didn't seem right.

"'Hold on. Why?' I asked, getting upset again.

"'Yeah. What if we don't want to share our blood?' Nicole chimed in.

"Francis snorted, rubbing his eyes, looking tired.

"Nicole and I looked at each other, unable to figure out what was going to happen next.

"'If we get your blood, we will share in your power. That simple. Why do you object?'

"'Because we don't want to share our power. At the moment, there's a good balance between ourselves and the humans. If the vampires suddenly become more powerful, it upsets the balance. Besides, don't you have enough power? Why is our blood so important?' I said.

"Now, Gawain spoke.

"'It is our belief that you two are part of a new breed of vampire. So far, you're the only two that we've seen, but it is possible that there are others.'

"'So, ask them. We will not give up our blood.' Nicole said.

"'Very well. I will warn you, however. This conversation may happen again. This council is fair and balanced, so we will not force you to give up your blood. We do have a need to constantly better ourselves as a species, though. Please give our request future consideration.'

"'That is fair.' I said, bowing again. Nicole imitated me.

"'Welcome to the Vampire Coven, ladies.' Francis said.

"'Thank you.' Nicole and I said simultaneously, doing the mouth-covering bow again.

"The chamber exploded in shrieks and screams of joy. Nicole and I were surrounded by vampires wanting to meet us and form a Cult with us.

"A Vampire Cult is like a sub-Coven. It consists, generally, of three to ten vampires that constantly share blood so that the entire Cult grows stronger. There's a leader that reports to the regional Overseer who reports to the Continental Council. Nicole and I spent at least an hour repeating over and over 'I'll think about it' or 'I'll take it into consideration' and 'Thank you for your offer.' This grew tiresome very quickly. I only wanted two things at that moment. One, to see the ancient Roman architecture in Europe.

"Two, answers from Nicole.

"After a while, I finally managed to corner her alone. When I did, I heard one of the most amazing tales I've ever heard.

"I'll summarize what she told me.

"The night that we were all executed, she was shot in the head like the rest of them, but she didn't die. According to her, she went into...a strictly observational state. She couldn't do anything but see and hear. It was like death without actually dying. I asked her how this was possible. The only thing she could think of was that she was not human. Never had been. This would explain her ability to use black magic in a way that none had ever been able to and her current condition.

"She said that after she was thrown in the fire, she began to burn like the rest of them, but couldn't feel it. She could see her skin melting and peeling and falling off and everything, but still wouldn't die. Then, at one point, she was pulled out of the fire and thrown in a cart, like myself. She was taken to the vampire meeting hall and given blood. Apparently, one of the vampires had noticed her eyes were still moving around and saw a great chance to conduct an experiment. She was given the blood of Sir Francis, the most powerful vampire in the area and healed immediately.

"As she was going through the training, her powers, both physical and magical, grew at an incredible rate. The way she described her physical powers sounded identical to mine, but her magical abilities were unheard of. She also noted that she was the first vampire mystic, which was a violation of the treaty between the two groups. As far as the Mystics' Guild was concerned, she was dead. She was sure they were rather pleased about the fact and she had no intention of upsetting them again.

"As for her magical powers, I was in awe. My trial, for example, was an illusion. I never left the main chamber. Black Mystics can cast small illusions, but nothing of that magnitude. Also, she no longer had to use grand hand gestures. All it took was the twitch of a finger, or in the case of low-level spells, she just had to think. That had never been done in the Mystics' Guild, either. The most amazing part, however was the power of her spells. She could do every spell ever imagined by the Mystics and more. She had created spells of her own. This had not been done in thousands of years. The common belief in the Guild was that every spell possible had already been documented. She was the first being to create a spell in thousands of years.

"Also, her training was quite different from mine. She was trained and refined by the Coven itself, and molded into a weapon. I had been trained by an individual. So, when it came time for our trials, hers was to show her powers to what they believed to be their greatest extent. She explained that she had hidden her greatest abilities from them for fear of being exploited. I understood this completely.

"As she was explaining all of this to me, I noticed a change in her demeanor. She seemed much calmer and...more mature then before. It appeared as though she was actually in control of herself. This was very nice since she seemed to be the most powerful person on the planet.

"Our conversation drifted to simple 'catching up' and laughing. She was so different than I remembered. So much easier to be around. Before, she was like a bull in a china shop, now she seemed like a real lady.

"She apologized for the harshness of my trial and explained that she figured I would pass it, in which case she would have an opportunity to apologize, as she was doing at that moment. I understood her warped logic and forgave her.

"Then, the past came up. She started it.

"'Look, Alex, I don't know about you, but I always considered you a friend.'

"'I agree.'

"'When I heard you were still alive...I was happy.'

"I could tell this wasn't the most comfortable thing for her to say.

"'Well, Nicole, I'm glad you're not dead, too, I guess.' I laughed.

"She laughed along with me and we finally embraced. It was so nice having someone from those days at my side. I can't tell you the comfort that offered me.

"We talked for a while longer before Aunica approached us. She walked up, hugged me and congratulated me and looked at Nicole questioningly.

"'Oh, how rude of me. Aunica, Nicole. Nicole, Aunica.' I gestured between the two of them.

"'I understand I'm looking at what's left of the Nine.' she said.

"I hated her sometimes. I really did.

"'Yes, I suppose you are.' Nicole said, her old self starting to surface. I remember thinking *please don't turn her into a cow or something, please don't.*

"'Care to accompany us to Europe?' Aunica asked, very graciously.

"Nicole looked at me, eyebrow cocked.

"Now, I'm going to add a little commentary here. Have you ever had a moment where you realize things that you thought were purely coincidental aren't, even remotely?"

"Yes, actually I have. Like when Milk Bone and I are at the liquor store and he has no money." Taran answered.

"Okay, well listen to this. When Aunica asked Nicole to go with us, I realized that it was not an odd, unplanned turn of events that reunited Nicole and me. I don't think that the entire Vampire Coven was in on this, I'm pretty sure it was just Aunica.

"'Aunica, what the hell are you planning?' I asked. I looked at Nicole. She had caught it, too.

"'Are you in, Nicole?' she asked.

"'Sure. What the hell? I've always wanted to see Rome.'

Alexandra stopped and stood up.

"So, let's take a break. What do you all say?"

Taran looked at Nigel. Nigel looked at Taran.

"Pantera's" Taran asked.

"Pantera's." Nigel concurred.

"What's Pantera's?" Sasha questioned Nigel.

"The best fucking pizza place in St. Louis." he mumbled.

"Second best," Taran corrected him, "Imo's is better, but Pantera's is great. Anyway, you wanna join us, Alex? I know you don't eat, but we'd love your company."

"We would?" Nigel looked at Taran.

"Yes, dickhead, we would." Taran returned the stare.

"Cool." Nigel agreed.

I WILL COME AS WELL THANKS FOR ASKING

They got up and walked outside to a moonless night. Taran noticed this and looked at Alexandra.

"I see it, too, babe." she said.

"What?" Sasha queried.

"Moonless night. Like the one from Alex's initiation into the Coven." Ghost pointed out.

"Shit. Guess this means we're all gonna die or meet some horrible fate or some shit." Nigel muttered.

"I'm going to stay here and meditate while you all go out, okay?" Ghost asked.

"Ah, meditate. Is that what they call it nowadays?" Nigel snickered.

"I don't grasp your meaning."

"Yeah, whatever. I'm sure you're gonna grasp something. Just don't get any cum stains on that nice, white ruffly shirt of yours."

"Don't get any on the couch, either, please." Milk Bone added from the hall.

Ghost swore under his breath and walked back inside, Alex holding the door for him.

They all piled into Nigel's car and headed out for Pantera's.

XI: The Imminent and Unavoidable

Raphael stood in the center of the Honor Hall and looked at the warriors that surrounded him. Very well built, tough, in control of themselves, and unwavering in their icy stares. Guild Master Joseph had done great work with these men. It was now time to have the best of them accompany him on a mission.

"Warriors, I need your full attention! Are all of you at least somewhat familiar with the legend of the Nine?"

The following grunts and yells seemed to indicate "yes."

"Very good. Well, they are reforming. You would think this is good. It is not. They are collaborating with vampires, one in particular. As many of you may or may not know, I have been tracking Alexandra Boliviere for a number of years. I had a confrontation with her and she got away tonight. Alexandra was part of the original team and is now part of the second team, or so it seems. I also question the motives of this 'Nine.' Their leader, once again Taran Walker, is a madman. He is obsessed with destroying me because of a disagreement he and I had a few years ago. He and I were once great friends, and I was going to disclose my true nature to him and attempt to forge an alliance between the Nine and the Vampire Hunters before our falling out. You see, until sometime recently, Taran had no idea who he really is. When he and I were friends, he was a mere child and was not aware of the truly strange workings of the world around him. He was unaware of his fate and my past. Now, the two are conflicting. I intend to wipe out the entire team and overthrow the evil deity myself. I will need assistance, however. Do I have any volunteers?"

Each men stepped forward.

"As I expected. Joseph, choose your five best men."

"Ramon, John, Alfred, Brian, and Steven, step forward! Look your best!" Joseph snapped. Five rugged-looking men marched forward and stopped. They stood motionless, glaring straight ahead, hands at their side, looking more like programmable death machines than human beings. Raphael paced back and forth in front of them, the sound of his boots on the hard floor echoing throughout the Honor Hall. He studied each man, looking for some sign of weakness. After a few minutes, he was satisfied. Time to meet the men. He approached the first warrior.

"Hunter! State your name and number of kills!" he barked.

"Alfred Ericson! Thirty-eight, Ancient!"

Raphael approached the second man.

"Hunter! State your name, number of kills, and the reason you became a Vampire Hunter!"

"John Killian! Twenty-nine! I wanted to carry on the family tradition of honor and respect, Ancient!"

The next man.

"Hunter! State your name, number of kills, the reason you became a Vampire Hunter, and the reason you want to accompany me on this mission!"

"Steven Epson! Fifty-three! I want to kill vampires! I want to kill vampires!"

The fourth Hunter.

"Hunter! State your name, number of kills, the reason you became a Vampire Hunter, the reason you want to accompany me on this mission, and the most notable vampire you've ever killed!"

"Alfred Spears! Thirty-seven! Revenge! It will be an honor to serve with you! And...uh...I'm not sure I understand the question, Ancient!"

"Hunter, your mind must be sharper than the blade you wield, otherwise the blade is useless. Rejoin your comrades that are not going on the mission. Joseph, replace this man!"

"Daniel!" Joseph yelled as Alfred marched back over to the group of Hunters. A very young man sprinted forward in his place.

"Hunter! Same question!"

"Daniel Smith! Sixteen! It is in my blood! I'm good at what I do and feel I would be very useful! Gawain Green, Ancient!"

Raphael paused. This "boy" had brought down the powerful Gawain. He was impressed.

"Well done, Hunter. You've done us all an honor." he turned to the last man, "Hunter, state your name, number of kills, your favorite flower, and your favorite Beatle!" This one always got them.

"Ramon Cortez! Forty-one! Daisies! Paul, Ancient!"

"Very good, all of you. I believe I have a team here. Joseph, you will be coming with us, too. Lead us to a meeting room of some kind so that we may plan out our attack."

"Hunters, you are dismissed! Those of you accepted by Raphael, on me! The rest of you, return to barracks! Follow me, please, Ancient." Joseph bellowed.

Raphael and the Hunters followed him down a rather uninteresting hall. Raphael observed all the other Hunters scrambling away, finding something to do while Raphael, Joseph, and the chosen Hunters planned their assault.

Rosaline raced down east-bound US-40 at a steady clip. She was probably doing 70 or 80, but her tears wouldn't let her see.

She had done this drive so many times, she didn't need to see.

"Taran?"
"Yes, Nigel?"
"Did you bring the beer?"
"Yes, Nigel."
"Can I have one?"
"No, Nigel."
"Why?"
"Because you're driving."

"Right. Cool." Nigel answered.

Sasha and Alexandra glanced at each other in the backseat and exchanged looks.

Nigel's car screamed into the parking lot, and nearly lost control of the back end. He masterfully guided the nearly airborne piece of crap into an empty space and popped the e-brake at the last second.

"And here we are." Nigel muttered.

"Yep." Taran said, slightly muffled by the cigarette between his lips.

The five of them stepped out of the car and took in the night.

You can still smell the dumpster from a mile away, Nigel thought.

He's annoying...but kinda cute, Sasha thought.

The moon...oh god, Alex thought.

Something is about to happen, Layne thought.

All those years ago, Taran thought...

"THAT right there is the fetus that was once in Rosaline, that I aborted. If you look closely enough, you might be able to make out your own features, but it's so tough in fetuses that early." Raphael explained matter-of-factly.

Raphael had invited Taran down to a secret chamber in their dojo, claiming he had something pertaining to Taran's fate to show him.

"Isn't it rather telling that Rosaline chose to talk to me instead of you regarding this...inconvenience? Taran, do you wish death upon her now?"

Taran stared at his aborted child.

His teeth rattled.

"No...not until...I know."

"Know what? That she would rather jettison your entire relationship than bear your child?'

Taran sunk to his knees and shut his eyes.

"NO! She would've involved me in any decision!"

"Taran? What's wrong?" Alex asked, shaking him as he sat there, staring into the concrete.

"Before I explain this, please know that one day you will understand why I did what I did."

"Taran? Who's dead? What are you talking about? Taran!" Alex shook him again as she crouched in front of him.

"Raphael..." Taran began to growl, staring his old friend in the eyes. Those cold, blue eyes...

"Alex, it's best if you leave him alone. He's just...talking nonsense

173

right now...I'll handle this. Taran? Come on, bud. It's in the past. Just forget about it. We got bigger fish to fry. It was bad, I know. I was here, too, remember?" Nigel said, trying to lift the man up.

"You already know, don't you? I don't even have to say it, do I? Did she tell you or are you just that smart?" Raphael asked, chuckling.

"Nigel, who died? What's he babbling about?" Sasha asked.
"Nothing. Forget you even heard it. TRUST ME, Sasha." Nigel barked, protecting the secret.

"I'll say it anyway. THEY'RE BOTH DEAD. One now, one later."

"Taran, we're here. He's not. Come on. It's 2001, not 1997. Let's go inside." Nigel urged his friend, pulling on his arm.
Taran suddenly looked around, gasping.
"Nigel! I..."
"I know...I remember...I...I'm sorry, bud...let's go get some pie and talk, alright?"
"Hold on! Remember what?" Sasha asked, getting frustrated.
"NOTHING!!! I mean..." Taran looked at Nigel, "I don't even really remember that. I know it happened, but it's almost like I remember someone else's account that was told to me. Lotsa 'memories' like that now. What the hell is happening?"
Taran looked at his companions and struggled to offer the next sentence. He knew he was supposed to offer some kind of good, powerful, leader-like statement here, to keep the troops' morale up, but had no idea how.
"Bad memories hurt. We all understand. Let's go inside and talk and have a good time, okay? I think we can all agree on that." Alex offered.
Nigel shrugged and headed in. Sasha hurried up behind him. Alex reached over and grabbed her lover's hand.
"It's cool, babe. You don't have to explain yourself to me. I love you. Come on." and Alex began strutting towards the door, with Taran in tow.
YOU ARE DONE WITH THE PAST BUT THE PAST IS NOT DONE WITH YOU I UNDERSTAND
"Don't even pretend to know what I know!" Taran cried at the floating corpse.
WE ARE ONE AND THE SAME
"We are NOT! Get the fuck outta my head and quit trying to relate your weakness to my...my..."
YOUR OWN WEAKNESS AS I SAID WE ARE ONE AND THE SAME WE ARE BOTH USERS OF THE CRUTCH
"I don't have a crutch anymore! I quit that shit!"

AND YET YOU WERE BROUGHT TO YOUR KNEES BY YOUR NEED TO HURT JUST AS I AM BROUGHT TO MY KNEES TO SATISFY MY HURT I WAS THE FOOL YOU MOCKED AND NOW YOU'VE REPLACED YOUR COCAINE WITH YOUR RAGE

Taran squinted and stared at Layne.

"I don't know you. Quit tryin' to act like you know me. You don't know a fuckin' thing about me."

TELL ME ABOUT YOUR FIRST KISS WITH ROSALINE

Taran's mouth hung open for a moment, then he straightened himself out while he thought.

YOU REMEMBER HER BETRAYAL PERFECTLY AS YOU'RE SUPPOSED TO BUT YOU CAN'T REMEMBER THAT FIRST KISS EVEN THOUGH IT HAPPENED

"Get the fuck outta my head!" Taran cried.

IT DID HAPPEN I ASSURE YOU

"Enough!" Alex yelled, placing a hand on both chests, "We have plenty of time to explore the oddness of each of our memories."

Taran shook the oddness off, and nodded at Alex.

I AM HERE TO HELP TARAN

Taran gave Layne the finger and turned his back.

They all walked in and picked a table, taking a seat. Nigel, Sasha, and Layne sat facing Alex and Taran, who was visibly shaken. A waiter came over quickly, carrying a tray of water glasses and menus.

"And how is everyone tonight?" he asked, wearing that professional grin quite well.

"Great. Two bud lights and..." Nigel trailed off, looking at Sasha.

"Oh! Uh...just a Coke for me. It's not that I don't like beer, I'm just not old enough, ya know? I'm sure it's quite good, but, well, I'm 18! You know how it is! You were 18 once, right? I mean, I could give into the peer pressure and-"

"He gets the idea, Sasha." Alex said.

"Oh, right! Just a Coke, thanks."

The waiter didn't even waiver in his professionalism. Gotta give this guy a good tip, Nigel thought.

"Two Bud Lights and a Coke, right. And for you, mam?" he asked Alex.

"Nothing, thank you. Not thirsty."

THE WEIRD ONE ISN'T THITSY EITHER KID

The waiter winced, and nodded.

"Alright. Be right back with your drinks." he said, folding the tray underneath his arm and walking to the kitchen.

"Anyway, how is everyone?" Sasha asked, smiling.

Nigel shrugged, lighting a cigarette. Alex ran her hands through Taran's hair, trying to comfort him. Taran sat, staring off into space, looking quite upset.

"Okay...well, in that case, let's get down to business. What's our next move?"

"Find other members, I guess." Alexandra said, stealing a cigarette from Taran.

"Alright. What do you guys think?" Sasha asked, directing the question to Taran and Nigel.

"Cool by me. We still gonna go to Cape Girardeau tomorrow?"

"I don't think we should." Sasha spoke.

"Why?" Nigel asked.

"Because it deviates from the mission."

"How do you know?" he asked.

"What makes you think we'll find anyone in Cape?"

"What makes you think we won't?"

"We've had no indicator that we'll find anyone there."

"Okay. What other places have you found indicators for?"

I SEE OUR FATE IN ST. LOUIS

"Our 'fate?' So we die here or we find the rest of the Nine here?" Nigel asked, glaring at Layne.

THERE IS A BATTLE HERE THAT IS ALL

"Two Bud Lights and a Coke?" the waiter chirped, approaching the table.

The group emitted no response.

The waiter set their drinks on the table and stood straight, smiling, and staring at them. Alex was the first to catch on.

"Uh...they'll have a large pepperoni, regular crust," she said indicating Taran and Nigel, "and you, Sasha?" she said.

Sasha snapped out of her trance-like state.

"Oh, a small mushroom with thin crust for me. Thanks."

"Alright. And nothing for you, mam?" he asked, looking at Alex.

"Oh, no thank you. Not hungry either, I guess." she said, shrugging and flashing a cute smile.

"Alright. One large pepperoni with regular crust and a small mushroom with thin crust. Be up in a flash, folks!" he grinned, snapping up the menus and hurrying off to the kitchen.

WAIT

The waiter snapped back to their table, almost like a puppet.

A SMALL PIZZA WITH THE BASICS OF A SHRIMP ALFREDO

"A...shrimp alfredo? But-"

A SHRIMP ALFREDO OR YOU WILL DIE IN YOUR OWN PISS

The team sat in silence again. Sasha shifted uncomfortably, Nigel glared at he movement, Alex stole another smoke from Taran, and he remained motionless.

The waiter snapped his smile back into place and whisked off to the kitchen.

"So, this has been a pretty heavy evening for everyone, and if anyone wants out now, just say so." Sasha offered, looking tired.

No one said anything initially.

Taran finally broke the silence.

"What we all need, Sasha, is a sign, as a group."

Nigel suddenly grabbed his temples and screamed.

I CAN TELL YOU ALL HIS SECRETS HE'S BEEN HIDING FROM YOU

"ENOUGH!!!" Taran roared at them, smashing his fist into the table. The other three stared at him, shocked.

"Taran, I-" Alex started.

"Alex, please just let me speak." he said, grabbing her hand, "We are going to Cape tomorrow. I feel that's the best course of action. Not only the off-chance that we find some people, but it was what I had originally planned to do this weekend, so maybe I'm suppoed to just keep following my path. Sasha, exactly how advanced are you in your Mystic training?"

She lit a cigarette and nearly spat her smoke out.

"Um, well, about three fourths of the way through it, though I am familiar with all the spells. The only training I really need to finish is mastering all of them. I am capable of fulfilling my White Mystic role, please don't doubt that."

"I don't. Nigel, how good are you with that pistol?"

"I could shave a girl's twat from fifty feet away without leaving any razor burn."

"Charming." Sasha snorted and shared an eye-roll with Alexandra.

"Good. Alex, are you confident in your ability to kick some ass if we get in a tight spot?"

"Yes."

"And, Layne, you're just scary as hell."

"Layne's head lolled forward in agreement.

"Alright, we're off to a good start. We have a pretty good team thus far. Tonight, we rest. Then, we head to Cape tomorrow. Now, there's an issue of how we transport Alex there. Any ideas?"

"Wrap her in a tarp?" Nigel offered.

"I will not be wrapped in a fucking tarp. I am not a piece of luggage or some 'thing' that is to be treated like an object. I am just as alive as any of you. I do not appreciate your sarcasm, Nigel."

"It wasn't sarcasm, Alex." he said, looking stung, "I'm being serious. We're going to need to find a way to keep you from getting fried out there. That seems to be a pretty good way of doing it. I welcome a better idea."

"He's right. I know it sounds uncomfortable and all, but we need to get you down there with the rest of us." Taran said, stroking her hand.

"Beggars can't be choosers, right? Wait a minute, you don't need me down there. I can stay here and keep an eye on things." she offered.

"No. We should stay together." Sasha said, looking at Taran for approval. He nodded and looked at his lady.

"Sorry, Alex. You're coming with us."

She sighed and put out the cigarette butt, mashing it into an unrecognizable form resembling anything but a filter. She blew out the last bit of smoke and looked at Taran.

"Alright. I trust you." she said sweetly, stroking his beard and leaning in to kiss him. The glint in her eye made her seem to be your standard college-age girl.

"I'll take care of you, Alexandra." he promised, returning the kiss.

"ANYWAY," Nigel interrupted, "what time do we leave tomorrow?"

"As soon as we wake up. We'll crash in your dorm room."

"We'll see what Hector has to say about that. He'll probably be cool with it."

"Who-, oh, your roommate, right. What's he like?"

"He's cool. He's a bit of a partier, so he'll probably be passed out drunk the majority of the time. What are we gonna do with her during the day?" Nigel asked, indicating Alex.

"Why don't you just stash me under your bed in the tarp along with the rest of your crap?" she cracked.

"Fine." Taran cut in, "Now, let's discuss the long term. We'll start with the Defenders of the Faith. Who do they report to?"

Alex, Sasha, and Nigel all looked at each other and shrugged. They were as clueless as he was. Taran continued.

GORATH

"Alright, well, it's a safe assumption that they report to someone who reports to someone else who reports to someone else, and so on and so forth. At the top of the chain has to be THE leader."

GORATH

"God." Nigel chimed in.

OR GORATH YOU RETARDS

"Or Gorath. Right. Or so we believe at the moment. If we can infiltrate the Defenders, we can work our way up and get to him." Taran said, gesturing like it was no big deal. Sasha spoke up.

"Wait. What do you have in mind when you say infiltrate? Do you mean, like one of us puts on a Defender costume and hopes that they don't find us out or do you mean something less cliché?"

"I mean we find out where they're based, get in, do some recon work, get out, and figure out what we can do with the information that we gathered. Follow me?"

"Yeah. When did you want to do this? Hopefully, when our group is slightly more sizable?" Nigel asked.

Taran chuckled.

"Yes, Nigel. I just think that we need a long term goal to shoot for. Anyway, first thing to figure out is where in the hell they're based."

"Rome." Alex blurted out.

Raphael listened as the Vampire Hunters looked at the topographical map of the area in which Taran's building was. He suspected that these men were good, but he had no idea that they were THIS good.

Each individual was familiar with every square inch of this city. They knew where each bush, sidewalk, and bus stop were. They knew the best way to insert into a building and withdraw in a matter of minutes, even seconds, if need be. He had definitely picked the best of the best for an operation in this city.

"Ancient, what do you think?" Joseph asked.

It went as follows. Men at the back door. Men at the front. Men in each alley. The men at the front door would ring the bell and talk with Taran, wanting a truce. The conversation would carry on for a bit, giving the men out back time to sneak in. The men in the alley would watch for escape attempts and bring down any individuals seen. The men in back would begin the assault, followed quickly by the men in front. The men in the alleys would join the fight only if the Remnants of the Nine began to (through some miracle) win the battle. That would probably not be necessary.

"It is a very solid plan. Get the necessary equipment and weaponry and have everyone ready in a half hour. Everyone clear?"

"Yes, Ancient!" they all barked in unison.

"Dismissed." he said, pleased with the level of skill of these men. He did, however, need to remember to not get ahead of himself, and wait to judge them in combat.

As the men were filing out of the room, Raphael grabbed Joseph's arm.

"Ancient, I'm sorry, have I-"

"It's alright, Joseph, just please be honest with me about these men. You feel they're good enough to handle this situation in a three minute window?"

"Yes, Ancient, I do."

"Very good. Please proceed." he said, releasing Joseph.

"Yes, Ancient." Joseph began to leave. Suddenly, a Hunter burst into the room, out of breath.

He had beads of sweat gleaming down his face, dripping off of his quivering lips. He nervously pushed his hair behind his ears, got his composure and addressed Raphael.

"Um...uh...Ancient, you have a visitor."

Raphael couldn't believe it. Never, in his life, had someone been able to track him. He had always eluded the public, flying in and out of shadows, never really knowing anyone personally. Except for Taran, of course, but he had good reason in that case. He had always been a master of the living world, outsmarting them right and left.

Joseph noticed Raphael's surprise.

"Ancient, would you like to me handle this?"

Raphael had to meet the man that had tracked him. He had a sneaking suspicion who this man was.

"No, Joseph, prepare for the assault. I'm very curious about who it is."

"Yes, Ancient." Joseph bowed, and walked briskly out of the room.

Raphael stood there, for a second, trying to contemplate how Taran could have found him. He also contemplated that it wasn't a good idea to be sure of anything. It could be Rosalaine. Or anyone. Who knows?

He climbed back up to the main floor of the bank, and headed towards the door.

As he was about to come into view, he froze.

Gut instinct kicked in.

This was bad. It was going to a very, very unpleasant surprise. He wasn't sure how to proceed. He knew, in his heart, it was someone he didn't want to see. Someone that was capable of injuring him somehow.

Hell with it. He was strong. He was a very skilled swordsman and warrior, perhaps the greatest in the world. No one in this world could defeat him. Unless-

Unless they were from-

Maybe it was happening.

Maybe it was finally happening.

Just go to the damn door and face whatever your fate is, Raphael, he thought.

Rosaline stood at the door of the bank that she had seen in her dream. She knew she could find Raphael here. He had told her last year, when they made their deal. The bank part was actually in the dream she had after he had knocked her out when they...

And, suddenly, there he was. Standing in the door, just like in her dream. He looked like something out of "Braveheart" or a movie about that period in history. He stared at her with an icy gaze. He seemed angry. Or at least, extremely surprised, but trying to hide it.

Rosaline became more than a little nervous. She knew what he was capable of. He was a man that could kill with a look, or even with that sword that had seemed to find its way into the sheath that now hung on his back. His cold blue eyes were more dazzling than ever. Even in such an odd moment, she found herself attracted to him.

Taran...

"How the hell do you know that?" Nigel barked.

"Alright, folks, food's up." the waiter called, approaching their table. He strolled over, balancing the large tray perfectly on his fingertips, and set it down on a fold-up stand he had been carrying in his other hand.

"Pepperoni for the guys...and veggies for the young lady."

AND

"And shrimp alfredo pizza for...this guy."

YOU SHALL LIVE

"Are you sure you wouldn't like anything, mam?" he asked Alexandra.

"Yeah, thanks."

"Alright, if you folks need anything, just let me know, okay?" he beamed.

"Thanks, man." Taran said, grinning the leave-now grin.

"Thank you, sir." he said, still smiling as he walked away.

Nigel returned to business.

"So, how do ya know they're in Rome?"

"I'll explain all that in a little while. I'll wait for you all to finish eating, since there are some parts that are...rather disagreeable. Anyway, their main base is in Rome, as is every other important building for their secret empire." Alex explained.

Taran cut in.

"What about other religions? Are any of them affiliated with the Defenders?"

"The Defenders represent no one but that 'god' of theirs. They in no way represent any Catholic or Christian churches, but they also enforce for them all. Same thing with governments. They pretty much have free reign to do anything they want. I don't know how they've gotten away with as much as they have with no action against them, but I suspect it has something do with either divine intervention or deep pockets. Or threats. In my observations, they are unstoppable. We have our work cut out for us, to say the least."

Everyone began eating in silence.

Nigel stared at his pizza. He really missed coming here with the guys. Those years had been a great time. It seemed like so long ago. They had all been happy. Care-free. Sure, they all had some rather difficult things going on from time to time, but overall, it had been a great time. Why was he thinking about this now? Stupid.

"After this, why don't we go down to where you two were executed? Maybe it'll stir something up. Memories, clues, something like that?" Nigel offered, trying to keep them on track.

"Good idea." Taran agreed.

"I...you're right...I haven't been back there since....anyway, yeah." Alexandra conceded.

"Okay." Sasha nodded.

"Rosaline. How interesting. Dare I ask how you found me here?"

"You told me. In a dream. You don't remember?"

"It's a dream. How the hell am I supposed to remember a dream that you had?"

"Good point. Anyway, can I come in and talk to you? It's about Taran."

"No. Good night, Rosaline. Come here again, and you will be killed. Understand?"

"Fine. Then kill me. Just tell me two things first."

"Maybe. What?"

"When's the last time you had any contact with him?"

Raphael started laughing.

"What?" Rosaline asked, confused.

"Nothing. Earlier today, actually. I tried to kill his new, well, old, well, whatever, anyway, I tried to kill his girlfriend. He intervened, naturally."

"You tried to kill someone? What's wrong with you? And, he has a GIRLFRIEND?! Do you have any idea who that bitch is that he's with now?"

Something clicked in Raphael's head.

"Want her gone?" he asked, smiling now.

Rosaline's eyes lit up.

"Yes, I do. Besides, as I recall, you owe me a favor. You're gonna help me win back Taran."

"Uh...wait...it's a bit more complicated than that. Come inside. We will talk, after all."

"Good. So, who is that bitch?" she asked, following him inside and flipping her hair back before checking her appearance in a mirror. Her bright red hair and sharp green eyes contrasted sharply with her pale skin.

"Alexandra Boliviere. Someone you don't want to mess with. Very, very dangerous woman. I'll get rid of her on one condition." Raphael said, taking a seat behind a desk.

"What? You're not gonna try to kill her again, are you?" she questioned him, taking a seat on the desk, to his left.

"I need you to pretend to be a hostage of ours. We're going to tell Taran that we will kill you if he doesn't turn over the vampire."

"Vampire? Is that a code name or something? Who the hell are you? Like, for real?"

"I am Raphael, the Ancient Vampire Hunter, sole surviving founder of the organization. Vampires are for real. God's darkest soldiers. I kill them."

"Whatever. Forget it. You're a fucking lunatic." she said, jumping up and heading for the door.

"Wait! Do you want him back or not?! If you don't, I'm killing him tonight!" Raphael exclaimed, sitting forward at the desk.

Rosaline stopped and turned to face him, tears beginning to fall.

"Raphael, what the hell is happening? It's like, one day, my life is completely normal, then everything flies apart. What are you and Taran not telling me? Is he really that nuts?"

"Yes."

Rosaline walked over to the desk and slammed her palms down.

"Who the fuck is he?" she hissed.

"He thinks he's going to save the universe."

"He's obviously wrong." she muttered.

"Yes, he is, because I'm going to."

She stood straight and backed away from him.

"You're both fucked up. Are we going to help each other or not?"

"Yes."

"And then, any connection between the two of us is severed, right?"

"Right."

"Cool, so show me what I gotta do and how you think this is going to work."

"Follow me." Raphael motioned, getting up and heading for the trapdoor.

Rosaline got up and walked behind him.

"By the way," he began, "we are going to wipe your memory of this place after all of this is over."

"I'm not going to tell any one!" she laughed.

"Yeah right. I remember all the times that you would worm your way into someone's life and then whisper about it, post-coitus, to Taran. You're a gossip."

"I am not!" she laughed again.

"Have your memory wiped or die." he nearly whispered, shooting her his death stare.

"Okay, okay. Fine. All I want is Taran back."

"Then we understand each other?"

"Yeah, sure." she said, digging her hands into her pockets to find her cigarettes.

"Good." and he opened the trap door.

"Damn! What kind of place is this?"

"You need not know. Come on down."

Rosaline climbed down with the unlit cigarette in her lips. When she set foot on the concrete floor in what was apparently the basement, she lit her smoke and looked around. A very, very poorly decorated place, but it was, after all, a basement, so whatever. Yells and laughs reverberated throughout the corridors. Freaky.

"Where the hell am I?" she asked again.

"A base. We're going to modify the plan, then we leave. Are you familiar with the layout of the building he's in?"

"The Halfway? Yeah."

"Good. You're going to help us modify the plan, then."

"Sure. Okay. Don't care. Just want my boyfriend back."

Rosaline followed him into the planning room, where stood six rugged-looking (but not bad looking) warriors.

"Ancient, are you ready?" Joseph asked.

"No. This young lady is going to help us. This is their leader's former lover."

"But soon to be non-former Or whatever!" she proclaimed, smiling.

"Ancient, I-" protested Joseph.

"She has tactical knowledge, Joseph. She will prove very useful." Raphael assured him.

"Yes, Ancient." he said.

"Alright, Rosaline, how much do you know exactly?"

Nigel, Taran, Alexandra, Layne, and Sasha all piled into Nigel's piece of shit Toyota. Nigel driving, Sasha sitting shotgun, and Taran, Layne, and Alex in the back. Nigel flew out of the parking lot and slammed it into gear.

Sasha found herself almost hypnotized by current events. She likened it to going from boot camp to combat. Nothing can ever prepare you for the chaos. She had almost romanticized the idea in her head, only to find it very difficult and trying, and they hadn't even gotten much done yet! Oh well. They had only begun a few hours ago. Surely, they would make more progress as time passed. She just didn't want to end up like Evangela...

Alex looked at Taran and observed him staring out the window. She wondered if he had any idea where they were about to go. A monument to failure. A shrine for evil. A mass grave.

She wondered how much of a connection there was between him and his predecessor. She wondered if he would ever remember what happened, if the two men were one and the same. He definitely seemed like the old one, only more controlled and disciplined. He almost seemed older. It didn't matter. She loved him already. She always had...

Taran stared out the window, wondering how he was going to accomplish so much in so little time. He knew he had leadership skills, but he didn't have experience. He wished they would understand that he had had spent the last several years being a fuck-up. He hadn't even tasted success. He had gone from being a zero to a revolutionary leader in a matter of hours. How the hell does that work? Another thing bugged him, too. Alexandra was too perfect...

Fuck, I'm thirsty, Nigel thought.

They flew down 40 in silence. Taran glanced at his sword and began to wonder if he should have it ready, just in case. He didn't know why he was even considering it, but something inside told him he might want to. Might be a good idea. Just in case.

"What?" Alex asked, following his gaze.

"Don't know. Gut instinct."

"My gut's never been wrong. Might wanna listen to it."

"Yeah, but if it's wrong, I'm gonna look like a fool wearing this thing on my back."

"Since when have you been concerned about image?" she asked, almost laughing.

"I dunno. I'm gonna leave it here."

"I'd bring it if I were you. Hell, if you don't, I will."

I DON'T HAVE TIME FOR YOUR IDIOTIC TENDENCIES BRING THE FUCKING SWORD

"It's just..." he trailed off, noticing that they had gotten off at the Broadway exit, and were approaching the riverfront.

"Just what?"

"Well, who in the hell is gonna be down there that we need to fear?"

"I don't know, Taran, just bring it."

YOU WILL NEED IT

"Fine."

Nigel looked back at them.

"I'm bringing my Beretta. You better come armed, too, Alex. I have a bad feeling about this."

"Thanks, Han Solo, I'm going to."

The two of them chuckled a little and settled back into their seats.

"Alright, Vampira, where's this place?" Nigel asked.

"Um, go towards the Eads Bridge."

"Eads Bridge, check." he said.

They raced down Broadway, watching all the "normal" people lead their "normal" lives. How depressing and how lucky, Taran thought.

As the minutes passed, that feeling of foreboding began to overwhelm Taran. He was almost in terror, but didn't know why. This was bad. They were about to face something bad.

"Guys, um, hold on a sec. I really actually do have a bad feeling about this." he spoke up.

"Yeah, me too." Alex agreed, sliding over and cuddling next to him.

"The fuck are you talking about?" Nigel asked, looking annoyed, "I really want to see this place."

I WISH TO FEEL THIS PLACE BUT DEATH IS HANGING IN THE AIR

"It's weird, man...I dunno, we'll go, but everybody, be on guard." Taran said, shifting.

"Whatever, man. Hey, Alex, we're coming up on Eads, so where exactly is this place?" Nigel asked, locking eyes through his rear-view.

"Um...right at the...base...of one of the first towers...supporting the bridge..." she said, sharing in Taran's terror.

"You cool?" he asked, still staring at her in his rear-view.

"You don't feel it, do you, Nigel?" she asked, shuddering.

"Feel what?" he answered, shrugging.

"Whatever you're referring to, I don't feel, either." Sasha said, looking back at Alexandra, who had her arms wrapped around herself, as though she was cold.

"Odd." Alex murmured, just for the sake of responding. Taran reached over and brushed her hair behind her ears, smiling at her. The old Taran was like that, too.

She really needed to stop comparing the two.

Why did she think such stupid thoughts in tough situations?

"Alright, folks, here's the infamous execution ground." Nigel muttered.

Alex leaned forward and stared. It was now mostly paved with bits of dead grass popping up through the cracks. Cigarette butts and shattered glass covered the ground, like some kids decided it would be "cool" to get drunk on the supposedly famous witch-burning ground. Throughout the years, Alexandra had been told that her ghost, Nicole's, and even others haunted this ground. Naturally, she couldn't have a ghost, nor could Nicole, since they were still "alive."

Along with the carnage from the party, bits of concrete littered the ground, broken out of the pavement and strewn randomly across the area.

Nigel pulled up and popped the e-brake.

"Ready?" he asked, oddly cheerful.

"Yep." Sasha piped up, seeming excited.

Taran and Alex looked at each other, both with rather concerned faces. They each found the other two's excitement unsettling and suspicious. They glanced at Layne.

His sunken, almost skeletal face betrayed no emotion, but his glassy, cataract eyes darted around in a manner that nearly conveyed nervousness.

"Fuck it. Let's do this." Taran said, sheathing his sword on his back and smiling.

"Yeah. Let's go." Alex agreed, returning his smile.

The four adventurers exited the Tercel and began walking on the forbidden ground of so many years ago. Alex felt an almost electricity-like feeling shoot through her.

Daddy, don't let me die!!!

Her vision began clouding.

I won't leave you.

The world began spinning.

I'm dead.

She wasn't falling.

I'm dead.

She was being held up.

I'm dead.

Someone was yelling.

I'm dead.

"Alex, pull yourself together! Come on! They're everywhere! We need your help!"

Sasha screamed.

"...and they spend a lot of time in the living room, so I'm guessing the majority of them will be there when we show up. By the way, let me get this straight. You want me to pretend to be a hostage?" Rosaline asked.

"Yes. Taran will do everything in his power to protect you and ensure your safety. He is a warrior, but highly predictable. Always the hero. Or so he wants to believe." Raphael said, grinning his old grin.

"Yeah, I remember. So, when do we leave?"

"Soon. Before we depart, though, I want to give you something."

"What's that?"

Raphael held up a finger and nodded at an assistant.

Rosaline glanced at Joseph who only shrugged. Now what, she thought. This is getting more and more whacked out moment by moment. She wasn't even sure she believed everything Raphael had told her. Taran was a weird guy, but not THAT weird. She was trying to imagine his out-of-shape punk ass holding a sword and actually doing something other than accidentally knicking himself with it. According to Raphael, he-

"Here." Raphael spoke, handing her a Walther P99.

"Wait." she said, not taking the gun.

"It's fixed with a detonation mechanism, so that if you turn on us, I can hit a button and it will explode. You're going to help us take the vampire bitch out."

"Hold on. I'm really not comfortable with this."

"Do you really want him back?! Are you willing to go all the way to prove your love?! You talk like an obsessive psychopath, but are you willing to do everything that love asks you to do?!" he yelled, holding the gun out to her.

She considered his words.

He had a good point.

She took the gun.

She knew she would use it.

"Joseph, are your men ready?" Raphael asked, staring at the five warriors who hadn't even moved a finger since assembling in the room.

"Yes, Ancient." he said proudly.

"Hold on, hold on, what's with all this 'ancient' stuff?" Rosaline asked, looking at Raphael.

"Madam, he's our most revered figure." Jospeh said, hoping she would shut up.

"First of all, I'm nowhere near married, so it's mademoiselle, thank you very much, and second, it's just Raphael."

"Anyway, Rosaline, I think it would be best if you just-" Raphael began.

"Nonono, wait. I wanna know why these guys practically worship you. You were Taran's dojo master. Nothing more. Why the weird cult thing?"

"A ruse." he said cracking a grin.

"How so?" she asked.

"I was never anything but the Ancient."

"I don't get it."

"I suspected as much. Look, I got close to Taran for one reason."

"That being?"

"I needed to know it if was really him."

"So, the reason that you made me-"

"Exactly." he said.

Rosaline put her hand just beneath her belly and began to feel sick.

Alex remembered the "whish!" of Taran's sword emerging from its sheath and the ringing of Nigel firing away with his pistol.

But, it was Sasha's bloodcurdling scream that snapped her out of her trance.

She shook her head a few times, trying to take in the moment. She saw all sorts of movement around her, unable to pinpoint exactly what was happening. She had been in such a deep trance, that the shift back to reality was very difficult to make. Like emerging from a pool and being expected to run a marathon right away.

She looked around for Sasha, trying to figure out what had caused her to emit such a horrible sound.

Then she saw and understood immediately.

A Defender of the Faith stood in front of her, his sword through her belly and out her back.

A black van pulled up down the street from the Halfway. Milk Bone noticed it from the living room couch. Big deal. The plastic manufacturer next door had vans stopping and picking up shit all the time. He turned his attention back to the issue at hand.

Mariah Carey's titties.

He had never known love until he laid eyes on her. She was the most beautiful woman he had ever seen. He worshiped her. He would live and die for a chance to squeeze those titties.

Movement in his peripheral vision.

He looked outside again and saw several men and some woman walking towards the Halfway. Men with guns and swords.

He recognized one of the guys from somewhere, from several of Taran's pictures.

He recognized the girl, too.

Rosaline.

She had a gun.

This was bad. Milk Bone burst upstairs to grab his Glock.

He thundered up the stairs, breathing heavily and started to rethink his smoking habits. He really wished his old crew was here. These motherfuckers would be no problem if his brother and the rest of the South City crew were here.

He reached the top floor and ran to his room, ramming open the door, throwing open his closet, fumbling through his old gym bag, and removing the pistol. He checked the clip. Loaded. He pulled out four more clips and lined them up in his waist band.

Time to show these motherfuckers how things are done in St. Louis city, he thought. Proper.

Nigel squeezed off one round after another into the Defender. The bullets were not only not penetrating, but being reflected completely. This was completely futile, and a waste of ammunition. The only reason he kept firing was because he wasn't going to let this girl die. He fired again and again. Nothing.

Taran circled around the beast trying to figure out a way to attack this armored abomination. There seemed to be no way to get at him with a sword. It suddenly hit Taran how worthless this weapon was when it wasn't coupled with a decent range weapon, like a shotgun.

Sasha writhed around, shrieking in pain at the blade that had penetrated her soft stomach.

"NIGEL!!!" she screamed between gritted teeth.

Nigel's blood pressure quadrupled. He was going to do something. He was going to kill this man. He had never killed a man, and had once sworn he never would, ever again.

He ejected his clip and slapped in a new one. The sound of the clips bouncing on the ground cut through Sasha's screams. Nigel began rushing at the Defender, gun raised.

The Defender saw him coming, put his foot on Sasha, and pushed her off of his sword. He turned to face his new opponent.

Nigel aimed for the eyes and blasted several rounds into the man.

The Defender laughed and raised his sword. Nigel kept charging, guns blazing, roaring at his enemy.

"You will die by HIS hand!" the Defender of the Faith bellowed, raising his sword in the air.

What seemed to be lightning shot out of the sky and lit up the sword like a hot iron.

"Die, little blasphemous shit!" he yelled again, thrusting the sword at Nigel. A ball of light shot out of it, hitting the gunman in the chest and knocking him out cold. His body crumpled to the ground, gun falling at his side.

Alex shook herself out of her terror and lunged for Taran.

"I can take him! Get Nigel and Sasha out of here!" she yelled.

"No, we're not doing this again." he said calmly, eying the Defender, who was turning to face them.

"TARAN!! ALEXANDRA!!" the Defender suddenly exclaimed.

They turned to look at the monster that was addressing them.

"We knew that our last encounter was not the last one. Alexandra and Nicole survived. We had no idea that you all were capable of being resurrected, but it is no problem. There are nine of you and millions of us. We offer you asylum as research subjects. We will not kill you, we just want to learn about you. Where you all came from, and other such things."

"Excuse me." Alex spoke up, talking to the Defender.

"What?" he responded, never taking his attention off of Taran.

"How did you find us here?"

"I was stationed here, in case any of the Nine should ever return."

"How long have you been here?"

"Sixteen years."

Alex cocked an eyebrow in surprise.

"You've gotta be kidding." she remarked.

"Alex, tend to the two of them. This shouldn't take long." Taran murmured, preparing to win again.

"Taran-"

"Now, goddamit!" he barked.

"I...fine." she murmured, ready to intervene, once Taran was wounded enough to get over his death-wish.

Alexandra rushed over to Sasha and Nigel. Both were still breathing. Nigel seemed okay, but she wasn't so sure about Sasha.

Sasha was bleeding everywhere. Alex's body began to scream for nourishment, from the sight of the beautiful, red pool.

"Sasha, can you hear me?" Alex whispered, slapping her teammate lightly on the cheek.

"Yeah. I'm alive, if that's...wondering..."

"Can you heal yourself?"

"Yeah. Just give me a second."

"Sasha, I'm not sure if you have that long. If you're able to, do it now."

"Alex...how's Nigel?"

"He's alive. He's fine. Just taking a nice, long, nap."

"What happened to him?"

"The Defender hit him with some kind of energy burst."

"Sounds...AH...ow...painful."

"Sasha, heal yourself, then take care of Nigel."

"Right...okay..." Sasha trailed off, raising her hands above her broken body, her eyes rolling back in her head.

"...l...i...f...e..." she hissed, each letter carrying a weight that Alexandra didn't quite understand, but was reassured by.

A soft glow began to form in each of Sasha's hands. The glow grew, a soft hum emanating from her palms. Suddenly, she plunged her hands into her belly. Electricity began to shoot through her. She writhed around for a second or two, then all activity ceased.

Sasha sat up, looked around, checked her stomach, and the bleeding had stopped. The wound was still visible, since no healer, but the very oldest and most skilled could heal instantaneously. It was closed up, but would still need regular medical attention as soon as possible.

"Not bad, kid." Alex smiled.

"Oh god, Nigel..." Sasha said, looking over at the fallen warrior.

Nigel lay on the hard pavement, breathing softly.

"What can you do?" the vampire asked.

"This is one of the oldest treatments known among Mystics. Watch closely."

Sasha crawled over to him and took his head in her hands.

"Wake up, motherfucker!" she said, smacking him repeatedly.

Nigel woke with a start.

"What the fu-" he snapped, seeing Taran and the Defender about to engage in battle.

Nigel leaped up, grabbed his gun, and throwing the girl off of him.

Just then, the Defender took advantage of Taran's slight distraction. He leaped at the fledgling warrior, swinging precisely and thoughtfully.

The first swing connected with Taran's side, causing a wound that would have been considerable had Taran not been fairly quick, despite his obvious out of shape build. Taran cried out, wanting to clutch his side, but knowing that doing so would seal his fate.

The second swing was blocked by Taran, but not too successfully. The superior strength of the Defender sent a vibration through Taran's hands and arms that almost caused him to drop his sword.

The third swing sliced across Taran's chest, sending a spray of blood and lost hope. Taran was sent reeling, falling to the ground.

"I win, heretic." the Defender hissed. He turned and looked at Nigel, who had still not come up with a good attack.

"Might as well die trying, right?" Nigel chuckled, raising his gun and opening fire.

The Defender raised his arm and began coming towards Nigel, Sasha, and Alexandra.

"Goddamit, no!" Taran screamed, trying to get back up.

Nigel pulled the trigger, repeatedly, watching his bullets ricochet right and left off of the monster's incredible armor.

The Defender came closer.

Alex stood up and knew her fate.

Nigel fired and fired.

Taran stood again, and raised his sword, right before something invisible pinned him to that spot.

Sasha tried to collect her thoughts.

The Defender grabbed Nigel by the neck, lifted him off the ground, and threw him into the concrete like a rag doll. He backhanded Sasha with a resounding "CRACK!"

And there stood Alexandra Boliviere, the Queen of the Night, his final opponent.

He snatched at her neck. She shot out of view, but soon made her presence known again. He felt himself being lifted, then heaved into one of the iron supports for the bridge above. When he finally hit the ground, he rolled and looked around. Taran stood in the distance, shuffling toward him, sword raised for battle. The vampire, however, was nowhere in sight. Suddenly, she was before him again. He somersalted back up. Just in time for her to slam a steel rod from the bridge right through the abdomen of his WarShell.

He pulled the steel rod out and threw it away, focusing all of his attention on killing the vampire. The Bishops had wanted her alive, to study, but would understand the need to defend himself in the extreme.

She was about to dart out of view again, but the Defender got a jump on her, already guessing her next move. He seized her by the arm, flipped her over, throwing her to the ground, and pinning her with one hand. She hissed and thrashed around, but her claws were no match for his tank-like armor. He took his other hand, placed it on her skull, and began squeezing.

A dent suddenly appeared in his helmet. The Defender leaned up and twitched his head a bit.

I LAUGH AT WHAT YOU PERCEIVE AS BLASPHEMY YOU OLD FOOL

"Layne, where the hell have you been?!" Alex cried out as the Defender released her and eyed his new challenge.

THERE WERE FOUR NOW THERE IS ONE

"Psycho Mystics are strictly forbidden according to the Papyrus. Surrender now and you will be treated well." the Defender growled.

I WILL NOT OFFER YOU A CHANCE TO SURRENDER I WILL SIMPLY KILL YOU

The Defender roared and began to claw at his body. Dents appeared on his armor, one after another.

Layne floated down, out of the sky, his arms outstretched. Rags, which had been his clothing, hung from his body as he descended. Distant thunder roared as lightning struck the bridge behind him. Rain began to fall.

"You don't know what you really are! Stop!" the Defender cried.

I DON'T CARE WHAT I REALLY AM I ONLY KNOW WHAT I AM BECOMING BUT THEN THAT IS TRUE FOR ALL

The Defender fell to one knee on that shattered concrete as his armor made an audible "clank."

Layne floated toward him. He had balled his whole body up, and a look of exhaustion hung on his face.

Taran found he could move again. He approached Layne.

"You okay, man? You look a little more shriveled than usual."

FUCK OFF I HAVE A MURDER TO COMMIT GET OUT OF HERE THEY'RE COMING

With a scream, the Defender's armor dented even further.

"Layne, enough! Finish it!" Alexandra cried, looking away. She hated both that he seemed to enjoy it and that she felt bad for the monster in that armor.

With a horrible "crunch-squish," the body went limp and fell face-first on the concrete, nearly hitting her.

Alexandra rolled away, grabbed Taran, and ran to collect the others. She had one of the worst headaches she had ever had, but was still "with it" enough to get them out of here.

"Taran! Freeze!" a male voice on a loudspeaker yelled. Taran looked around.

"Now what?" he asked, looking at Alex.

She didn't respond. She just kept dragging him toward Nigel and Sasha, who was just now shaking her head and looking very groggy.

"Taran and company! Stay where you are! We are coming to collect you now!"

Wait a minute. Alex knew that voice. Never mind. Keep running.

"Alex! You carry Sasha! Nigel, you're with me!" Taran yelled.

"Layne, is that who I think it is?" Alex asked.

JUST GO

Alex picked up Sasha, while Taran put himself under one of his friend's arms, and they were off toward the car.

Alex began to detect movement in the shadows.

"Members of the Nine! This is your final warning! If you do not stop, we will open fire!"

Gorath.

"Taran, we're in BIG trouble!" Alex called out.

"No kidding!" Taran cried.

"Taran, that's-"

Suddenly, a blinding white bubble appeared right in front of them.

"What the hell is this?!" Taran yelled, stumbling back.

He began to see a small form walking out of the bubble.

"Who-" he began, just when the form emerged.

A dwarf.

"Bendle Ruffentuff at your service. Please come with me. I'm saving your lives." the dwarf said, and began walking back into the bubble.

Alex looked at Taran. He simply shrugged, and began leading Nigel into the bubble.

"Oh, killer, the white light thing is true." Nigel muttered.

"Shut up." Taran snapped, heading into the bubble.

Alex, carrying Sasha, followed them in.

Layne cautiously floated in after them.

The doorbell rang again, making it five times in five minutes.

These motherfuckers have some patience, Milk Bone thought. He crouched on the landing between the first and second floors, Glock aimed at the door, waiting for them to try and bust the two inch-thick solid steel door down.

He waited.

Thirty seconds gone by.

He noticed that he didn't see them in the little glass window at the top of the door anymore.

One minute.

Shit.

Minute thirty.

The windows.

Milk Bone tore down the stairs, trying to figure out the best way for them to enter. The mess hall would make the most sense, since it had two huge bay windows and lots of space to navigate. He took a right at the bottom of the stairs, down the hall and burst through the door to the mess hall.

Nothing. Just endless rows of tables and benches.

He was about to swear out loud when it occurred to him that would give up his position. So would standing in the middle of a large, empty room. Milk Bone ducked behind the open door and waited. He was sure they would enter through here.

He heard a crash in the distance. Shit, wrong room.

He slid out from behind the door and followed the noise, his Glock trained straight ahead.

Where the fuck was Taran and everyone else? He could really use their help right about now.

Milk Bone checked the living room. Windows and boards intact.

He checked the first empty room. Nothing.

He proceeded toward the kitchen.

Something caught his eye in the kitchen. Movement.

He inhaled sharply, preparing for the assault.

1...2...3!

He flew into the kitchen, hammering on the trigger as fast as he could.

Rosaline fell to the ground as she gasped.

"Oh!" Milk Bone yelled, running over to her, "Rosaline...I thought you was some bad mothafuckas or some shit. Oh, man, this is bad." he continued, rolling her onto her back. There was blood coming from her left side and her left shoulder.

"You planned this, didn't you, Raphael?!" she cried.

"Raphael?" Milk Bone asked. She must be going into shock or something, he thought.

"No. I should have, though. It would've made a great diversionary plan." a thin, silky voice spoke from outside. Milk Bone looked up, towards the back door that was part of the kitchen. It was wide open, the light posts from outside outlining a human shadow in the doorway. Milk Bone wasn't sure why, but he knew this guy could kick his ass.

That's why he ran like his brother should have. Fast and with a purpose. The figure in the doorway was giving chase. Milk Bone couldn't

194

hear him (what's with that?) but he knew he was there.

However, this dark figure had underestimated the little man. If anything, Milk Bone had proven that he could run. He was a thin, wiry guy, and had no physical strength anywhere but his legs. Milk Bone ran and ran and ran. He ran up the stairs. He ran down the hall of the top floor. He ran out the fire escape.

And jumped.

Oh, man, that was dumb, Milk Bone thought.

In mid-air, he knew he was dead.

If it weren't for the fact that the back yard was overgrown with trees.

He landed with a resounding "thud" on a branch. The branch knocked the wind out of him, but not the escape. He turned to glance at his pursuer for the first time.

That was dumb, too, he thought.

The dark figure stood perched on the fire escape railing like a cat, ready to pounce. Long, black hair, a horribly beautiful scaly, green cloak, and a deadly, serious look in his eye.

"Boy, I do not intend to kill you." the dark man spoke, "I simply need to hold you hostage. Do not continue your escape. Wherever you run, we will follow. We are relentless. We will never let you go. I will, however, release you eventually. I only need you for a few hours or so. I would very much appreciate your cooperation. May I please have it?"

Milk Bone thought about this. The only reason he was running was because he didn't want to die. However, he owed Taran his life and had a feeling that's who this psycho was here to see.

"Can I think about it for a sec without you all jumpin' up in my face and shit?" Milk Bone asked.

"You may."

"Uh...thanks, man."

Milk Bone realized he was still hanging on this tree branch on his stomach, which had grown quite uncomfortable. He pulled himself up and straddled it. Now he needed to figure out how to get out of here. He looked down and saw a couple of really dirty looking long-hairs in the yard staring back up at him. He saw another at the back door, tending to Rosaline. Another one was standing by the back gate. Another was scaling the tree he was in.

"Hey, man, tell your boy over there to get the fuck down out my tree!" Milk Bone yelled to the dark man.

"Ramon, down!"

The Hunter scampered back down the tree.

"Boy, may we talk now?" Raphael asked.

"We can talk from here!"

"Why don't you trust me?"

"You broke into my fuckin' crib, man!"

"I apologize for that, but we didn't think you'd open the door for us."

"Anyway, man, I think ya'll better leave."

"Boy, we very much need your help. Will you at least hear us out?"

Milk Bone looked at his options again. He still had the gun, and it looked like they wanted him alive, but would kill if necessary.

"Boy, are you listening? We will take you by force, if needed."

"Go ahead, mothafucka!" Milk Bone yelled, and squeezed off a shot at the dark man.

It ricocheted off of his cloak. The dark man began laughing.

"What the f-" Milk Bone began before the tranquilizer kicked in.

"I told you not to kill him!" Rosaline yelled, shoving one of the Hunters.

"I didn't, young lady." Alfred mumbled, crouched in the bushes, the muzzle from his dart gun still smoking.

"He's tranquilized, Rosaline." Raphael said, descending the fire escape, "Now, we wait for Taran. Revenge is at hand."

"Welcome to Praxidia." Bendle said, greeting them as they walked into what appeared to be a cave.

"Thank you. So, um, where's Praxidia?" Taran asked, helping Nigel to sit down.

"I'll let Lord Dell explain that. First, let's tend to your wounded."

"Good idea." Alexandra agreed, frowning at Sasha's condition.

"Ointy!" Bendle called out. Suddenly, several female dwarves appeared out of the shadows and began caring for Nigel and Sasha. One dwarf approached Taran.

"No, I'm fine, thank you." he said, as graciously as possible.

"Don't be retarded." Bendle barked at him.

"I-" Taran began to protest

"Taran, don't be rude!" Alex said.

"I...okay, okay. Whatever." he sat down, and let the female dwarf start dabbing his scrapes and cuts with a wet rag.

A few hours later, Taran awoke on the most comfortable bed he had ever slept on. He looked around, trying to gauge when, where, and how long he had been where he was. He seemed to be in a rather rudimentary hut. There was a coal oven and stove in the corner, with flowers and miniature dragons decorating every bare spot. There were also some rather beautiful swords hung on the wall, with dry blood covering the blades. Next to those were some almost frightening looking heads of creatures he had never seen on Animal Planet.

Well, it was time to get back to their adventure, he decided. He stood up and looked for the door. What had been that dwarf's name? Benny? Ben...Bendover? He chuckled to himself and opened the rather small door. He bent down, went through the opening and took in the utter beauty of the scene.

Endless, rolling hills. Blue sky. Little, wooden huts with dwarven children playing and laughing. Odd little creatures running in the distance. And Alexandra, the most beautiful sight of all. He realized that he had never seen her in the bright of light before. She was standing in front of one of the huts, talking to their dwarf friend. The sunlight reflected off of her hair so beautifully.

The sunlight.

"NO!!! ALEX, NO!!!" Taran yelled, breaking into a run.

Alex looked up at him and began laughing.

"Taran, I'm-"

He tackled her, carried her into the hut, and slammed the door behind them. She was still laughing.

"Are you okay? Did you forget or something? What the hell were you thinking?" he yelled, still gasping from the sudden explosion of energy.

"Taran, I was fine."

Suddenly, the little door creaked open and Bendle appeared.

"Everything alright, Miss Boliviere?"

"Yes, Bendle, everything's okay. Can you give us a sec?"

"Yes, mam." he said, creaking the door closed.

"The sun doesn't affect me here."

"What?"

"It doesn't affect me here. Bendle said...well, actually, I kinda already knew this. Anyway, just believe me when I say the rules that we know don't apply here."

"Where the hell are we?"

"You have a lunch meeting with Lord Dell in four hours. Apparently, we're getting a lot of our answers then."

"Oh. Good." Taran laughed, not quite believing it would be that easy.

He shook off the skepticism, the negativity, and just focused his mind on her beautiful bare feet.

He stared at her well-formed toes and thought, maybe that's a remnant of a time gone by, 'cause most girls nowadays got some funky-ass toes.

He focused on her toes and cleared his brain of the bullshit. He moved his eyes up her foot, and noted how how lovely her ankles were. They were angular without being skeletal.

He thought about Alexandra, Nigel, Sasha, and Layne, then thought about Ghost and Milk Bone.

Then, he thought about his parents and siblings and all the friends that he had bailed on.

He thought about Rosaline, Jill, and the nearly stupid depth of feeling he'd had for way too many girls in his young life.

His stomach bottomed out and everything felt false. His heart was suddenly put on display for his mind to observe objectively, and he longed to feel nothing. His reality was shunted under a dispassionate microscope and his brain was calling bullshit.

And yet, he stood in a hut with a hot female vampire that he was in love with, inexplicably, and dwarves were playing outside with weird creatures that didn't exist on his planet.

Suck it up and move forward, he thought.

He took her hand, kissed it, and rubbed it against his stubbly cheek.

"I love you, Alexandra."

"I love you, too, Taran."

They both took a moment to hold each other. The world stopped for a second, and allowed the two lovers to exist only in each other's hearts. The love shared by the two lovers had suddenly become the only believable thing in their hearts and minds.

Taran suddenly jerked away.

"What's wrong?" Alex asked.

"Nigel? Sasha? Layne? Where are they?"

"Nigel and Sasha are still resting. They're fine. Layne is taking care of himself."

"Okay. Sorry, it's just...still adjusting to...shit, everything."

"I know. Let me take your mind off of it. Wanna see something fucked up?"

"Sure."

Alexandra opened her mouth.

"Oh my god." Taran gasped.

Perfect, human teeth.

"Where'd they go?"

"I told you. The rules don't apply here. I don't know why, and neither does Bendle."

"Does this mean that you're 'cured?'"

"I doubt it."

"Can I take a gander at something here?" Taran asked, cracking a wicked smile.

"Sure."

"We're not only not in Missouri anymore, but we're not even in our universe here."

"That's my estimation."

"Okay, how do we get back?"

"Ask Lord Dell when you have lunch with him."

"Cool. Anything else we need to discuss?"

"Nothing. Well, except that I'd like to get laid as a human while we're here, if you don't mind."

"No better time than the present, right?" he smiled.

"Not on Bendle's bed!"

Suddenly, they heard a voice from outside.

"You fuck her on my bed and I'll kick your scrawny, human ass!"

"Seems someone's been eavesdropping on us."

"Actually, dwarves are known for their hearing." Alex giggled.

"You bet your hairless fucking ass!" the dwarf bellowed from outside.

"Wanna meet our host?" she asked.

"Sure."

She grabbed his hand and led him outside. Still holding his hand, they approached the dwarf. He was quite an interesting sight, now that Taran finally got a good look at him. He looked a little like the little guy in the movie, "The Labyrinth." Hobble, or whatever that guy's name was. The attire was somewhat different.

Bendle Ruffentuff, as Alexandra introduced him, stood at about four feet tall, with short, gray hair, a little goatee at his chin, a huge nose and puffy cheeks, with small beady eyes adorning his face. He wore a simple tunic and brown leather pants, with an AK-47 strung across his back.

"Taran Walker, meet Bendle Ruffentuff."

"A pleasure." Taran said, extending his hand. Bendle took it.

"I'm sure." Bendle said, shaking his hand.

"Now, if you don't mind my asking, where did you get that AK?"

"Took it off prey that I hunted."

"Excuse me?"

"I hunt humans for sport. I took it off one that I killed. I'm an avid hunter. Humans are the most fun, because they actually shoot back."

"Tell me you're kidding." Taran laughed in disbelief.

"Not at all. Want your sword back?"

"Uh...yeah." Taran said, embarrassed that he hadn't even noticed it was missing.

"Sorry, but the kids thought it was neat, so, I've been letting them play with it."

"Right..." Taran said, shooting a curious glance at Alex, who only shrugged.

Bendle walked over to an open space between two of the huts and returned a second later with the sword. It sparkled brilliantly in the sun. He approached Taran and handed it over.

"Thank you." Taran responded, sheathing it.

"Not a problem."

"Taran, you up for a walk through the countryside?" Alex asked, smiling at the trees, grass, and sun.

"Absolutely, babe."

"Bendle, we'll be back in an hour." she said, rubbing the dwarf on the head.

"Yes, ma'am."

Taran and Alexandra grasped each other's hands and began walking.

"When will he wake?" Rosaline asked, glaring at Raphael and wincing as one of the Hunters bandaged her.

"In the next ten minutes or so. Why are you so anxious?"

"I wanna find out who that girl is to Taran."

"She's the one he was destined for. Didn't we go over this?"

"What do you mean, 'destined for?'"

"They were created for each other." Raphael said, smiling.

"You are so fucked up."

"Don't believe me? Ask Ravindranathan."

"Who's Ravindra.....whatever?"

"You will meet him. I'm sure of it."

"Who is he?"

"Your master."

Taran and Alex came upon a beautiful lake that seemed to stretch for eternity. The other side was barely hidden in the distant horizon. There were gorgeous multi-colored fish that resembled scaled-down (no pun intended) catfish dipped in tie-die jumping out of the water in all over the lake.

"Taran, where the hell are we?" Alex asked.

"I...I have no idea."

"I don't want to go back."

Taran looked at her, questioningly. She looked back at him, surprised that he didn't get it.

"Taran, I'm normal here. We can make a life here."

"And we will. We have a mission to fulfill back there first."

"We might not survive it."

"Better to die well than to live with needess guilt."

"I guess. Anyway, want to hear the rest?"

"The rest of what?"

"My 'epic' tale?"

"Shouldn't we wait for Nigel and Sasha?"

"I'll recount it to them when you're meeting with Lord Dell."

"Okay."

"It's long."

"We have time."

"Alright. Here goes...."

XII: From Then 'til Now

"So, Aunica, Nicole, and I went by ship to England. From there, Aunica demanded that we head immediately to Italy. Nicole was really eager to do some unwinding and sightseeing, but Aunica wouldn't have it. So, after a fair amount of evil eying between Aunica and Nicole, we headed for Italy.

"We arrived in Rome a bit after three in the afternoon, so we were forced to hide on the train for several hours. In that time, a very shocking discovery was made.

"We were in one of the cargo cars when Nicole started getting very antsy.

"'Hey.' she whispered to us.

"'Keep quiet, insolent girl!' Aunica hissed.

"'I wish to see the sunlight once again.'

"'Don't be crazy!' I barked at her.

"'A second or two of exposure won't kill me. A minor burn, but I'll be healed by tomorrow.'

"'Nicole, this is neither the time nor the place to start experimenting with mortality.' Aunica snapped.

"'Hell with both of you, I'm gonna do it.'

"'Nicole, you'll give up our hiding spot!' I began to raise my voice.

"Aunica put her finger on her lips, signaling for me to quiet down. She turned to Nicole.

"'Very well, young lady, do as you wish. You will learn your lesson rather quickly, I imagine.'

"Nicole merely shrugged, went to the large sliding door, and used her strength to yank the door open.

"Sunlight streamed through.

"I lay there, shielding my eyes and staying behind the boxes that were being stored in there to protect my body.

"'Nicole, you idiot! You'll-' Aunica yelled, from behind boxes at the other end of the cargo hold.

"Suddenly, a shrill sound emerged from our loony companion.

"'NICOLE, NO!' I yelled, leaping up to save her from her own madness. I felt the sun begin to tear through me.

"But, she was laughing and dancing around.

"I fell back down, unable to handle the pain.

"'Alex, I...oh god, child, are you okay? What were you thinking?' she asked running over to me and crouching next to me.

"'Nicole, close the damn door!' Aunica yelled.

"'Right...' she said, rather absentmindedly, and got up to do so. As soon as the door slammed shut, Aunica ran over to me.

"'Alexandra,' she said, lovingly, 'stay still. The wounds should be gone in a week or two.'

"'A week or two? I heal much faster than that.' I whispered, becoming delirious with pain.

"'Not with light burns. Light burns are the worst wound for a vampire. They are the most painful and the slowest to heal. The best thing for you right now is vampire blood. Drink from me.'

"'Aunica, you haven't fed in days, you'll grow weak...'

"'Nonsense, I refuse to let my little girl suffer anymore than she must. Drink from me.'

"She grabbed me by the back of my hair and thrust my mouth toward her throat. My body screamed in pain at the sudden movement, then the heartbeat drove me mad until I bit into her, but then I felt the high from vampire blood. All the pain ceased for a minute. When I forced myself to stop, I felt the burning begin to creep in again, but a tiny bit less than before.

"It was then that I finally passed out from the agony.

"I awoke what must have been a few hours later. Nicole was shaking me.

"'Alex, we gotta move. It's dark now, so you and Aunica can go outside.'

"'So, the sun doesn't hurt you, huh?'

"'I guess not. Let's go.'

"I pulled myself up, grimacing at each slight movement.

"'I've already secured us a hotel room and everything, so let's get moving.' Nicole said, very serious.

"Aunica pulled the car door open, and the three of us hopped out. We began to head into town. As we walked through the city streets, I took in all the Roman architecture. They had such an understanding of strength and power in their buildings. Even the newer, more modern Christian buildings showed off their designer's visions of beauty. The churches were gorgeous. Even in the extreme pain I was, I could still appreciate such an impressive display of art.

"The three of us made our way into the hotel room and got settled. It was decided that Nicole and Aunica would explore the city and gather the needed information for our strike. I was to stay in the room and read through some books that Nicole had picked up about the Catholic faith and other related topics.

"All in all, it was a wasted night. I learned nothing from the stupid books that Nicole had picked up, and all they learned was that there was no sign of the Defenders anywhere. Once they got back, Nicole wanted to go back out and enjoy the day, but Aunica ordered that we all rest.

"The next night, they went out to feed, and brought me back a pretty little Italian boy that had been slitting throats for purses, drunk off wine. I enjoyed him quite a bit. We sat up and discussed our options.

"'A frontal assault is out of the question, I can tell you that much.' Aunica offered.

"'I disagree. There's not a single serious threat between us and infiltrating the Vatican.' Nicole said.

"'Who says the Vatican is even our target?' I asked.

"'Why don't we just admit that we have no idea what the hell we're supposed to be doing here? Why are we even here?' Nicole complained.

"'To do what we were created to do. Back to the point, we need to do some serious reconnaissance work. We need to send one person into the Vatican, one person into some of the governmental buildings, and one person into other locations. More than one would draw too much attention. Just have one of us get in there, look around, and assess the situation. Quite simple. Are we agreed?' I asked.

"'Sounds good. How are you feeling?' Nicole asked.

"'Better. Not one-hundred percent yet, but a lot better.'

"'There's one other thing that I'd like to suggest.' Nicole said, looking a little nervous.

"'What's that?' Aunica asked, growing impatient with the girl.

"'Sunlight has no effect on me. This gives me a serious edge. If I-'

"'Nonsense. When would you regenerate?' Aunica snapped.

"'Whenever! It doesn't matter!'

"'Ladies, if I may, there's another thing I'd like to point out. The Defenders aren't expecting any kind of trouble from vampires, which means they're not expecting the kind of attack we would offer at night, the only time we could strike. We should definitely strike at night, if we ever do 'strike,' especially since we have no choice. Right now, though, we should rest. Good day.'

"And we slept."

"The next night, I awoke with a jolt.

"'Alex, wake up! Get out of bed, now! She's gone!' Aunica was shaking me.

"'Aunica, what? What's going on?'

"'Nicole's gone!'

"BOOM!

"'An explosion went off in the distance. Aunica and I looked at each other and had a pretty good idea what was going on. We dressed hurriedly and dashed out the door. With our enhanced speed and vision, we were able to traverse the city in no time. We began to approach the Vatican.

"We skidded to a stop, inches from the lip of a crater in front of it.

"A familiar giggle.

"'So much for any resistance they had to offer. I must say, being imbued with these vampire abilities has definitely improved my magical abilities.'

"'Nicole, you idiot!' Aunica shrieked. She leaped into the air, seized Nicole by the hair, and dragged her back over to our position.

"'Then, I had a bad thought.

"It was still early evening, the earliest a vampire would dare venture out. Where were all the people? Where was the commotion that was to be expected after such a loud explosion in a crowded city? Where were all the police, trying to beat Nicole down?

"'Hisss...'

"The three of us whirled around, trying find the location of the noise. It continued, all around us.

"'Hisss...'

"'Alex, what is that?' Nicole asked.

"'Vampire.' I whispered.

"Movement. In the shadows. Had I still been human, I would not have noticed, but now, I definitely detected something.

"Then, he was in front of us. Just seemed to drop down, out of the sky. He landed, crouched on one knee, covered in a black cloak.

"I knew him.

"Nicole raised her hand, preparing to vaporize him.

"'No, wait!' I commanded.

"'What?' she balked.

"'Thank you for staying her hand, Miss Boliviere.' the cloaked figure spoke, beginning to stand.

"Frederik, the great Vampire Hunter, revealed himself as he threw back his hood.

"'And you, Miss Anderson, I am not so pleased with you. You wiped out all my men. Do you know that you are the most sought after out of all the vampires in the world? The price on your head could never afford to be paid.' he turned to me, 'May I kill her?'

"'No, Frederik, you may not. She is my friend. How did you make that hissing noise seem to be all around us?'

"'That was my second order of business. I didn't. There's a group of vampires surrounding us, waiting for us to leave so that they can kill the lovely Miss Anderson here. I was going to try to beat them to the prize, but since I am indebted to Miss Boliviere, I won't.'

"'Why do they want to kill me?'

"'Because you frighten them. You are, as far as anyone knows, the most powerful vampire in the world. If they kill you and take your blood, they gain some of your power. I would turn tail and run if I were you all.'

"Just then, a horrible roaring began, all around us.

"'What the hell is that?' Aunica asked.

"'These vampires do not use language, they communicate much like animals, using vocal tones. They are growing impatient, getting ready to attack.'

"'Why haven't they tried already?' Nicole asked.

"'As I said, they fear you.'

"'Well, I don't fear them! Let them come! Attack me if you will, you stupid wretches!'

"As she said that, they did

"Dark, scaly, hissing creatures leaped from rooftops and tree branches and bushes.

"Frederik charged forward, slicing one in half. Aunica grabbed

204

one by it's neck, punched her hand through one, ripped it's innards out, and snapped the head off. Nicole began setting various creatures on fire.

"These vampires were unlike any other vampire I had ever seen. They resembled lizards more than anything else. Green, scaly skin, flicking tongues, spiny fins down their back.

"The battle ensued at a lightning fast pace. I could see Frederick, his blade flashing, seeming to almost do a dance among the creatures, blood spilling right and left. Aunica stood in one place, literally ripping one lizard vampire after another apart. Nicole was laughing, sending one discharge after another at the creatures. I continued fighting as well.

"After several minutes of nonstop carnage, I think Frederick and I came to the same realization. We both looked around and realized that the streets, rooftops, and every inch of any structure was covered with these creatures. They had sent an entire army after Nicole!

"'Miss Boliviere, this is hopeless! We must retreat!' he called out.

"'I know! Nicole, Aunica, let's-'

"'Alex!!! I-' then a splattering sound.

"I looked over at Aunica, and realized one of the creatures had decapitated her with a sharpened stone, like a caveman would use. He and several others began lapping up her blood. I froze. My mentor, my teacher, my best friend, she who had fixed me, was dead.

"'AUNICA!!!' I shrieked. In blind fury, I charged in, clawing at the creatures, ripping out one throat after another, insuring not a single one who had received her blood lived. They would all die. All of them. I continued on my rampage, decimating their numbers, singlehandedly.

"'Miss Boliviere, WE NEED TO LEAVE!!!' Frederik cried out. I heard him, but didn't. My lover had already been stolen from me, I wasn't going to let them take my best friend, too. I rushed over, scooped up her body, and took to the roof. And ran. They gave chase. Quite a good one, too. But, they were never able to catch me. After several hours, they resumed their pursuit of Nicole. I cradled Aunica's headless body and drained it of every last drop of blood. If she were to continue in anyway, it was going to be through me. I would ensure her legacy lived on though me. I would stop at nothing to complete our mission. I had too many lives to avenge now.

"I sat with her all night. I cried to her all night. Kissed her all over all night. Then the sun came.

"I lifted her body above my head and fed it to the ever-hungry sun. We began to burn together. Her body, drained of all it's blood, burst into flames, giving itself back to the world it had stolen from so many times.

"'AUNICA!!!' I screamed.

"The sun began to consume me as well. I felt myself being lifted into the air. The pain overwhelmed me. I lost consciousness.

"Then, I awoke again. I was back on my bed in the hotel. I was naked. I looked down. My skin was a fairly dark shade, looking almost

Egyptian. I tried to sit up, but the pain took over, and I dropped back down. I cried out.

"'Hello?! Nicole?!'

"No answer.

"I must have laid there for days, starving, writhing, screaming, before I was well enough to move again. I found my bloody, scorched clothes, and put them on, they being all that I had, and I set out on my mission again. Alone. I had no idea what had become of Frederik, Nicole, or the reptile vampires. There was no indication that it had ever happened. Even the crater that Nicole had made was gone. I soon began to believe I was going mad. Then, something else grabbed my attention. I found their base."

"The Defender's base?!" Taran asked, his jaw dropping.

"Yes. It's underneath a little shack in the countryside surrounding Rome. I trailed a lone Defender there."

"Wait, hold on. Who brought you back to the hotel?"

Alexandra shrugged.

"Did you ever find out?"

"Shut up, please."

"Okay, sorry."

"Anyway, I followed this Defender into a little shack, through a trap door, into a...a...shit, I don't even know how to describe it. Remember in Star Wars, Episode IV, when the Millennium Falcon gets towed into the Death Star, and C-3PO and R2-D2 are in that little control room?"

"Yeah." Taran said, eyes lighting up.

"The whole place looked like that. Keep in mind, this was a LONG time ago. They had this technology back then. The underground facility has to be a least several miles across, on any side. It's huge, Taran."

"So, what'd you do?"

"I spied a little, took mental notes, etcetera. I have an entire report on my PC at one of my homes, but to make a long story short, it looks like a very compact military base that would be easily win WWIII. There was one chamber I couldn't get into, though. It was never opened the entire time I was there."

"Did they have any clue that you were there?"

"None, as far as I knew, which I have a hard time believing, given the technology that they apparently had. If they knew I was there, they simply didn't care. I don't know. After that, I left. I had no one around anymore, and I was hanging in some weird space between depression and excitement. I could do anything I wanted, but I had no one to share it with. I left and wandered until the other day, when you found me."

"What brought you to St. Louis?"

"I don't know. Wanted to finally go home. There are all sorts of adventures that I'm skipping over, but none of them are relevant to our dilemma. Anyway, can we just make love, please? I want to do it at least once, while I am actually alive."

206

"Of course, m'lady." Taran smiled, and then kissed her. Both were pawing at each other's clothes within seconds.

They engaged in no foreplay, whatsoever, wanting only the sensation of being united. They pulled each other's clothes off, she shoved him down, and slid down on his pulsing organ. She felt it fill her. It touched the back of her and caused a slight twinge of pain. She gasped. She began to move slowly. Forward and backward. Up and down. All simultaneously.

Taran stared up at her. He had no idea how he, a creature, who contained so much ugliness and hatred, could ever be loved by such a woman. A woman who's heart contained nothing but love and sadness.

Her riding increased in speed. Her breasts bounced, her back arched, her lips formed in a grimace.

"Oh god, Taran, yes!" she hissed.

Taran grabbed her sides, forcing himself deeper into her, as if he could go any deeper.

"Taran, cum in me! Please! I want to feel your life force in me!"

He flipped, spun her around, and began to make love to her from behind. He began pounding into her, using every bit of strength he could draw from himself. He had a hand on each hip, almost pulling her onto him, crashing against her. She quivered, let out another gasp, and almost collapsed. She might have, had he not had such a grip on her lower section.

Suddenly, he felt it. It was his time. She was on her third climax, digging her nails into the dirt.

He exploded into her. The volcano in his groin filled her with his hot seed. He let go of her, and the two collapsed side by side, holding each other.

"They're fucking, I know they are." Nigel snickered, gazing at Sasha.

"Right. I know Taran, and he is totally focused on the mission right now." she said, blowing out a smoke ring.

"I'm sure you're right." he said, almost wanting to smack her over the back of the head, and go "duh!"

"You interpret things too literally. Relax. Life speaks in metaphors a lot."

"It's never good news when it does."

"You speak as if you believe you've lived life enough to say that."

"Maybe I have."

"You're only 21." she muttered, shrugging.

"Age doesn't matter."

"Only the young say that."

"I'm older than you are. And why do you always argue?" he snapped.

"Why do you always provoke arguments?"

"Forget it."

"Easily forgotten."

Nigel shook his head in frustration. He didn't dare to admit his deep, deep attraction to her. She was so beautiful and and had that perfect balance of confidence and humility. Sasha Stone was definitely a catch. A catch almost certainly out of his reach.

Maybe he should try not being such an ass all the time. Of course, she could lighten up quite a bit herself, couldn't she?

If there was one thing Nigel Poe struggled with, it was defining himself to others. He knew he came off as ugly and jaded, but he almost enjoyed it. He liked being pissed-off and brooding all the time. It seemed to drive everyone but Taran nuts, but at the same time, he guessed he wasn't really like that with Taran, since he didn't really need that defense with Taran. Taran had known him before Kat had left him. True guilt and loss are things that can really kill a man inside.

Nigel felt himself sinking again. He and Taran were experiencing different things here. Taran seemed to be rebuilding. Nigel was feeling worse.

He also felt bold.

He reached over and grabbed Sasha's hand. She gasped and almost recoiled, but quickly understood.

"Nigel, I'm sor-"

"No. No words right now." he whispered.

Nigel and Sasha sat in front one of the huts, hand in hand, watching life go by. He took in his surroundings. Like something out of one of those fantasy books that Taran used to always read.

Is this a "tender moment?" Why am I feelng better already? How is it bottle after bottle and song after song and conversation after conversation with Taran can't yield this potent a result? The touch of this woman seems to numb my pain receptors. I think I might just leave this little quest of theirs and simply sit here holding her hand for the rest of my life.

Nigel thought all this and closed his eyes, waiting for the weeping to begin.

And, it never came. Thank god.

A human man approached them. He had long brown hair pulled back in a ponytail and stared at them seriously.

Nigel was already annoyed with him.

"What can I do for ya, bro?"

Ponytail man smiled viciously at them.

"YOU CAN TELL ME WHAT LIES YOU ARE TELLING HER NOW SO THAT I MAY WARN HER OF YOUR ILL INTENTIONS I HATE NOT HAVING POWER WHEN CAN WE LEAVE." the man bellowed at them, then reverted to his stare.

Nigel and Sasha glanced at each other.

Sasha leaned over to Nigel.

"He's almost kinda cute without the corpse-look." she whispered.

"Yeah, but he still talks like a retarded robot." Nigl turned from Sasha to Layne, "Guess what, asswipe? I'm here, and I've always had a fully functional body, and I don't talk like the dumbest fucking Borg ever, so how 'bout you go frighten some dwarf children with your scary yelling shit?"

Layne smiled, considered Nigel, then Sasha, then Nigel again.

"I CAN'T READ YOUR MIND, BUT I CAN STILL ENSURE THAT YOU HAVE NO SEX IN THE IMMEDIATE FUTURE." Layne barked again.

"What?" Nigel spat, twisting his face in annoyance.

Layne's eyes suddenly took on a menacing glare as he focused and stared at Nigel. Suddenly, he nodded his head sharply and Nigel shit his own pants.

"Ah, fuck me!" Nigel cried, about to jump up before he stopped himself.

"PSYCH IT'S AN ILLUSION YOU BE GOOD TO HER OR I'LL MAKE YOU VOMIT OUT YOUR OWN INTESTINES!"

With that, Layne skulked away.

Nigel felt the phantom turd disappear, but rammed his hands down his own pants just to be sure.

"What? Are you okay?" Sasha asked, looking at him concernedly.

"Yeah. I'm cool. He's just a twisted fuck. What were we talking about?" Nigel asked, calming himself.

"How did you and Taran meet?" Sasha suddenly asked.

Nigel snapped out of his distracted state and looked at her. He thought for a moment, realizing it had been literally years since anybody had asked him about his past and really cared. He quickly dusted the memories off and began the telling the truth, also for the first time in years.

"I was a freshman in high school and he was a sophomore. I had just turned fifteen and he was about sixteen. We were both guitarists, bouncing from one band to another, and sort of wound up in the same one. We've been friends ever since."

"When did Raphael enter the picture?"

"I honestly don't know. That guy is a scary motherfucker, and someone I told Taran to stay away from."

"What happened with Taran and Raphael? Will you please tell me?"

"I can't. Understand, I made a promise to Taran. I can't break it."

"Okay, okay." Sasha trailed off, frustrated.

"What about you?" Nigel asked, smiling for the first time.

"How do you mean?"

"What's your story?"

Sasha sat up, retrieved her hand from his, ran her hands over her knees, and looked a little taken aback by the question. She exhaled, slumped back down, and looked at him.

"I'm kinda weird, Nigel, I really am."

"So am I, it's okay."

"Yeah, but I'm...okay, here ya go. I was born July 1st, 1983 in South Africa to a pair of archaeologists, hence my full name."

"Which is?"

"Sasha Rosetta Stone."

"Clever."

"Very. Anyway, shortly after my birth, my parents and I went back to America, where I was raised. We started out in Baltimore, then D.C., then Terre Haute, Indiana, then St. Louis. I've lived here, I mean, St. Louis, since I was six."

"How did you meet Ghost?"

"I was eight years old when the Coven found me. I would do things like slightly illuminate a dark room and stuff like that, and magic users can sense each other, and so I was whisked away in the middle of the night to appear before the Council to have my future decided, and he happened to be there. They were asking me all sorts of questions, and he was standing there, just watching. I kept looking at him, and we made eye contact. He freaked. The next day, he found me, asked me if I could see him, I said yes, and it sort of went from there. The Coven began one training, and he began another. I've never really had any friends because of this."

"What about your parents?"

"They're always out digging, so I live alone, funded by them."

"School, work, anything?"

"School. I'm in my senior year at Clayton High School."

"High school?! Damn, you're a baby."

"Yep."

Sasha and Nigel looked around again. It was starting to hit midday.

"What about your younger years?" Sasha asked.

"I was born in Kansas City on February 12th, 1980 to a couple of teenagers. Mom bailed, Dad and I moved to St. Louis, so that he could take a job doing maintenance on vending machines. He used to get drunk every night and beat the shit out of me, until one day, I grew up and got drunk and beat the shit out of him. Now we get along fine. I've been going to school at SEMO (Southeast Missouri State) for about three years now."

"Looks like this might be the last year of school for both of us." Sasha said.

"I don't know. I kinda wanna die an educated man when the world blows up."

"I think I've caught onto the key difference between you and Taran."

"Is that so?" Nigel laughed, "What is it?"

"You're much more down to earth than he is. Taran's very

concerned with things inside himself and not letting down his guard. You seem a little more relaxed."

"I guess. Except Taran's a little too whacked out right now make that kind of judgment. He's much worse when he's sane. He's slowly coming unraveled right now. This Raphael business has overtaken every thought at this moment. As soon as we get to Cape, he and I are going to have a nice, long chat. If he keeps this up, Raphael's gonna kill him."

"Agreed."

"Ow." Rosaline murmured.

"You've been shot, what do you expect? Let me finish patching this up, and the pain will subside a bit." Raphael said as was bandaging her shoulder.

"I can't believe you let me get shot at."

"It wasn't anticipated. I didn't realize that crazed thug was the only one here. I thought the person holding the gun would be Taran or someone else who wouldn't have fired on you."

"Whatever."

Rosaline and Raphael were sitting in the kitchen in the halfway. It was quite a picture to behold. There couldn't have been a stranger alliance in the history of mankind.

Ramon walked into the kitchen.

"Ancient, he's awake, sir!" Ramon barked.

Raphael chuckled.

"Want to see how a proper interrogation is done?" he asked the girl.

"I don't care."

"You will."

XIII: Answers

Taran and Alexandra approached the little village again. As they walked up, they noticed no one was outside. Taran began to reach back for his blade.

"Wait." Alex said, hushed, "You don't know what's going on. Don't be rash."

"Sorry, babe. Better safe than sorry." he said, unsheathing it.

They continued approaching the village. Nothing really looked strange, just the lack of people.

Where the hell were Nigel and Sasha?

Where was Bendle?

They began to approach Bendle's hut.

A voice.

"Ah, yes, I see. You are one of the old code." it boomed, sounding huge and reverberating.

It had come from inside Bendle's hut.

Taran leaped forward, tossing the flap aside and launching inside, ready to kill.

And there sat Jesus Christ. Or a slight variation of. Instead of the raggedy, brown clothes commonly associated with Christ's usual wardrobe, he wore a more regal outfit. A king's clothes, the crown and everything.

"...wow..." Taran uttered, amazed. Alex walked in behind him and gasped.

"I am Lord Dell, deity of this universe. You must be Taran and Alexandra, pleased to make your acquaintance." he spoke, standing and shaking their hands.

"I'm sorry, your lord, I don't want to be rude, but are you...uh..." Alex spoke, quivering.

"God? Yes and no. To these creations, yes. To you all, no. But, yes. Anyway, all will be explained. I promised you all food, so let's go."

Taran spoke up.

"Um, excuse me, but where are my friends?"

"They are already eating, I'd imagine. Come, let's not waste precious time. The clock is ticking back in your universe, too."

The three walked outside the hut. A huge caravan of horse-like creatures and guards were waiting outside. The best way to describe the horses is hairless horses with dark brown skin and elephant trunks, and slightly larger than clydesdales. A mighty carriage sat in the middle of the caravan. Lord Dell, Taran, and Alexandra got in. The caravan began moving.

"Taran, Alexandra, just to bring you all up to speed, I am Lord Dell, god of this universe. This universe is not parallel to yours whatsoever. This universe, your universe, and about three billion others are all that exist. Nothing else in reality exists. There are about three billion universes and about three billion "gods" as you all call us. Ages and ages ago, and I apologize for lack of exact numbers, but time is commonly based on a planet's revolutions around a sun, and we have no common frame or reference here, so settle for the phrase "a long, long time ago," okay? Anyway, a long, long time ago, there was one universe. Within that universe, there were many, many galaxies, with many, many stars, and many, many planets. On one of those planets, a society sprang up. That societies' inhabitants evolved for billions and billions of our years and eventually evolved to the point where we could outdo physics. We learned to do two key things: One, manipulate genetics, and two, create and destroy matter. After many thousands of years of this, we fused the two. We began to genetically engineer our own people to be able to create and destroy matter with thought. Eventually, we began to create our own universes and go inside them and start playing god. Oh by the way, you're wondering who created our universe, the universe of the gods, right? To answer your question, we're not sure. We're pretty sure nobody, but who knows? Anyway, this went on for quite some time, and after a while we all got really good at it. Now, in most cases, the god actually lives inside his universe. This has advantages and disadvantages. One advantage is that you actually get to enjoy your hard work and interact with the people, but there are two drawbacks. One, is that you lose your omniscient abilities. You can't see everywhere and anywhere, and also, you become subject to your own rules that you've set up. On the other hand, if you rule from outside, you can't really interact or change anything. You can jump back and forth from inside to outside, but it's a very difficult process, and very exhausting. It also takes literally years in our years, which can be a day or a millennium, depending on which planet you're going to appear on. Any questions so far?"

"Is this why it seems like god is only paying attention occasionally? Because he's so inundated with so many planets to manage and keeps jumping back and forth from in and out of our universe?" Alex asked, intrigued.

"Yes. Though, with Ravindranathan, you can never be sure."

"Who's Ravindranathan?" Taran asked.

"The god of the universe you've been in."

Taran and Alexandra looked at each other, more uncertain than ever of their future.

"All will be explained during lunch, fret not."

"What's your name, boy?" Raphael asked, staring Milk Bone in the eye.

Milk Bone glared back at him.

"I said, what's your name?"

"His name's Milk Bone." Rosaline said.

"I didn't ask you. Stay quiet, girl. Okay, Milk Bone, I'll get right to the point. Where are Taran and Alexandra?"

"I dunno." Milk Bone sighed, not seeming worried at all.

"Glad to see you've found you're voice, but I'm a little disappointed by your answer, and trust me, Mr. Bone, I'm not a good person to disappoint."

"Taran's pretty clever, Raphael, and might've purposely hidden that from Milk Bone, just in case you came asking." Rosaline offered.

"Rosaline, if you speak one more time, I will make your experience with me from a few years ago seem like a fucking picnic! Shut up!!!" Raphael roared.

"What'd you do to her a couple of years ago?" Milk Bone asked, genuinely curious.

"What?" Raphael asked, amazed at the size of the balls on this kid.

"What'd you do that was supposedly so fuckin' bad, dude? I mean, you walk around here, struttin' your shit, you got these dirty-ass Braveheart-lookin' motherfuckers so wound up and afraid of you and shit, and I'm just wonderin' why you think you're so fuckin' hard? What the fuck makes you so cool?"

Raphael studied the kid with great interest. It had been a few years since anybody had spoken to him like that. Taran was the last one.

"You're familiar with abortion, right, Milk Bone?"

"Yeah."

"Well, you see, your buddy Taran accidentally knocked up his girlfriend, Rosaline, and well, it was of greatest importance to me that he never procreated, so you see, I took that away from him."

"Huh?"

"She was pregnant with his twins and I ripped them out of her."

Rosaline bunched up her face and walked out of the room.

"You violated the code, Ancient."

Raphael whirled around and stared at Ramon. Ramon had just violated the code himself.

"Joseph, strip him of his gear and bind him next to the kid." Raphael ordered.

Ramon willingly surrendered his weapons and allowed himself to be bound, knowing he would die later. At least he would die with purpose, having spoken down to a madman.

"Hold up, if you didn't want Taran to have no kids, why didn't you just kill him?" Milk Bone asked.

"Because there was no honor in that."

"Oh and there's SO MUCH honor in forcing a woman down and rippin' fuckin' fetuses outta her!"

"Ancient, you have gone too far. Guild Master, relieve him. You know it's the right thing to do. This is not an honorable mission, it's about satisfying his need for revenge. He's abusing the guild and using it for selfish means." Ramon stated coldly, staring Raphael in the eye.

"No, Ramon, the last of the Ancients is infallible. He does not make mistakes." Joseph spoke, never wavering.

"Anyway," Raphael began, "we deviate from the purpose here.

Milk Bone, where are Taran and Alexandra?"

"Look, man, they didn't fuckin' tell me!"

Raphael reared back and back handed Milk Bone, sending blood rushing out of his mouth. He whimpered, fighting back tears.

Rosaline raised the gun to her head.

Lord Dell, Taran, Alexandra, Nigel, Sasha, Layne, and Bendle sat around a huge table, servants dashing in and out bringing in food. It was quite an elegant place. Huge domed ceilings, beautiful paintings on the walls (all of Lord Dell, apparently), and beautiful rugs adorning the floor.

Something resembling bagels were served along with a rather mushy, but wonderfully tasting oatmeal-like substance. All in all, a great meal.

"Lord Dell, this is wonderful, thank you." Alexandra spoke up.

"You're quite welcome, Alexandra. And, I'm willing to bet you all are just dying to know just what is actually going on, aren't you?"

All except Bendle nodded vigorously.

"Okay, here goes. A civil war is at hand among my race. Ravindranathan is at the helm of the "bad guys," if you will, and you all were created to stop him. A long time ago, all of my people agreed to non-interference among the universes. Ravindranathan grudgingly agreed. See, if a lot of interference goes on and universes mingle, it creates paradoxes in their respective time lines and the universe destroys itself. We all agreed that our creations were just as alive as we were and should be treated as such. Ravindranathan and several others don't agree. They see their people as toys to be played with. We all agreed to a strict set of rules governing how to be "god." Ravindranathan and his allies have been breaking those rules by sabotaging other universes and building armies in their own."

"Why not simply kill Ravi...nath...whatever?" Nigel asked, looking skeptical.

"We can't. We physically can't kill each other. For one, we are far too powerful on our homeworld to be killed there, and second we can't physically enter each other's universes to slay each other. We can, however, dispatch assassins into each other's universes. Ravindranthan has already proved that by killing a couple of us, and merging their universes with his."

"You see, the biggest problem is that, unfortunately, our native universe is beginning to collapse in on itself. We don't know why, but it is, which means we must escape into the ones we've created, which will greatly limit our power. In short, he who has the biggest universe wins. Ravindranathan's goal is to kill all three billion of the others and be THE GOD in one HUGE universe. If he succeeds, it will be similar to the hell he has created for the universe in which you've been living."

"Lord Dell, if I may, who created us?" Taran asked.

"It isn't apparent to you yet?" he retorted, smiling, "I did."

"The first team as well?" Alex piped up.

"Yes."

"What happened to Evangela's and Wil's souls?" she asked, staring into her drink.

"They...are trapped...they are in Ravindranthan's hell. I fought as hard as I could in the senate to get them back, but I lost, since I had violated the law by sending you all in there. Also, is it true that you are a vampire over there?"

"Yes...yes..." she sighed, "What do you mean, 'they're trapped?' Why can't you retrieve them? Can I?"

"You would have to descend into the depths of hell to do it, and I don't even know if that's possible. I don't fully understand his arrangement there. His setup is rather cruel, if you ask me. Here, souls are recycled. Reborn."

"Reincarnated." Sasha chimed in.

"OH AREN'T YOU SO FUCKING SMART." Layne yelled.

"Yes. Now, here's the bad news. I don't know the names of the others in your group. Keep in mind, the parents always decide a soul's name. After that, it's subconsciously implanted into the subsequent parents' minds. Since I can't see into other universes, I always have to rely on scouts. I am able to implant you all with a need to find each other, but I can't outright tell you where they are, unless I have a scout do all the looking and talking for me. I apologize that I can't make this mission easier for you all, but...I know you will do your best. Anyway, here's the rules. You all will be able to return here once a year, and only for a few days at a time, in order to heal up or rest or relax. Taran, you have the timepiece and key, right?"

Taran blinked at him, and opened his mouth to speak.

"Okay. Anyway, the secret to opening it is that Alexandra is the only one who can do it. I did that for security reasons. It opens a portal here. Any questions on that?"

Taran raised his hand.

"Yeah, um, what the hell are you talking about?"

Dell regarded Taran for a moment.

"You really don't know what I'm talking about?"

Taran shook his head.

"Dude, I have no fucking idea what this timepiece is, so how 'bout you tell me how to locate it?"

Dell looked very sad for a moment.

"Your mother never gave you a timepiece?"

Taran shook his head even more vigorously.

"Nope."

Dell sagged his shoulders.

"You need to ask her about it. She'll know what you're talking about. No matter what she says or does, you need to get this timepiece from her."

Taran nodded, then looked away.

Alexandra glanced at him.

"What? What is it?" she asked, placing a hand on one of his.

"My family situation is complicated. I'll tell ya about it later."

"Now, for the good news. I have all the information you need to complete your quest. First, round up the group. They should all be in roughly the same places as before. Second, once the group's together, you must find and slay the four top-ranking generals in his army. I don't know who they are or their names, my scouts couldn't find out. The reason why they must be slayed is because they posses some of his power and can actually resurrect him if need be. After that, you must travel to our homeworld, with which I will help you and begin to switch his universe over to my control, and do this without his knowing. Then, you must find a way to draw him down into the universe and fight him there. You stand no chance if you do it on the homeworld. He is far too powerful there. Oh, and in case you were wondering why I'm taking his universe, it's so that his creations don't perish, along with you all when he blinks out. Any final questions?"

"Who created Raphael?" Taran asked, looking very serious.

Lord Dell looked shocked.

"How do you know that name?" he asked, visibly shaken.

"We used to be close friends, and now we're not. Who is he, or better, what is he?"

"I sincerely apologize, but I must consult the others before I answer that question. I'm not entirely sure what he is, but he has interfered with us before, and has even killed a few of us. Let me make sure I understand first, though, Raphael is still alive? Long black hair, black body armor,-"

"Long green dragon scale cloak, yes."

"That is incredible. I'll let you know as soon as I understand all the facts. A word of warning, Taran. He is far more powerful than you. Stay away from him. By the way, you did receive your sword already, right?"

"Yes."

"I thought that was pretty clever. I delivered your abilities to you with those samurai. They were a good training excercise, huh?"

"Raphael delivered it to me."

Lord Dell's jaw dropped.

"This is very confusing. This is bad. Something is afoot. Listen, to put it very bluntly, Raphael is the most powerful being on that planet right now. STAY AWAY FROM HIM! This mission is far too important for you to get yourself killed going on some ridiculous quest for personal salvation. Anyway, unless you have any more questions, I will deliver you back home."

"Let's do it." Nigel said rising, checking the clip in his gun.

"Okay, listen carefully, where do want me to deliver you? Keep in mind, time has been passing there, approximately three hours or so. More has passed here, but you have to factor in that time is relative, so...anyway, where?"

"Well, my car's downtown, but I can get it later." Nigel said.

"The roof of the halfway." Taran said.

"WHAT? What about my car?" Nigel asked.

"I don't know. We need to get home. Now." Taran muttered, gazing into nothingness.

"Okay. Now all of you lock arms."

The five of the Nine did as he asked, joining together, arms locked. Lord Dell approached them, putting his hand on Taran's head. As soon as he let go, Taran looked up at him.

XIV: The Dance

And he saw the night sky of St. Louis city. He looked around. Everyone was present and accounted for.

And, Alexandra was a vampire again. His heart sank at this realization.

Layne collapsed to the ground. He slowly floated back up, but he was barely alive once again.

Taran checked the surroundings. He saw the van out front.

"I think Milk Bone has a few guests." he said.

Nigel walked over and looked.

"It could be for the plastics place next door."

"No, it's not." Alexandra said, "I ran down there and checked. He's here, Taran. Sebastian's dead in the foyer and Milk Bone's damn close if Raphael keeps beating on him like that.

Taran's knees nearly buckled.

"Taran, we must leave. There's no point to staying here. It's not essential to the mission." Sasha spoke.

WRONG

"No, it's not. You all go ahead to Cape. I'm going to finish this now. I'll meet you there."

"Taran, she's right." Nigel offered.

NO WRONG

"Nigel, you of all people should understand loyalty. Chances are, Milk Bone and Sebastian were being tortured to discover my whereabouts. And they wouldn't give in. I owe them this."

"Taran, they died so that you could escape." Sasha stated, getting worried.

"Milk Bone's not dead yet. I won't let him die."

"Don't make their sacrifices in vain. Escape and avenge their deaths later. This is not what we were sent here to do. Let's leave." Sasha argued.

HEARLTESS BITCH AND RETARD ALCOHOLIC ARE WRONG

Taran nodded at Layne.

"Final word. You all leave. I will get Milk Bone out and join you all down there. That is an order. Nigel, you are charged with protecting Alex during the day. Good bye." and Taran leaped down onto the fire escape.

"Milk Bone, one more blow will kill you. Don't throw away your life. TELL ME!!!"

Milk Bone looked up, sobbing blood and tears. He didn't want to die like this. He didn't deserve to die like this, but Taran had been his big brother for the past year, and he wasn't going to forget that now.

"Milk Bone...your friend Sebastian has already died, and you're going to join him soon."

Taran crept down the third floor hall, heading toward the stairs. He had never, never been in this kind of situation before, but somehow understood it, almost like instinct. He wondered if this was one of his natural abilities.

Noise. Down the hall. Last door on the right.

He sneaked down the hall, neared the door, unsheathed his sword, and looked in briefly. Rosaline. With a gun to her head.

Fuck, he mouthed. This was the last thing he needed right now.

He began whispering.

"Rosaline, what the hell are you doing?"

She looked up, and smiled.

"Oh my god, it's you! Taran! I...wait a minute!" she ran out to the stairs, "Raphael! He's here! He's here!" she screamed, running down the stairs.

"Shit!" Taran yelled, ducking into an empty room to hide, except all the rooms were empty here. It was an abandoned halfway house. Nowhere to hide. He heard a single set of feet come running back up the stairs.

Taran steeled himself.

This was it.

Raphael vs. Taran.

The final showdown.

The door burst open.

In a split second, Taran thought, it was really dumb of me to close that door, considering that all the others were wide open.

A figure crashed through.

Taran looked at him strangely.

"Who are you?"

"Daniel."

Taran hesitated.

"Are you here to kill me or what?"

"No."

Daniel withdrew a shotgun and aimed it at Taran. Taran shot over to the side and at the guy, so as to avoid the spray, spinning around and decapitating him so quickly he never even got a shot off.

"Next!" Taran yelled downstairs. He couldn't wait to get his hands on the next protégé of Raphael's. He wondered if-

Raphael grabbed him and threw him into a wall, making a sizable dent. He calmly withdrew his elegant blade and waited for Taran to stand back up. The two men stood only a few feet apart, waiting for the other to make the first move.

Taran very willingly obliged Raphael. And, so the dance began.

Joseph studied Ramon. He didn't understand how one of his best had failed so miserably.

"Raphael will die up there, Guild Master." Ramon spoke up, "It is

the moral thing."

"The moral thing, young man, is neither always the right thing or what necessarily happens." Joseph said, almost comfortingly.

Suddenly, the back door slammed open.

"Hey boys! Nice party!" he heard someone yell followed by gunfire. Then, the window behind him exploded. Joseph whipped around, knowing he didn't even have to look and opened fire. The being kept coming. He tossed his gun to the ground and pulled out his sword.

It was her. Alexandra.

She hissed at him, baring her fangs.

"Don't play games with me, blood drinker! I can strike you down in a matter of seconds and you know it!"

She laughed.

"Guild Master, I'm here!" spoke one of the remaining Hunters, standing behind him.

"Hunter, back out through the door. We are going to fight her in a less constrictive environment." Joseph ordered, both of them backing through the door.

Click.

Joseph felt a warm piece of metal next to his head, along with a cocking noise.

"Freeze, dicksmack." a voice spoke up, "Oh, and go ahead and drop the sword."

Joseph and the Hunter complied.

"Hunter, you know what to do, correct?" Joseph stated.

"Yes, sir."

"What the hell are talking about?" Nigel asked, annoyed.

Suddenly, Joseph seized his arm, spun around, and pulled his arm down. Nigel fired in vain, while the Hunter wrestled his gun away from him.

Alexandra lunged at them. She picked the Hunter up by the back of his pants and hurled him across the foyer. She punched Joesph in the face several times before he finally let go of Nigel. He and the Hunter scrambled into the mess hall, to regroup, presumably. Sasha walked in through the front door and approached the other two.

Nigel picked his gun back up.

"Sasha, Milk Bone could really use your help." Nigel glanced at Sebastian's crumpled body, "Dammit...he was a great guy, too. I guess he's beyond our help."

"Wait a minute, who's he?" Alex asked, pointing at Ramon.

"I dunno. We'll find out later. I'm gonna take care of these assholes first." Nigel said, motioning towards the mess hall.

"I'm gonna go check on Taran." Alex said, already heading up the stairs.

Sasha began to check on Milk Bone.

Taran was dripping with sweat. So was Raphael.

Taran lunged at him, almost knocking him down. He swung his blade low, so as to connect with the jugular while he was down, but Raphael shot up in the air, bringing his foot up to kick Taran in the face. Taran put his hand out, grabbed the bottom of Raphael's boot and sent him flipping. Raphael, amazingly landed on his feet, and the fighting continued.

Their blades sliced through the air, barely making and kind of sounds.

Raphael swung at Taran, put too much force into it, and stumbled a bit. Taran whipped around and spin kicked him into the hall, sending him crashing into a wall, making a dent comparable to Taran's. Taran stabbed forward, intending to pierce his neck. Raphael rolled, kicking Taran's feet out from under him, but he simply somersalted back. They began hacking away at each other, cutting through the plaster walls to their right and left. Bits and chunks of the walls were flying out all over the place.

After a while, Taran realized how pathetic this was, and bolted down the hall to the fire escape, and climbing to the roof.

Layne floated around the building, his rage fighting his depression. He had loved the physical form he had in Dell's world, even if he had hated not being able to access minds.

He saw one of the Hunters around a corner. With a thought, he severed the young man's spinal cord, and he dropped dead.

Layne continued to float, his agony building. He missed that body. There had been no physical pain or embarrassment.

Taran even allowed Raphael to climb up unharmed, though he had little choice in the matter. Raphael sort of launched himself up and lunged at Taran. The sword duel resumed.

"You must be Alexandra." a sexy, soft female voice spoke from behind her.

Alexandra turned. A rail-thin, busty, beautiful red-head stood behind her, pointing a pistol at her.

"Yes, I am." Alex said, lunging at what was obviously a very poorly-trained Vampire Hunter, and draining every last bit of blood in her. The girl squeezed a couple of shots, but they were almost like mosquito bites to the vampire. As she was draining the girl, images began to flood into her mind. This always happened with every victim Alex had drained. This girl, however, was odd. She kept seeing images of Taran, like in a romantic manner. When the girl was dead, it occured to her:

She had just killed Rosaline. Oh god.

As Nigel came creeped around the corner, Joseph cold-cocked him.

Nigel fell to the floor and dropped his gun.

Goddamit, not again, he thought as he saw his Walther P99 skid across the floor.

Joseph calmly looked down at Nigel and strolled out of the room.

"Hey, wait! What?! You can't...hey, get back here!" Nigel yelled, going after his opponent. He ran into the kitchen just in time to see Joseph go out the back door and up the fire escape, carrying an uzi.

The warriors were on the roof of the building, as cliches demand, thought Taran.

Taran and Raphael were an even match. They had both begun to wonder if this duel would ever end. Raphael jabbed at Taran. Taran blocked. Raphael lunged forward, pushing on his blade, trying to force Taran down. Taran pushed back. Their faces were a few inches apart. They could smell the stink of each other. Just then, they both heard clanging on the fire escape. They both turned to look, and Taran took advantage of this. He dropped down on his rear, slid his legs underneath Raphael, and kicked forward, sending Raphael flying over his head. He kicked back up, flipped around and sent his sword flying in that direction.

It found its home in Raphael's heart, piercing through his armor. The beast and both swords flew off the roof.

"ANCIENT, NO!!!" Joseph screamed, beginning to unload the uzi clip at Taran. He had no choice but to follow the shortcut that Raphael had discovered. Taran threw himself off the top of the three story building.

"Hey, Branch Davidian boy!" somebody right behind Joseph yelled, right before they put four bullets into his chest. Joseph crumpled on the fire escape. Nigel grinned. Killing mindless followers that happened to be shooting at his best friend was fun.

He ran onto the roof.

"Taran! Taran!" Nigel walked around the roof, trying to find his friend. The wind began to pick up blowing his hair and clothes around. He walked to the opposite edge, his hand carrying his gun at his side. He looked over the edge.

There, on the grass, lay Taran and Raphael side by side.

"....no..."Nigel whispered.

"I'm okay, fucknuts!" Taran yelled up, still lying there, "Layne broke my fall. I'm just taking a breather."

"Did we win?" Nigel yelled down.

"I think so...I'm not sure. No one's trying to kill us anymore, so I take that as a good sign. Where are the girls?"

"I don't know. I'll check and meet ya out there."

"Awesome."

Nigel hopped onto the fire escape on the other side and entered on the third floor, to sweep the building and make sure no one else was around. He walked from room to room, holding his gun like they do on all those cop shows, where the leg and gun formed a 45 degree angle. He felt really cool when he did that.

Third floor was clear.

He ran down the stairs to the second floor. First room clear. Second room clear. Third room-

There sat Alexandra weeping, cradling Rosaline. Rosaline appeared very, very dead, with fang marks on her neck.

"Oh god, Alexandra, what have you done?" Nigel asked.

"She attacked me, I needed to feed anyway, I didn't realize who she was until it was done. It's okay, though. Her soul was one of the most tortured I have ever seen. I think I finally gave her what Taran never could."

"What's that?"

"Peace."

She convulsed into even more sobbing.

"How am I going to tell Taran? He's gonna hate me."

"I doubt that. Come on, let's get the fuck out of here."

"But-"

"Alex, we need to leave before we're put in jail."

"Oh. Yeah. Okay." she said gently setting Rosaline's head on the floor, then following Nigel.

She stopped, went into Rosaline's purse, and withdrew a very old-fashioned looking key.

Taran lay next to his dead enemy, smoking a cigarette and wiping the sweat from his forehead.

"I can't believe I beat you, Raphael. You were always better in the dojo. I finally beat you in something, and it had to be the big one."

Nigel, Alex, and Sasha emerged from the front door and approached Taran.

"Bud, we gotta go." Nigel said, offering his hand.

"Yeah, we do. Where's Milk Bone?"

"He's alive. Pretty beat up, but I called the police and an ambulance for him, and gave him a cover-up story to tell the cops. I also released Ramon." Sasha said.

"Who's Ramon?" Taran asked.

"A vampire Hunter that talked back to Raphael." she answered.

"We have a few hours before the sun comes up, and we can make in that time. Milk Bone will be fine. Let's leave." Alex said.

"Right, right." Taran said, taking Nigel's hand and standing up. He retrieved his sword from Raphael's dead body as they started to head to Sasha's Celica.

"Shit! We still gotta pick up my car downtown. We're gonna be cutting this close." Nigel said, waving his arms in frustration.

"Chill. It'll be no problem. We'll get to Cape, crash in Nigel's dorm room, get some sleep, then go looking for the rest of the team." Taran said.

226

Taran looked back at the Halfway and paused for a moment. He was sure of only one thing at this point.

This stupid chapter of his life had closed. He still had almost nothing, but he did have the most valuable thing.

TO BE CONTINUED

Blaine Atkinson

October 1998-April 23rd, 2000
June 2009 (final edit)
August 2009 (final final edit)
June 2011 (font revision + ISBN addition)

Afterword

I put this book out with some very mixed feelings. On one hand, underneath all the rage with which it was written, there is a good story. On the other, it's kinda written like shit.

If you know me, I've talked endlessly about how strange it was to pick up something that I'd written when I was 20 & 21, and edit it when I was 30 & 31.

When I wrote this, I was perhaps the angriest little man the world had ever seen, and though I'm calmer, balder, and fatter now, I still carry a hint of that rage with me, though not nearly in the toxic levels I used to. I understand that young man, and feel compassion for him, and while I don't agree with everything he believed back then, I still wish to honor him by publishing the book in the form he would've most liked.

There are certain stylistic choices I made when I wrote this, and while I've cleaned up quite a bit of the book, I've tried to leave intact the book my 20-year old self wanted to write.

It's written very much like one is telling the story out loud, and while it kinda works, this is the last time I'm using that voice for this series.

If you like the story, but hate part of the way it's written, I understand. I love the story and hate the way it's written, too. I just hope you, faithful reader, understand my need to honor an old version of myself that maybe never got a fair shake before I killed him.

Anyway, if you made it this far, I appreciate it, and promise that there is more to come for these characters. The second novel in the series is already underway, and it has been fantastic to pick this series back up and run with it. It's the first time I've written truly new material for these characters in eight years, and I'm loving it thus far, and hope you will, too.

If you want to keep up with me, you can follow my blog at http://filthywriter.blogspot.com or email me @ taranwalker@gmail.com. All I ask is that you be cool in any communications with me.

Feel free to drop me a line with any questions or thoughts you might have. Please DO NOT SEND ME ANY FUCKING STORY IDEAS OR SUGGESTIONS. Thanks, and I hope to hear from ya!

Go Cardinals!

-Blaine

2009/8/8

About the Author

Blaine Atkinson is a writer (sort of.) He lives in Manchester, MO and finds it very uncomfortable to write about himself in the third person. He is married to the screenwriter, Cori Crouch. She is very pretty and was responsible for editing and giving feedback on this mess of a book. They have a son, and you may not have his name because you are probably a dangerous pervert.

Blaine received his B.A. In Fiction Writing from Columbia College Chicago, where he won no awards and did nothing at all remarkable except shoot off his mouth at wildly inappropriate times. He did throw the best parties in all of Chicago.

Go Cards! Fuck the Cubs!

there is nothing interesting on this page